ALISTAIR MacLEAN

san ANDReas

FAWCETT CREST • NEW YORK

A Fawcett Crest Book
Published by Ballantine Books
Copyright © 1984 by Alistair MacLean

Library of Congress Catalog Card Number: 85-4395

ISBN 0-449-20970-9

This edition published by arrangement with Doubleday & Co., Inc.

Manufactured in the United States of America

First Ballantine Books Edition: September 1986

PROLOGUE

THERE ARE THREE DISTINCT BUT INEVITABLY interlinked elements in this story: the British Merchant Navy (officially the Mercantile Marine) and the men who served in it; Liberty Ships; and the units of the German forces, underseas, on the seas and in the air, whose sole mission was to seek out and destroy the vessels and crews of the Merchant Navy.

1) At the outbreak of war in September 1939 the Merchant Navy was in a parlous state indeed—"pitiable" would probably be a more accurate term. Most of the ships were old, a considerable number unseaworthy, and some no more than rusting hulks plagued by interminable mechanical breakdowns. Even so, the vessels were in good shape compared to those whose misfortune it was to serve aboard those ships, in appalling living conditions.

The reason for the savage neglect of both ships and men could be summed up in one word: greed. The fleet owners of yesteryear—and there are more than

1

a few around today—were grasping, avaricious and wholly dedicated to their high priestess—profits at all costs, provided that all of the costs did not fall on them. Centralization was the watchword of the day, the gathering in of overlapping monopolies into a few rapacious hands. While crews' wages were cut and living conditions reduced to barely subsistence levels, the owners grew fat, as did some of the less desirable directors of those companies and a considerable number of carefully hand-picked and favored shareholders.

The dictatorial powers of the owners, discreetly exercised, of course, were little short of absolute. Their fleets were their satraps, their feudal fiefdoms, and the crews were their serfs. If a serf chose to revolt against the established order, that was his misfortune. His only recourse was to leave his ship, to exchange it for virtual oblivion. Apart from the fact that he was automatically blackballed, unemployment was high in the Merchant Navy and the few vacancies available were for willing serfs only. Ashore, unemployment was even higher, and even if it had not been so seamen find it notoriously difficult to adapt to a landlubber's way of life. The rebel serf had no place left to go. Rebels were few and far between. The vast majority knew their station in life and kept to it. Official histories tend to gloss over this state of affairs or, more commonly, ignore it altogether, an understandable myopia. The treatment of the merchant seamen between the wars and, indeed, during the Second World War, does not form one of the more glorious chapters in British naval annals.

Successive governments between the wars were perfectly aware of the conditions of life in the Merchant Navy—they would have had to be more than ordinarily stupid not to be so aware—so, in largely hypocritical face-saving exercises, a series of governments passed regulations laying down minimum specifications regarding accommodation, food, hygiene and safety. Both governments and owners were perfectly aware—in the case of the shipowners no doubt cheerfully aware—that regulations are not laws and that a regulation is not legally enforceable. The recommendations, for they amounted to no more than that, were almost wholly ignored. A conscientious captain who tried to enforce them was liable to find himself without a command.

Recorded eyewitness reports of the living conditions aboard Merchant Navy ships in the years immediately prior to the Second World War—there is no reason to question those reports, especially as they are all so depressingly unanimous in tone—describe the crews' living quarters as being so primitive and atrocious as to beggar description. Medical inspectors stated that in some instances the crews' living quarters were unfit for animal, far less human, habitation. The quarters were cramped and bereft of any form of comfort. The decks were wet, the men's clothes were wet, and the mattresses and blankets, where such luxuries were available, were usually sodden. Hygiene and toilet facilities ranged from the primitive to the nonexistent. Cold was pervasive and heating of any form—except for smoky and evil-smelling coal stoves—was rare, as, indeed, was ventilation. And the food, which as one writer said would not have been tolerated in a home for the utterly destitute, was even worse than the living quarters.

The foregoing may strain the bounds of incredulity or, at least, seem far-fetched, but respectively they should not and are not. Charges of imprecision and exaggeration have never been laid at the doors of the London School of Hygiene and Tropical Medicine or the Registrar General. The former, in a prewar report, categorically stated that the mortality rate below the age of fifty-five was twice as high for seamen as it was for the rest of the male population, and statistics issued by the latter showed that the death rate for seamen of all ages was 47 percent in excess of the national average. The killer was not the sea but tuberculosis, cerebral haemorrhage or gastric or duodenal ulcers. The incidence of the first and last of those is all too understandable, and there can be little doubt that the combination of those contributed heavily to the abnormal occurrence of strokes.

The prime agent of death was unquestionably tuberculosis. When one looks around Western Europe today, where TB sanatoria are a happily and rapidly vanishing species, it is difficult to imagine just how terrible a scourge tuberculosis was just over a generation ago. It is not that tuberculosis, worldwide, has been eliminated: in many underdeveloped countries it still remains that same terrible scourge and the chief cause of death, and as recently as the early years of this century TB was still the number-one killer in Western Europe and North America. Such is no longer the case since scientists came up with the agents to tame and destroy the tubercle bacillus. But in 1939 it was still very much the case: the discovery of the chemotherapeutic agents rifampin, para-aminosalicylic acid, isoniasid and especially streptomycin, still lay far beyond a distant horizon.

It was upon those tuberculosis-ridden seamen, illhoused and abominably fed, that Britain depended to bring food, oil, arms and ammunition to its shores and to those of its allies. They were the sine qua non conduit, the artery, the lifeline upon which Britain was absolutely dependent: without those ships and men Britain would have gone under. It is worth noting that those men's contracts ended when the torpedo, mine or bomb struck. In wartime as in peacetime the owners protected their profits to the end: the seaman's wages were abruptly terminated when his ship was sunk, no matter where, how or in what circumstances. When an owner's ship went down he shed no salt tears, for his ships were insured, as often as not grossly overinsured; when a seaman's ship went down he was fired.

The Government, Admiralty and shipowners of that time should have been deeply ashamed of themselves; if they were, they manfully concealed their distress: compared to profits, prestige and glory the conditions of life and the horrors of death of the men of the Merchant Navy were a very secondary consideration indeed.

The people of Britain cannot be condemned. With the exception of the families and friends of the Merchant Navy and the splendid volunteer charitable organizations that were set up to help survivors—such humanitarian trifles were of no concern to owners or

Whitehall—very few knew or even suspected what was going on.

2) As a lifeline, a conduit and an artery, the Liberty Ships were on a par with the British Merchant Navy: without them, too, Britain would have assuredly gone down in defeat. All the food, oil, arms and ammunition that overseas countries—especially the United States—were eager and willing to supply were useless without the ships in which to transport them. After less than two years of war it was bleakly apparent that because of the deadly attrition of the British Merchant fleets there must soon be no ships left to carry anything and that Britain would, inexorably and not slowly, be starved into surrender. In 1940, even the indomitable Winston Churchill despaired of survival, let alone ultimate victory. Typically, the period of despair was brief, but heaven only knew that he had cause for it.

In nine hundred years, Britain, of all the countries in the world, had never been invaded, but in the darkest days of the war such invasion seemed not only perilously close but inevitable. Looking back today over a span of forty and more years it seems inconceivable and impossible that the country survived: had the facts been made public, which they weren't, it almost certainly would not have.

British shipping losses were appalling beyond belief and beggar even the most active imagination. In the first eleven months of the war Britain lost 1,500,000 tons of shipping. In some of the early months of 1941, losses averaged close to 500,000 tons. In 1942, the bleakest period of the war at sea, 6,250,000 tons of shipping went to the bottom. Even working at full stretch, British shipyards could replace only a small fraction of those enormous losses. That, together with the fact that the number of operational U-boats in that same grim year rose from 91 to 212, made it certain that, by the law of diminishing returns, the British Merchant Navy would eventually cease to exist unless a miracle occurred.

The name of the miracle was the Liberty Ship. To anyone who can recall those days the term "Liberty Ships" was automatically and immediately linked with Henry Kaiser. Kaiser—in the circumstances it was ironic that he should bear the same name as the title of the late German Emperor—was an American engineer of genius. His career until then had been a remarkably impressive one; he had been a key figure in the construction of the Hoover and Grand Coulee Dams and San Francisco's Bay Bridge. It is questionable whether Henry Kaiser could have designed a row-boat, but that was of no matter. He almost certainly had a better understanding of prefabrication based on a standard and repeatable design than any other person in the world at the time and did not hesitate to send out contracts for part-construction to factories in the United States that lay hundreds of miles from the sea. Those sections were transmitted to shipyards for assembly, originally to Richmond, California, where Kaiser directed the Permanente Cement Company, and eventually to other shipyards under Kaiser's control. Kaiser's turnover and speed of production stopped just short of the incredible: he did for the production of merchant vessels what Henry Ford's assembly lines had done for the Model T Ford. Until then, as far as oceangoing vessels were concerned, mass production had been an alien concept.

Mistakenly but understandably there existed a widely held belief that the Liberty Ships originated in the design offices of the Kaiser shipyards. The design and prototypes were, in fact, English and were conceived by the design staff of the ship-builders J. L. Thompson of North Sands, Sunderland. The first of what was to become a very long line indeed, the *Embassage*, was completed in 1935. (The prefix "Liberty" did not come into existence for another seven years, and only for some of the Kaiser-built vessels.) The *Embassage*, 9,300 tons, with a raked stem and rounded stern and three triple-expansion coal-burning engines, was a non-starter in the aesthetic stakes, but then the J. L. Thompson firm was not interested in aesthetics: what it had aimed at was a modern, practical and economical cargo vessel, and in this it succeeded admirably. Twenty-four more similar vessels were built before the outbreak of war.

Those ships were built in Britain, the United States and Canada, the great preponderance in the Kaiser yards. Hull designs remained identical but the Americans, and only the Americans, introduced two changes which they regarded as refinements. One of those changes, using oil instead of coal as fuel, may well have been; the other, which concerned the accommodation of officers and crew, was not. While the Canadians and British retained the original concept of having the living quarters both fore and aft, the Americans elected to have all the crew, officers and men—and the navigating bridge—in a superstructure surrounding the funnel. In retrospect—bitter experience makes for a splendid conductor to belated wisdom— it was a blunder. The Americans had all their eggs in one basket.

Those vessels were armed, after a fashion. They had four-inch low-angle and twelve-pound anti-aircraft guns, neither of which was particularly effective, together with Bofors guns and rapid-firing Oerlikons. The Oerlikons were deadly in trained hands—but there were few trained hands around. They also had weird devices such as rocket-fired parachutes and cables carrying coils of war and grenades: those were as dangerous to those using them as the aircraft they were supposed to bring down. Some few of these ships had catapult-launched Hurricane fighters—the nearest equivalent to the suicidal Japanese kamikaze planes that Britain ever had. The pilots could not, of course, return to their ships: they had the uncomfortable option of either bailing out or ditching. In the Arctic, in winter, their survival rate was not high.

3) From the air, on the sea and under the sea the Germans, often with brilliance, always with tenacity and ruthlessness, used every means in their power to destroy the Merchant Navy convoys.

Basically, they used five main types of aircraft. Their standard or conventional bomber was the Dornier, which flew at predetermined heights and released their bombs in predetermined patterns; they were useful planes and had their successes but were not particularly effective.

Much more feared, in ascending order, were the Heinkel, the Heinkel III and the Stuka. The Heinkel was a torpedo bomber, which attacked at wave-top level, its pilot releasing the torpedo at the last possible moment then using the lightened weight of his aircraft to lift over the ship it was attacking. Those planes had an unusual degree of immunity from destruction: when the anti-aircraft gunners on the merchant ships peered over the sights of their Oerlikons, Bofors or pom-poms—two-pounders—the thought that he gets me or I get him didn't make for the degree of cool detachment which would have been helpful in the circumstances. In the Arctic winter, those torpedo bombers were not infrequently at a disadvantage, especially for the unfortunate pilots who flew them: ice could freeze up their torpedo release mechanisms and their burdened aircraft were unable to lift off over their targets. This made little difference to the equally unfortunate crews of the merchant vessels: whether the torpedo was running free or still attached to the aircraft when it crashed into the ship, the results were equally devastating.

The Heinkel III used glider bombers. Those were highly effective; they exposed their pilots to a much lesser degree of risk, and the bombs, once released, were virtually impossible to shoot down. Fortunately for the Merchant Navy, the Germans did not have many of those highly specialized planes.

The Stukas, the dihedral-gull-winged Junker 87 dive-bombers were the most feared of all. It was their customary practice to fly at high altitude in level formation, then peel off successively in near-vertical dives. Forty years later, seamen and soldiers—the Germans used the Junker 87 in every theater of war—who survived those attacks and are still alive will never forget the sound of the banshee shrieking as the Stuka pilots switched on their sirens in their plummeting dive. The sound, to say the least, was unnerving and considerably reduced the effectiveness of antiaircraft gunners. The Royal Navy used searchlights, customarily of the forty-four-inch variety, in an attempt to blind the Stuka pilot until it was pointed out to them that the pilots, well aware of this tactic, used dark glasses to reduce the blinding glare to mere pinpoints of light which enabled them to home in even more accurately on their targets. From the German point of view the Stukas had just one drawback: they were essentially short-range planes and could operate effectively only against convoys moving to the north of Norway en route to Murmansk and Archangel.

Oddly enough, the most effective air weapon the Germans had was the essentially noncombative Focke-Wulf Condor 200. True, it could and did carry 250-kilo bombs and had a fairly formidable array of machine guns, but with bombs removed and extra fuel tanks fitted in their place it became an invaluable reconnaissance plane. For that comparatively early flying era, in the early forties, its flying range was remarkable. Condors flew almost daily from Trondheim, in German-occupied Norway, around the Western coast of the British Isles to German-occupied France; more important, they were capable of patrolling the Barents Sea, the Greenland Sea and, most damagingly of all, the justly dreaded Denmark Strait, between Iceland and Greenland, for it was through that strait that the Russian-bound convoys from Canada and the United

States passed. For such a convoy, the sight of a Condor was the guarantee of disaster.

Flying high and safely out of reach of anti-aircraft fire, the Condor would literally circle the convoy, its crew noting the number of ships and the convoy's speed, course and precise latitude and longitude. This information was radioed to Alta Fjord or Trondheim and then transmitted to Lorient, the French headquarters of Admiral Karl Doenitz, almost certainly the best submarine Commander in Chief of his or any time. From there the information was retransmitted to the growing number of submarine wolfpacks, instructing them when and where to position themselves to intercept the convoy.

As far as surface warships were concerned, the Germans were more than adequately prepared at the outbreak of war. By the Anglo-German agreement of 1937 Germany could build one hundred percent of the British equivalent of submarines but only thirty-five percent of surface ships. In fact they built twice as many submarines and completely ignored the other thirty-five-percent restriction. The *Deutschland*, *Admiral Graf Spee* and *Admiral Scheer* were nominally 10,000-ton cruisers: they were, in fact, fast and powerful commerce raiders, in effect pocket battleships of a far greater tonnage than purported. The *Scharnhorst* and *Gneisenau*, 26,000-ton battle cruisers, were completed in 1938, and it was in that year that the *Bismarck* and *Tirpitz* were laid down in the Blohm and Voess shipyards in Hamburg. Those were the best and most powerful battleships ever built, a statement that remains true to this day. By treaty limitations they were restricted to 35,000 tons; they were, in fact, 53,000 tons.

The *Bismarck* had a brief but spectacular career, the *Tirpitz* no career at all. It spent its war holed up in northern Norway, where it nonetheless performed the invaluable function of tying up major units of the British Home Fleet, which feared that the giant battleship might slip its moorings in Alta Fjord and break out into the Atlantic. It was at those moorings that the *Tirpitz* was ultimately destroyed by ten-ton bombs from R.A.F. Lancasters.

Although the British had a very considerable advantage in battleships, they were, individually, no match for those of the Germans as was tragically proven when the *Bismarck* sank the battle cruiser *Hood*, pride and darling of the Royal Navy, with a single salvo.

Underwater, the Germans used mines and submarines. Less than three months after the outbreak of war the Germans had come up with a rather unpleasant device, the magnetic mine. Unlike the standard type, which had to come into physical contact with a vessel before being activated, the magnetic mine was set off by the electrical current generated by the ship's hull. Those mines could be laid by either ships or aircraft, and in the first four days after their introduction no fewer than fifteen ships were sent to the bottom. The fact that the ships were nearly all neutrals seemed of no great concern to the Germans; magnetic mines are very clever devices but not clever enough to discriminate between a neutral and an enemy. The British managed to retrieve one intact, took it to pieces—not without considerable danger to those engaged in the dismantling—and came up with electronic countermeasures which enabled minesweepers to detonate the magnetic mine at a respectable distance.

Submarines, of course, were the most deadly enemies the Merchant Navy had to face. The toll taken in the first three and a half years of war was savage beyond belief. It wasn't until the early summer of 1943 that the menace was brought under some form of control, and it wasn't until the end of 1944—during 1943 and 1944, 480 German submarines were destroyed— that those stealthy pursuers and silent killers ceased to be a factor of consequence.

It was inevitable that the U-boat crews should be selected as *the* target for hatred and depicted, both during the war and subsequently, as cunning, treacherous and ice-cold murderers, fanatical Nazis to a man, who hunted down unsuspecting innocents, closed in unheard and unseen, destroyed their victims without mercy or compunction, then moved on again, still unheard and unseen. To a limited extent, this view was valid. The structure for this belief was set on the very first day of the war, when the liner *Athenia* was torpedoed. In no way could the *Athenia* have been mistaken for anything other than it was, a peaceful passenger vessel crammed with civilians—men, women and children. This must have been known to the far from gallant Oberleutnant Fritz-Julius Lemp, commander of the German U-boat that sent the *Athenia* to the bottom. There is no record that Lemp was ever reprimanded for his action.

The same charge of ruthlessness, of course, might have been leveled against Allied submariners—to a lesser extent, admittedly, but only because they had a much more limited choice of targets.

The popular overall U-boat picture is false. Ruthless Nazis there may have been among the crews, but they were a tiny minority; many men were motivated principally by intense pride in the traditions of the Imperial German Navy. Certainly there were acts of brutality by individual U-boat commanders, but there were also acts of humanity, gallantry and compassion. What was undeniable was the immense personal courage and spirit of self-sacrifice of those men. It has to be remembered that, out of a total of 40,000 U-boat submariners, 30,000 died, the most shocking casualty rate in the history of naval warfare. While the actions of those men are not to be condoned, the men themselves are not to be condemned. Ruthless they were—the nature of their job demanded it—but they were brave beyond belief.

Such then were the conditions in which the men of the Merchant Navy had to live and die: such too were their enemies, who sought, implacably, to destroy them. The chances that the health and lives of the merchantmen would survive, respectively, their living conditions and the attentions of the enemy were low indeed: theirs was a classic no-win situation. In the circumstances it was an astonishing fact that men who had survived two or three torpedoings and sinkings would immediately, on their return to Britain, seek out another ship to take them to sea again. By definition those men were noncombatants but their endurance, tenacity and determination—they would have laughed at words like gallantry and courage—matched those of the men who hunted them down.

1

SILENTLY, UNDRAMATICALLY, WITHOUT FORE-warning, as in any abrupt and unexpected power cut in a city, the lights aboard the *San Andreas* died in the hour before the dawn. Such blackouts were rare but not unknown and gave rise to no particular alarm as far as the handling and navigation of the vessel were concerned. On the bridge, the binnacle light that illuminated the compass, the chart light and the essential telephone line to the engine room remained unaffected because, operating as they did on a lower voltage, they had their own separate generator. The overhead lights were on the main generator but this was of no consequence, as those lights were switched off: the bridge, any bridge, was always dark-ened at night. The only item on the bridge that did fail was the Kent screen, an inset circular plate of glass directly ahead of the helmsman which spun at high speed and offered a clear view in all conditions.

Third Officer Batesman, the officer of the watch,

was unworried: to the best of his belief there was neither land nor other ship within a hundred miles of him, with the exception of the frigate H.M.S. *Andover*. He had no idea where the frigate was and it didn't matter; the frigate always knew where he was, for it was equipped with highly sophisticated radar.

In the operating theater and recovery room it was a case of business as usual. Although the surrounding sea and sky were still dark as midnight, the hour was not early: in those high latitudes and at that time of year daylight, or what passed for daylight, arrived about 10 A.M. In those two rooms, the most important in a hospital ship—for that was what the *San Andreas* was—battery-powered lights came on automatically when the main power failed. Throughout the rest of the ship emergency lighting was provided by hand-hung nickel-cadmium lamps; a twist of the base of such a lamp provided at least a bare minimum of illumination.

What did give rise to concern was the complete failure of the upper deck lights. The hull of the *San Andreas* was painted white—more correctly, it had been white but time and the sleet, hail, snow and ice spicules of Arctic storms had eroded the original to something between a dingy off-white and an equally dingy light gray. A green band ran all the way around the hull. Very big red crosses had been painted on both her sides, as well as on the fore and after decks. During nighttime those red crosses were illuminated by powerful floodlights; at that season darkness accounted for twenty hours out of the twenty-four.

Opinion as to the value of those lights was fairly

evenly divided. According to the Geneva conventions, the red crosses guaranteed immunity against enemy attacks. As the *San Andreas* had so far been reassuringly immune, those aboard her who had never been subjected to an enemy attack of any kind tended to believe in the validity of the Geneva conventions. But the crew members who had served aboard before her conversion from a Liberty cargo carrier to her present status regarded those conventions with a very leery eye. To sail at night lit up like a Christmas tree went against all the instincts of men who for years had been conditioned to believe, rightly, that to light a cigarette on the upper deck was to attract the attention of a wandering U-boat. They didn't trust the lights. They didn't trust the red crosses. Above all, they didn't trust the U-boats. There was justification for their cynicism; other hospital ships, they knew, had been less fortunate than they had been, but whether all of those attacks had been deliberate or accidental had never been established. There are no courts of law on the high seas and no independent witnesses. Either from reasons of delicacy or because they thought it pointless, the crew never discussed the matter with those who lived in what they regarded as a fool's paradise—the doctors, the sisters, the nurses and the ward orderlies.

The starboard screen door on the bridge opened and a figure, torch in hand, entered. Batesman said: "Captain?"

"Indeed. One of these days I'll get to finish my breakfast in peace. Some lamps, will you, Third?"

Captain Bowen was of medium height, running to fat—"well-built" was his preferred term—with a cheerful white-bearded face and periwinkle-blue eyes. He was also well past retirement age but had never asked to retire and had never been asked to: in both ships and men the Merchant Navy had suffered crippling losses, and a new ship could be made in a tiny fraction of the time it took to make a new captain; there weren't too many Captain Bowens left around.

The three emergency lamps didn't give much more light than a similar number of candles, but it was enough to see just how quickly the captain's coat had been covered in snow in the brief seconds it had taken him to cover the distance from the saloon. He removed the coat, shook it out through the doorway and hurriedly closed the door.

"Bloody generator having one of its fits again," Bowen said. He didn't seem particularly upset about it, but then no one had ever seen the captain upset about anything. "Kent screen on the blink, of course. No odds. Useless anyway. Heavy snow, thirty-knot wind and visibility zero." There was a certain satisfaction in Bowen's voice, and neither Batesman nor Hudson, the helmsman, had to ask why. All three belonged to the group who thought that minimal belief in the Geneva conventions was too much: no plane, ship or submarine could hope to locate them in those conditions. "Been through to the engine room?"

"I have not." Batesman spoke with some feeling and Bowen smiled. Chief Engineer Patterson, a northeasterner from the Newcastle area, had pride in his undoubted technical skills, a temper with a notoriously short fuse and a rooted aversion to being questioned by anyone as lowly as a third officer. "I'll get the chief, sir."

He got the chief. Bowen took the phone and said: "Ah, John. Not having much luck this trip, are we? Overload coil? Brushes? Fuse? Ah! The standby, then— I do hope we're not out of fuel again." Captain Bowen spoke in tones of grave concern and Batesman smiled; every member of the crew, down to the pantry boy, knew that Chief Patterson was devoid of any sense of humor. Bowen's reference to fuel referred to the occasion when, with Chief Patterson off duty, the main generator had failed and the young engineer in charge had forgotten to turn the cock on the fuel line to the auxiliary. Patterson's comments were predictable. With a pained expression on his face, Bowen held the phone a foot from his ear until the crackling in the earpiece had ceased, spoke briefly again, then hung up and said diplomatically: "I think Chief Patterson is having rather more trouble than usual in locating electrical faults. Ten minutes, he says."

Only two minutes later the phone rang.

"Bad news, for a fiver." Bowen lifted the phone, listened briefly, then said, "You want a word with me, John? But you *are* having a word with me.... Ah. I see. Very well." He hung up. "The chief wants to show me something."

Bowen did not, as Batesman might have assumed, go to the engine room. He went, instead, to his cabin, where he was joined within a minute by the chief engineer. A tall lean man, with an unremarkable face and a permanent five-o'clock shadow, Patterson was, like a number of men who are humorless and unaware of it, given to smiling at frequent intervals, almost always at inappropriate moments. He was not, however, smiling at that moment. He produced three pieces of what appeared to be black carbon and arranged them on the captain's table until they formed an oblong shape.

"What do you make of that, then?"

"You know me, John, just a simple seaman. An armature brush for a dynamo or generator or whatever?"

"Exactly." Patterson was much better at being grim than he was at smiling.

"Hence the power failure?"

"Nothing to do with the power failure. Overload coil thrown. Short somewhere. Jamieson's taken a bridge-megger and gone off to look for it. Shouldn't take him long to locate it."

This Bowen was prepared to believe. Jamieson, the Second Engineer, was a bright young man with the unusual distinction of being an A.M.I.E.E.—an associate member of the Institute of Electrical Engineers. He said: "So this brush comes from the auxiliary generator, it's broken, and you seem unhappy about it. I take it this is unusual."

"Unusual? It's unknown. At least I've never known of it. The brush is under constant spring-loaded pressure against the face of the armature. There is no way it could have broken in this particular fashion."

"Well, it did happen. First time for everything." Bowen touched the broken pieces with his fingers. "A one-off job? Flaw in manufacture?"

Patterson didn't answer. He dug into an overall

pocket, brought out a small metal box, removed the lid and placed the box on the table beside the broken brush. The two brushes inside were identical in shape and size to the one that Patterson had reassembled. Bowen looked at them, then at Patterson, and pursed his lips.

"Spares?"

Patterson nodded. Bowen picked one up but only one half came away in his hand: the other half remained in the bottom of the box.

"Our only two spares," Patterson said.

"No point in examining the other?"

"None. Both generators were examined and in good shape when we were in Halifax—and we've used the auxiliary twice since leaving there."

"One broken brush could be an extraordinary fluke. Three broken ones don't even make for a ludicrous coincidence. Doesn't even call for thoughtful chin-rubbing, John. We have an ill-intentioned crank in our midst."

"Crank! Saboteur, you mean."

"Well, yes, I suppose. At least, someone who is ill-disposed to us. Or toward the *San Andreas*. But saboteur? I wonder. Saboteurs go in for varied forms of wholesale destruction. Breaking three generator brushes can hardly be classified as wholesale. And unless the character responsible is deranged he's not going to send the *San Andreas* to the bottom—not with him inside it. Why, John, why?"

They were still sitting there, pondering why, when a knock came at the door and Jamieson entered. Young, red-headed and with a carefree attitude to life, he was being anything but ebullient at that moment: he had about him an air of gravity and anxiety, both alien intruders on his nature.

"Engine room told me I'd find you here. I thought I should come at once."

"As the bearer of bad news," Captain Bowen said. "You've discovered two things—the location of the short and evidence of, shall we say, deliberate destruction?"

"How the hell—I'm sorry, sir, but how could you possibly—"

"Tell him, John," Bowen said.

"I don't have to. Those broken brushes are enough. What did you find, Peter?"

"For'ard. Carpenter's shop. Lead cable passing through a bulkhead. Clips on either side seemed to have worked loose where it passed through the hole in the bulkhead."

Bowen said: "Normal ship's vibration, weather movement—doesn't take much to chafe through soft lead."

"Lead's tougher than you think, sir. In this case a pair of hands helped the normal chafing along. Not that that matters. Inside the lead sheathing the rubber around the power cable has been scorched away."

"Which one would expect in a short?"

"Yes, sir. Only, I know the smell of electrically burned rubber and it doesn't smell like sulphur. Some bright lad had used an igniting match-head or heads to do the trick. I've left Ellis on the repair job. It's simple and he should be about through now."

"Well, well. So it's as easy as that to knock out a ship's electrical power."

"Almost, sir. He'd one little other job to do. There's a fuse box just outside the carpenter's shop and he removed the appropriate fuse before starting work. Then he returned to the fuse box and shorted out the line—insulated pliers, ditto screwdriver, almost anything would do—then replaced the fuse. If he'd replaced the fuse before shorting out the line it would have blown, leaving the rest of the electrical system intact. Theoretically, that is—on very rare occasions the fuse is not so obliging and doesn't go." Jamieson smiled faintly. "Fact of the matter is, if I'd had a cold in the nose he might have got away with it."

The phone rang. Captain Bowen lifted it and handed it over to Patterson, who listened, said: "Sure. Now," and handed the phone back. "Engine room. Power coming on."

Perhaps half a minute passed; then Captain Bowen said mildly: "You know, I don't think the power *is* coming on."

Jamieson rose and Bowen said: "Where are you going?"

"I don't know, sir."

Bowen raised an eyebrow.

"Well, first of all I'm going to the engine room to pick up Ellis and the bridge-megger and then I don't know. It seems that old Flannelfoot has more than one string to his bow."

The phone rang again and Bowen, without answering, handed it over to Patterson, who listened briefly, said: "Thank you. Mr. Jamieson is coming down," and handed the phone back. "Same again. I wonder how many places our friend *has* jinxed and is just waiting for the opportunity to activate them."

Jamieson hesitated at the door. "Do we keep this to ourselves?"

"We do not." Bowen was positive. "We broadcast it far and wide. Granted, Flannelfoot, as you call him, will be forewarned and forearmed but the knowledge that a saboteur is at large will make everyone look at his neighbor and wonder what a saboteur looks like. If nothing else it will make this lad a great deal more circumspect and, with any luck, may restrict his activities a bit."

Jamieson nodded and left.

Bowen said: "I think, John, you might double the watch in the engine room or at least bring on two or three extra men, not, you understand, for engine-room duties."

"I understand. You think, perhaps—"

"If you wanted to sabotage a ship, to incapacitate it completely, where would you go?"

Patterson rose, went to the door and, as Jamieson had done, stopped there and turned. "Why?" he said. "Why?"

"I don't know why. But I have an unpleasant feeling about the where and the when. Here or hereabouts and sooner than we think, quicker than we want. Somebody," Captain Bowen said, as if by way of explanation, "has just walked over my grave."

Patterson gave him a long look and closed the door quietly behind him.

Bowen picked up the phone, dialed a single number and said: "Archie, my cabin." He had no sooner replaced the receiver when it rang again. It was the bridge. Batesman didn't sound too happy.

"Snowstorm's blowing itself out, sir. *Andover* can see us now. Wants to know why we're not showing any lights. I told them we had a power failure, then another message just now, why the hell are we taking so long to fix it?"

"Sabotage."

"I beg your pardon, sir."

"Sabotage. S for Sally, A for Arthur, B for Bobby, O for—"

"Good God! Whatever—I mean, why, who..."

"I do not know why or who." Captain Bowen spoke with a certain restraint. "Tell them that. I'll tell you what I know—which is practically nothing—when I come up to the bridge. Five minutes. Maybe ten."

Archie McKinnon, the bosun, came in. Captain Bowen regarded the bosun—as indeed many other captains regarded their bosuns—as the most important crew member aboard. He was a Shetlander, about six feet two in height and built accordingly, forty years of age, with a brick-colored complexion, blue-gray eyes and flaxen hair—the last two almost certainly inheritances from Viking ancestors who had passed by, or through, his native island a millennium previously.

"Sit down, sit down," Bowen said. He sighed. "Archie, we have a saboteur aboard."

"Have we now." No raised eyebrows, no startled oaths from the bosun, not ever. "And what has he been up to, Captain?"

Bowen told him what had been found and said:

"Can you make any more of it than I can, which is zero?"

"If you can't, Captain, I can't." The regard in which the captain held the bosun was wholly reciprocated. "He doesn't want to sink the ship, not with him aboard and the water temperature below freezing. But he doesn't want to stop the ship—there's half a dozen ways a clever man could do that. I'm thinking myself that all he wanted to do is to douse the lights."

"What would the object be?"

"Well, as I don't have to tell you, the lights—at night time, anyway—identify us as a hospital ship."

"And why would he want to do that, Archie?" It was part of their unspoken understanding that the captain always called him "Bosun" except when they were alone.

"Well." The bosun pondered. "You know I'm not a Highlander or a Western Islander so I can't claim to be fey or have sound sight." There was just the faintest suggestion of an amalgam of disapproval and superiority in the bosun's voice, but the captain refrained from smiling; essentially, he knew, Shetlanders did not regard themselves as Scots and restricted their primary allegiance to the Shetlands. "But like yourself, Captain, I have a nose for trouble and I can't say I'm very much liking what I can smell. Half an hour—well maybe forty minutes—anybody will be able to see that we are a hospital ship." He paused and looked at the captain with what might possibly have been a hint of surprise, which was the nearest the bosun ever came to registering emotion. "I have the feeling that someone is going to have a go at us before dawn. At dawn, most likely."

"I have the same feeling myself, Archie. Alert the crew, will you? Ready for emergency stations. Spread the word that there's an illegal electrician in our midst."

The bosun smiled. "So that they can keep an eye on each other. I don't think, Captain, that we'll find the man among the crew. They've been with us for a long time now."

"I hope not and I think not. That's to say I'd like to think not. But it was someone who knew his way around. Their wages are not exactly on a princely scale. You'd be surprised what a bag of gold can do to a man's loyalty."

"After twenty-five years at sea, there isn't a great deal that can surprise me. Those survivors we took off that tanker last night—well, I wouldn't care to call any of them my blood brother."

"Come, come, bosun, a little of the spirit of Christian charity, if you please. It was a Greek tanker—Greece is supposed to be an ally, if you remember—and the crew would be Greek. Well, Greek, Cypriot, Lebanese, Hottentot if you like. Can't expect them all to look like Shetlanders. I didn't see any of them carrying a pot of gold."

"No. But some of them—the uninjured ones, I mean—were carrying suitcases."

"And some of them were carrying overcoats."

"And at least three of them were wearing ties."

"And why not? The *Argos* spent six hours there wallowing around after being mined: time and enough for anyone to pack his worldly possessions or such few possessions as Greek seamen appear to have. It would be a bit much, I think, Archie, to expect a crippled Greek tanker in the Barents Sea to have aboard a well-dressed crewman with a bag of gold who just happened to be a trained saboteur."

"Aye, it's not a combination that one would expect to find every day. Do we alert the hospital?"

"Yes. What's the latest down there?" The bosun knew the state of everything aboard the *San Andreas* whether it concerned his department or not.

"Dr. Singh and Dr. Sinclair have just finished operating. One man with a broken pelvis, the other with extensive burns. They're in the recovery room now and should be okay. Nurse Magnusson is with them."

"Archie, you do appear to be singularly well-informed, even for you."

"Nurse Magnusson is a Shetlander," the bosun said, as if that explained everything. "Seven patients in Ward A, not fit to be moved. Worst is the Chief Officer of the *Argos*, but not in danger, Janet says."

"Janet?"

"Nurse Magnusson." The bosun was a difficult man to put off his stride. "Ten in recuperating Ward B. The *Argos* survivors are in the bunks on the port side."

"I'll go down there now. Go and alert the crew. When you've finished come along to the sick bay—and bring a couple of your men with you."

"Sick bay?" The bosun regarded the deckhead. "You'd better not let Sister Morrison hear you call it that."

Bowen smiled. "Ah, the formidable sister. All right,

hospital. Twenty sick men down there. Not to mention sisters, nurses and ward orderlies who—"

"And doctors."

"And doctors who have never heard a shot fired in their lives. A close eye, Archie."

"You are expecting the worst, Captain?"

"I am not," Bowen said heavily, "expecting the best."

The hospital area of the *San Andreas* was remarkably airy and roomy, remarkably but not surprisingly, for the *San Andreas* was primarily a hospital and not a ship. Well over half of the lower deck space had been given to its medical facilities. The breaching of watertight bulkheads—a hospital ship, theoretically, did not require watertight bulkheads—increased both the sense and the actuality of spaciousness. The area was taken up by two wards, an operating theater, recovery room, medical store, dispensary, galley—quite separate from and independent of the crew's galley—cabins for the medical staff, two messes—one for the staff, the other for recuperating patients—and a small lounge. It was toward the last of those that Captain Bowen now made his way.

He found three people there, having tea: Dr. Singh, Dr. Sinclair and Sister Morrison. Dr. Singh was a good-natured man of Pakistani descent, middle-aged and wearing a pince-nez—he was one of the few people who looked perfectly at home with such glasses. He was a qualified and competent surgeon who disliked being called Mister. Dr. Sinclair, sandy-haired and every bit as amiable as his colleague, twenty-six years old, had quit in his second year as an intern in a big teaching hospital to volunteer for service in the Merchant Navy. Nobody could ever have accused Sister Morrison of being amiable: about the same age as Sinclair, she had auburn hair, big brown eyes and a generous mouth, all three of which accorded ill with her habitually prim expression, the steel-rimmed glasses which she occasionally affected and a faint but unmistakable aura of hauteur. Captain Bowen wondered what she looked like when she smiled; he wondered if she ever smiled.

He explained, briefly, why he had come. Their reactions were characteristic. Sister Morrison tightened her lips, Dr. Sinclair raised his eyebrows and Dr. Singh, half-smiling, said: "Dear me, dear me. Saboteur or saboteurs, spy or spies aboard a British vessel. Quite unthinkable." He meditated briefly. "But then not everybody aboard is strictly British. I'm not, for one."

"Your passport says you are." Bowen smiled. "As you were operating in the theater at the time as our saboteur was operating elsewhere that removes you from the list of potential suspects. Unfortunately, we don't have a list of suspects, potential or otherwise. We do indeed, Dr. Singh, have a fair number of people who were not born in Britain. We have two Indians—lascars—two Goanese, two Singhalese, two Poles, a Puerto Rican, a Southern Irishman and, for some odd reason, an Italian who, as an official enemy, ought to be a prisoner of war or in an internment camp somewhere. And, of course, the survivors of the *Argos* are non-British to a man."

"And don't forget me," Sister Morrison said coldly. "I'm half German."

"You are? With a name like Margaret Morrison?"

She put her chin forward, an exercise which seemed to come naturally to her. "How do you know that my name is Margaret?"

"A captain holds the crew lists. Like it or not, you are a member of the crew. Not that any of this matters. Spies, saboteurs, can be of any nationality and the more unlikely they are—in this case British—the more efficiently they can operate. As I say, that's at the moment irrelevant. What is relevant is that the bosun and two of his men will be here shortly. Should an emergency arise he will assume complete charge except, of course, for the handling of the very ill. I assume you all know the bosun?"

"An admirable man," Dr. Singh said. "Very reassuring, very competent, couldn't imagine anyone I'd rather have around in times of need."

"We all know him." Sister Morrison was good with her clipped tones. "Heaven knows he's here often enough."

"Visiting the sick?"

"Visiting the sick! I don't like the idea of an ordinary seaman pestering one of my nurses."

"Mr. McKinnon is not an ordinary seaman. He's an extraordinary seaman and he's never pestered anyone in his life. Let's have Janet along here to see if she bears out your preposterous allegations."

"You—you know her name."

"Of course I know her name." Bowen sounded weary. It was not the moment, he thought, to mention the fact that until five minutes ago he had never heard of anyone on board called Janet. "They come from the same island and have much to talk about. It would help, Miss Morrison, if you took as much interest in your staff as I do in mine."

A good exit line, Bowen thought, but he wasn't particularly proud of himself. In spite of the way she spoke he rather liked the girl because he suspected that the image she projected to the world was not the real one and that there might be some very good reason for this.

The Chief Officer, Geraint Kennet—an unusual name but one that he maintained came from an ancient aristocratic lineage—was awaiting Bowen's arrival on the bridge. Kennet was a Welshman, lean of figure and of countenance, very dark and very irreverent.

"You are lost, Mr. Kennet?" Bowen said.

"When the hour strikes, sir, Kennet is there. I hear of alarums and excursions from young Jamie here." "Young Jamie" was Third Officer Batesman, who didn't much like the designation. "Something sinister afoot, I gather."

"You gather rightly. Just how sinister I don't know." He described what had happened. "So, two electrical breakdowns, if you could call them that, and a third in the process of being investigated."

"And it would be naïve to think that the third is not connected with the other two?"

"Quite naïve."

"This presages something ominous."

"Didn't they teach you English in those Welsh schools?"

"No, sir. I mean, yes sir. You have reached a conclusion, not, perhaps, a very nice one?"

The phone rang. Batesman took it and handed the phone to Bowen, who listened briefly, thanked the caller and hung up.

"Jamieson. In the cold room, this time. How could anyone get into the cold room? Cook's got the only key."

"Easily," Kennet said. "If a man was a saboteur, as you suggest, trained in his art—if that's the word I want—one would expect him to be an expert picklock or at least to carry a set of skeleton keys around with him. With respect, sir, I hardly think that's the point. When will this villain strike again?"

"When indeed. Flannelfoot—that's Jamieson's term for him—seems to be a bastard of some resource and foresight. It is more than likely that he has some further surprises. Jamieson is of the same mind. If there's another power failure when they switch on again he says he's going to go over every inch of wiring with his bridge-megger, whatever that is."

"Some sort of instrument for detecting voltage leaks—you know, breaks in a circuit. It's occurred to me—"

Chief Radio Officer Spenser appeared at the hatchway of his wireless office, paper in hand. "Message from the *Andover*, sir."

Bowen read out: "Continued absence of lights very serious. Essential expedite matters. Has saboteur been apprehended?"

Kennet said: "Cue, I think, for angry spluttering."

"Man's a fool," Bowen said. "Commander Warrington, I mean, captain of the frigate. Spenser, send: 'If you have any members of the Special Branch or C.I.D. with you they are welcome aboard. If not, kindly refrain from sending pointless signals. What the hell do you think we're trying to do?'"

Kennet said: "In the circumstances, sir, a very restrained signal. As I was about to say—"

The phone rang again. Batesman took the call, listened, acknowledged, hung up and turned to the captain.

"Engine room, sir. Another malfunction. Both Jamieson and Third Engineer Ralson are on their way up with meggers."

Bowen brought out his pipe and said nothing. He gave the impression of a man temporarily bereft of words. Kennet wasn't, but then Kennet never was.

"Man seldom gets to finish a sentence on this bridge. Have you arrived at any conclusion, sir, however unpleasant?"

"Conclusion, no. Hunch, suspicion, yes. Unpleasant, yes. I would take odds that by or at dawn someone is going to have a go at us."

"Fortunately," Kennet said, "I am not a betting man. In any event I wouldn't bet against my own convictions, which are the same as yours, sir."

"We're a hospital ship, sir," Batesman said. He didn't even sound hopeful.

Bowen favored him with a morose glance. "If you are immune to the sufferings of the sick and dying and care to exercise a certain cold-blooded and twisted logic, then we are a man-of-war even though we are completely defenseless. For what do we do? We take our sick and wounded home, fix them up and send them off again to the front or to the sea to fight the Germans once more. If you were to stretch your conscience far enough, you could make a good case out of maintaining that to allow a hospital ship to reach its homeland is tantamount to aiding and abetting the enemy. Oberleutnant Lemp would have torpedoed us without a second thought."

"Oberleutnant who?"

"Lemp. Chap who sent the *Athenia* to the bottom, and Lemp knew that the *Athenia* carried only civilians as passengers, men, women and children who—he knew this well—would never be used to fight against the Germans. The *Athenia* was a case much more deserving of compassion than we are, don't you think, Third?"

"I wish you wouldn't talk like that, sir." Batesman was now not only as morose as the captain had been, but positively mournful. "How do we know that this fellow Lemp is not lurking out there, just over the horizon?"

"Fear not," Kennet said. "Oberleutnant Lemp has long since been gathered to his ancestors, for whom one can feel only a certain degree of sympathy. However, he has brothers or some kindred souls out there. As the captain so rightly implies, we live in troubled and uncertain times."

Batesman looked at Bowen. "It is permitted, Captain, to ask the chief officer to shut up?"

Kennet smiled broadly, then stopped smiling as the phone rang again. Batesman reached for the phone but Bowen forestalled him. "Master's privilege, Third.

The news may be too heavy for a young man like you
to bear." He listened, cursed by way of acknowledgment and hung up. When he turned round he looked,
and sounded, disgusted.

"Bloody officers' toilet!"

Kennet said: "Flannelfoot?"

"Who do you think it was. Santa Claus?"

"A sound choice," Kennet said judiciously. "Very
sound. Where else could a man work in such peace,
privacy and for an undetermined period of time, bliss-
fully immune, one might say, from fear of interruption.
Might even have time to read a chapter of his favorite
thriller as is the habit of one young officer aboard this
ship, who shall remain nameless."

"The third officer has the right of it," Bowen said.
"Will you kindly shut up?"

"Yes, sir. Jamieson?"

"Yes."

"We should be hearing from Ralson any time now."

"Jamieson has already heard from him. Seamen's
toilet this time, port side."

For once, Kennet had no observation to make and
for almost a minute there was silence on the bridge
for the sufficient reason that there didn't seem to be
any comment worth making. When the silence was
broken it was, inevitably, by Kennet.

"A few more minutes and our worthy engineers
might as well cease and desist. Or am I the only person
who has noticed that the dawn is in the sky?"

Already, to the southeast, off the port beam, the sky
had changed from black, or as black as it ever becomes
in northern waters, to a dark gray and was steadily

lightening. The snow had stopped now, the wind had dropped to twenty knots, and the *San Andreas* was pitching, not heavily, in the head seas coming up from the northwest.

Kennet said: "Shall I post a couple of extra lookouts, sir? One on either wing?"

"And what can those lookouts do? Make faces at the enemy?"

"They can't do a great deal more, and that's a fact. But if anyone is going to have a go at us, it's going to be now. A high-flying Condor, for instance—you can almost see the bombs leaving the bay and there's an even chance in evasive action." Kennet didn't sound particularly enthusiastic or convinced.

"And if it's a submarine, dive bomber, glider bomber or torpedo bomber?"

"They can still give us warning and time for a prayer. Mind you, probably a short prayer, but still a prayer."

"As you wish, Mr. Kennet."

Kennet made a call and within three minutes his lookouts arrived on the bridge, duffel-coated and scarfed to the eyebrows as Kennet had instructed. McGuigan and Jones, a Southern Irishman, and a Welshman, were only boys, neither of them a day over eighteen. Kennet issued them binoculars and posted them on the bridge wings, Jones to port, McGuigan to starboard. Seconds only after closing the port door, Jones opened it again.

"Ship, sir! Port quarter." His voice was excited, urgent. "Warship, I think."

"Relax," Kennet said. "I doubt whether it's the *Tirpitz*." Less than half a dozen people aboard knew that the *Andover* had accompanied them during the night. He stepped out onto the wing and returned almost immediately. "The good shepherd," he said. "Three miles."

"It's almost half-light now," Captain Bowen said. "We could be wrong, Mr. Kennet."

The radio-room hatchway panel banged open and Spenser's face appeared.

"*Andover*, sir. Bandit, bandit, one bandit...045... ten miles...five thousand."

"There now," Kennet said. "I knew we weren't wrong. Full power, sir?" Bowen nodded and Kennet gave the necessary instructions to the engine room.

"Evasive action?" Bowen was half smiling. Knowledge, however unwelcome that knowledge, always comes as a relief after uncertainty. "A Condor, you would guess?"

"No guess, sir. In these waters, only the Condor flies alone." Kennet slid back the port wing door and gazed skyward. "Cloud cover's pretty thin now. We should be able to see our friend coming up—he should be practically dead astern. Shall we go out on the wing, sir?"

"In a minute, Mr. Kennet. Two minutes. Gather flowers while we may—or at least keep warm as long as possible. If fate has abandoned us we shall be freezing to death all too soon. Tell me, Mr. Kennet, has any profound thought occurred to you?"

"A lot of thoughts have occurred to me, but I wouldn't say any of them are profound."

"How on earth do you think that Condor located us?"

"Submarine? It could have surfaced and radioed Alta Fjord."

"No submarine. The *Andover*'s sonar would have picked him up. No plane, no surface ships, that's a certainty."

Kennet frowned for a few seconds, then smiled. "Flannelfoot," he said with certainty. "A radio."

"Not necessarily even that. A small electrical device, probably powered by our own mains system, that transmits a continuous homing signal."

"So if we survive this lot it's out with the fine-tooth comb?"

"Indeed. It's out with—"

"*Andover*, sir." It was Spenser again. "Four bandits, repeat four bandits...310...eight miles...three thousand."

"I wonder what we've done to deserve this?" Kennet sounded almost mournful. "We were even more right than we thought, sir. Torpedo bombers or glide bombers, that's for sure, attacking out of the darkness to the northwest and us silhouetted against the dawn."

The two men moved out on the port wing. The *Andover* was still on the port quarter but had closed in until it was less than two miles distant. A low bank of cloud, at about the same distance, obscured the view aft.

"Hear anything, Mr. Kennet? See anything?"

"Nothing, nothing. Damn that cloud. Yes, I do. I hear it. It's a Condor."

"It's a Condor." Once heard, the desynchronized clamor of a Focke-Wulf 200's engine is not readily forgotten. "And I'm afraid, Mr. Kennet, that you'll have to postpone your evasive action practice for another time. This lad sounds as if he is coming in very low."

"Yes, he's coming in low. And I know why." Most unusually for Kennet, he sounded very bitter. "He intends to do some pinpoint precision bombing. He's under orders to stop us or cripple us but not sink us. I'll bet that bastard Flannelfoot feels as safe as houses."

"You have it to rights, Mr. Kennet. He could stop us by bombing the engine room, but doing that is a practical guarantee that we go to the bottom. There he comes, now." The Focke-Wulf Condor had broken through the cloud and was heading directly for the stern of the *San Andreas*. Every gun on the *Andover* that could be brought to bear had opened up as soon as the Focke-Wulf had cleared the cloud bank, and within seconds the starboard side of the *Andover* was wreathed in smoke. For a frigate, its anti-aircraft fire power was formidable: low-angle main armament, pompoms, Oerlikons and the equally deadly Boulton-Paul Defiant turrets, which loosed off a devastating 960 rounds a minute. The Focke-Wulf must have been hit many times, but the big Condor's capacity to absorb punishment was legendary. Still it came on, now no more than two hundred feet above the waves. The sound of the engines had risen from the clamorous to the thunderous.

"This is no place for a couple of honest seamen, Mr. Kennet." Captain Bowen had to shout to make himself heard. "But I think it's too late now."

"I rather think it is, sir."

Two bombs, just two, arced lazily down from the now smoking Condor.

2

HAD THE AMERICANS RETAINED THE ORIGINAL British design concept for accommodations aboard the Liberty ships, the tragedy, while still remaining such, would at least have been minimized. The original Sunderland plans had the accommodations both fore and aft: Henry Kaiser's designers, in their wisdom—blind folly as it turned out—had *all* their accommodations, for both officers and men, including also the navigating bridge, grouped in a single superstructure surrounding the funnel.

The bosun, Dr. Sinclair by his side, had reached the upper deck before the Condor reached the *San Andreas* and was almost immediately joined by Patterson, for whom the *Andover*'s barrage had sounded like a series of heavy metallic blows on the side of his engine room.

"Down!" the bosun shouted. Two powerful arms around their shoulders bore them to the deck, for the Focke-Wulf had reached the *San Andreas* before the bombs did and the bosun was well aware that the Focke-Wulf carried a fairly lethal array of machine guns. On this occasion, however, the guns remained silent, possibly because the gunners were under instructions not to fire, more probably because the gunners were already dead, for it was plain that the Condor, trailing a huge plume of black smoke, whether from fuselage or engines it was impossible to say, and veering sharply to starboard, was itself about to die.

The two bombs, contact and not armor-piercing, struck fore and aft of the funnel, exploded simultaneously and just immediately after passing through the unprotected deckheads of the living quarters, blowing the shattered bulkheads outward and filling the air with screaming shards of metal and broken glass, none of which reached the three prone men. The bosun cautiously lifted his head and stared in disbelief as the funnel, seemingly intact but sheared off at its base, toppled slowly over the port side and into the sea. Any sound of a splash that there may have been was drowned out by the swelling roar of more engines.

"Stay down, stay down!" Flat on the deck, the bosun twisted his head to the right. There were four of them in line-abreast formation, Heinkel torpedo bombers, half a mile away, no more than twenty feet above the water and headed directly for the starboard side of the *San Andreas*. Ten seconds, he thought, twelve at the most, and the dead men in the charnel house of that shattered superstructure would have company and to spare. Why had the guns of the *Andover* fallen silent? He twisted his head to the right to look at the frigate and immediately realized why. It was impossible that the gunners on the *Andover* could not hear the sound of the approaching Heinkels but it was equally impossible that they could see them. The *San Andreas* was directly in line between the frigate and the approaching bombers which were flying below the height of its upper deck.

He shook his head in exasperation, then looked right again and to his momentary astonishment saw that this was no longer the case. The Heinkels were lifting clear of the water, and it suddenly became clear that their intention was to fly over the *San Andreas*, which they did seconds later, not much more than ten feet above the deck, two on each side of the twisted superstructure. The hospital ship was not the target now, only the shield for the Heinkels: the frigate was the target and the bombers were halfway between the *San Andreas* and frigate before the bemused defenders aboard the *Andover* understood what was happening.

When they did understand, their reaction was sharp and violent. The main armament was virtually useless. It takes time to train and elevate a gun of any size, and against a close-in and fast-moving target there just isn't time. The anti-aircraft guns, the two-pounders, the Oerlikons and the Defiants did mount a heavy barrage, but torpedo bombers were notoriously difficult targets, not least because the gunners were acutely aware that death was only seconds away, a realization that made for less than a controlled degree of accuracy.

The bombers were less than three hundred yards away when the plane on the left side of the formation pulled up and banked to its left to clear the stern of the *Andover*; almost certainly neither the plane nor the pilot had been damaged: as was not unknown, the torpedo release mechanism had iced up, freezing the torpedo in place. Almost at the same instant the plane on the right descended in a shallow dive until it touched the water—almost certainly the pilot had been shot. A victory but a Pyrrhic one. The other two Heinkels released their torpedoes and lifted clear of the *Andover*.

Three torpedoes hit the *Andover* almost simultaneously, the two that had been cleanly released and the one that was still attached to the plane that had crashed into the water. All three torpedoes detonated, but there was little enough in the way of thunderclaps of sound or shock waves: water always has this same muffling effect on an underwater explosion. What they did produce, first, was a great sheen of water and spray which rose to two hundred feet into the sky and then slowly subsided. When it finally disappeared the *Andover* was on its beam ends and deep in the water. Within twenty seconds, with only a faint hissing as the water flooded the engine room and with curiously little in the way of bubbles, the *Andover* slid beneath the surface of the sea.

"My God, my God, my God!" Dr. Sinclair, swaying slightly, was on his feet. As a doctor, he was acquainted with death, but not in this shocking form; he was still dazed, not quite aware of what was going on around him. "Good God, that big plane is coming back again!"

The big plane, the Condor, was coming back again, but it offered a diminished threat to them. Dense smoke pouring from all four engines, it completed a half circle approaching the *San Andreas*. Less than half a mile away it touched the surface of the sea, momentarily dipped beneath it, then came into sight again. There was no more smoke.

"God rest them," Patterson said, looking at where the *Andover* had been. He was almost abnormally calm. "Damage control party first. See if we're making water, although I shouldn't have thought so."

"Yes, sir." The bosun stared at what was left of the superstructure. "Perhaps a fire-control party. Lots of blankets, mattresses, clothes, papers in there—God only knows what's smoldering away already."

"Do you think there will be any survivors in there?"

"I wouldn't even guess, sir. If there are, thank heavens we're a hospital."

Patterson turned to Dr. Sinclair and shook him gently. "Doctor, we need your help." He nodded toward the superstructure. "You and Dr. Singh—and the ward orderlies. I'll send some men with sledges and crowbars."

"An oxyacetylene torch?" said the bosun.

"Of course."

"We've got enough medical equipment and stores aboard to equip a small-town hospital," Sinclair said. "If there are any survivors, all we'll require is a few hypodermic syringes." He seemed back on balance again. "We don't take in the nurses?"

"Good God, no." Patterson shook his head vehemently. "I tell you, *I* wouldn't like to go in there. If there are any survivors the nurses will have their share of horrors later."

McKinnon said: "Permission to take away the lifeboat, sir?"

"Whatever for?"

"There could be survivors from the *Andover*."

"Survivors! She went down in thirty seconds."

"The *Hood* blew apart in one second. There were three survivors."

"Of course, of course. I'm not a seaman, bosun. You don't need permission from me."

"Yes, I do, sir." The bosun gestured toward the superstructure. "All the deck officers are there. You're in command."

"Good God!" The thought, the realization, had never struck Patterson. "What a way to assume command!"

"And speaking of command, sir, the *San Andreas* is no longer under command. She's slewing rapidly to port. Steering mechanism on the bridge must have been wrecked."

"Steering can wait. I'll stop the engines."

Three minutes later the bosun eased the throttle and edged the lifeboat toward an inflatable life raft which was roller-coasting heavily near the spot where the now vanished Condor had been. There were only two men in the raft; the rest of the air crew, the bosun assumed, had gone to the bottom with the Focke-Wulf. Probably dead anyway. One of the men, no more than a youngster, very seasick and looking highly apprehensive—he had every right, the bosun thought, to be apprehensive—was sitting upright and clinging to a lifeline. The other lay on his back in the bottom of the raft; in the regions of his left upper chest, left upper arm and right thigh his flying overalls were saturated with blood. His eyes were closed.

"Jesus' sake!" Able Seaman Ferguson, who had a powerful Liverpool accent and whose scarred face spoke eloquently of battles lost and won, mainly in barrooms, looked at the bosun with a mixture of disbelief and outrage. "Jesus, bosun, you're not going to pick those bastards up? They just tried to send us to the bottom. Us! A hospital ship!"

"Wouldn't you like to know *why* they bombed a hospital ship?"

"There's that, there's that." Ferguson reached out with a boat hook and brought the raft alongside.

"Either of you speak English?"

The wounded man opened his eyes; they, too, seemed to be filled with blood. "I do."

"You look badly hurt. I want to know where before we try to bring you aboard."

"Left arm, left shoulder, I think, right thigh. And I believe there's something wrong with my right foot." His English was completely fluent, and if there was any accent at all it was a hint of southern standard English, not German.

"You're the Condor captain, of course."

"Yes. Still want to bring me aboard?"

The bosun nodded to Ferguson and the two other seamen he had along with him. The three men brought the injured pilot aboard as carefully as they could, but with both lifeboat and raft rolling heavily in the beam seas it was impossible to manage it smoothly. They laid him in the thwarts close to where the bosun was sitting by the controls. The other survivor huddled miserably amidships. The bosun opened the throttle and headed for the position where he estimated the *Andover* had gone down.

Ferguson looked down at the injured man, who was lying motionless on his back, arms spread-eagle. The red stains were growing. It could have been that he was still bleeding heavily; but it could have been the effect of sea water.

"Reckon he's a goner, Bosun?"

McKinnon reached down and touched the side of the pilot's neck and after a few seconds located the pulse, fast, faint and erratic, but still a pulse.

"Unconscious. Fainted. Couldn't have been an easy passage for him."

Ferguson regarded the pilot with a certain grudging respect. "He may be a bloody murderer, but he's a bloody tough bloody murderer. Must have been in agony, but never a squawk. Shouldn't we take him back to the ship first? Give him a chance, like?"

"I thought of it. No. There just may be survivors from the *Andover* and if there are they won't last long. Sea temperature is about freezing or just below it. A man's usually dead inside a minute. If there's anyone at all, a minute's delay may be a minute too late. We owe them that chance. Besides, it's going to be a very quick trip back to the ship."

The *San Andreas*, still slewing to port, had come around in a full half-circle and, under reverse thrust, was slowing to a stop. Patterson had almost certainly done this so as to maneuver the temporarily rudderless ship as near as possible to the spot where the *Andover* had been torpedoed.

Only a pathetic scattering of flotsam and jetsam showed where the frigate had gone down, balks of timber, a few drums, carley floats, lifebuoys and life jackets, all empty—and four men. Three of the men were together. One of them, with what appeared to be a gray stocking hat, was keeping the head of another man, either unconscious or dead, out of the water: with his other hand he waved at the approaching life-boat. All three men were wearing life jackets and, much more important, all three were wearing wet-suits—the only reason they were still alive after fifteen minutes in the lethally cold waters of an Arctic winter.

All three were hauled inboard. The young, bare-headed man who had been supported by the man with the gray stocking hat was unconscious, not dead. There was a great swelling bruise still oozing blood just above his right temple. The third man—it seemed most incongruous in the circumstances—wore the peaked braided cap of a naval commander. The cap was completely saturated. The bosun made to remove it, then changed his mind when he saw the blood at the back of the cap: the cap was probably stuck to his head. The commander was conscious, he had courteously thanked the bosun for being pulled out of the sea, but his eyes were vacant, glazed and sightless. McKinnon passed a hand before his eyes, but there was no reaction: for the moment, at any rate, the commander was blind.

Although he knew he was wasting his time, the bosun headed toward the fourth man in the water but backed off when he was still five yards away. Although the man's face was deep in the water he hadn't died from drowning but from freezing: he wasn't wearing a wet-suit. The bosun turned the lifeboat back to the *San Andreas* and touched the commander gently on the shoulder.

"How do you feel, Commander Warrington?"

"What? How do I feel? How do you know I'm Commander Warrington?"

"You're still wearing your cap, sir." The commander made as if to touch the peak of his cap but the bosun restrained him. "Leave it, sir. You've cut your head. We'll have you in hospital inside fifteen minutes. Plenty of doctors and nurses there for that sort of thing, sir."

"Hospital." Warrington shook his head as if trying to clear it. "Ah, of course. The *San Andreas*. You must be from her."

"Yes, sir. I'm the bosun."

"What happened, Bosun? The *Andover*, I mean." Warrington touched the side of his head. "I'm a bit foggy up here."

"No bloody wonder. Three torpedoes, sir, almost simultaneously. You must have been blown off the bridge, or fell off it or, most likely been washed off it when your ship went down. She was on her beam ends then, sir, and it took only just over twenty seconds."

"How many of us—well, how many have you found?"

"Just three, sir. I'm sorry."

"God above. Just three. Are you sure, Bosun?"

"I'm afraid I'm quite sure, sir."

"My yeoman of signals—"

"I'm here, sir."

"Ah. Hedges. Thank heavens for that. Who's the third?"

"Navigating officer, sir. He's taken a pretty nasty clout on the head."

"And the first lieutenant?"

Hedges didn't answer; he had his head buried in his hands and was shaking it from side to side.

"I'm afraid Hedges is a bit upset, Commander. Was the first lieutenant wearing a red kapok jacket?"

Warrington nodded.

"Then we found him, sir. I'm afraid he just froze to death."

"He would, wouldn't he? Freeze to death, I mean." Warrington smiled faintly. "Always used to laugh at us and our wet-suits. Carried a rabbit's foot around with him and used to say that was all the wet-suit he'd ever need."

Dr. Singh was the first man to meet the bosun when he stepped out of the lifeboat. Patterson was with him, as were two orderlies and two stokers. The bosun looked at the stokers and wondered briefly what they were doing on deck, but only very briefly: they were almost certainly doing a seaman's job because there were very few seamen left to do it. Ferguson and his two fellow seamen had been in the for'ard fire-control party and might well be the only three left: all the other seamen had been in the superstructure at the time of the attack.

"Five," Dr. Singh said. "Just five. From the frigate and the plane, just five."

"Yes, Doctor. And even they had the devil's own

luck. Three of them are pretty wobbly. Commander looks all right but I think he's in the worst condition. He seems to have gone blind and the back of his head has been damaged. There's a connection, isn't there, Doctor?"

"Oh dear. Yes, there's a connection. We'll do what we can."

Patterson said: "A moment, Bosun, if you will." He walked to one side and McKinnon followed him. They were halfway toward the twisted superstructure when Patterson stopped.

"As bad as that is it, sir?" the bosun said. "No eaves-droppers. I mean, we have to trust someone."

"I suppose." Patterson looked and sounded tired. "But damned few. Not after what I've seen inside that superstructure. Not after one or two things I've found out. First things first. The hull is still structurally sound. No leaks. I didn't think there would be. We're fixing up a temporary rudder control in the engine room: we'll probably be able to reconnect to the bridge, which is the least damaged part of the superstructure. There was a small fire in the crew's mess, but we got that under control." He nodded to the sadly twisted mass of metal ahead of them. "Let's pray for calm weather to come. Jamieson says the structural supports are so weakened that the whole lot is liable to go over the side if we hit heavy seas. Would you like to go inside?"

"Like? Not like. But I have to." The bosun hesitated, reluctant to hear the answer to the question he had to ask. "What's the score so far, sir?"

"Up to now we've come across thirteen dead." Patterson grimaced. "And bits and pieces. I've decided to

leave them where they were meantime. There may be
more people left alive."

"More? You have found some?"

"Five. They're in a pretty bad way, some of them.
They're in the hospital." He led the way inside the
twisted entrance at the after end of the superstructure.
"There are two oxyacetylene teams in there. It's slow
work. No fallen beams, no wreckage as such, just
twisted and buckled doors. Some of them, of course—
the doors, I mean—were just blown off. Like this one
here."

"The cold room. Well, at least there would have been
nobody in there. But there were three weeks' supply
of beef, all kinds of meat, fish, and other perishables
in there: in a couple of days time we'll have to start
heaving them over the side." They moved slowly along
the passageway. "Cool room intact, sir, although I don't
suppose a steady diet of fruit and veg will have much
appeal. Oh God!"

The bosun stared into the galley, which lay across
the passage from the cool room. The surfaces of the
cooking stoves were at a peculiar angle, but all the
cupboards and the two work tables were intact. What
had caught the bosun's horrified attention was not the
furniture but the two men who lay on the floor. They
seemed unharmed except for a trickle of blood from
the ears and noses.

"Netley and Spicer," the bosun whispered. "They
don't seem—they're *dead*?"

"Concussion. Instantaneous," Dr. Sinclair said.

The bosun shook his head and moved on.

"Tinned food store," he said. "Intact. It would be.

And the liquor store here, not a can dented or a bottle broken." He paused. "With your permission, sir, I think this a very good time to breach the liquor store. A hefty tot of rum all round—or at least for the men working in here. Pretty grim work, and it's the custom in the Royal Navy when there's grim work to be done."

Patterson smiled, a smile that did not touch the eyes. "I didn't know you were in the Royal Navy, Bosun."

"Twelve years. For my sins."

"An excellent idea," Patterson said. "I'll be your first customer." They made their way up a twisted but still serviceable companionway to the next deck, the bosun with a bottle of rum and half a dozen mugs strung on a wire in the other.

The crew accommodation deck was not a pretty sight. The passageway had a distinct S-bend to it, the deck was warped so that it formed a series of undulations. At the for'ard end of the passageway, two oxyacetylene teams were at work, each attacking a buckled door. In the short space between the head of the companionway and where the men were working were eight doors, four of them hanging drunkenly on their hinges, four that had been been cut open by torches: seven of those cabins had been occupied, and the occupants were still there, twelve in all. In the eighth cabin they found Dr. Sinclair stooping over and administering a morphine injection to a prone but fully conscious patient, a consciousness testified to by the fact that he was addressing nobody in particular in an unprintable monologue.

The bosun said: "How do you feel, Chips?" Chips was Rafferty, the ship's carpenter.

"I'm dying." He caught sight of the rum bottle in the bosun's hand and his stricken expression vanished. "But I could make a rapid recovery—"

"This man is not dying," Dr. Sinclair said. "He has a simple fracture of the tibia, that's all. No rum—morphine and alcohol make for bad bedfellows. Later." He straightened and tried to smile. "But I could do with a tot, if you would, Bosun—a generous one. I feel in need of it." With his strained white face he unquestionably looked in need of it; nothing in Dr. Sinclair's brief medical experience had even remotely begun to prepare him for the experience he was undergoing. The bosun poured him the requisite generous measure, did the same for Patterson and himself, then passed the bottle and mugs to the men with the torches and the two ward orderlies who were standing unhappily by, strapped stretcher at the ready: they looked in no better condition than Dr. Sinclair but cheered up noticeably at the scent of rum.

The deck above held the officers' accommodation. It too had been heavily damaged, but not so devastatingly as the deck below. Patterson stopped at the first cabin they came to; its door had been blown inward and the contents of the cabin looked as if a maniac had been let loose there with a sledgehammer. The bosun knew it was Chief Patterson's cabin.

The bosun said: "I don't much care for being in an engine room, sir, but there are times when it has its advantages." He looked at the empty and almost as badly damaged third engineer's cabin opposite. "At least Ralson is not here. Where is he, sir?"

"He's dead."

"He's dead," the bosun repeated slowly.

"When the bombs struck he was still in the seaman's toilet fixing that short circuit."

"I'm most damnably sorry, sir." He knew that Ralson had been Patterson's only close friend aboard the ship.

"Yes," Patterson said vaguely. "He had a young wife and two kids—babies, really."

The bosun shook his head and looked into the next cabin, that belonging to the second officer. "At least Mr. Rawlings is not here."

"No. He's not here. He's up on the bridge." The bosun looked at him, then turned away and went into the captain's cabin, which was directly opposite and which, oddly enough, seemed almost undamaged. The bosun went directly to a small wooden cupboard on the bulkhead, produced his knife, opened up the marlin spike and inserted its point just below the cupboard lock.

"Breaking and entering, Bosun?" The chief engineer's voice held puzzlement but no reproof: he knew McKinnon well enough to know that the bosun never did anything without a sound reason.

"Breaking and entering is for locked doors and windows, sir. Just call this vandalism." The door sprang open and the bosun reached inside, bringing out two guns. "Navy Colt .445s. You know about guns, sir?"

"I've never held a gun in my hand in my life. *You* know about guns—as well as rum?"

"I know about guns. This little switch here—you press it so. Then the safety catch is off. That's really all you require to know about guns." He looked at the broken cupboard and then the guns and shook his head again. "I don't think Captain Bowen would have minded."

"Won't. Not wouldn't. Won't."

The bosun carefully laid the guns on the captain's table. "You're telling me that the captain is not dead?"

"He's not dead. Neither is the chief officer."

The bosun grinned for the first time that morning, then looked accusingly at the chief engineer. "You might have told me this, sir."

"I suppose. I might have told you a dozen things. You would agree, Bosun, that we each have a great deal on our minds. They're both in the sick bay, both pretty savagely burned about the face but not in any danger, not, at least, according to Dr. Singh. It was being far out on the port wing of the bridge that saved them—they were away from the direct effects of the blast."

"How come they got so badly burned, sir?"

"I don't know. They can hardly speak, their faces are wrapped in bandages, they look more like Egyptian mummies than anything else. I asked the captain and he kept mumbling something like Essex or Wessex or something like that."

The bosun nodded. "Wessex, sir. Rockets. Distress flares. Two lots kept on the bridge. The shock must have triggered some firing mechanism and it went off prematurely. Damnable ill luck."

"Damnably lucky, if you ask me, Bosun. Compared to practically everybody else in the superstructure."

"Does he—does he know yet?"

"It hardly seemed the time to tell him. Another thing he kept repeating, as if it was urgent. 'Home signal, home signal,' something like that. Over and over again. Maybe his mind was wandering, maybe I couldn't make him out. Their mouths are the only part of their faces that aren't covered with bandages, but even their lips are pretty badly burned. And, of course, they're loaded with morphine. 'Home signal.' Mean anything to you?"

"At the moment, no."

A young and rather diminutive stoker appeared in the doorway. McCrimmon, in his middle twenties, was a less than lovable person, his primary and permanent characteristics being truculence, a fixed scowl, a filthy tongue and the interminable mastication of chewing gum; at that moment all four were in abeyance.

"Bloody *awful*, so it is, down there. Just like a bloody cemetery."

"Morgue, McCrimmon, morgue," Patterson said. "What do you want?"

"Me? Nothing, sir. Jamieson sent me. He said something about the phones no' working and you would be wanting a runner, maybe."

"Second engineer to you, McCrimmon." Patterson looked at the bosun. "Very thoughtful of the second engineer. Nothing we require in the engine room— except to get that jury rudder fixed. Deckside, Bosun?"

"Two lookouts, although God knows what they'll be looking out for. Two of your men, sir, the two ward orderlies below, Able Seaman Ferguson and Curran. Curran is—used to be—a sailmaker. Don't fancy him his job, but I'll give him a hand. Curran will know what to bring. I suggest, sir, we have the crew's mess deck cleared."

"Our mortuary?"

"Yes, sir."

"You heard, McCrimmon? How many men?"

"Eight, sir."

"Eight. Two lookouts. The two seamen to bring up the canvas and whatever required. The other four to clear the crew's mess. Don't you try to tell them, they'd probably throw you overboard. Tell the second engineer and he'll tell them. When they're finished have them report to me, here or on the bridge. You too. Off you go."

McCrimmon left.

The bosun indicated the two Colts lying on the table. "I wonder what McCrimmon thought of those."

"Probably old hat to him. Jamieson picked the right man—McCrimmon's tough and hasn't much in the way of finer feelings. Irish Scots from some Glasgow slum. Been in prison. In fact, if it wasn't for the war that's probably where he'd be now."

The bosun nodded and opened another small wall locker—this one had a key to it. It was a small liquor cupboard, and from a padded velvet retainer McKinnon removed a rum bottle and laid it on the captain's bunk.

"I don't suppose the captain will mind that either," Patterson said. "For the stretcher bearers?"

"Yes, sir." The bosun started opening drawers in the captain's table and found what he was looking for in the third drawer, two leather-bound folders, which he handed to Patterson. "Prayer book and burial service, sir. But I should think the burial service would be enough. Somebody's got to read it."

"I'm not a preacher, Bosun."

"No, sir. But you're the officer commanding."

"Good God," Patterson said. He placed the folders reverently on the captain's table. "I'll look at those later."

"'Home signal,'" the bosun said slowly. "That's what the captain said, wasn't it? 'Home signal.'"

"Yes."

"Homing signal is what he was trying to say. Homing signal. Should have thought of it before—but I suppose that's why Captain Bowen is a captain and I'm not. How do you think the Condor managed to locate us in the darkness? All right, it was half-dawn when he attacked, but he *must* have been on the course when it was still night. How did he know where we were?"

"U-boat?"

"No U-boat. The *Andover's* sonar would have picked him up." The bosun was repeating the words that Captain Bowen had used.

"Ah." Patterson nodded. "Homing signal. Our saboteur friend."

"Flannelfoot, as Mr. Jamieson calls him. Not only was he busy fiddling around with our electrical circuits, he was transmitting a continuous signal. A directional signal. The Condor knew where we were to the inch. I don't know whether the Condor was equipped to receive such signals, I know nothing about planes, but it wouldn't have mattered, some place like Alta Fjord could have picked up the signal and transmitted our bearing to the Condor."

"You have it, of course. Bosun, you have it to rights." Patterson looked at the two guns. "One for me and one for you."

"If you say so, sir."

"Don't be daft, who else would have it?" Patterson picked up a gun. "I've never even held one of those things in my hand, far less fired one. But you know, Bosun, I don't really think I would mind firing a shot once. Just one."

"Neither would I, sir."

Second Officer Rawlings was lying beside the wheel and there was no mystery as to how he had died: what must have been a flying shard of metal had all but decapitated him.

"Where's the helmsman?" the bosun asked. "Was he a survivor, then?"

"I don't know. I don't know who was on. Maybe Rawlings had sent him to get something. But there were two survivors up here, apart from the captain and chief officer—McGuigan and Jones."

"McGuigan and Jones? What were they doing up here?"

"It seems Mr. Kennet had called them up and posted them as lookouts, one on either wing. I suppose that's why they survived, just as Captain Bowen and Mr. Kennet survived. They're in the hospital too."

"Badly hurt?"

"Unharmed, I believe. Shock, that's all."

The bosun moved out to the port wing and Patterson followed. The wing was wholly undamaged, no signs of metal buckling anywhere. The bosun indicated a once gray but now badly scorched metal box which was attached just below the windbreaker; its top and one side had been blown off. "That's where they kept the Wessex rockets," he said.

They went back inside and the bosun moved toward the wireless office hatchway: the sliding wooden door was no longer there.

"I wouldn't look if I were you," Patterson said.

"The men have got to, haven't they?"

Chief Radio Officer Spenser was lying on the deck, but he was no longer recognizable as such. He was just an amorphous mass of bone and flesh and torn, blood-saturated clothing: had it not been for the clothing it could have been the shattered remnants of any animal lying there. When McKinnon looked away Patterson could see that some color had drained from the deeply tanned face.

"The first bomb must have gone off directly beneath him," the bosun said. "God, I've never seen anything like it. I'll attend to him myself. Third Officer Batesman. I know he was the officer of the watch. Any idea where he is, sir?"

"In the chart room. I don't advise you to go there either."

Batesman was recognizable, but only just. He was still on his chair, half leaning, half lying on the table, what was left of his head pillowed on a blood-stained chart. McKinnon returned to the bridge.

"I don't suppose it will be any comfort to their relatives to know that they died without knowing. I'll fix him up myself, too. I couldn't ask the men." He looked ahead through the shattered windscreens. At least, he thought, they wouldn't be needing a Kent clear-view screen any more. "Wind's backing to the east," he said absently. "Bound to bring more snow. At least it might help to hide us from the wolves—if there are any wolves around."

"You think, perhaps, they might come back to finish us off?" The chief was shivering violently, but that was only because he was accustomed to the warmth of the engine room: the temperature on the bridge was about 6° F.—twenty-six degrees of frost—and the wind held steady at twenty knots.

"Who can be sure, sir? But I really don't think so. Even one of those Heinkel torpedo bombers could have finished us off if they had had a mind to. Come to that, the Condor could have done the same thing."

"It did pretty well as it was, if you ask me."

"Not nearly as well as it could have done. A Condor normally carries 250-kilo bombs—that's about 550 pounds. A stick of those—say three or four bombs— would have sent us to the bottom. Even two might have been enough—they'd have certainly blown the superstructure out of existence, not just crippled it."

"The Royal Navy again, is that it, Bosun?"

"I know explosives, sir. Those bombs couldn't have been any more than 50 kilos each. Don't you think, sir, that we might have some interesting questions to ask that Condor captain when he regains consciousness?"

"In the hope of getting some interesting answers, is that it? Including the answer to the question as to why he bombed a hospital ship in the first place."

"Well, yes, perhaps."

"What do you mean, perhaps?"

"There's just a chance—a faint one, I admit—that he didn't know he was bombing a hospital ship."

"Don't be ridiculous, Bosun. Of course he knew. How big does a red cross have to be before you see it?"

"I'm not trying to make any excuses for him, sir." There was a touch of asperity in McKinnon's voice and Patterson frowned, not at the bosun but because it was most unlike the bosun to adopt such a tone without reason. "It was still only half-dawn, sir. Looking down, things look much darker than they do at sea level. You've only got to go up to a crow's-nest to appreciate that." As Patterson had never been in a crow's-nest in his life he felt ill-equipped to comment on the bosun's observations. "As he was approaching from dead astern he couldn't possibly have seen the markings on the ship's sides, and as he was flying very low he couldn't have seen the red cross on the foredeck—the super-structure would have blocked off his view."

"That still leaves the red cross on the after deck. Even though it might have been only half-light, he *must* have seen that."

"Not with the amount of smoke you were putting up under full power."

"There's that. There is a possibility." He was unconvinced and watched with some impatience as the bosun spun the now useless wheel and examined the binnacle compass and the standby compass, smashed beyond any hope of repair.

"Do we have to remain up here?" Patterson said. "There's nothing we can do here at the moment, and I'm freezing to death. I suggest the captain's cabin."

"I was about to suggest the same, sir."

The temperature in the cabin was no more than freezing point, but that was considerably warmer than it had been on the bridge and, more important, there was no wind there. Patterson went straight to the liquor cabinet and extracted a bottle of scotch.

"If you can do it I can do it. We'll explain to the captain later. I don't really like rum and I need it."

"A specific against pneumonia?"

"Something like that. You will join me?"

"Yes, sir. The cold doesn't worry me, but I think I'm going to need it in the next hour or so. Do you think the steering can be fixed, sir?"

"It's possible. Have to be a jury job. I'll get Jamieson on to it."

"It's not terribly important. I know all the phones are out, but it shouldn't take too long to reconnect them, and you're fixing up a temporary rudder control in the engine room. Same with the electrics—it won't take long to run a few rubber cables here and there. But we can't start on any of those things until we get this area—well, cleared."

Patterson lowered the contents of his glass by half. "You can't run the *San Andreas* from the bridge. Two minutes up there was enough for me. Fifteen minutes and anyone would be frozen to death."

"You can't run it from any other place. Cold is the problem, I agree. So we'll board it up. Plenty of plywood in the carpenter's shop."

"You can't see through plywood."

"Could always pop our heads through the wing doors

from time to time, but that won't be necessary. We'll let some windows into the plywood."

"Fine, fine," Patterson said. The scotch was apparently restoring his circulation. "All we need is a glazier and some windows, and we haven't got either."

"A glazier we don't need. We don't need to have cut glass or fitted windows. You must have rolls and rolls of insulating tape in your electrical department."

"I've got a hundred miles of it and I still don't have any windows."

"Windows we won't need. Glass, that's all. I know where the very best glass is—and plate glass at that. The tops of all those lovely trolleys and trays in the hospital."

"Ah! I do believe you have it, Bosun."

"Yes sir. I suppose Sister Morrison will let you have them."

Patterson smiled one of his rare smiles. "I believe I'm the officer commanding, however temporary."

"Indeed, sir. Just don't let me be around when you put her into irons. Those are all small things. There are three matters that give a bit more concern. First, the radio is just a heap of scrap metal. We can't contact anyone and no one can contact us. Secondly, the compasses are useless. I know you had a gyro installed, but it never worked, did it? But worst of all is the problem of navigation."

"Navigation? Navigation! How can that be a problem?"

"If you want to get from A to B, it's the biggest problem of all. We have—we had—four navigating officers aboard this ship. Two of those are dead and the other two are swathed in bandages—in your own words, like Egyptian mummies. Commander Warrington could have navigated, I know, but he's blind, and from the look in Dr. Singh's eyes I should think the blindness is permanent." The bosun paused for a moment then shook his head. "And just to make our cup overflowing, sir, we have the *Andover's* navigating officer aboard and he's either concussed or in some sort of coma—we'll have to ask Dr. Singh. If a poker player got dealt this kind of hand of cards, he'd shoot himself. Four navigating officers who can't see, and if you can't see you can't navigate. That's why the loss of the radio is so damned unfortunate. There must be a British warship within a hundred or two miles which could have lent us a navigating officer. Can you navigate, sir?"

"Me? Navigate?" Patterson seemed positively affronted. "I'm an engineer officer. But you, McKinnon. You're a seaman—*and* twelve years in the Royal Navy."

"It doesn't matter if I had been a hundred years in the Royal Navy, sir. I still can't navigate. I was a torpedo petty officer. If you want to fire a torpedo, drop a depth charge, blow up a mine or do some elementary electrics, I'm your man. But I'd barely recognize a sextant if I saw one. Such things as sun sights, moon sights— if there is such a thing—and star sights are just words to me. I've also heard of words like deviation and variation and declination, and I know more about Greek than I do about those.

"We do have a little hand-held compass aboard the motor lifeboat, the one I took out today, but that's useless. It's a magnetic compass, of course, and that's useless because I do know the magnetic north pole is nowhere near the geographical north pole; I believe it's about a thousand miles away from it. Canada, Baffin Island or some such place. Anyway, in the latitudes we're in now the magnetic pole is more west than north." The bosun sipped some whisky and looked at Patterson over the rim of his glasses. "Chief Patterson, we're lost."

"Job's comforter." Patterson stared moodily at his glass, then said without much hope: "Wouldn't it be possible to get the sun at noon? That way we'd know where the south was."

"The way the weather is shaping up we won't be able to *see* the sun at noon. Anyway, what's noon, sun time? It's certainly not twelve o'clock on our watches. Supposing we were in the middle of the Atlantic, where we might as well be, and knew where south was. Would that help us find Aberdeen, which is where I believe we are going? The chronometer, incidentally, is kaput, which doesn't matter at all—I still wouldn't be able to relate the chronometer to longitude. And even if we did get a bearing on due south, it's dark up here twenty hours out of the twenty-four, and the auto-pilot, of course, is as wrecked as everything else on the bridge. We wouldn't, of course, be going around in circles— the hand compass would stop us from doing that— but we still wouldn't know in what direction we were heading."

"If I want to find some optimism, Bosun, I'll know where not to look. Would it help at all if we knew approximately where we were?"

"It would help, but all we know, approximately, is

that we're somewhere north or northwest of Norway. Anywhere, say, in twenty thousand square miles of sea. There are only two possibilities, sir. The captain and chief officer must have known where we were. If they're able to tell us, I'm sure they will."

"Good God, of course! Not very bright, are we? At least, I'm not. What do you mean 'if'? Captain Bowen was able to talk about twenty minutes ago."

"That was twenty minutes ago. You know how painful burns can be. Dr. Singh is sure to have given them painkillers, and sometimes the only way they can work is by knocking you out."

"And the other possibility?"

"The chart house. Mr. Batesman was working on a chart—he still had a pencil in his hand. I'll go."

Patterson grimaced. "Sooner you than me."

"Don't forget Flannelfoot, sir."

Patterson touched his overalls where he had concealed his gun.

"Or the burial service."

Patterson looked at the leather-covered folder in distaste. "And where am I supposed to leave that? On the operating table?"

"There are four empty cabins in the hospital, sir. For recuperating V.I.P.s. We don't have any at the moment."

"Ah. Ten minutes, then."

The bosun was back in five minutes, the chief engineer in fifteen, with an air of almost palpable gloom hanging over him.

"No luck, sir?"

"No, damnit," Patterson said. "You guessed right. They're under heavy sedation, may be hours before they come to. And if they do start coming to, Dr. Singh says, he's going to sedate them again. Apparently they were trying to tear the bandages off their faces. He's got their hands swathed in bandages—an unconscious man, the doctor says, will try to scratch away at whatever irritates him. Anyway, their hands *were* burned—not badly, but enough to justify the bandages."

"They've got straps for tying wrists to the bed frames."

"Dr. Singh did mention that. He said he didn't think Captain Bowen would take too kindly to waking up and finding himself in irons on his own ship. By the way, the missing helmsman was Hudson. Broken ribs, and one pierced his lung. Doctors says he's very ill. What luck did *you* have?"

"Same as you, sir. Zero. There was a pair of parallel rules lying beside him, so I assume he must have been penciling out a course."

"You couldn't gather anything from the chart?"

"It wasn't a chart any more. It was just a blood-stained rag."

3

IT WAS SNOWING HEAVILY AND A BITTER WIND BLEW from the east as they buried their dead in the near-Stygian darkness of the early afternoon. They did have a form of illumination, for the saboteur, probably more than satisfied with the results of his morning's activities, was now resting on his laurels and the deck floodlights were working again. But in that swirling blizzard, the light given off was weak, fitful, almost ineffectual, serving only to intensify the ghoulish effect of the burial party hastening about their macabre task and the ghostlike appearance of the dozen snow-covered mourners. Flashlight in hand, Chief Engineer Patterson read out the burial service, but he might as well have been quoting the latest prices on the stock exchange, for not a word could be heard: one by one the dead, in their weighted canvas shrouds, slipped down the tilted plank, out from under the union flag and vanished silently into the freezing water of the Barents Sea. No bugle calls, no Last Post for the Merchant Navy, not ever: the only requiem was the lost and lonely keening of the wind through the frozen rigging and the jagged gaps that had been torn in the superstructure.

Shivering violently and mottled blue and white with the cold, the burial party and mourners returned to the only reasonably warm congregating space left on the *San Andreas*—the dining and recreational area in the hospital between the wards and the cabins.

"We owe you a very great debt, Mr. McKinnon," Dr. Singh said. He had been one of the mourners and his teeth were still chattering. "Very swift, very efficient. It must have been a gruesome task."

"I had six willing pairs of hands," the bosun said. "It was worse for them than it was for me." The bosun did not have to explain what he meant: everybody knew that anything would always be worse for anybody than for that virtually indestructible Shetlander. He looked at Patterson. "I have a suggestion, sir."

"A Royal Naval one?"

"No, sir. Deep-sea fisherman's. Anyway, it's close enough, those are the waters of the Arctic trawlers. A toast to the departed."

"I endorse that, and not for traditional or sentimental reasons." Dr. Singh's teeth still sounded like castanets. "Medicinal. It doesn't really warm you, but there's the illusion, and I don't know about the rest of you, but my red corpuscles are in need of some assistance."

The bosun looked at Patterson, who nodded his approval. McKinnon turned to an undersized, freckle-faced youth who was hovering at a respectful distance. "Wayland."

Wayland came hurrying forward. "Yes, Mr. McKinnon, sir?"

"Go with Mario to the liquor store. Bring back some refreshments."

"Yes, Mr. McKinnon, sir. Right away, Mr. McKinnon, sir." The bosun had long given up trying to get Wayland Day to address him in any other fashion.

Dr. Singh said: "That won't be necessary, Mr. McKinnon. We have supplies here." He pointed.

"Medicinal, of course?"

"Of course." Dr. Singh watched as Wayland went into the galley. "How old is that boy?"

"He claims to be seventeen or eighteen, says he's not sure which. In either case, he's fibbing. I don't believe he's ever seen a razor."

"He's supposed to be working for you, isn't he? Pantry boy, I understand. He seems to spend nearly all his day here."

"I don't mind, Doctor, if you don't."

"No, not at all. He's an eager lad, willing and helpful."

"He's all yours. Besides, we haven't a pantry left. He's making eyes at one of the nurses?"

"You underestimate the boy. Sister Morrison, no less. At a worshipful distance, of course."

"Good God!" the bosun said.

Mario entered, bearing, one-handed and a few inches above his head, a rather splendid silver salver laden with bottles and glasses, which, in the circumstances, was no mean feat, as the *San Andreas* was rolling noticeably. With a deft twirling movement Mario had the tray on the table without as much as the clink of a glass against glass. Where the salver had come from was unexplained and Mario's business. As became the popular conception of an Italian, Mario was darkly and magnificently mustachioed, but whether he possessed the traditional flashing eyes was impossible to say, as he invariably wore sun glasses. There were those who purported to see in those glasses a connection with the Sicilian Mafia, an assertion that was always good-humoredly made, as he was well liked. Mario was over-weight, of indeterminate age, and claimed to have served in the Savoy Grill, which may have been true. What was beyond dispute was that there lay behind Mario, a man whose rightful home Captain Bowen considered to be either a prisoner-of-war or internment camp, a more than usually checkered career.

After no more than two fingers of scotch, but evidently considering that his corpuscles were back on the job, Dr. Singh said: "And now, Mr. Patterson?"

"Lunch, Doctor. A very belated lunch, but starving ourselves isn't going to help anyone. I'm afraid it will have to be cooked in your galley and served here."

"Already under way. And then?"

"And then *we* get under way." He looked at the bosun. "We could, temporarily, have the lifeboat's compass in the engine room. We already have rudder control there."

"It wouldn't work, sir," McKinnon said. "There's so much metal in your engine room that any magnetic compass would have fits." He pushed back his chair and rose. "Think I'll pass up lunch. You will agree, Mr. Patterson, that a telephone line from the bridge

to the engine room and electric power on the bridge—
so that we can see what we are doing—are the two
first priorities?"

Jamieson said: "That's already being attended to,
Bosun."

"Thank you, sir. But the lunch can still wait." He
was speaking now to Patterson. "Board up the bridge
and let some light in. After that, sir, we might try to
clear up some of the cabins in the superstructure, find
out which of them is habitable and try to get power
and heating back on. A little heating on the bridge
wouldn't come amiss, either."

"Leave all that other stuff to the engine-room staff—
after we've had a bite, that is. You'll be requiring some
assistance?"

"Ferguson and Curran will be enough."

"Well, that leaves only one thing." Patterson regarded
the deckhead. "The plate glass for your bridge windows."

"Indeed, sir. I thought you—"

"A trifle." Patterson waved a hand to indicate how
much of a trifle it was. "You have only to ask, Bosun."

"But I thought you—perhaps I was mistaken."

"We have a problem?" Dr. Singh said.

"I wanted some plate glass from the trolleys or trays
in the wards. Perhaps, Dr. Singh, you would care—"

"Oh, no." Dr. Singh's reply was as quick as it was
decisive. "Dr. Sinclair and I run the operating theater
and look after our surgical patients, but the running
of the wards has nothing to do with us. Isn't that so,
Doctor?"

"Indeed it is, sir." Dr. Sinclair also knew how to sound decisive.

The bosun surveyed the two doctors and Patterson with an impassive face that was much more expressive than any expression could have been and passed through the doorway into Ward B. There were ten patients in this ward and two nurses, one very much a brunette, the other very much a blonde. The brunette, Nurse Irene, was barely in her twenties, hailed from Northern Ireland, was pretty and of such a warm and happy disposition that no one would have dreamed of calling her by her surname, which no one seemed to know anyway. She looked up as the bosun entered, and for the first time since she'd joined she failed to give him a welcoming smile. He patted her shoulder gently and walked to the other end of the ward, where Nurse Magnusson was rebandaging a seaman's arm.

Janet Magnusson was a few years older than Irene and taller, but not much. She had a more than faintly windswept, Viking look about her and was unquestionably good-looking: she shared the bosun's flaxen hair and blue-gray eyes but not, fortunately, his burned-brick complexion. Like the younger nurse, she was much given to smiling; like her colleague's, the smile was in temporary abeyance. She straightened as the bosun approached, reached out and touched his arm.

"It was terrible, wasn't it, Archie?"

"Not a thing I would care to do again. I'm glad you weren't there, Janet."

"I didn't mean that—the burial, I mean. It was you who sewed up the worst of them—they say that the radio officer was, well, all bits and pieces."

"An exaggeration. Who told you that?"

"Johnny Holbrook. You know, the young orderly. The one that's scared of you."

"There's nobody scared of me," the bosun said absently. He looked around the ward. "Been quite some changes here."

"We had to turf some of the so-called recuperating patients out. You'd have thought they were being sent to their deaths. Siberia, at least. Nothing the matter with them. Not malingerers, really; they just liked soft beds and being spoiled."

"And who was spoiling them, if not you and Irene? They just couldn't bear to be parted from you. Where's the lioness?"

Janet gave him a disapproving look. "Are you referring to Sister Morrison?"

"She's the one I mean. I have to beard her in her den."

"You don't know her, Archie. She's very nice really. Maggie's my friend. Truly."

"Maggie?"

"When we're off duty, always. She's in the next ward."

"Maggie! Good lord. I thought she disapproved of you because she disapproved of me talking to you."

"Fiddlesticks. And Archie?"

"Yes?"

"A lioness doesn't have a beard."

The bosun didn't deign to answer. He moved into the adjacent ward. Sister Morrison wasn't there. Of the eight patients, only two, McGuigan and Jones, were visibly conscious. The bosun approached their adjacent beds and said: "How's it going, boys?"

"Ach, we're fine, Bosun," McGuigan said. "We shouldn't be here at all."

"You'll stay here until you're told to leave." Eighteen years old. He was wondering how long it would take them to recover from the sight of the almost decapitated Rawlings lying by the wheel when Sister Morrison entered by the far door.

"Good afternoon, Sister."

"Good afternoon, Mr. McKinnon. Making your medical rounds, I see."

The bosun felt the stirrings of anger but contented himself with looking thoughtful; he was probably unaware that his thoughtful expression, in certain circumstances, could have a disquieting effect on people.

"I just came to have a word with you, Sister." He looked around the ward. "Not a very lively bunch, are they?"

"I hardly think this is the time or place for levity, Mr. McKinnon." The lips were not as compressed as they might have been, but there was an appreciable lack of warmth behind the steel-rimmed spectacles.

The bosun looked at her for long seconds, during which time she began to show distinct signs of uneasiness. Like most people—with the exception of the timorous Johnny Holbrook—she regarded the bosun as being cheerful and easygoing, with the additional rider, in her case, that he was probably a bit simple: it required only one glance at that cold, hard, bleak face to realize how wrong she had been. It was an unsettling experience.

The bosun spoke in a slow voice. "I am not in the mood for levity, Sister. I've just buried fifteen men. Before I buried them I had to sew them up in their sheets of canvas. Before I did that I had to gather up their bits and stick their guts back inside. Then I sewed them up. Then I buried them. I didn't see you among the mourners, Sister."

The bosun was more than aware that he shouldn't have spoken to her like that and he was also aware that what he had gone through had affected him more than he had thought. Under normal circumstances it was impossible that he should have been so easily provoked; but the circumstances were abnormal and the provocation too great.

"I've come for some plate glass, such as you have on the tops of your trolleys and trays. I need them urgently and I don't need them for any lighthearted purposes. Or do you require an explanation?"

She didn't say whether she required an explanation or not. And she did nothing dramatic like sinking into a chair, reaching out for the nearest support or even putting a hand to her mouth. Only her color changed. Sister Morrison had the kind of complexion that, like her eyes and lips, was in marked contrast to her severe expression and steel-rimmed glasses, the kind of complexion that would have had the cosmetic tycoons sending their scientists back to the bench; at that moment, however, the peaches had faded from the traditional if rarely seen peaches and cream to the traditional if equally rare English rose.

The bosun removed the glass top from a table by

Jones's bedside, looked around for trays, saw none, nodded to Sister Morrison and went back to Ward B.

Janet Magnusson looked at him in surprise. "Is that what you went for?"

The bosun nodded.

"Maggie—Sister Morrison—had no objection?"

"Nary an objection. Have you any glass-topped trays?"

Chief Patterson and the others had already begun lunch when the bosun returned, five sheets of plate glass under his arm. Patterson too looked faintly surprised.

"No trouble then, Bosun?"

"One has only to ask. I'll need some tools for the bridge."

"Fixed," Jamieson said. "I've just been to the engine room. There's a box gone up to the bridge—all the tools you'll require, nuts, bolts, screws, insulating tape, a power drill and a power saw."

"Ah. Thank you. But I'll need power."

"Power you have. Only a temporary cable, mind you, but the power is there. And lights, of course. The phone will take some time."

"That's fine. Thank you, Mr. Jamieson." He looked at Patterson. "One other thing, sir. We have a fair number of nationalities in our crew. The captain of the Greek tanker—Andropolous, isn't it?—might have a mixed crew too. I should think there's a fair chance, sir, that one of our men and one of the Greek crew might have a common language. Perhaps you could make inquiries, sir."

"And how would that help, Bosun?"

"Captain Andropolous can navigate."

"Of course, of course. Always the navigation, isn't it, Bosun?"

"There's nothing without it, sir. Do you think you could get hold of Naseby and Trent? They're the two men who were with me here when we were attacked. Weather's worsening, sir, and we have ice forming on the deck. Would you have them rig up lifelines between here and the superstructure?"

"Worsening?" Dr. Singh said. "How much worse, Mr. McKinnon?"

"Quite a bit, I'm afraid. Bridge barometer is smashed, but I think the one in the captain's cabin is intact. I'll check." He brought out the hand compass that he'd removed from the lifeboat. "This thing's virtually useless, but at least it does show changes in direction. We're wallowing in the troughs port side to, so that means the wind and the sea are coming at us on the port beam. Wind direction is changing rapidly, we've backed at least five degrees since we came down here. Wind's roughly northeast. If experience is any guide that means heavy snow, heavy seas and a steadily dropping temperature."

"No slightest light in the gloom, is that it, Mr. McKinnon?" Dr. Singh said. "Where every prospect pleases and only man is vile. Except the other way round."

"A tiny speck of light, Doctor. If the temperature keeps falling like this, the cold room is going to stay cold and the frozen meat and fish should stay that way. And we do have a vile man—or men—aboard or we shouldn't be in the state we are. You're worried about your patients, aren't you, Doctor—especially the ones in Ward A?"

"Telepathy, Mr. McKinnon. If conditions deteriorate much more they're going to start falling out of their beds—and the last thing I want to do is to start strapping wounded men to their beds."

"And the last thing I want is for the superstructure to topple over the side."

Jamieson had pushed back his chair and was on his feet. "I have my priorities right, no, Bosun?"

"Indeed, Mr. Jamieson. Thank you very much."

Jamieson left. Dr. Singh half-smiled. "Not more telepathy?"

The bosun smiled back. Dr. Singh appeared to be very much the right man in the right place. "I think he's gone to have a word with the men rigging up the telephone line from the bridge to the engine room."

"And then I press the button," Patterson said.

"Yes, sir. And then southwest. I don't have to tell you why."

"You might tell a landlubber why," Dr. Singh said.

"Of course. Two things. Heading southwest will mean that the wind and the seas from the northeast are dead astern. That should eliminate all rolling so that you don't have to put your patients in straitjackets or whatever. There'll be some pitching, of course, but not much, and even then Mr. Patterson can smooth that out by adjusting the ship's speed to the wave speed. The other big advantage is that by heading southwest there's no land we can bump into for hundreds of miles to come. If you will excuse me, gentlemen." The bosun left, together with his sheets of plate glass and hand compass.

"Doesn't miss much, does he?" Dr. Singh said. "Competent, you would say, Mr. Patterson?"

"Competent? He's more than that. Certainly the best bosun I've ever sailed with—and I've never known a bad bosun yet. If we ever get to Aberdeen—and with McKinnon around I rate our chances better than even—I won't be the man you'll have to thank."

The bosun arrived on the bridge, a bridge now over-illuminated with two garish arc-lamps, to find Ferguson and Curran already there, with enough plywood of various shapes and sizes to build a modest hut. Neither of the two men could be said to be able to walk, not in the proper sense of the term. Muffled to the ears and with balaclavas and hoods pulled low over their foreheads, they were so swaddled in layers of jerseys, trousers, and coats that they were barely able to waddle; given a couple of white fur coats they would have resembled nothing as much as a pair of polar bears that had given up on their diet years ago. As it was, they were practically white already: the snow, driving almost horizontally, swept, without let or hindrance, through the yawning gaps where the port for'ard screens and the upper wing door screen had once been. Conditions weren't improved by the fact that, at a height of some forty feet above the hospital, the effects of the rolling were markedly worse than they had been down below—so bad, in fact, that it was very difficult to keep one's footing, and that only by hanging on to something. The bosun carefully laid the plate glass in a corner and wedged it so that it wouldn't slide all over the deck. The rolling didn't bother the bosun, but the creaking and groaning of the superstructure supports and the occasional shuddering vibration that shook the bridge bothered him a very great deal.

"Curran! Quickly! Chief Engineer Patterson. You'll find him in the hospital. Tell him to start up and turn the ship either into the wind or away from the wind. Away is better—that means hard a-starboard. Tell him the superstructure is going to fall over the side any minute."

For a man usually slow to obey any order and handicapped though he was by his constricted lower limbs, Curran made off with remarkable alacrity. It could have been that he was a good man in an emergency. More likely, he didn't fancy being on the bridge when it vanished into the Barents Sea.

Ferguson eased two layers of scarf from his mouth. "Difficult working conditions, Bosun. Impossible, a man might say. And have you seen the temperature?"

The bosun glanced at the bulkhead thermometer which was about the only thing still working on the bridge. "Two above," he said.

"Ah! Two above. But two above what? Fahrenheit, that's what it's above. That means thirty degrees of frost." He looked at the bosun in what he probably regarded as a meaningful fashion. "Have you ever heard of the chill factor, eh?"

The bosun spoke with commendable restraint. "Yes, Ferguson, I have heard of the chill factor."

"For every knot of wind the temperature, as far as the skin is concerned, falls by one degree." Ferguson had something on his mind and as far as he was concerned the bosun had never heard of the chill factor. "Wind's at least thirty knots. That means it's *sixty* below on this bridge. Sixty!" At that moment, at the end of an especially alarming roll, the superstructure gave a loud creak, more of a screech than a creak, and it didn't require any kind of imagination to visualize metal tearing under lateral stress.

"If you want to leave the bridge," the bosun said, "I'm not ordering you to stay."

"Trying to shame me into staying, eh? Trying to apeal to my better nature? Well, I got news for you. I ain't got no better nature, mate."

The bosun said, mildly: "Nobody aboard this ship calls me 'mate.'"

"Bosun." Ferguson made no move to carry out his implied threat and he wasn't even showing any signs of irresolution. "Do I get danger money for this? Overtime, perhaps?"

"A couple of tots of Captain Bowen's special malt scotch. Let's spend our last moments usefully, Ferguson. We'll start with some measuring."

"Already done." Ferguson showed the spring-loaded steel measuring tape in his hand and tried hard not to smile in smug self-satisfaction. "Me and Curran have already measured the front and side screens. Written down on that bit of plywood there."

"Fine, fine." The bosun tested both the electric drill

and electric saw. Both worked. "No problem. We'll cut the plywood three inches wider and higher than your measurements to get the overlap we need. Then we'll drill holes top, bottom and sides, three quarters of an inch in, face the plywood up to the screen bearers, mark the metal and drill the holes through the steel."

"That steel is three-eighths of an inch. Take to next week to drill all those holes."

The bosun looked through the tool box and came up with three packets of drills. The first he discarded. The drills in the second, all with blue tips, he showed to Ferguson.

"Tungsten. Goes through steel like butter. Mr. Jamieson doesn't miss much." He paused and cocked his head as if listening, but it was a purely automatic reaction. Any sound from the after end of the ship was carried away by the wind. But there was no mistaking the throbbing that pulsed through the superstructure. He looked at Ferguson, whose face cracked into what might have been a smile.

The bosun moved to the starboard wing door—the sheltered side of the ship—and peered through the gap where the screen had been in the upper half of the door. The snow was so heavy that the seas moving away from the *San Andreas* were as much imagined as seen. The ship was still rolling in the troughs. A vessel of any size that has been lying dead in the water can take an unconscionable time—depending, of course, on the circumstances—to gather enough momentum to have steerage way on, but after another minute the bosun became aware that the ship was sluggishly answering to the helm. He couldn't see this but he could feel it: a definite quartering motion had entered into the rolling to which they had been accustomed for some hours.

McKinnon moved away from the wing door. "We're turning to starboard. Mr. Patterson has decided to go with the wind. We'll soon have both sea and snow behind us. Fine, fine."

"Fine, fine," Ferguson said. This was about twenty seconds later and the tone of his voice indicated that everything was all but fine. He was, instead, acutely uneasy and with reason. The *San Andreas* was heading almost due south, the heavy seas bearing down on her port quarter were making her corkscrew violently and the markedly increased creaking and groaning of the superstructure was doing little enough for his morale. "God's sake, why couldn't we have stayed where we were?"

"A minute's time and you'll see why." And shortly he did see why. The corkscrewing and rolling gradually eased and ceased altogether, as did the creaking in the superstructure and the *San Andreas*, on an approximately southwest course, was almost rock steady in the water. There was a slight pitching, but, compared to what they had just experienced, it was so negligible as not to be worth the mentioning. Ferguson, with a stable deck beneath his feet, the fear of imminent drowning removed and the snowstorm so squarely behind them that not a flake reached the bridge, had about him an air of profound relief.

Shortly after the bosun and Ferguson had started sawing out the rectangles of plywood, four men arrived on the bridge—Jamieson, Curran, McCrimmon and another stoker called Stephen. Stephen was a Pole and was called always by his first name: nobody had ever been heard to attempt the surname of Przynyszewski. Jamieson carried a telephone, Curran two black heaters, McCrimmon two radiant heaters and Stephen two spools of rubber-insulated cable, one thick, one thin, both of which he unreeled as he went.

"Well, this is more like it, Bosun," Jamieson said. "A mill pond, one might almost call it. Done a power of good for the morale down below. Some people have even rediscovered their appetites. Speaking of appetites, how's yours? You must be the only person aboard who hasn't had lunch today."

"It'll keep." The bosun looked to where McCrimmon and Stephen were already attaching wires from the heaters to the heavy cable. "Thanks for those. They'll come in handy in an hour or two, when we've managed to keep all this fresh air out."

"More than handy, I should have thought." Jamieson shivered. "My word, it is fresh up here. What's the temperature?"

The bosun looked at the thermometer. "Zero. That's two degrees it's dropped in a few minutes. I'm afraid, Mr. Jamieson, that we're going to be very cold tonight."

"Not in the engine room," Jamieson said. He unscrewed the back of the telephone and started connecting it to the slender cable. "Mr. Patterson thinks this is an unnecessary luxury and that you just want it so that you can talk to someone when you feel lonely. Says that keeping the stern on to wind and seas is child's play and that he could do it for hours without deviating more than two or three degrees off course."

"I've no doubt he could. That way we'll never see Aberdeen. You can tell Mr. Patterson that the wind is backing and that if it backs far enough and he still keeps stern on to the wind and sea we'll end up by making a small hole in the north of Norway and a large hole in ourselves."

Jamieson smiled. "I'll explain that to the chief. I don't think the possibility has occured to him—it certainly didn't to me."

"And when you go below, sir, would you send up Naseby? He's an experienced helmsman."

"I'll do that. Need any more help up here?"

"No, sir. The three of us are enough."

"As you say." Jamieson screwed the back of the telephone in place, pressed the call-up button, spoke briefly and hung up. "Satisfaction guaranteed. Are you through, McCrimmon? Stephen?" Both men nodded, and Jamieson called the engine room again, asked for power to be switched on and told McCrimmon and Stephen to switch on one heater apiece, one black, one radiant. "Still require McCrimmon as a runner, Bosun?"

The bosun nodded toward the telephone. "Thanks to you, I've got my runner."

One of McCrimmon's radiant heaters had started to glow a dim red. Stephen removed a hand from the black heater and nodded.

"Fine. Switch off. It would seem, Bosun, that Flannelfoot has knocked off for the day. We'll go below now, see what cabins we can make habitable. I'm afraid there won't be many. The only way we can make a cabin habitable—the clearing up won't take long, I've already got a couple of our boys working on that—is to replace defective heating systems. That's all that matters. Unfortunately, most of the doors have been blasted off their hinges or cut away by the oxyacetylene torches, and there's no point in replacing heating if we can't replace the doors. We'll do what we can." He spun the useless wheel. "When we've finished below and you've finished here—and when the temperature is appropriate for myself and other hothouse plants from the engine room—we'll come and have a go at this steering."

"Big job, sir?"

"Depends upon what damage in the decks below. Don't hold me to it, Bosun, but there's a fair chance that we'll have it operational, in what you'll no doubt regard as our customary crude fashion, some time this evening. To give me some leeway, I won't specify what time."

The temperature on the bridge continued to drop steadily, and because numbing cold slows up a man both physically and mentally it took McKinnon and his two men well over two hours to complete their task; had the temperature been anything like normal they could have done it in less than half the time. About three-quarters of the way through the repairs they had switched on all four heaters and the temperature had begun to rise, albeit very slowly.

McKinnon was well enough satisfied with their end product. Five sheets of hardboard had been bolted into position, each panel fitted with an inlet oblong of plate glass, one large, the other four, identical in shape, about half the size. The large one was fitted in the center, directly ahead of where the helmsman normally stood; two of the others were fitted on either side of this and the remaining two on the upper sections of the wing doors. The inevitable gaps between the glass and the plywood and between the plywood and the metal to which they were bonded had been sealed off with Hartley's compound, a yellow plastic material normally used for waterproofing external electrical fittings. The bridge was as draft-proof as it was possible to make it.

Ferguson put away the last of the tools and coughed. "There was some mention of a couple of tots of Captain Bowen's malt."

McKinnon looked at him and at Curran. Their faces were mottled blue and white with cold and both men were shivering violently; chronic complainers, neither had complained once.

"You've earned it." He turned to Naseby. "How's she bearing?"

Naseby looked at his hand-held compass in distaste. "If you can trust this thing, two-twenty. Give or take. So the wind's backed five degrees in the past couple of hours. We don't bother the engine room for five degrees?"

George Naseby, a solid, taciturn, black-haired and swarthy Yorkshireman—he hailed from Whitby, Captain Cook's home town—was McKinnon's alter ego and closest friend. A bosun himself on his two previous ships, he had elected to sail on the *San Andreas* simply because of the mutual regard that he and McKinnon shared. Although he held no official ranking, he was regarded by everyone, from the captain down, as the number two on the deck side.

"We don't bother them. Another five, perhaps, ten degrees off, then we bother them. Let's go below— ship can look after itself for a few minutes. Then I'll have Trent relieve you."

The level of scotch in the captain's bottle had fallen quite rapidly—Ferguson and Curran had their own ideas as to what constituted a reasonably sized tot. McKinnon, in between rather more frugal sips, examined the captain's sextant, thermometer and barometer. The sextant, as far as the bosun could tell, was undamaged; the felt lining of its wooden box would have cushioned it from the effects of the blast. The thermometer, too, appeared to be working: the mercury registered 17° F., which was about what McKinnon reckoned the cabin temperature to be. The captain's cabin was one of the few with its door still intact, and Jamieson had already had a black heater installed.

He gave the thermometer to Naseby, asking that it be placed on one of the bridge wings, then turned his attention to the barometer. This was functioning normally, for when he tapped the glass the black needle fell sharply to the left.

"Twenty-nine point five," the bosun said. "Nine-ninety-nine millibars and falling."

"Not good, eh?" Ferguson said.

"No. Not that we need a barometer to tell us that."

McKinnon left and went down from deck to the

officers' quarters. He found Jamieson at the end of the passageway.

"How's it coming, sir?"

"We're about through. Should be five cabins fit for human habitation—depending, of course, upon what your definition of human is."

The bosun tapped the bulkhead beside him. "How stable do you reckon this structure is, sir?"

"Highly unstable. Safe enough in these conditions, but I gather you think these conditions are about to change."

"If the wind keeps backing and we keep holding to this course then we're going to have the seas on the starboard quarter and a lot of nasty corkscrewing. I was thinking perhaps—"

"I know what you were thinking. I'm a ship's engineer, Bosun, not a construction engineer. I'll have a look. Maybe we can bolt or weld a few strengthening steel plates at the weakest points. I don't know. There's no guarantee. First of all, we'll go have a look at the steering on the bridge. How are things up top?"

"Draft-free. Four heaters. Ideal working conditions."

"Temperature?"

"Fifteen."

"Above freezing, or below?"

"Below."

"Ideal. Thank you very much."

McKinnon found four people in the staff dining area—Chief Engineer Patterson, Dr. Singh, and Nurses

Janet Magnusson and Irene. The nurses were off duty—the *San Andreas*, as did all hospital ships, carried an alternate nursing staff. The bosun went to the galley, asked for coffee and sandwiches, sat at the table and made his report to the chief engineer. When he was finished he said: "And how did you get on, sir? Finding a translator, I mean?"

Patterson scowled. "With our luck?"

"Well, I didn't really have any hope, sir. Not, as you say, with our luck." He looked at Janet Magnusson. "Where's Sister Morrison?"

"In the lounge." Neither her voice nor her eyes held much in the way of warmth. "She's upset. You upset her."

"She upset me." He made an impatient, dismissive gesture with his hand. "Tantrums. This is neither the time nor the place. If ever there is a time and a place."

"Oh, come now." Dr. Singh was smiling. "I don't think either of you is being quite fair. Sister Morrison is not, as you suggest, Mr. McKinnon, sulking in her tent and, Nurse, if she's feeling rather unhappy, it's not primarily the bosun's fault. She and Mr. Ulbricht are not quite seeing eye to eye."

"Ulbricht?" the bosun said.

"Flight-Lieutenant Karl Ulbricht, I understand. The captain of the Condor."

"He's conscious?"

"Very much so. Not only conscious but wanting out of bed. Quite remarkable powers of recuperation. Three bullet wounds, all flesh, all superficial. Bled a great deal, mind you, but he's had a transfusion; one hopes that the best British blood goes well with his own native Aryan stock. Anyway, Sister Morrison was with me when he came to. She called him a filthy Nazi murderer. Hardly makes for the ideal nurse-patient relationship."

"Not very tactful, I agree," Patterson said. "A wounded man recovering consciousness might expect to be entitled to a little more sympathy. How did he react?"

"Very calmly. Mild, you might say. Said he wasn't a Nazi and had never murdered anyone in his life. She just stood and glared at him—if you can imagine Sister Morrison glaring at anybody—and—"

"I can imagine it very easily," the bosun said with some feeling. "She glares at me. Frequently."

"Perhaps," Nurse Magnusson said, "you and Lieutenant Ulbricht have a lot in common."

"Please." Dr. Singh held up a hand. "Lieutenant Ulbricht expressed deep regrets, said something about the fortunes of war, but didn't exactly call for sackcloth and ashes. I stopped it there—it didn't look like a profitable discussion. Don't be too hard on the sister, Bosun. She's no battleaxe, far less a termagant. She feels deeply and has her own way of expressing her feelings."

McKinnon made no reply, caught Janet's still far from friendly eye and changed his mind. "How are your other patients, Doctor?"

"The other air-crew member—a gunner, it seems, by the name of Helmut Winterman—is okay, just a scared kid who expects to be shot at dawn. Commander Warrington, as you guessed, Mr. McKinnon, is badly hurt. How badly, I don't know. His occiput is fractured, but only surgery can tell us how serious it is. I'm a surgeon but not a brain surgeon. We'll have to wait until we get to a mainland hospital to ease the pressure on the sight center and find out when, if ever, he'll see again."

"The *Andover*'s navigator?"

"Lieutenant Cunningham?" Dr. Singh shook his head. "I'm sorry—in more ways than one, I'm afraid this may be your last hope gone—that the young man won't be doing any more navigating for some time to come. He's in a coma. X-ray shows a fracture of the skull, and not a hairline fracture either. Pulse, respiration, temperature show no sign of organic damage. He'll live."

"Any idea when he might come to, Doctor?"

Dr. Singh sighed. "If I were a first-year intern, I'd hazard a fairly confident guess. Alas, it's twenty-five years since I was a first-year intern. Two days, two weeks, two months—I simply don't know. As for the others, the captain and chief officer are still under sedation and when they wake up I'm going to put them to sleep again. Hudson, the one with the punctured lung, seems to have stabilized—at least, the internal bleeding has stopped. Rafferty's fractured tibia is no problem. The two injured crewmen from the *Argos*, one with a broken pelvis, the other with multiple burns, are still in the recovery room, not because they're in any danger but because Ward A was full and it was the best place to keep them. And I've discharged two young seamen, I don't know their names."

"Jones and McGuigan."

"That's the two. Shock, nothing more. I understand they're lucky to be alive."

"We're all lucky to be alive." McKinnon nodded his thanks as Mario put coffee and sandwiches before him, then looked at Patterson. "Do you think it might help, sir, if we had a word with the Lieutenant Ulbricht?"

"If you're halfway right on your way of thinking, Bosun, it might be of some help. At least, it can be of no harm."

"I'm afraid you'll have to wait a bit," Dr. Singh said. "The lieutenant was getting a little bit too active—or beginning to feel too active—for his own good. It'll be an hour, perhaps two. A matter of urgency, Mr. McKinnon?"

"It could be. He might be able to tell us *why* we're all so lucky as to be still alive. And if we knew, then we might have some idea, or a guess at least, as to what lies in store for us."

"You think the enemy is not yet finished with us?"

"I should be surprised if they are, Doctor."

McKinnon, alone now in the dining area, had just finished his third cup of coffee when Jamieson and three of his men entered, to the accompaniment of much arm-flapping and teeth-chattering. Jamieson went to the galley, ordered coffee for himself and his men and sat beside McKinnon.

"Ideal working conditions, you said, Bosun. Snug as a bug in a rug, one might say. Temperature's soaring—it's almost ten degrees up there. Minus."

"Sorry about that, sir. How's the steering?"

"Fixed. For the moment, at least. Not too big a job. Quite a bit of play on the wheel, but Trent says it's manageable."

"Fine. Thank you. We have bridge control?"

"Yes. I told the engine room to cease and desist. Chief Patterson seemed quite disappointed—seems to think that he can do a better job than the bridge. What's next on the agenda?"

"Nothing. Not for me, that is."

"Ah! I take your point. Our idle hands, is that it? We'll have a look at the chances of bracing the super-structure in a moment—a moment depending on how long it takes us to get defrosted."

"Of course, sir." The bosun looked over his shoulder. "I have noticed that Dr. Singh doesn't bother to keep the hospital's private liquor cabinet locked."

"Well, now. A little something in our coffee, per-haps?"

"I would recommend it, sir. Might help to speed up the defrosting process."

Jamieson gave him an old-fashioned look, rose and crossed toward the cabinet.

Jamieson drained his second cup of reinforced cof-fee and looked at McKinnon. "Something bothering you, Bosun?"

"Yes." McKinnon had both hands on the table, as if preparing to rise. "Motion's changed. A few minutes back the ship started quartering a little, not too much, as if Trent was making a slight course adjustment, but now she's quartering too damn much. It could be that the steering has failed again."

McKinnon left at speed, Jamieson close behind him. Reaching the now smoothly ice-coated deck, McKinnon grabbed a lifeline and stopped.

"Corkscrewing," he shouted. He had to shout to make himself heard above the near gale force wind. "Twenty degrees off course, maybe thirty. Something far wrong up there."

And when they arrived on the bridge, there was something wrong. Both men paused, momentarily, and McKinnon said: "My apologies, Mr. Jamieson. It wasn't the steering after all."

Trent was lying, face up, just behind the wheel, which was mindlessly jerking from side to side in response to the erratic seas striking against the rudder. Trent was breathing, no doubt about that, his chest rising and falling in a slow, rhythmic fashion. McKinnon bent over to examine his face, looked more closely, sniffed, wrinkled his nose in distaste and straightened.

"Chloroform." He reached out for the wheel and began to bring the *San Andreas* back on course again.

"And this." Jamieson stooped, picked up the fallen compass and showed it to McKinnon. The glass was smashed, the needle irremediably twisted out of position. "Flannelfoot strikes again."

"So it would appear, sir."

"Ah. You don't seem particularly surprised, Bosun?"

"I saw it lying there. I didn't have to look. There are quite a few other helmsmen aboard. That was our only compass."

4

"WHOEVER WAS RESPONSIBLE FOR THIS MUST have had access to the dispensary," Patterson said. He was with Jamieson and McKinnon in the hospital's small lounge.

"That won't help, sir," McKinnon said. "Since ten o'clock this morning everybody aboard this ship—except, of course, the wounded, the unconscious and those under sedation—have had access to the dispensary. There's not a single person who hasn't been in the hospital area, either to eat, sleep or just rest."

"Maybe we're not looking at it in the right way," Jamieson said. "*Why* should anyone want to smash the compass? It can't just be to stop us from following whatever course we were following or that we might outrun someone. The chances are high that Flannelfoot is still transmitting his homing signal and that the Germans know exactly where we are."

"Maybe he's hoping to panic us," McKinnon said. "Maybe he's hoping we'll slow down, rather than travel around in circles, which could easily happen if the weather deteriorates, the sea becomes confused and if we have no compass. Perhaps there's a German submarine in the vicinity and he doesn't want us to get too far away. There's an even worse possibility. We've been assuming that Flannelfoot has only a transmitter. Maybe he has a transceiver—what if he's in radio contact with Alta Fjord or a U-boat or even a reconnaissance Condor? There could be a British warship in the vicinity and the last thing they would want is that we make contact with it. Well, we couldn't contact it, but its radar could pick us up ten, fifteen miles away."

"Too many 'ifs,' 'maybes' and 'perhaps this and perhaps thats.'" Patterson's voice was decisive, that of a man who has made up his mind. "How many men do you trust aboard this ship, Bosun?"

"How many—" McKinnon broke off in speculation. "The three of us here and Naseby. And the medical staff. Not that I have any particular reason to trust them—nor do I have any particular reason to distrust them—but we *know* that they were here, all present and accounted for, when Trent was attacked, so that rules them out."

"Two doctors, six nursing staff, three orderlies and the four of us. That makes fifteen," Jamieson said. He smiled. "Apart from that, everyone is a suspect?"

The bosun permitted himself a slight smile in return. "It's difficult to see kids like Jones, McGuigan and Wayland Day as master spies. Those apart, I wouldn't put my hand in the fire for any of them, that's to say I've no reason to trust them in a matter of life and death."

Patterson said: "The crew of the *Argos*? Survivors? Guests by happenstance?"

"Ridiculous, I know, sir. But I just don't trust anyone." The bosun paused. "Am I wrong in thinking that it is your intention to search through the quarters and possessions of everyone aboard?"

"You are not wrong, Bosun."

"With respect, sir, we'll be wasting our time. Anyone as smart as Flannelfoot is too smart to leave anything lying around, or at least to leave it in any place where it might be remotely associated with him. There are hundreds of places aboard where you can hide things, and we are not trained rummagers. On the other hand, it's better than doing nothing. But I'm afraid that's what we'll find, Mr. Patterson. Nothing."

They found nothing. They searched every living quarter, every wardrobe and cupboard, every case and duffel bag, every nook and cranny. A rather awkward moment arose when Captain Andropolous, a burly, bearded and seemingly intemperate character who had been given one of the empty cabins normally reserved for recuperating patients, objected violently and physically to having his quarters searched: McKinnon, who had no Greek, resolved this impasse by pointing his Colt at the captain's temple, after which, probably realizing that McKinnon wasn't acting for his own amusement, the captain had been cooperation itself, even to going to the extent of accompanying the bosun and ordering his crew to open up their possessions for scrutiny.

* * *

The two Singhalese cooks in the hospital galleys
were more than competent, and Dr. Singh, who
appeared to be something of a connoisseur in such
matters, produced some Bordeaux that would not have
been found wanting in a Michelin-approved restau-
rant. But poor justice was done to the food and, more
surprisingly, the wine at dinner that evening. The
atmosphere was somber. There was an uneasiness
about, even a faint air of furtiveness. It is one thing
to be told that there is a saboteur at large: it is quite
another to have your luggage and possessions searched
on the basis of the possibility that you might be the
saboteur in question. Even, or perhaps especially, the
hospital staff seemed unduly uncomfortable: their possessions had not been searched so they were not, officially, in the clear. An irrational reaction it may have
been but, in the circumstances, understandable.

Patterson pushed back his unfinished plate and said
to Dr. Singh: "This Lieutenant Ulbricht. Is he awake?"

"He's more than awake." Dr. Singh sounded almost
testy. "Remarkable recuperative powers. Wanted to join
us for dinner. Forbade it, of course. Why?"

"The bosun and I would like to have a word with him."

"No reason why not." He pondered briefly. "Two
possible minor complications. Sister Morrison is
there—she's just relieved Sister Maria for dinner." He
nodded toward the end of the table where a fair-haired,
high-cheek-boned girl in a sister's uniform was having
dinner. Apart from Stephen Przybyszewski she was
the only Polish national aboard, and as people found

her surname of Szarzynski, like Stephen's, impassable, she was "Sister Maria."

"We'll survive," Patterson said. "The other complication?"

"Captain Bowen. Like Lieutenant Ulbricht, he has a high tolerance to sedatives. Keeps surfacing—longer and longer spells of consciousness, and when he is awake he's in a very bad humor. Who has ever seen Captain Bowen in ill humor?"

Patterson rose. "If I were the captain I wouldn't be very much in the mood for singing and dancing. Come on, Bosun."

They found the captain awake, very much so, and in a more than irritable frame of mind. Sister Morrison was seated on a stool by his bedside. She made to rise, but Patterson waved to her to remain where she was. Lieutenant Ulbricht was half sitting, half lying in the next bed, his right hand behind his neck; Lieutenant Ulbricht was wide awake.

"How do you feel, Captain?"

"How do I feel, Chief?" Briefly Bowen told him how he felt. He would no doubt have expressed himself even more forcefully had he not been aware that Sister Morrison was sitting by his side. He raised a bandaged hand to cover a cough. "All's gone to hell and breakfast, isn't it, Chief?"

"Well, yes, things could be better."

"Things couldn't be worse." Captain Bowen's words were blurted and indistinct; speaking through those blistered lips had to be agonizing. "Sister has told me. Even the boat compass smashed. Flannelfoot."

"Flannelfoot?" said Sister Morrison.

"He's still around. Flannelfoot."

"Flannelfeet," McKinnon said.

"Archie!" It said much for the captain's state of mind that, for the first time ever, he had, in company, addressed the bosun by his first name. "You're here."

"Bad pennies, sir."

"Who's on watch, Bosun?"

"Naseby, sir."

"That's all right. Flannelfeet?"

"There's more than one, sir. There has to be. I know. I don't know how I know, but I know."

"You never mentioned this to me," Patterson said.

"That's because I didn't think about it until now. And there's another thing I didn't think about. Captain Andropolous."

"The Greek master," Bowen said. "What about him?"

"Well, sir, you know we're having a little trouble with the navigation?"

"A *little*? That's not how Sister Morrison tells it."

"Well, then, a lot. We thought Captain Andropolous might give us a hand if we could communicate with him. But we can't. Maybe we don't have to. Maybe if we just show him your sextant, Captain, and give him a chart, that might be enough. Trouble is, the chart's ruined. Blood."

"No problem. The only problem we don't have," Bowen said. "We always carry duplicates. It'll be under the table or in the drawers at the after end of the chart room."

"I should be back in fifteen minutes," the bosun said.

* * *

It took him considerably longer, and when he did return his set face and the fact that he was carrying with him the sextant in its box and a chart bespoke a man who had come to report the failure of a mission.

Patterson said: "No cooperation?"

"Flannelfoot. Captain Andropolous was lying on his bunk, snoring his head off. I tried to shake him, but I might as well have shaken a sack of potatoes. My frist thought was that the same person who had been to attend to Trent had also been to see the captain, but there was no smell of chloroform. I fetched Dr. Singh, who said Andropolous had been heavily drugged."

"Drugged!" Bowen tried to express astonishment but his voice came out as a croak. "God's sake, is there no end to it? How in heaven's name could he have been drugged?"

"Easily, it would seem, sir. Dr. Singh didn't know what drug it was, but he said he must have taken it with something he'd eaten or drunk. We asked Achmed, the head cook, if the captain had had anything different to eat from the rest of us, and he said he hadn't, but also said that he had coffee afterward. Captain Andropolous had his own idea as to how coffee should be made—half coffee, half brandy. Dr. Singh said that that amount of brandy would have disguised the taste of any drug he knows of. There was a cup and saucer by the captain's bunkside table. It was empty."

"Ah." Patterson looked thoughtful. "There must have been dregs. I know nothing about those things, of course, but couldn't Dr. Singh have analysed those dregs?"

"There were none. The captain could have done it himself—washed the cup, I mean. More likely, I think it was Flannelfoot covering his tracks. No point in making inquiries about who might or might not have been seen going into or leaving the captain's cabin."

"No communication, is that it?" Patterson said.

"That's it. Only his own crew were around at the time."

Patterson said: "Assuming that our saboteur has been at work again—and I don't think we can assume anything else—where the hell would he have got hold of powerful drugs like this?"

"Where did he get hold of the chloroform? I would think that Flannelfoot is well stocked with what he considers essentials. Maybe he's not only a bit of a chemist, too. Maybe he knows what to look for in the dispensary."

"No," Bowen said. "I asked Dr. Singh. The dispensary is kept locked."

"Yes sir," McKinnon said. "But if this person is a professional, a trained saboteur, then among what he rates essentials I would think that a set of skeleton keys comes pretty high on his list."

"My cup overfloweth," Bowen mumbled. "As I said, all gone to hell and breakfast. If the weather breaks down much more, and I understand it's doing just that, we can end up any place. Coast of Norway, most like."

"May I speak, Captain?"

Bowen twisted his head to one side, an ill-advised move that made him grunt in pain. "Is that Lieutenant Ulbricht?" There was little encouragement in his voice and, had his eyes not been bandaged, it was quite certain that there would have been none there either.

"Yes, sir."

"Speak."

"I can navigate."

"You are very kind, Lieutenant." Bowen tried to sound icy but his blistered mouth wasn't up to it. "You're also the last person in the world I would ever turn to for help. You have committed a crime against humanity." He paused for some seconds, but it was no pause for reflection; a combination of anger and pain was making speech very difficult. "If we get back to Britain you will be shot. You? God!"

McKinnon said: "I can understand how you feel, sir. Because of his bombs, fifteen men are dead. Because of his bombs, you are the way you are. So are the Chief Officer, Hudson and Rafferty. But I still think you should listen to him."

The captain was silent for what seemed an unconscionably long time. It said much for the regard in which he held the bosun that probably no other man could have given him pause for so long. When he spoke, his voice was thick with bitterness. "Beggars can't be choosers. That's it, isn't it?" McKinnon made no reply. "Anyway, navigating a plane is quite different from navigating a ship."

"I can navigate a ship," Ulbricht said. "In peacetime I was at a *Marine Schule*—a marine school. I have a marine navigation certificate." He smiled briefly. "Not with me, of course, but I have one. Besides, I have many times taken star sights from a plane. That is much more difficult than taking sight from the bridge of a ship. I repeat, I can navigate."

"Him! That monster!" Sister Morrison sounded even more bitter than the captain, but maybe that was because her lips weren't blistered. "I'm quite sure he can navigate, Captain Bowen. I'm also sure that he would navigate us straight to Alta Fjord or Trondheim or Bergen—some place in Norway, anyway."

Ulbricht said: "That's a silly statement, Sister. Mr. McKinnon may not be a navigator but he must be a very experienced seaman, and it would require only one glimpse of the sun or the polestar to let him know whether we were steering roughly southeast instead of roughly southwest."

"I still don't trust him an inch," Sister Morrison said. "If what he says is true, then I trust him even less." Her eyes were coldly appraising, her lips firmly compressed. One could see that she had missed out on her profession, she was well on the way to being the headmistress of a strict school, with Ulbricht cast in the unlikely role of a trembling and errant pigtailed thirdgrader. "Look what happened to Trent. Look what happened to that Greek captain. Why shouldn't the same thing happen to Mr. McKinnon?"

"With respect, Sister," McKinnon said in a voice notably lacking in respect, "I have to repeat what Lieutenant Ulbricht said—that's a very silly statement indeed. It's silly for two reasons. The first is Naseby is also a bosun and a very fine one, too. Not that I would expect you to know that." The bosun put an unnecessary emphasis on the word "you." "Trent, Ferguson and Curran can also tell the difference between north and south. So, I'm sure, can Chief Patterson and Mr. Jamieson. There could be half a dozen others among the crew. Are you suggesting that by some mysterious means that passes my comprehension— but not, it would seem, yours—Lieutenant Ulbricht is going to have us *all* immobilized?"

Sister Morrison parted lips that had been tightly, even whitely, compressed. "And the second reason?"

"If you think that Lieutenant Ulbricht is in cahoots with the persons who were responsible for the destruction of his plane and, near as a whisker, the loss of his own life—well, if you believe that, you'll believe anything."

If it is possible to clear a throat in a soothing fashion, Patterson did just that. "I think, Captain, that the lieutenant here might not be quite as black a villain as you and Sister think."

"Not a villain! That black-hearted—" Bowen broke off, and when he spoke again his voice was quiet and almost thoughtful. "You would not say that without a reason, Chief. What makes you think so?"

"It was the bosun who first came up with the suggestion. I think I agree with him. Bosun, tell the captain what you told me."

"I've had time to think about this," McKinnon said apologetically. "You haven't. From what Dr. Singh tells me about the pain you must be suffering, it must be a damn hard job to think at all. It's my belief, sir, that the Lieutenant's Luftwaffe have sold him down the river."

"Sold him down—what the devil is that meant to mean?"

"I don't think he knew he was attacking a hospital

ship. Sure, he knows now. But he didn't when he dropped the bombs."

"He didn't know! Bomber pilots, I would remind you, Bosun, are supposed to have excellent eyesight. All those red crosses—"

"I don't think he saw them, sir." Once more, he explained. "The lights were off. It was half-dark. As he was approaching from dead astern, he certainly couldn't have seen the crosses on the sides and he was so low the superstructure would have blocked off any view of the for'ard cross. As for the cross aft, we were making so much smoke at the time that it must have been obscured. And I can't imagine for a moment that Lieutenant Ulbricht would have made so suicidal an approach, so suicidal an attack on the *San Andreas*, if he had known there was a British frigate only a couple of miles away. I wouldn't have put his chances of survival very high."

"Neither did I." Lieutenant Ulbricht spoke with some feeling.

"And the clincher, sir. Those four Heinkel torpedo bombers. I know you didn't see them, sir, even hear them—you were unconscious at the time. But Chief Patterson and I saw them. They deliberately avoided us—lifted over us—and headed straight for the *Andover*. So what do you make of it, sir? A Condor attacks us—I'm sure it must have been with low-power bombs—and the Heinkels, who could have sent us to the bottom, didn't. The Heinkel pilots *knew* the *Andover* was there: Lieutenant Ulbricht did not. The Luftwaffe, Captain, would seem to have two hands, with the left hand not telling the right hand what it was doing. I'm more than ever convinced that the lieutenant was sold down the river, sold by his own high command and the saboteur who blacked out our red-cross lights.

"Besides, he doesn't *look* like a man who would bomb a hospital ship."

"How the hell can I tell, what in hell do I care what he looks like?" Bowen spoke with, understandably, some irritation. "A baby-face with a harp can be no less of a murderer, no matter what he looks like. But, yes, I agree, Bosun, it does raise some very odd questions. Questions that seem to call for some very odd answers. Don't you agree, Sister?"

"Well, yes, perhaps." Her tone was doubtful, grudging. "Mr. McKinnon could be right."

"He *is* right." The voice was Kennet's, and it was very firm.

"Mr. Kennet." Bowen turned to the bed on the other side of him and cursed, not too sotto voce, as his neck and head reminded him that sudden movements were not advisable. "I thought you were asleep."

"Never more awake, sir. Just that I don't feel too much like talking. Of course the bosun's right. Has to be."

"Ah. Well." More carefully, this time, Bowen turned back to face Ulbricht. "All right. I hear no apologies for what you have done. But maybe you're not the black-hearted murderer we thought you were. Bosun, Chief tells me that you've been smashing furniture in my cabin."

"No more than I had to, sir. Couldn't find the keys."

"The keys are in the back left-hand corner of the left drawer in my desk. Look in the right-hand locker under my bunk. There's a chronometer there. See if it's working."

"A *spare* chronometer, sir?"

"Many captains carry one. I always have. If the sextant has survived the blast, maybe the chronometer has too. The sextant is functioning, isn't it?"

"As far as I can tell."

"May I see it?" Lieutenant Ulbricht said. He examined it briefly. "It works."

McKinnon left, taking the sextant and chart with him.

When he returned, he was smiling. "Chronometer is intact, sir. I've put Trent back on the wheel and Naseby in your cabin. There he can see anybody who tries to go up the bridge ladder and, more important, clobber any unauthorized person who tries to come into your cabin. I've told him the only authorized people are Mr. Patterson, Mr. Jamieson and myself."

"Excellent," Bowen said. "Lieutenant Ulbricht, we may yet call upon your services." He paused. "You are aware, of course, that you will be navigating yourself into captivity?"

"A firing squad?"

"That would be a poor return for your—ah—professional services. No."

"Better a live prisoner of war than floating around and frozen to death in a rubber raft, which I would have been but for Mr. McKinnon here." Ulbricht propped himself up in his bed. "Well, no time, as you British say, like the present."

McKinnon placed a restraining hand on his shoulder. "Sorry, Lieutenant, it'll have to wait."

"You mean—Dr. Singh?"

"He wouldn't be too happy. But it's not that. Blizzard. Zero visibility. No stars, and there'll be none tonight."

"Ah." Ulbricht lay back in bed.

It was then that, for the third time that day, the lights failed. McKinnon switched on his flashlight, located and switched on four nickel-cadmium emergency lights and looked thoughtfully at Patterson. Bowen said: "Something up?"

"Sorry, sir," Patterson said. He had momentarily forgotten that the captain couldn't see. "Another blasted power cut."

"Another...Jesus!" The captain sounded less concerned and angry than disgusted. "No sooner do we think we have cleared up one problem than we have another. That bastard."

"Maybe, sir," McKinnon said. "Maybe not. I don't imagine the lights have failed because someone has been drugged or chloroformed. I don't imagine they've failed because someone wanted to douse our topside red-cross lights because visibility is zero and it would serve no point. If it' sabotage, it's sabotage for some other reason."

"I'll go see if they can tell me anything in the engine room," Patterson said. "Looks like another job for Mr. Jamieson."

"He's working in the superstructure," McKinnon said. "I was going there anyway. I'll get him for you. Meet you back here, sir?"

Patterson nodded and hurried from the ward.

On the now relatively stable upper deck the lifelines were no longer needed as such but were invaluable as guidelines, for, with the absence of deck lights and in the driving snow, McKinnon literally could not see an inch before his face. He was brought up short as he bumped into someone.

"Who's that?" His voice was sharp.

"McKinnon? Jamieson. Not Flannelfoot. He's been at it again."

"Looks like it, sir. Mr. Patterson would like to see you in the engine room."

On the deck level of the superstructure the bosun found three of the engine-room crew welding a cross-plate to two beams, the harsh glare of the oxyacetylene flame contrasting eerily with the utter blackness around. Two decks up he came across Naseby in the captain's cabin, a marlin spike, butt end cloth-wrapped, in his hand and a purposeful expression on his face.

"No visitors, George?"

"Nary a visitor, Archie, but it looks as if someone has been visiting somewhere on this ship."

The bosun nodded and went up to the bridge, checked with Trent and descended the ladder again. He stopped outside the captain's cabin and looked again at Naseby. "Notice anything?"

"Yes, I notice something. I notice that the engine revs have dropped, we're slowing. This time, perhaps, a bomb in the engine room?"

"No. We'd have heard it in the hospital."

"A gas grenade would have done just as well."

"You're getting as bad as I am," McKinnon said.

He found Patterson and Jamieson in the hospital dining area. They were accompanied, to McKinnon's momentary surprise, by Ferguson, who had just arrived. But the surprise was only momentary.

"Engine room's okay, then?" McKinnon said.

Patterson said: "Yes. Reduced speed as a precaution. How did you know?"

"Ferguson here was holed up with Curran in the carpenter's shop, which is as far for'ard as you can get in this ship. So the trouble must be up near the bows—nothing short of an earthquake would normally get Ferguson out of his bunk—or whatever he's using for a bunk up there."

Ferguson looked and sounded aggrieved. "Just dropping off, I was, when Curran and me heard this explosion. Felt it, too. Directly beneath us. Not so much an explosion as a bang or a clang. Something metallic, anyway. Curran shouted that we'd been mined or torpedoed but I told him not to be daft. If a mine or torpedo had gone off beneath us we wouldn't have been alive to talk about it. So I came running aft—well, as fast as you can run on that deck—it's like a skating rink."

McKinnon said to Patterson: "So you think the ship's hull is open to the sea?"

"I don't know what to think, but if it is, then the slower we go the less chance of increasing the damage to the hull. Not too slow, of course. If we lose steerage way, then we'll start rolling or corkscrewing or whatever, and that would only increase the strain on the hull. Would Captain Bowen have the structural plans in his cabin?"

"I don't know. I suppose he has but it doesn't matter. I know the layout. I'm sure Mr. Jamieson does as well."

"That means I don't?"

"Didn't say that, sir. Let me put it this way. Next time I see a chief engineer crawling around the bilges will be the first time. Besides, you have to stay up top, sir. If an urgent decision has to be taken, the bilges are no place for the commanding officer to be."

Patterson sighed. "I often wonder, Bosun, where one draws a line between common sense and diplomacy."

"This is it, you think, Bosun?"

"It has to be, sir." Jamieson and the bosun, together with Ferguson and McCrimmon, were in the paint store, a lowermost deck compartment on the port side forward. Facing them was an eight-clamped door set in a watertight bulkhead. McKinnon placed the palm of his hand against the top of the door and then against the bottom. "Normal temperatures above—well, almost normal—and cold, almost freezing, below. Sea water on the other side, sir—not more than eighteen inches, I would think."

"Figures," Jamieson said. "We're not more than a few feet below the water line here, and that's as much as the compressed air will let in. That's one of the ballast rooms, of course."

"That's *the* ballast room, sir."

"And this is *the* paint store." Jamieson gestured at the irregularly welded patch of metal on the ship's side.

"Chief Engineer never did have any faith in what he called those Russkie shipwrights."

"That's as may be, sir. But I don't see any Russian shipwrights leaving a time bomb in the ballast room."

Russian shipwrights had, indeed, been aboard the *San Andreas*, which had sailed from Halifax, Nova Scotia, as the freighter *Ocean Belle*, *Ocean* being a common prefix for American-built Liberty ships. At the time of sailing, the *Ocean Belle* was neither fish nor fowl but was, in fact, a three-fourths-completed hospital ship. Its armament, at that stage, had been removed, its magazines emptied, all but the essential watertight bulkheads breached or partially cut away, the operating theater completed, as were the cabins for the medical staff and the dispensary, already fully stocked; the medical store was almost finished, the galley partially so, whereas work had not yet begun on the wards, the recovery room and messes. The medical staff, which had come from Britain, were already on board.

Orders were received from the Admiralty that the *Ocean Belle* was to join the next fast convoy to northern Russia, which had already assembled at Halifax. Captain Bowen had not refused—refusal of an admiralty order was not a wonderful notion—but he had objected in a fashion so strongly as to be tantamount to refusal. He was damned, he said, if he was going to sail to Russia with a shipload of civilians aboard. He was referring to the medical staff aboard and, as they constituted only a round dozen, they could hardly have

been called a shipload; he was also conveniently overlooking the fact that every member of the crew, from
himself downward, was also technically a civilian.

The medical staff, Bowen had maintained, were a
different kind of civilian. Dr. Singh had pointed out to
him that 90 percent of the medical staff of the armed
forces were civilians, only they wore different kinds of
uniforms: the medical staff wore uniforms which happened to be white.

Captain Bowen had then fallen back on his last
defense: he was not, he said, going to take women
through a war zone—he was referring to the six nurses
aboard. A by now thoroughly irritated escort commander forcibly made three points that had been made
to him by the Admiralty: thousands of women and
children had been in war zones while being trans-
ported as refugees to the United States and Canada;
in the current year, as compared to the previous two
years, U-boat losses had quadrupled while mercantile
marine losses had been cut by 80 percent; and the
Russians had requested, or rather insisted, that as many
wounded Allied personnel as possible be removed from
their overcrowded Archangel hospitals. Captain Bowen,
as he should have done at the beginning, capitulated,
and the *Ocean Belle*, still painted in wartime gray but
carrying adequate supplies of white, red and green
paint, had sailed with the convoy.

As convoys to northern Russia went, it had been an
exceptionally uneventful one. Only two incidents had
occurred, and both had involved the *Ocean Belle*. Some
way south of Jan Mayen Island they had come across
a venerable V-and-W-class destroyer, stopped in the

water with an engine breakdown. This destroyer had been a unit of the destroyer screen escorting a previous convoy and had stopped to pick up survivors from a sinking cargo vessel, which had been heavily on fire. The time had been about 2:30 P.M., well after sunset, and the rescue operation had been interrupted by a brief air attack. The attacker had not been seen but had obviously no difficulty in seeing the destroyer, silhouetted as it was against the blazing cargo ship. It had been assumed that the attacker was a reconnaissance Condor, for it had dropped no bombs and contented itself with raking the bridge with machine-gun fire, which had effectively destroyed the radio office. Thus, when the engines had broken down some hours later—the breakdown had nothing to do with the Condor, the V-and-Ws were superannuated, overworked and much plagued by mechanical troubles—they had been unable to contact the vanished convoy.*

The wounded survivors were taken aboard the *Ocean Belle.* The destroyer itself, together with its crew and

*NOTE: Throughout the wartime convoy sailings to Murmansk and Archangel, the use of rescue ships remained a bone of contention between the Royal Navy at sea and the Royal Navy on land—the latter being the London-based Admiralty, which acquitted itself with something less than distinction during the long years of the Russian convoys. In the earlier days, the use of rescue ships was the rule, not the exception. After the loss of the *Zafaaran* and the *Stockport*, which was lost with all hands, including the many survivors that had been picked up from other sunken vessels, the Admiralty forbade the further use of rescue ships.

This was a rule that was observed in the breach. In certain convoys a self-selected number of the escort group, usually a destroyer or smaller, would assign itself the role of rescue ship, an assignment in which the force commander would acquiesce or to which he turned a blind eye. The task of the rescue ships was a hazardous one. There was never any question of a convoy's stopping or of escorts leaving the convoy, so that almost invariably the rescue ship was left alone and unprotected. The sight of a Royal Naval vessel stopped in the water alongside a sinking vessel was an irresistible target for many U-boat commanders.

unwounded survivors, were taken in tow by an S-class destroyer. It was later learned that both vessels had reached Scapa Flow intact.

Three days afterward, somewhere off North Cape, they had come across an equally ancient Kingfisher corvette, which had no business whatever in those distant waters. It too was stopped, and so deep in the water astern that its poop was already awash. It too had survivors aboard—the survivors of the crew of a Russian submarine that had been picked up from a burning oil-covered sea.* The Russians, for the most part badly burned, had been transferred to the *Ocean Belle*, the crew being transferred to an escort destroyer. The corvette was sunk by gunfire. It was during this transfer that the *Ocean Belle* had been holed twice, just below the water line, on the port side, in the paint store and ballast room. The reason for the damage had never been established.

The convoy had gone to Archangel, but the *Ocean Belle* had put in to Murmansk—neither Captain Bowen nor the escort commander had thought it wise that the *Ocean Belle* should proceed any farther than necessary in its then present condition—slightly down by the head and with a list to port. There were no dry-dock facilities available, but the Russians were masters of improvisation—the rigors of war had forced them to be. They filled up the after tanks, drained the for'ard tanks and removed the for'ard slabs of concrete ballast

---

*NOTE: It was neither appreciated nor reported that the Russians had a few submarines operational in the area at that time. One of them almost certainly damaged the *Tirpitz* sufficiently to make it return to its moorings in Alta Fjord.

until the holes in the paint store and ballast room were just clear of the water, after which it had taken them only a few hours to weld plates in position over the holes. The equalization of the tanks and the replacement of ballast had then brought the *Ocean Belle* back to an even keel.

While those repairs were being effected, a small army of Russian carpenters had worked, three shifts in every twenty-four hours, in the hospital section of the ship, fitting out the wards, recovery room, messes, galley and medical store. Captain Bowen was astonished beyond measure. On his previous visits to the two Russian ports he had encountered from his allies, blood brothers who should have been in tears of gratitude for the dearly bought and vital supplies being ferried to their stricken country, nothing but sullenness, indifference, a marked lack of cooperation and, not occasionally, downright hostility. The baffling sea change he could only attribute to the fact that the Russians were only showing their heartfelt appreciation that the *Ocean Belle* had brought their wounded submariners back home.

When they sailed it was as a hospital ship—Bowen's crew, paint brushes in hand, had worked with a will during their brief stay in Murmansk. They did not, as everyone had expected, proceed through the White Sea to pick up wounded servicemen in Archangel. The Admiralty's orders had been explicit: they were to proceed, and at all speed, to the port of Aberdeen in Scotland.

* * *

Jamieson replaced the cover of the small electrical junction box, having effectively isolated the ballast room from the main power system. He tapped the watertight door. "Short in there—could have been caused by the blast or sea water, it doesn't matter—should have blown a fuse somewhere. It didn't. Somewhere or other there's a fuse that's been tampered with—fuse wire replaced by a nail or some such. That doesn't matter either. I'm not going to look for it. McCrimmon, go ask the engine room to try the generator."

McKinnon tapped the same door. "And what do we do here?"

"What indeed?" Jamieson sat on a paint drum and thought. "Three choices, I would say. We can get an air compressor down here, drill a hole through the bulkhead at about shoulder level and force the water out, which would be fine if we knew where the level of the hole in the hull is. We don't. Besides, the chances are that the compressed air in the ballast room would escape before we could get the nozzle of the compressed-air hose into the hole we drilled, which could only mean that more water would pour into the ballast room. Or we could reinforce the bulkhead. The third choice is to do nothing. I'm for the third choice. It's a pretty solid bulkhead. We'd have to reduce speed, of course. No bulkhead is going to stand up to the pressure at full speed if there's a hole the size of a barn door in the hull."

"A barn door would not be convenient," McKinnon said. "I think I'll go and have a look."

It was a cold and bruised McKinnon who half climbed and was half pulled up to the foredeck of the *San Andreas*, which, engines stopped, was wallowing heavily in quartering seas. In the pale half-light given by the again functioning deck arc-lamps they presented a strange quartet, Jamieson, Ferguson and McCrimmon wraithlike figures completely shrouded in snow, McKinnon a weirdly gleaming creature, the sea water on his rubber suit, aqualung and waterproof torch already, in that 35-below temperature, hardening into ice. At a gesture from Jamieson, McCrimmon left for the engine room while Ferguson pulled in the rope ladder: Jamieson took McKinnon's arm and led him, the newly formed ice on the rubber suit crackling as he stumbled along, toward the shelter of the super-structure, where McKinnon pulled off his aqualung. His teeth were chattering uncontrollably.

"Pretty bad down there, Bosun?"

"Not that, sir. This damned rubber suit." He fingered a waist-high gash in the material. "Tore it on a jagged piece of metal. From here down the suit is filled with water."

"Good God! You'll freeze to death, man. Hurry, hurry!" In what was left of his cabin McKinnon began to strip off his rubber suit. "You located the damage?"

"No problem—and no barn door. Just a ragged hole about the size of my fist."

Jamieson smiled. "Worth risking pneumonia to find

that out. I'm going to the bridge. See you in the captain's cabin."

When McKinnon, in dry clothing but still shivering violently, joined Jamieson and Naseby in the captain's cabin, the *San Andreas* was back on course and steadily picking up speed. Jamieson pushed a glass of scotch across to him.

"I'm afraid the captain's supplies are taking a fearful beating, Bosun. This shouldn't increase the risk of pneumonia—I've left the water out. I've been speaking to Mr. Patterson and the captain—we've got a line through to the hospital now. When I told him you'd been over the side in this weather, he didn't say thank you or anything like that, just said to tell you that you're mad."

"Captain Bowen is not often wrong, and that's a fact." McKinnon's hands were shaking so badly that he spilled liquid from his brimming glass. "Any instructions from the captain or Mr. Patterson?"

"None. Both say they're quite happy to leave the topside to you."

"That's kind of them. What they really mean is that they have no option—there's only George and myself."

"George?"

"Sorry, sir. Naseby, here. He's a bosun, too. We've been shipmates on and off, friends for twenty years."

"I didn't know." Jamieson looked thoughtfully at Naseby. "I can see it now. You've made arrangements for up here, Bosun?"

"About to, sir. George and I will take turns here, looking after the family jewels, so to speak. I'll have Trent, Ferguson and Curran spell one another on the wheel. I'll tell them to give me a shake—if I'm asleep—when or if the weather clears."

"Cue for Lieutenant Ulbricht?"

"Indeed. I would like to make a suggestion, sir, if I may. I would like to have some people keeping watch at the fore and aft exits of the hospital, just to make absolutely certain that nobody's going to start sleep-walking during the night."

"Who's going to watch the watchers?"

"A point, sir. The watchers I would suggest are Jones, McGuigan, McCrimmon and Stephen. Unless they're wonderful actors, the first two are too young and innocent to be criminals. McCrimmon may indeed have a criminal bent of mind, but I think he's an honest criminal. And Stephen strikes me as being a fairly trustworthy lad. More important, he's not likely to forget that it was a naval mine sweeper that picked him up out of the North Sea."

"I didn't know that either. You seem to be better informed about my own department than I am. I'll arrange for Stephen and McCrimmon, you look after the others. Our resident saboteur is not about to give up all that easily?"

"I would be surprised if he did. Wouldn't you?"

"Very much. I wonder what form his next attempt to nobble us will take?"

"I just have no idea. But another thought occurs, sir. The person you have keeping an eye on the aft exit from the hospital might also keep an eye on the entrance to A Ward."

"A Ward? That bunch of crooks? Whatever for?"

"The person or persons who are trying to slow us

and are doing their best to get us lost might think it a rather good idea to disable Ulbricht."

"Indeed they might. I'll stay in the ward myself tonight. There's a spare bed. If I do drop off, the duty nurse can always give me a shake if anyone comes in who shouldn't be coming in." Jamieson was silent for a few moments. "What's behind it all, Bosun?"

"I think you know as well as I do, sir. Somebody, somewhere, wants to take over the *San Andreas*, although *why* anyone should want to take over a hospital ship I can't even begin to imagine."

"No more can I. A U-boat, you think?"

"It would have to be, wouldn't it? I mean you can't capture a ship from the air, and they're hardly likely to send the *Tirpitz* after us." McKinnon shook his head. "A U-boat? Any fishing boat, with a few armed and determined men, could take us over whenever they felt like it."

5

McKINNON, DEEP IN SLEEP THOUGH HE WAS, was instantly awake at Naseby's shake and swung his legs over the edge of Captain Bowen's bunk.

"What's the time, George?"

"Six A.M. Curran's just been down from the bridge. Says the blizzard has blown itself out."

"Stars?"

"He didn't say."

The bosun pulled on an extra jersey, duffel coat and sea boots, made his way up to the bridge, spoke briefly to Curran and went out on the starboard wing. Within only a second or two, bent double and with his back to the gale-force wind, coughing and gasping as the ice-chilled air reached down into his lungs, he was beginning to wish himself anywhere except where he was. He switched on his torch and picked up the thermometer. It showed —8° —40° of frost on the Fahrenheit scale. Combined with the strong wind the temperature, expressed in terms of the chill factor on exposed skin, was in the region of —80° F.

He straightened slowly and looked out toward the bows. In the light of the red cross arc-lamps on the foredeck it was at once clear, as Curran had said, that, despite the wind, the blizzard had blown itself out. Against the deep indigo of the sky, the stars were preternaturally bright and clear. Breathing through a mittened hand that covered both mouth and nose, McKinnon turned into the wind and looked aft.

At first he could see nothing, for the bitter wind brought instantaneous tears to his eyes. He ducked below the shelter of the canvas windbreaker, fumbled a pair of goggles from his coat pocket, strapped them on under his duffel hood, straightened again, and, by dint of wiping the back of his free mitten against the glasses, was able to see, intermittently, what was going on astern of him.

The waves—the weather had not yet worsened to the extent that the seas had become broken and confused—were between twelve and fifteen feet in height, their lee sides whitely streaked in spume and half hidden in flying spray as the wind tore their tops away. The stars were as brilliant as they had been in the other direction and McKinnon soon located the pole, off the starboard quarter. The wind was no longer backing to the north and the *San Andreas*, as far as he could judge, was still heading roughly between southwest and south-southwest.

McKinnon moved back into the bridge, thankfully closed the wing door and pondered briefly. Their present course, it was safe to assume, offered no danger;

on the other hand, it was not safe to assume that they would or could maintain their present course. The weather, in this gray and undefined area between the Barents and Norwegian Seas, was notoriously fickle. He had not, for instance, expected—and had said as much—that the skies would clear that night; there was equally no guarantee that they would remain clear and that the wind would not back farther to the north. He descended two decks, selected an armful of warm clothing from the now mostly abandoned crew's quarters and made for the hospital area. Crossing the dangerously slippery upper deck and guided only by the lifeline, he became acutely and painfully aware that a change was already under way, a factor that he had not experienced on the starboard wing only a few minutes ago. Needle-pointed ice spicules were beginning to lance into the unprotected areas of his skin. It augured ill.

In the hospital mess deck he came across both Jones and McGuigan, both of whom assured him that no one was or had been abroad. He passed into B Ward, at the far end of which Janet Magnusson was seated at her desk, her elbows propped on it, her chin propped on her hands and her eyes closed.

"Aha!" McKinnon said. "Asleep on the job, Nurse Magnusson."

She looked up, startled, blinked and tried to sound indignant. "Asleep? Of course not." She peered at his armful of clothing. "What on earth is that for? Have you moved into the old rags trade, Archie? No, don't tell me. It's for that poor man in there. Maggie's in there too—she won't be pleased."

"As far as your precious Maggie is concerned, I would have thought that a little suffering for Lieutenant Ulbricht would be preferable to none. No salt tears for either Sister Morrison or the lieutenant."

"Archie!" She was on her feet. "Your face. Blood!"

"As far as the lieutenant and myself are both concerned, that should please your friend." He wiped the blood off his face. "It's not nice up top."

"Archie." She looked at him uncertainly, concern in her tired eyes.

"It's all right, Janet." He touched her shoulder and passed into A Ward. Sister Morrison and Lieutenant Ulbricht were both awake and drinking tea, the sister at her desk, Ulbricht sitting up in bed; clear-eyed and rested, the German pilot, as Dr. Singh had said, unquestionably had remarkable recuperative powers. Jamieson, fully clothed and stretched out on the top of a bed, opened an eye as McKinnon passed by.

"Morning, Bosun. It *is* morning, isn't it?"

"Six-twenty, sir."

"Good lord. Selfishness, that's what it is—I've been asleep for seven hours. How are things?"

"A quiet night up top. Here too?"

"Must have been—no one gave me a shake." He looked at the bundle of clothing that McKinnon was carrying, then at Ulbricht. "Stars?"

"Yes, sir. At the moment, that is. I don't think they'll be there for long."

"Mr. McKinnon!" Sister Morrison's voice was cold with a touch of asperity, as it usually was when addressing the bosun. "Do you intend to drag that poor man out of bed on a night like this? He's been shot several times."

"I know he's been shot several times—or have you forgotten who picked him out of the water?" The bosun was an innately courteous man but never at his best when dealing with Sister Morrison. "So he's a 'poor man,' now—well, it's better than being a filthy Nazi murderer. What do you mean, on a night like this?"

"I mean the weather, of course." Her fists were actually clenched.

Jamieson surveyed the ward deckhead. "What do you know about the weather? You haven't been out of here all night. If you had been, I would have known." He turned a dismissive back on her and looked at Ulbricht. "How do you feel, Lieutenant?"

"I have an option?" Ulbricht smiled. "I feel well enough. Even if I didn't I'm still coming. Don't be too hard on the ward sister, Bosun—even your lady with a lamp in the Crimea had a pretty short way with difficult patients—but she's overlooking my natural selfishness. I'm on this ship too." He climbed stiffly out of bed and, with the assistance of McKinnon and Jamieson started to pull clothing on over his pajamas while Sister Morrison looked on in frigid disapproval. The disapproval finally culminated in the drumming of fingertips on the table.

"I think," she said, "that we should have Dr. Singh in here."

McKinnon turned slowly and looked at her, and when he spoke his voice was as expressionless as his face. "I don't think it matters very much what you think, Sister. I suggest you just give a shake to Captain

Bowen there and find out just how much your thinking matters."

"The captain is under heavy sedation. When he regains consciousness, I shall report you for insolence."

"Insolence?" McKinnon looked at her with indifference. "I think he would prefer that to stupidity—the stupidity of a person who is trying to endanger the *San Andreas* and all those aboard her. It's a pity we don't have any irons on this ship."

She glared at him, made to speak, then turned as Dr. Sinclair came into the ward. Sleepy-eyed and tousle-haired, he looked in mild astonishment at the spectacle before him.

"Dr. Sinclair! Thank heavens you're here!" Rapidly and urgently she began to explain the situation to him. "Those—those men want star sights or navigation or something, and in spite of all my protests they insist on dragging a seriously ill man up to the bridge or wherever and—"

"I can see what's happening," Sinclair said mildly. "But if the lieutenant is being dragged he's not putting up much in the way of resistance, is he? And by no stretch of the imagination can you describe him as being seriously ill. But I do take your point, Sister. He should be under constant medical supervision."

"Ah! Thank you, Doctor." Sister Morrison came very close to permitting herself a smile. "So it's back to bed for him."

"Well, no, not quite. A duffel coat, a pair of seaboots, my bag of tricks and I'll go up with them. That way the lieutenant will be under watchful medical eyes."

Even with three men lending what assistance they could, it took twice as long as expected to help Lieutenant Ulbricht as far as the captain's cabin. Once there, he sank heavily into the chair behind the table.

"Thank you very much, gentlemen." He was very white, his breathing shallow and abnormally rapid. "Sorry about that. It would seem that I am not as fit as I thought I was."

"Nonsense." Dr. Sinclair was brisk. "You did splendidly. It's that inferior English blood that we had to give you this morning, that's all." He made free with Captain Bowen's supplies. "Here. Superior Scotch blood. Effects guaranteed."

Ulbricht smiled faintly. "Isn't there something about opening pores?"

"You won't be out in the open long enough to give your pores a chance to protest."

Up on the bridge McKinnon adjusted Ulbricht's goggles, then scarfed him so heavily above and below the goggles that not a square millimeter of skin was left exposed. When he was finished, Lieutenant Ulbricht was as immune to the weather as it was possible for anyone to be: two balaclavas and a tightly strung duffel hood made sure of that.

McKinnon went out on the starboard wing, hung a trailing lamp from the canvas windbreaker, went back inside, picked up the sextant, took Ulbricht by his right arm—the undamaged one—and led him outside. Even though he was so cocooned against the elements, even though the bosun had warned him and even though he had already had an ominous foretaste of what lay in store in their brief journey across the upper deck, he was totally unprepared for the power and savagery of the wind that caught him as soon as he stepped out on the wing. His weakened limbs were similarly unprepared. He took two short, sharp steps forward and though he managed to clutch the top of the windbreaker would probably have fallen but for McKinnon's sustaining hand. Had he been carrying the sextant he would almost certainly have dropped it.

With McKinnon's arm around him, Ulbricht took three star sights, to the south, west and north, clumsily noting down the results as he did so. The first two sights were comparatively quick and simple; the third, to the north, took much longer and was far more difficult because Ulbricht had to keep clearing away the ice spicules from his goggles and the sextant. When he had finished he handed the sextant back to McKinnon, leaned his elbows on the after edge of the wing and stared out toward the stern, occasionally and mechanically wiping his goggles with the back of his hand. After about twenty seconds of this McKinnon took his good arm and almost literally dragged him back into the shelter of the bridge, banging the door to behind him. Handing the sextant to Jamieson, he quickly removed Ulbricht's duffel hood, balaclavas and goggles.

"Sorry about that, Lieutenant, but there's a time and a place for everything, and daydreaming or sightseeing out on that wing is not one of them."

"The funnel." Ulbricht looked slightly dazed. "What's happened to your funnel?"

"It fell off."

"I see. It fell off. You mean—I—"

"What's done is done," Jamieson said philosophically. He handed a glass to the lieutenant. "To help you with your calculations."

"Thank you. Yes." Ulbricht shook his head as if to clear it. "Yes. My calculations."

Weak though he was and shivering constantly—despite the fact that the bridge temperature was already over 55° F.—Ulbricht left no doubt that, as a navigator, he knew precisely what he was about. Working from star sights he had no need to worry about the vagaries of deviation and variation. With a chart, dividers, parallel rules, pencils and chronometer he completed his calculations in remarkably short order and made a tiny cross on the chart after consulting navigational tables.

"We're here. Well, near enough—68.05 north, 7.20 east—more or less due west of the Lofotens. Our course is 218. Is one permitted to ask our destination?"

Jamieson smiled. "Quite frankly, Lieutenant, you wouldn't be much use to us if you didn't. Aberdeen."

"Ah! Aberdeen. They have a rather famous prison there, do they not? Peterhead, isn't it? I wonder what the cells are like."

"It's a prison for civilians. Of the more intractable kind. I should hardly think you'd end up there. Or in any prison." Jamieson looked at him with some curiosity. "How do you know about Peterhead, Lieutenant?"

"I know Scotland well. I know England even better." Ulbricht did not seek to elaborate. "So, Aberdeen. We'll stay on this course until we get to the latitude of Trondheim, then south until we get to the latitude of Bergen—or, if you like, Mr. McKinnon, the latitude of your home islands."

"How did you know I'm a Shetlander?"

"Some members of the nursing staff don't seem to mind talking to me. Then on a more westerly course. That's speaking roughly, we'll work out the details as we go along. It's a very simple exercise and there's no problem."

"Of course it's no problem," Jamieson said, "neither is playing Rachmaninoff, as long as you are a concert pianist."

Ulbricht smiled. "You overrate my simple skills. The only problem that will arise is when we make our landfall, which, of course, will have to be in daylight. At this time of the year North Sea fogs are as common as not, and there's no way I can navigate in a fog without a radio and compass."

"With any luck, there shouldn't be all that much of a problem," McKinnon said. "War or no war, there's still pretty heavy traffic on the east coast, and there's more than an even chance that we can pick up a ship and be guided into harbor."

"Agree," Ulbricht said. "A red cross ship is not easily overlooked—especially one with its funnel missing." He sipped his drink, pondered briefly, then said: "Is it your intention to return me to the hospital?"

"Naturally," Sinclair said. "That's where you belong. Why do you ask?"

Ulbricht looked at Jamieson. "I would, of course, be expected to do some more navigating?"

"Expected, Lieutenant? 'Depended' is the word you're after."

"And at frequent intervals, if cloud or snow conditions permit. We never know when the set of the sea and the wind may change without our being aware of it. Point is, I don't much fancy dragging myself back down to the hospital, then coming back up here again every time I have to take star sights. Couldn't I just lie down in the captain's cabin?"

"I have no objections," Jamieson said. "Dr. Sinclair?"

"Makes sense. Lieutenant Ulbricht is hardly on the critical list, and it could only help his recuperation. I'll pop up every two or three hours to see how he's getting on."

"Bosun?"

"Fine by me."

"I shall have company, of course?"

"Company?" Sinclair said. "You mean a nurse, Lieutenant?"

"I don't mean a nurse. With all respect to your charming young ladies, Dr. Sinclair, I don't think any of them would be much use if this fellow you call Flannelfoot came up to remove or destroy the sextant and chronometer, and the way I'm feeling I couldn't fight off a determined fly. Also, of course, he'd have to dispose of witnesses, and I don't much fancy that."

"No problem, Lieutenant," the bosun said. "He'll have to try to dispose of either Naseby or myself, and I don't much think he would fancy that. We would, though."

Sinclair shook his head sadly. "Sister Morrison isn't

going to like this one little bit. Further usurpment of her authority. After all, the lieutenant is her patient, not mine."

"No problem," McKinnon said. "Just tell her the lieutenant fell over the side."

"And how are your patients this morning, sir?" McKinnon was having breakfast with Dr. Singh.

"No dramatic changes, Bosun. The two *Argos* crewmen in the recovery room are much of a muchness—as well as can be expected when one has a fractured pelvis and the other massive burns. The condition of Commander Warrington and his navigating officer is unchanged—Cunningham is still in deep coma and is being fed intravenously. Hudson is stabilized—the lung bleeding has stopped. Chief Officer Kennet is definitely on the mend, although heaven knows how long it will be before we can take those bandages off his face. The only one that gives some cause for worry is the captain. It's nothing critical, not even serious, just worrisome. You saw how he was when you last saw him—breathing hellfire and brimstone in all directions. He's gone strangely quiet now, almost lethargic. Or maybe he's just more calm and relaxed now that he knows the ship's position and course. That was a fine job you did there, Bosun."

"No credit to me, sir. It was Lieutenant Ulbricht who did it."

"Be that as it may, Captain Bowen appears to be in at least a more philosophical mood. I suggest you come along and see him."

When a man's face is completely obscured by bandages it is difficult to say what kind of mood he is in. He had the stem of an evil-smelling briar stuck between his burned lips, and again it was impossible to say whether he was enjoying it or not. When he heard McKinnon's voice he removed the pipe.

"We still afloat, Bosun?" The enunciation was clearer than it had been and was costing him less effort.

"Well, sir, let's say we're no longer all gone to hell and breakfast. No more alarms and excursions either. As far as I can tell, Lieutenant Ulbricht is an expert— I don't think you'd hesitate to have him as your navigating officer. He's lying down on the bunk in your cabin, sir—but you will have been told that and the reasons why."

"Broaching my rapidly dwindling supplies, I have no doubt."

"He did have a couple of tots, sir. He needed it. He's still a pretty sick man and very weak, and the cold out there on the wing bridge was vicious. I don't think I've ever known it worse in the Arctic. Anyway, he wasn't doing any broaching when I left him. He was sound asleep."

"As long as he keeps on acting in this fashion he can do as much broaching as he likes. Give him my sincere thanks."

"I'll do that. Have you any instructions, sir?"

"Instructions, Bosun? Instructions? How can I give any instructions?"

"I wouldn't know, sir. I've never been a captain."

"You bloody well are now. I'm in no position to give anyone instructions. Just do what you think best—

and from what I've heard to date your best seems to be very good indeed. Not," Bowen added deprecatingly, "that I would have expected anything else of Archie McKinnon."

"Thank you, sir. I'll try." McKinnon turned to leave the ward, but was stopped by Sister Morrison. For once she was looking at him as if he might even belong to the human race.

"How is he, Mr. McKinnon?"

"The lieutenant? Resting. He's a lot weaker than he says he is, but he'd never admit it. A very brave man. And a fine navigator. And a gentleman. When he says he didn't know the *San Andreas* was a hospital ship I believe him absolutely. I don't believe many people absolutely."

"I'm quite sure you don't." The return to the old asperity proved to be momentary. She paused, thinking. "... I don't think I believe it either. In fact, I *don't* believe it."

"That's nice." McKinnon smiled at her, the first time, he reflected with some astonishment, that he'd ever smiled at her. "Janet—Nurse Magnusson—tells me you come from the east coast. Would it be impertinent to ask where exactly?"

"Of course not." She smiled, and McKinnon realized with an even greater sense of shock that this was the first time she'd ever smiled at him. "Aberdeen. Why?"

"Odd. Lieutenant Ulbricht seems to know Aberdeen rather well. He certainly seems to know about Peterhead prison and isn't all that keen on ending up there."

A brief flicker of what could have been concern registered on her face. "Will he?"

"Not a chance. If he brings this ship back to Aberdeen they'll probably send him to a prisoner-of-war camp. Unless they decide to give him a medal. Both your parents from Aberdeen, Sister?"

"My father is. My mother's from Kiel."

"Kiel?"

"Yes. Didn't you know?"

"Of course not. How should I have known? Now that I do know, is that supposed to make a difference?"

"I'm half German." She smiled again. "Aren't you surprised, Mr. McKinnon? Shocked, perhaps?"

"No, I'm not shocked." McKinnon looked gloomy. "I have troubles of my own in that direction. My sister Jean is married to an Italian. I have a niece and a nephew, two bambinos who can't—or couldn't before the war—speak a word of English to their old uncle."

"It must make—must have made—communication a bit difficult."

"Luckily, no. I speak Italian."

She removed her glasses as if to examine him more closely. "You speak Italian, Mr. McKinnon?"

"Yes. And Spanish. And German. You must be able to speak German—you can try me any time. Surprised, Sister? Shocked?"

"No." She shook her head slowly and smiled a third time. It was borne in upon McKinnon that a smiling Margaret Morrison, with her warm, friendly brown eyes, was a totally different creature from the Sister Morrison he thought he had known. "No, I'm not. Really."

"You come from seafaring people, Sister?"

"Yes." This time she was surprised. "How did you know?"

"I didn't. But it was a fair guess. It's the Kiel connection. Many British sailors know Kiel well—I do myself—and it has, or did have, the finest regatta in Europe. Your father's from Aberdeen. A fisherman? A seaman of some sort?"

"A seaman of some sort."

"What sort?"

"Well." She hesitated.

"Well what?"

"He's a captain in the Royal Navy."

"Good Lord!" McKinnon looked at her in mild astonishment, then rubbed an unshaven chin. "I shall have to treat you with more respect in future, Sister Morrison."

"I hardly think that will be necessary, Mr. McKinnon." The voice was formal but the smile that followed was not. "Not now."

"You sound almost as if you were ashamed of being the daughter of a Royal Navy captain."

"I am not. I'm very proud of my father. But it can be difficult. Do you understand?"

"Yes. I think I do."

"Well, now, Mr. McKinnon." The glasses were back in position and Sister Morrison was back in business. "You'll be seeing Lieutenant Ulbricht up top?"

McKinnon nodded.

"Tell him I'll be up to see him in an hour, maybe two."

McKinnon blinked, which was about as far as he

ever permitted himself to go in the way of emotional expression. "You?"

"Yes. Me." If bridling hadn't gone out of fashion she would have bridled.

"But Dr. Sinclair said he would come—"

"Dr. Sinclair is a doctor, not a nurse." Sister Morrison made it sound as if there were something faintly discreditable in being a doctor. "I'm the lieutenant's sister-in-charge. He'll probably require to have his bandages changed."

"When exactly will you be coming?"

"Does it matter? I can find my own way."

"No, Sister, you won't. You don't know what it's like up top. There's a full gale blowing, it's forty below, black as the earl of hell's waistcoat, and the deck's like a skating rink. No one goes up top without my permission, and most certainly not nurses. You will phone and I will come for you."

"Yes, Mr. McKinnon," she said primly. She gave a slight smile. "The way you put it, it doesn't leave much room for argument."

"I'm sorry. No offense. Before you come up, put on as much warm clothing as you think you will need. Then double the amount."

Janet Magnusson was in B Ward when he passed through it. She took one quick look at his face and said: "What's the matter with you?"

"Prepare thyself, Nurse Magnusson. The end is nigh."

"What on earth do you mean, Archie?"

"The dragon next door." He jerked a thumb toward A Ward. "She has just—"

"Dragon? Maggie? Yesterday she was a lioness."

"Dragon. She's stopped breathing fire. She *smiled* at me. First time since leaving Halifax. Smiled. Four times. Unsettles a man."

"Well." She shook his shoulders. "I *am* pleased. So you admit you misjudged her."

"I admit it. Mind you, I think she may have misjudged me a bit, too."

"I told you she was nice, Archie. Remember?"

"Indeed I remember. And indeed she is."

"Very nice. Very."

McKinnon regarded her with suspicion. "What's that meant to mean?"

"She smiled at you."

The bosun gave her a cold look and left.

Lieutenant Ulbricht was awake when McKinnon returned to the captain's cabin.

"Duty calls, Mr. McKinnon? Another fix?"

"Rest easy, Lieutenant. No stars. Overcast. More snow, I'm thinking. How do you feel?"

"Well enough. At least when I'm lying down. That's physically, I mean." He tapped his head. "Up here, not so well. I've been doing a lot of wondering and thinking."

"Wondering and thinking why you're lying here?"

"Exactly."

"Haven't we all. At least I've been doing nothing else but wondering about it. Haven't got very far, though. In fact, I haven't got anywhere."

"I'm not saying it would help any, just call it curiosity if you like, but would you mind very much telling me what's been happening to the *San Andreas* since you left Halifax. Not, of course, if it means telling me naval secrets."

McKinnon smiled. "I don't have any. Besides, even if I did have and told you, what would you do with them?"

"You have a point. What indeed?"

McKinnon gave a brief résumé of what had happened to the ship since leaving Nova Scotia, and when he had finished Ulbricht sat up, thinking it out. Then he said: "Well, now let me see if I can count. As far as I can make out there were seven different parties involved in the movements of the *San Andreas*—actually aboard it, that is. To begin with, there was your own crew. Then there were the wounded survivors picked up from this crippled destroyer. After that came the Russian submarine survivors you took from this corvette you had to sink. Then you picked up some wounded servicemen in Murmansk. Since leaving there you've picked up survivors from the *Argos*, the *Andover* and Helmut and myself. That makes seven?"

"That makes seven."

"We can eliminate the survivors from the broken-down destroyer and the sinking frigate. Their presence aboard your ship could only have been due to sheer happenstance, nothing else. We an equally forget Commander Warrington and his two men and Helmut Winterman and myself. That leaves just your crew, the survivors from the *Argos* and the sick men you picked up in Murmansk."

"I couldn't imagine a more unlikely trio of suspects."

"Neither could I, Bosun. But it's not imagination that concerns us here, it's logic. It has to be one of those three. Take the sick men you picked up in Murmansk. One of them could have been suborned. I know it sounds preposterous, but war itself is preposterous. The most unbelievable things happen in preposterous circumstances, and if there is one thing that is for certain it is that we are not going to find the answer to this enigma in the realms of the obvious. How many sick men are you repatriating from Russia?"

"Seventeen."

"Do you happen to know the nature of their injuries?"

McKinnon regarded the lieutenant speculatively. "I have a fair idea."

"All seriously wounded?"

"There are no seriously wounded, far less critically injured patients aboard. If they were, they wouldn't be here. Poorly, you might call them, I suppose."

"But bed-ridden? Immobile?"

"The wounded are."

"They are not all wounded?"

"Only eight."

"Good God! Eight? You mean to tell me that there are nine who are *not* injured?"

"It all depends upon what you mean by injured. Three are suffering from advanced cases of exposure—frostbite, if you like. Then there are three with tuberculosis and the remaining three have suffered mental breakdowns. Those Russian convoys take a pretty vicious toll, Lieutenant, in more ways than one."

"You have no cause to love our U-boats, our Luft-waffe, Mr. McKinnon."

The bosun shrugged. "We do send the occasional thousand bombers over Hamburg."

Ulbricht sighed. "I suppose this is no time for phi-losophizing about how two wrongs can never make a right. So we have nine wounded. Are all of them mobile?"

"The three exposure cases are virtually immobile. You've never seen so many bandages. The other six— well, they can get around as well as you and I. Well, that's not quite accurate—as well as I can and a damned sight better than you can."

"So. Six mobiles. I know little enough of medicine, but I do know just how difficult it is to gauge how severe a case of TB is. I also know that a man in a pretty advanced stage can get around well enough. As for mental breakdowns, those are easy enough to sim-ulate. One of those three may be as rational as we are—or think we are. Come to that, all three of them may be. I don't have to tell you, Mr. McKinnon, that there are those who are so sick of the mindlessness, the hellishness of war that they will resort to any means to escape from it. Malingerers, as they are commonly and quite often unfairly called. Many of them have quite simply had enough and can take no more. During the First World War quite a number of British soldiers were affected by an incurable disease that was a sure-fire guarantee for a one-way ticket to Blighty. D.A.H. it was called—Disorder Affecting the Heart. The more unfeeling of the British doctors commonly referred to it as Desperate Affection for Home."

"I've heard of it. Lieutenant, I'm not by nature an inquisitive person, but may I ask you a personal question?"

"Of course."

"Your English. So much better than mine. Thing is, you don't sound like a foreigner talking English. You sound like an Englishman talking English, an Englishman who's been at an English public school. Funny."

"Not really. You don't miss much, Mr. McKinnon, and that's a fact. I was educated in an English public school. My mother is English. My father was for many years an attaché in the German Embassy in London."

"Well, well." McKinnon shook his head and smiled. "It's too much. It's really too much. Two shocks like this inside twenty minutes."

"If you were to tell me what you are talking about—"

"Sister Morrison. You and she should get together. I've just learned that she's half German."

"Good God! Goodness gracious me!" Ulbricht could hardly be said to be dumfounded, but he was taken aback. "German mother, of course. How extraordinary! I tell you, Bosun, this could be a serious matter. Her being my nurse, I mean. Wartime. International complications."

"I don't know and I don't see it. You're both just doing your job. Anyway, she's coming up to see you shortly."

"Coming to see me? The ruthless Nazi killer?"

"Maybe she's had a change of heart."

"Under duress, of course."

"It's her idea and she insists on it."

"It'll be a hypodermic syringe. Lethal dose of morphine or some such. To get back to our six walking unwounded. Widens the field a bit, doesn't it? A suborned malingerer or ditto TB patient. How do you like it?"

"I don't like it at all. How many suborned men, spies, saboteurs, do you think we've picked up among the survivors from the *Argos*? Another daft thought, I know, but as you've more or less said yourself we're looking for daft answers to daft questions. And speaking of daft questions, here's another one. How do we know the *Argos* really was mined? We know that tankers are extremely tough, heavily compartmented, and that this one was returning with empty tanks. Tankers don't die easily, and even laden tankers have been torpedoed and survived. We don't even *know* the *Argos* was mined. How do we know it wasn't sabotaged so as to provide the opportunity to introduce a saboteur or saboteurs aboard the *San Andreas*? How do you like that?"

"Like yourself, I don't like it at all. But you're not seriously suggesting that Captain Andropolous would deliberately—"

"I'm not suggesting anything about Captain Andropolous. For all I know, he may be as double-dyed a villain as is sailing the seas those days. Although I'm willing to consider almost any crazy solution to our questions, I can't go along with the idea that any captain would sacrifice his ship for any imaginable purpose. But a person or persons to whom the *Argos* meant nothing might quite happily do just that. It would be interesting to know whether Andropolous had taken on any extra crew members in Murmansk, such as fellow nationals who had survived a previous sinking. Unfortunately, Andropolous and his crew speak nothing but Greek and nobody else aboard speaks Greek."

"I speak a little Greek, very little, schoolboy stuff— English public schools are high on Greek—and I've forgotten most of that. Besides, it was classical Greek. Not that I can see that it would do much good anyway, even if we were to find out that a person or X number of persons joined the *Argos* at Murmansk. They would only assume expressions of injured innocence, say they don't know what we are talking about, and what could we do then?" Ulbricht was silent for almost a minute, then suddenly said: "The Russian shipwrights."

"What Russian shipwrights?"

"The ones that fixed the damage to the hull of your ship and finished off your sick bay. But especially the hull repairers."

"What about them?"

"Moment." Ulbricht thought some more. "I don't know just how many undercover agents there may be aboard the *San Andreas*, but I'm all at once certain that the original one was a member of your own crew."

"How on earth do you figure that out? Not, mind you, that anything would surprise me."

"You sustained this hull damage to the *San Andreas* while you were alongside the sinking corvette, *before* you sank her by gunfire. That is correct?"

"Correct."

"How did it happen?"

"I told you. We don't know. No torpedoes, no mines, nothing of that nature. A destroyer was along one side of the corvette, taking off her crew, while we were on the other taking off the survivors of the sunken Russian submarine. There was a series of explosions inside the corvette before we could get clear. One was a boiler going off, the others could have been guncotton, two-pounders, anything—there was some sort of fire inside. It was at that time that the damage must have happened."

"I suggest it didn't happen that way at all. I suggest, instead, that it was then that a trusty member of your crew detonated a charge in the port ballast room. I suggest that it was someone who knew precisely how much explosive to use to insure that it didn't sink the ship but enough to inflict sufficiently serious damage that it would have to make for the nearest port where repair facilities were available, which, in this case, was Murmansk."

"Makes sense. It could have happened that way. But I'm not convinced."

"In Murmansk, did anyone see the size or type of hole that had been blown in the hull?"

"No."

"Did anyone try to see?"

"Yes. Mr. Kennet and I."

"But surprise, surprise, you didn't. You didn't because you weren't allowed to see it."

"That's how it was. How did you know?"

"They had tarpaulins rigged all around and above the area under repair?"

"They had." McKinnon was beginning to look intently at Ulbricht.

"Did they give any reasons?"

"To keep out the wind and snow."

"Was there much in the way of those?"

"Very little."

"Did you ask to get behind the tarpaulins, see behind them?"

"We did. They wouldn't let us. Said it was too dangerous and would only hold up the work of the shipwrights. We didn't argue because we didn't think it was all that important. There was no reason why we should have thought so. If you know the Russians at all, you must know how mulish they can be about the most ridiculous things. Besides, they were doing us a favor and there was no reason why we should have been suspicious. All right, all right, Lieutenant, there's no reason to beat me over the head with a two-by-four. You don't have to be an engineer or a metallurgist to recognize a hole that has been blown from the inside out."

"And does it now strike you as strange that the second damage to the hull should have occurred in precisely the same ballast compartment?"

"Not now it doesn't. Our gallant—ours, not yours— our gallant allies almost certainly left the charge in the ballast room with a suitable length of fuse conveniently attached. You have the right of it, Lieutenant."

"So all we have to do now is to find some member of your crew with a working knowledge of explosives. You know of any such, Mr. McKinnon?"

"Yes."

"What!" Ulbricht propped himself up on an elbow. "Who?"

McKinnon raised his eyes to the deckhead. "Me."

"That's a help." Ulbricht lowered himself to his bunk again. "That's a great help."

6

I T WAS SHORTLY AFTER TEN O'CLOCK IN THE MORN-
ing that the snow came again. McKinnon had spent
another fifteen minutes in the captain's cabin, leaving only when he saw the lieutenant was having difficulty in keeping his eyes open, then had spoken in turn
with Naseby, Patterson and Jamieson, who was again
supervising the strengthening of the superstructure. All
three had agreed that Ulbricht could be correct in the
assessment he had made; and all three agreed with the
bosun that this fresh knowledge, if knowledge it was,
served no useful purpose whatsoever. McKinnon had
returned to the bridge when the snow came.

He opened a wing door in duly circumspect fashion
but, for all his caution, had it torn from his grasp to
crash against the leading edge of the bridge, such was
the power of the wind. The snow, light as yet, was
driving along nearly horizontally. It was quite impossible to look into it, but with his back to it and looking
out over the bows he could see that the wave pattern

had changed; the dawn was in the sky now, and in its light he could see that the last semblance of serried ranks had vanished and that the white-veined, white-spumed seas were now broken walls of water, tending this way and that in unpredictable formlessness. Even without the evidence of his eyes he would have known that this was so: the deck was beginning to shake and shudder beneath his feet disconcertingly. The cold was intense. Even with his very considerable weight and strength McKinnon found it no easy task to heave the wing door shut behind him as he stepped back into the bridge.

He was in desultory conversation with Trent, who had the helm, when the phone rang. Sister Morrison said she was ready to come up to the captain's cabin.

"I wouldn't recommend it, Sister. Things are pretty unpleasant up top."

"I would remind you that you gave me your promise." She was speaking in her best sister's voice.

"I know. It's just that conditions have worsened."

"Really, Mr. McKinnon—"

"I'm coming. On your own head."

In Ward B, Janet Magnusson looked at him with disapproval. "A hospital is no place for a snowman."

"Just passing through. On a mission of mercy. At least, your mule-headed friend imagines she is."

She kept her expression in place. "Lieutenant Ulbricht?"

"Who else? I've just seen him. Looks fair enough to me. I think she's daft."

"The trouble with you, Archie McKinnon, is that you have no finer feelings. Not as far as caring for the sick is concerned. In other ways too, like as not. And if she's daft, it's only because she's been saying nice things about you."

"About me? She doesn't know me."

"True, Archie, true." She smiled sweetly. "But Captain Bowen does."

McKinnon sought briefly for a suitable comment about captains who gossiped to ward sisters, found none and moved into Ward A. The sister, suitably bundled up, was waiting. There was a small medical case on a table by her side. McKinnon nodded to her.

"Would you take those glasses off, Sister?"

"Why?"

"It's the Lothario in him," Kennet said. He sounded almost his old cheerful self again. "He probably thinks you look nicer without them."

"It's no morning for a polar bear, Mr. Kennet, far less a Lothario. If the lady doesn't remove her glasses the wind will do the job for her."

"What's the wind like, Bosun?" It was Captain Bowen.

"Force two, sir. Blizzard. Eight below, 990 millibars."

"And the seas breaking up?" Even in the hospital the shuddering of the vessel was unmistakable.

"They are a bit, sir."

"Any problems?"

"Apart from Sister here seeming bent on suicide, none." Not, he thought, as long as the superstructure stayed in place.

* * *

Sister Morrison gasped in shock as they emerged onto the upper deck. However much she had mentally prepared herself, she could not have anticipated the savage power of that near hurricane force wind and the driving blizzard that accompanied it, could not even have imagined the lung-searing effect of the abrupt 80° F. drop in temperature. McKinnon wasted no time. He grabbed Sister Morrison with one hand, the lifeline with the other, and allowed the two of them to be literally blown across the treacherous ice-sheathed deck into the shelter of the superstructure. Once under cover, she removed her duffel hood and stood there panting, tenderly massaging her ribs.

"Next time, Mr. McKinnon—if there is a next time— I'll listen to you. My word! I never dreamed—well, I just never dreamed. And my ribs!" She felt carefully as if to check they were still there. "I've got ordinary ribs, just like anyone else. I think you've broken them."

"I'm sorry about that," McKinnon said gravely. "But I don't think you'd have much fancied going over the side. And there will be a next time, I'm afraid. We've got to go back again and against the wind, and that will be a great deal worse."

"At the moment, I'm in no hurry to go back, thank you very much."

McKinnon led her up the companionway to the crew's quarters. She stopped and looked at the twisted passageway, the buckled bulkheads, the shattered doors.

"So this is where they died." Her voice was husky.

"When you see it, it's all too easy to understand how they died. But you have to see it first to understand. Ghastly—well, ghastly couldn't have been the word for it. Thank God I never saw it. And you had to clear it all up."

"I had help."

"I know who did all the horrible bits. Mr. Spenser, Mr. Rawlings, Mr. Batesman, those were the really shocking cases, weren't they? I know you wouldn't let anyone else touch them. Johnny Holbrook told Janet and she told me." She shuddered. "I don't like this place. Where's the lieutenant?"

McKinnon led her up to the captain's cabin. Naseby was keeping an eye on the recumbent lieutenant.

"Good morning again, Lieutenant. I've just had a taste of the kind of weather Mr. McKinnon has been exposing you to. It was awful. How do you feel?"

"Low, Sister. Very low. I think I'm in need of care and attention."

She removed oilskins and duffel coat. "You don't look very ill to me."

"Appearances, appearances. I feel very weak. Far be it from me to prescribe for myself, but what I need is a tonic, a restorative." He stretched out a languid hand. "Do you know what's in that wall cupboard there?"

"No." Her tone was severe. "I don't know. I can guess, though."

"Well, I thought, perhaps—in the circumstances, you understand—"

"Those are Captain Bowen's private supplies."

"May I repeat what the captain told me?" Mr.

McKinnon said. "'As long as Lieutenant Ulbricht keeps navigating he can keep on broaching my supplies.' Words to that effect."

"I don't see him doing any navigating at the moment. But very well. A small one." McKinnon poured and handed him a glass of scotch; the expression on Sister Morrison's face was indication enough that she and the bosun placed different interpretations on the word "small."

"Come on, George," McKinnon said. "This is no place for us."

Sister Morrison looked faintly surprised. "You don't have to go."

"We can't stand the sight of blood. Or suffering, come to that."

Ulbricht lowered his glass. "You would leave us to the mercy of Flannelfoot?"

"George, if you wait outside I'll go and give Trent a spell on the wheel. When you're ready to go back, Sister, you'll know where to find me."

McKinnon would have expected that her ministrations might have taken ten minutes, fifteen at the most. Instead, almost forty minutes elapsed before she put in an appearance on the bridge. McKinnon looked at her sympathetically.

"More trouble than you expected, Sister? He wasn't just joking when he said he felt pretty low?"

"There's very little the matter with him. Especially not with his tongue. How that man can talk!"

"He wasn't talking to an empty bulkhead, was he?"

"What do you mean?"

"Well," McKinnon said reasonably, "he wouldn't have kept on talking if you hadn't kept on listening."

Sister Morrison seemed to be in no hurry to depart. She was silent for some time. Then she said with a slight trace of a smile: "I find this—well, not infuriating but annoying. Most people would be interested in what we were saying."

"I am interested. Just not inquisitive. If you wanted to tell me, you'd tell me. If I asked you to tell me and you didn't want to, then you wouldn't tell me. But, fine, I'd like you to tell me."

"I don't know whether that's infuriating or not." She paused. "Why did you tell Lieutenant Ulbricht that I'm half German?"

"It's not a secret, is it?"

"No."

"And you're not ashamed of it. You told me so yourself. So why—ah! Why didn't I tell you that I'd told him? That's what you're asking. Just never occurred to me."

"You might at least have told me that *he* was half English."

"That didn't occur to me either. It's unimportant. I don't care what nationality a person is. I told you about my brother-in-law. Like the lieutenant, he's a pilot. He's also a lieutenant. If he thought it his duty to drop a bomb on me, he'd do it like a shot. But you couldn't meet a finer man."

"You're a very forgiving man, Mr. McKinnon."

"Forgiving?" He looked at her in surprise. "I've nothing to forgive. I mean, he hasn't dropped a bomb on me yet."

"I didn't mean that. Even if he did, it wouldn't make any difference."

"How do you know?"

"I know."

McKinnon didn't pursue the matter. "Doesn't sound like a very interesting conversation to me. Not forty minutes' worth, anyway."

"He also took great pleasure in pointing out that he's more British than I am. From the point of view of blood, I mean. Fifty percent British to start with plus two more British pints yesterday."

McKinnon was polite. "Indeed."

"All right, so statistics aren't interesting either. He also says that his father knows mine."

"Ah. That *is* interesting. Wait a minute. He mentioned that his father had been an attaché at the German Embassy in London. He didn't mention whether he was a commercial or cultural attaché or whatever. He didn't just happen to mention to you that his father had been the naval attaché there?"

"He was."

"Don't tell me that his old man is a captain in the German navy."

"He is."

"That makes you practically blood brothers. Or brothers and sisters. Mark my words, Sister," McKinnon said solemnly, "I see the hand of fate here. Something preordained, you might say?"

"Pfui!"

"Are they both on active service?"

"Yes." She sounded forlorn.

"Don't you find it funny that each of your respective

fathers should be prowling the high seas figuring out ways of doing each other in?"

"I don't find it at all funny."

"I didn't mean funny in that sense." If anyone had ever suggested to McKinnon that Margaret Morrison would one day strike him as a woebegone figure he would have questioned his sanity; but not any longer. He found her sudden dejection inexplicable. "Not to worry, lassie. It'll never happen." He wasn't at all sure what he meant by that.

"Of course not." Her voice carried a total lack of conviction. She made to speak, hesitated, looked down at the deck, then slowly lifted her head. Her face was in shadow, but he felt almost certain that he saw the sheen of tears. "I heard things about you today."

"Oh. Nothing to my credit, I'm sure. You can't believe a word anyone says those days. What things, Sister?"

"I wish you wouldn't call me that." The irritation was as unaccustomed as the dejection.

McKinnon raised a polite eyebrow. "Sister? But you are a sister."

"Not the way you make it sound. Sorry, I didn't mean that, you don't make it sound different from anyone else. It's like those cheap American films where the man with the gun goes around calling everyone sister."

He smiled. "I wouldn't like you to confuse me with a hoodlum. Miss Morrison?"

"You know my name."

"Yes. I also know that you started out to say something, changed your mind and are trying to stall."

"No. Yes. Well, not really. It's difficult, I'm not very good at those things. I heard about your family this morning. Just before we came up. I'm sorry, I am terribly sorry."

"Janet?"

"Yes."

"It's no secret."

"It was a German bomber pilot who killed them." She looked at him for a long moment, then shook her head. "Along comes another German bomber pilot, again attacking innocent civilians, and you're the first person to come to his defense."

"Don't go pinning any halos or wings on me. Besides, I'm not so sure that's a compliment. What did you expect me to do? Lash out in revenge at an innocent man?"

"You? Don't be silly. Well, no, maybe I was silly to say it, but you know very well what I mean. I also heard Petty Officer McKinnon, B.E.M., D.S.M. and goodness knows what else, was in a Malta hospital with a broken back when he heard the news. An Italian Air Force bomber got your submarine. You seem to have an affinity for enemy bombers."

"Janet didn't know that."

She smiled. "Captain Bowen and I have become quite friendly."

"Captain Bowen," McKinnon said without heat, "is a gossipy old woman."

"Captain Bowen is a gossipy old woman. Mr. Kennet is a gossipy old woman. Mr. Patterson is a gossipy old woman. Mr. Jamieson is a gossipy old woman. They're all gossipy old women."

"Goodness me! That's a very serious allegation, Sister. Sorry. Margaret."

"Gossipy old women speak in low voices or whispers. Whenever any two of them or three of them, or indeed all four, are together they speak in low voices or whispers. You can feel the tension, almost smell the fear—well, no, that's the wrong word, apprehension, I should say. Why do they whisper?"

"Maybe they've got secrets."

"I deserve better than that."

"We've got saboteurs aboard."

"I know that. We all know that. The whisperers know that we all know that." She gave him a long steady look. "I still deserve better. Don't you trust me?"

"I trust you. We're being hunted. We think that somebody aboard the *San Andreas* has a transmitter radio that is sending out a continuous location signal. The Luftwaffe, the U-boats know exactly where we are. Somebody wants us. Somebody wants to take over the *San Andreas*, for reason or reasons unknown."

For long moments she looked at his eyes as if searching for an answer to a question she couldn't formulate. McKinnon shook his head and said: "I'm sorry. That's all I know. You must believe me."

"I do believe you. Who could be sending out this signal?"

"Anybody. My guess is that it is a member of our own crew. Could be a survivor from the *Argos*. Could be any of the sick men we picked up in Murmansk. Each idea is quite ridiculous, but one has to be less ridiculous than the others. Which, I have no idea."

"Why would anyone want us?"

"If I knew that, I'd know the answer to a lot of things. Once again, I have no idea."

"How would they take us over?"

"Submarine. U-boat. No other way. They have no surface ships, and an aircraft is out of the question. Praying, that's what your whisperers are probably at— praying. Praying that the snow will never end. Our only hope lies in concealment. Praying, as the old divines used to say, that we will not be abandoned by fortune."

"And if we are?"

"Then that's it."

"You're not going to *do* anything?" She seemed more than faintly incredulous. "You're not even going to *try* to do anything?"

It was quite some hours since McKinnon had made up his mind where his course of action would lie, but it seemed hardly the time or the place to explain or elaborate his decision. "What on earth do you expect me to do? Send them to the bottom with a salvo of stale bread and old potatoes? You forget, this is a hospital ship. Sick, wounded, and all civilians."

"Surely there's *something* you can do." There was a strange note in her voice, one almost of desperation. She went on bitterly: "The much-bemedaled Petty Officer McKinnon."

"The much-bemedaled Petty Officer McKinnon," he said mildly, "would live to fight another day."

"Fight them now!" Her voice had a break in it. "Fight them! Fight them! Fight them!" She buried her face in her hands.

McKinnon put his arm round her shaking shoulders and regarded her with total astonishment. A man of almost infinite resource and more than capable of dealing with anything that came his way, he was at an utter loss to account for her conduct. He sought for words of comfort and consolation, but as he didn't know what he was supposed to be comforting or consoling about he found none. Nor did repeating phrases like "Now, now, then" seem to meet the case either, so he finally contented himself with saying: "I'll get Trent up and take you below."

After a particularly harrowing trip across the upper deck between superstructure and hospital—they had to battle their way against the great wind and the driving blizzard—he led her to the little lounge and went in search of Janet Magnusson. When he found her he said: "I think you'd better go and see your pal Maggie. She's very upset." He raised a hand. "No, Janet, not guilty. I did not upset her."

She said accusingly: "But you were with her when she became upset."

"She's disappointed with me, that's all."

"Disappointed?"

"She wants me to commit suicide. I don't see it her way."

She tapped her head. "One of you is touched. I don't much doubt who it is." McKinnon sat down on a stool by a mess table while she went into the lounge. She emerged some five minutes later and sat down opposite him. Her face was troubled.

"Sorry, Archie. Not guilty. And neither of you is touched. She's got this ambivalent feeling toward the Germans."

"Ambi what?"

"Mixed up. It doesn't help that her mother is German. She's had rather a bad time. A very rough time. Oh, I know you have, too, but you're different."

"Of course I'm different. I have no finer feelings."

"Oh, do be quiet. You weren't to know—in fact, I think I'm the only person who does know. About five months ago she lost both her only brother and her fiancé. Both died over Hamburg. Not in the same plane, not even in the same raid. But within weeks of each other."

"Oh, Jesus." McKinnon shook his head slowly and was silent for some moments. "Poor bloody kid. Explains a lot." He rose, crossed to Dr. Singh's private source of supplies and returned with a glass. "The legendary McKinnon will power. You were with Maggie when this happened, Janet?"

"Yes."

"You knew her before then?"

"Of course. We've been friends for years."

"So you must have known those two boys?" She said nothing. "Known them well, I mean?" Still she said nothing, just sat there with her flaxen head bowed, apparently gazing down at her clasped hands on the table. As much in exasperation as anything McKinnon reached out, took one of her wrists and shook it gently. "Janet."

She looked up. "Yes, Archie?" Her eyes were bright with unshed tears.

"Oh dear, oh dear." McKinnon sighed. "You, too." Again he shook his head; again he remained silent for some time. "Look, Janet, those boys knew what they were doing. They knew the risks. They knew that, if they could at all, the German anti-aircraft batteries and night-fighter pilots would shoot them down. And so they did and so they had every right to do. And I would remind you that those were no mere pinpoint raids— it was saturation bombing, and you know what that means. So while you and Maggie are crying for yourselves you might as well cry for the relatives of all the thousands of innocent dead that the R.A.F. left behind in Hamburg. Cry, if you want; you might as well cry for all mankind."

Two tears trickled down her cheeks. "You, McKinnon, are a heartless fiend."

"I'm all that." He rose. "If anyone wants me I'll be on the bridge."

Noon came and went, and as the day lengthened the wind strengthened until it reached the screaming intensity commonly found in the hurricanes and typhoons of the more tropical parts of the world. By two o'clock in the afternoon, when the light which, at best, had never been more than a gray half-light was beginning to fade, what little could be seen of the mountainous seas abeam and ahead of the *San Andreas*—the blizzard made it quite impossible to see anything abaft of the bridge—were as white as the driving snow itself, the shapeless troughs between the towering walls of water big enough to drown a suburban house or, to the more apprehensive eye, big enough to drown a suburban church including a fair part of its steeple. The *San Andreas* was in trouble. At 9300 tons it was not a small vessel, and the bosun had had engine revolutions reduced until the ship had barely steerage way on, but still she was in trouble, and the causes for this lay neither in the size of the ship nor the size of the seas, for normally the *San Andreas* could have ridden out the storm without much difficulty. The two main reasons for concern lay elsewhere.

The first of those was ice. A ship in a seaway can be said to be either stiff or tender. If it is stiff, it is resistant to roll and, when it does roll, recovers sharply; when it is tender it rolls easily and recovers slowly and reluctantly. Tenderness arises when a vessel becomes top-heavy, raising the center of gravity. The prime cause of this is ice. As the thickness of ice on the upper decks increases, so does the degree of tenderness; when the ice becomes sufficiently thick the vessel will fail to recover from its roll, turn turtle and founder. Even splendidly seaworthy oceangoing trawlers, specially built for Arctic operations, have succumbed to the stealthily insidious and deadly onslaught of ice; and for aircraft carriers operating in the far north, ice on their vast areas of open upper decks provided a constant threat to stability.

McKinnon was deeply worried by the accumulation of ice on the decks of the *San Andreas*. Compacted snow from the blizzard had formed a certain thickness of ice but not much, for, apart from the area abaft of the superstructure, most of the snow had simply been blown away by the powerful wind; but for hours now, according to the ever-changing direction of the constantly shifting masses of water, the *San Andreas* had been shipping copious amounts of water and spray, water and spray that turned to ice even before it hit the decks. The vessel occasionally rode on an even keel, but more and more frequently it lurched into a sudden roll and each time recovered from it more and more slowly. The critical limit, he was well aware, was still some time away, but without some amelioration in the conditions, it would inevitably be reached. There was nothing that could be done: sledgehammers and crowbars would have had but a minimal effect and the chances were high that people wielding those would have ended up, in short order, over the side; on those lurching ice-rink decks footing would have been impossible to maintain. For once, McKinnon regretted that he was aboard an American-built oil-burning ship instead of a British-built coal-burning one: boiler ashes spread on the deck would have given a reasonably secure footing and helped considerably toward melting the ice. There was nothing that one could do with Diesel oil.

Of even more immediate concern was the superstructure. Except when on even keel the overstressed metal, shaking and shuddering, creaked and groaned and protested its torture, and when the ship fell into the depths of a trough the entire structure shifted perceptibly. At the highest point, the bridge on which he was standing, McKinnon estimated the lateral movement to be between four and six inches a time. It was an acutely uncomfortable sensation and a thought-provoking one: how much of a drop and how acute an angle would be required before the shear factor came into operation and the superstructure parted company with the San Andreas? With this in mind, McKinnon went below to see Lieutenant Ulbricht.

Ulbricht, who had lunched on sandwiches and scotch and slept a couple of hours thereafter, was propped up in the captain's bunk and was in a reasonably philosophical mood.

"Whoever named this ship the *San Andreas*," he said, "named it well. I don't know who the first San Andreas was, but you know, of course, that the San Andreas is a famous—or notorious—earthquake fault." He grabbed the side of his bunk as the ship fell into a trough and shuddered alarmingly. "At the moment I feel I'm living through an earthquake."

"It was Mr. Kennet's idea. Mr. Kennet has, at times, a rather peculiar sense of humor. A week ago this was still the *Ocean Belle*. When we changed our paint from gray to the red-cross colors of white, green and red, Mr. Kennet thought we should change the name too. This ship was built in Richmond, California. Richmond is on the Hayward's Fault, which is a branch of the San Andreas. He was of the opinion that *San Andreas* was much more of a romantic name than *Hayward's Fault*. He also thought it was an amusing idea to name it after a potential disaster area." McKinnon smiled. "I wonder if he still thinks it amusing."

"Well, he's had plenty of time for reflection since I dropped those bombs on him yesterday morning. I should rather think he's had second thoughts on the matter." Ulbricht tightened his grip on the side of his bunk as the *San Andreas* fell heavily into another trough. "The weather does not improve, Mr. McKinnon?"

"The weather does not improve. That's what I came to talk about, Lieutenant. Force twelve wind. With the darkness and the blizzard—it's as strong as ever—visibility is zero. Not a chance of a star sight for hours. I think you'd be far better off in the hospital."

"Certainly not. I'd have to fight my way against a hurricane to reach the hospital. A man in my weakened condition? Not to be thought of."

"It's warmer down there, Lieutenant. More comfortable. And the motion, naturally, is much less."

"Mr. McKinnon, how could you overlook the most important inducement—all those pretty nurses. No, thank you. I prefer the captain's cabin, not to mention the captain's scotch. The truth of the matter is, of course, that you suspect that the superstructure may go over the side at any moment and that you want me out of here before that happens. Isn't that so?"

"Well." McKinnon touched the outer bulkhead. "It is a bit unstable."

"While you remain, of course."

"I have a job to do."

"Unthinkable. The honor of the Luftwaffe is at stake. You stay, I stay."

McKinnon didn't argue. If anything, he felt obscurely pleased by Ulbricht's decision. He tapped the barometer and lifted an eyebrow. "Three millibars?"

"Up?"

"Up."

"Help is at hand. There's hope yet."

"Take hours for the weather to moderate—if it does.

Superstructure could still go at any time. Even if it doesn't, our only real hope lies with the snow."

"And when the snow goes?"

"Then your U-boats come."

"You're convinced of that?"

"Yes. Aren't you?"

"I'm afraid I am, rather."

Three hours later, shortly after five o'clock in the afternoon and quite some time before McKinnon had expected it, the weather began to moderate, almost imperceptibly at first, then with increasing speed. The wind speed dropped to a relatively benign force six, the broken and confused seas of the early afternoon resolved themselves, once again, into a recognizable wave pattern, the *San Andreas* rode on a comparatively even keel, the sheeted ice on the decks no longer offered the same threat, and the superstructure had quite ceased its creaking. But best of all, from McKinnon's point of view, the snow, though driving much less horizontally than it had earlier on, still fell as heavily as ever. He was reasonably certain that when an attack did come it would come during the brief hours of daylight, but was well aware that a determined U-boat captain would not hesitate to press home an attack in moonlight. In his experience most U-boat captains were very determined indeed—and there would be a moon later that night. Snow would avail them nothing in daytime, but during the hours of darkness it was a virtual guarantee of safety.

He went to the captain's cabin where he found Lieutenant Ulbricht smoking an expensive Havana—Captain Bowen, a pipe man, permitted himself one cigar a day—and sipping an equally expensive malt, both of which, combined with the changes outside, no doubt helped to contribute to his comparatively relaxed mood.

"Ah, Mr. McKinnon. This is more like it. The weather, I mean. Moderating by the minute. Still snowing?"

"Heavily. A mixed blessing, I suppose. No chance of star sights, but at least it keeps your friends out of our hair."

"Friends? Yes. I spend quite some time wondering who my friends are." He waved a dismissive hand. "Is Sister Morrison ill?"

"I shouldn't think so."

"I'm supposed to be her patient. One could almost term this savage neglect. A man could easily bleed to death."

"We can't have that." McKinnon smiled. "I'll get her for you."

He phoned the hospital, and by the time he arrived there Sister Morrison was ready. She said: "Something wrong? Is he unwell?"

"He feels cruelly neglected and says something about bleeding to death. He is, in fact, in good spirits, smoking a cigar, drinking whisky, and appearing to be in increasingly excellent health. He's just bored or lonely or both and just wants to talk to someone."

"He can always talk to you."

"When I said someone, I didn't mean anyone. I am

not Margaret Morrison. Crafty, those Luftwaffe pilots. He can always have you up for dereliction of duty."

He took her to the captain's cabin, told her to call him at the hospital when she was through, took the crew lists from the captain's desk, left and went in search of Jamieson. Together they spent almost half an hour going over the papers of each member of the deck and engine-room crews, trying to recall every detail they knew of their past histories and what other members of the crew had said about any particular individual. When they had finished consulting both the lists and their memories, Jamieson pushed away the lists, leaned back in his chair and sighed.

"What do you make of it, Bosun?"

"Same as you do, sir. Nothing. I wouldn't even begin to know where to point the finger of suspicion. Not only are there no suitable candidates for the role of saboteur, there's nobody who's even remotely likely. I think we'd both go into court and testify as character witnesses for the lot of them. But if we accept Lieutenant Ulbricht's theory—and you, Mr. Patterson, Naseby and I do accept it—that it must have been one of the original crew that set off that charge in the ballast room when we were alongside that corvette, then it must have been one of them. Or, failing them, one of the hospital staff."

"The hospital staff?" Jamieson shook his head. "Sister Morrison as a seagoing Mata Hari? I have as much imagination as the next man, Bosun, but not that kind of imagination."

"Neither have I. We'd both go to court for them, too. But it *has* to be someone who was aboard this ship when we left Halifax. When we retire, Mr. Jamieson, I think we'd better not be applying for a job with Scotland Yard's C.I.D. Then there's the possibility that whoever it is may be in cahoots with someone from the *Argos* or one of the nine invalids we picked up in Murmansk."

"About all of whom we know absolutely nothing. A great help."

"As far as the crew of the *Argos* is concerned, that's true. As for the invalids we have, of course, their names, ranks and numbers. One of the TB cases, man by the name of Hartley, is an E.R.A.—Engine Room Artificer. He would know about electrics. Another, Simons, a mental breakdown case, or an alleged mental breakdown case, is an L.T.O.—Leading Torpedo Operator. He would know about explosives."

"Too obvious, Bosun."

"Far too obvious. Maybe we're meant to overlook the obvious."

"Have you seen those two? Spoken to them, I mean?"

"Yes. They're the two with the red hair."

"Ah. Those two. Bluff, honest sailormen. Don't look like criminal types at all. But then, I suppose, the best criminals never do. Look that way, I mean." He sighed. "I agree with you, Bosun. The C.I.D. are in no danger from us."

"No, indeed." McKinnon rose. "I think I'll go and rescue Sister Morrison from Lieutenant Ulbricht's clutches."

Sister Morrison was not in the lieutenant's clutches, nor did she show signs of wanting to be rescued. "Time to go?" she said.

"Of course not. Just to let you know I'll be on the bridge when you want me." He looked at Ulbricht, then at Sister Morrison. "You managed to save him, then?"

Compared to what it had been only a few hours previously, the starboard wing of the bridge was now almost a haven of peace and quiet. The wind had dropped to not more than force four and the seas, while far from being a millpond, had quieted to the extent that the San Andreas, when it did at all, rarely rolled more than a few degrees. That was on the credit side. On the debit side was the fact that the snow had thinned so that McKinnon had no difficulty in making out the arc-lit shape of the red cross on the foredeck reflecting palely under its sheathing of ice. He went back inside the bridge and called up Patterson in the engine room.

"Bosun here, sir. Snow's lightening. Looks as if it's going to stop altogether pretty soon. I'd like permission to switch off all exterior lights. Seas are still too high for any U-boat to see us from periscope depth, but if it's on the surface, if the snow has stopped and we still have the red cross lights on, we can be seen miles away from its conning tower."

"We wouldn't want that, would we. No lights."

"One other thing. Could you have some men clear a pathway—hammers, crowbars, whatever—in the ice between the hospital and the superstructure. Two feet should be wide enough."

"Consider it done."

Fifteen minutes later, still without any sign of Margaret Morrison, the bosun moved out on the wing again. The snow had stopped completely. There were isolated patches of clear sky above and some stars shone, although the polestar was hidden. The darkness was still pretty complete: with the deck lights extinguished McKinnon couldn't even see as far as the fo'c's'le. He returned inside and went below to the captain's cabin.

"The snow's stopped, Lieutenant. There are a few stars around, not many, and certainly not at the moment the pole, but a few. I don't know how long those conditions might last so I thought you might like to have a look now. I assume that Sister Morrison has stanched the flow of blood."

"There never was any flow of blood," she said. "As you know perfectly well, Mr. McKinnon."

"Yes, Sister."

She winced, then smiled. "Archie."

"Wind's dropped a lot," McKinnon said. He helped Ulbricht on with outer clothing. "But those are just as necessary as they were before. The temperature is still below zero."

"Fahrenheit?"

"Sorry. You don't use that. It's about twenty below, Centigrade."

"May his nurse come with him? After all, Dr. Sinclair went with him last time."

"Of course. Wouldn't advise you to come on the wing bridge, though." McKinnon gathered up sextant and chronometer and accompanied them up to the bridge. This time Ulbricht made it unaided. He went out on both wing bridges in turn and chose the starboard from which to make his observations. It took him longer than it had on the previous occasion, for he found it necessary to take more sights, presumably because the polestar was hidden. He came back inside, worked on the chart for some time and finally looked up.

"Satisfactory. In the circumstances, very satisfactory. Not my navigation. The course we've been holding. No idea if we've been holding it all the time, of course, and that doesn't matter. We're south of the Arctic Circle now, near enough 66.20 north, 4.20 east. Course 213, which seems to indicate that the wind's backed only five degrees in the past twelve hours. We're fine as we are, Mr. McKinnon. Keeping the sea and the wind to the stern should see us through the night, and even if we do wander off course we're not going to bump into anything. This time tomorrow morning we'll lay off a more southerly course."

"Thank you very much, Lieutenant," McKinnon said. "As the saying goes, you've earned your supper. Incidentally, I'll have that sent up inside half an hour. You've also earned a good night's sleep—I won't be troubling you any more tonight."

"Haven't I earned something else, too? It was mighty cold out there, Mr. McKinnon."

"I'm sure the captain would approve. As he said, as long as you're navigating." He turned to the young woman. "You coming below?"

"Yes, yes, of course, she must," Ulbricht said. "I've been most remiss, most." If remorse were gnawing it didn't show too much. "All your other patients—"

"All my other patients are fine. Sister Maria is looking after them. I'm off duty."

"Off duty! That makes me feel even worse. You should be resting, my dear girl, that or sleeping."

"I'm wide awake, thank you. Are *you* coming below? It's no trouble now, ship's like a rock and you've just been told you won't be required any more tonight."

"Well, now." Ulbricht paused judiciously. "On balance, I think I should remain. Unforeseeable emergencies, you understand."

"Luftwaffe officers shouldn't tell fibs. Of course I understand. I understand that the only foreseeable emergency is that you run short of supplies and the only reason you're not coming below is that we don't serve whisky with ward dinners."

The lieutenant shook his head in sadness. "I am deeply wounded."

"Wounded!" she said. They had returned to the hospital mess deck.

"I think he is." McKinnon looked at her in amusement. "And you, too."

"Me? Oh, really!"

"Yes. Really. You're hurt because you think he prefers scotch to your company. Isn't that so?" She made no reply. "If you believe that, then you've got a very low opinion of both yourself and the lieutenant. You were with him for about an hour tonight. What did he drink in that time?"

"Nothing." Her voice was quiet.

"Nothing. He's not a drinker and he's a sensitive lad. He's sensitive because he's an enemy, because he's a captive, a prisoner of war and, of course, he's sensitive above all because he's now got to live all his life with the knowledge that he killed fifteen innocent people. You asked him if he was coming down. He didn't want to be asked if. He wanted to be persuaded, even ordered. 'If' implies indifference, and the way he's feeling it could be taken for a rejection. So what happens? The ward sister tells her feminine sympathy and intuition to take a holiday and delivers herself of some cutting remarks that Margaret Morrison would never have made. A mistake, but easy enough to put right."

"How?" The question was a tacit admission that a mistake had indeed been made.

"Ninny. You take his hand and say sorry. Or are you too proud?"

"Too proud?" She seemed uncertain, confused. "I don't know."

"Too proud because he's a German? Look, I know about your fiancé and brother and I'm terribly sorry but that doesn't—"

"Janet shouldn't have told you."

"Don't be daft. You didn't object to her telling you about my family."

"And that's not all." She sounded almost angry. "You said they went around killing thousands of innocent people and that—"

"Those were not my words. Janet did not say that You're doing what you accused the lieutenant of doing—fibbing. Also, you're dodging the issue. Okay, so the Germans killed two people you knew and loved. I wonder how many hundreds *they* killed before *they* were shot down. But that doesn't matter really, does it? You never knew them or their names. How can you weep over people you've never met, husbands, wives, sweethearts and children, without faces or names? It's quite ridiculous, isn't it, and statistics are so boring. Tell me, did your brother ever tell you how he felt when he went out in his Lancaster bomber and slaughtered his mother's fellow countrymen? But, of course, he'd never met them so that made it all right, didn't it?"

She said in a whisper: "I think you're horrible."

"You think I'm horrible. Janet thinks I'm a heartless fiend. *I* think you're a pair of splendid hypocrites."

"Hypocrites?"

"You know—Dr. Jekyll and Mr. Hyde. The ward sister and Margaret Morrison. Janet's just as bad. At least I don't deal in double standards." McKinnon made to leave, but she caught him by the arm and indulged, not for the first time, in the rather disconcerting practice of examining each of his eyes in turn.

"You didn't really mean that, did you? About Janet and myself being hypocrites?"

"No."

"You *are* devious. All right, all right, I'll make it right with him."

"I knew you would, Margaret Morrison."

"Not Ward Sister Morrison?"

"You don't look like Mrs. Hyde." He paused. "When were you to have been married?"

"Last September."

"Janet. Janet and your brother. They were pretty friendly, weren't they?"

"Yes. She told you that?"

"No. She didn't have to."

"Yes, they were pretty friendly." She was silent for

a few moments. "It was to have been a double wedding."

"Oh, hell," McKinnon said and walked away.

He checked all the scuttles in the hospital area—even from the relatively low altitude of a submarine conning tower the light from an uncovered porthole can be seen from several miles—went down to the engine room, spoke briefly to Patterson, returned to the mess deck, had dinner, then went into the wards. Janet Magnusson, in Ward B, watched his approach without enthusiasm.

"So you've been at it again."

"Yes."

"Do you know what I'm talking about?"

"No. I don't know and I don't care. I suppose you're talking about your friend Maggie—and yourself. Of course I'm sorry for you both, terribly sorry, and maybe tomorrow or when we get to Aberdeen I'll break my heart for yesterday. But not now, Janet. Now I have one or two more important things on my mind such as, say, *getting* to Aberdeen."

"Archie." She put a hand on his arm. "I won't even say sorry. I'm just whistling in the dark, don't you know that, you clown? I don't want to think about tomorrow." She gave a shiver, which could have been mock or not. "I feel funny. I've been talking to Maggie. It's going to happen tomorrow, isn't it, Archie?"

"If by tomorrow you mean when daylight comes, then yes. Could even be tonight, if the moon breaks through."

"Maggie says it has to be a submarine. So you said."

"Has to be."

"How do you fancy being taken a prisoner?"

"I don't fancy it at all. If it comes to that."

"But you will be, won't you?"

"I hope not."

"How can you hope not? Maggie says you're going to surrender. She didn't say so outright because she knows we're friends—we *are* friends, Mr. McKinnon?"

"We are friends, Miss Magnusson."

"Well, she didn't say so, but I think she thinks you're a bit of a coward, really."

"A very—what's the word, perspicacious?—a very perspicacious girl is our Maggie."

"She's not as perspicacious as I am. You really think there's a chance we'll reach Aberdeen?"

"There's a chance."

"And after that?"

"Aha! Clever, clever Janet Magnusson. If I haven't got any plans for the future then I don't see any future. Isn't that it? Well, I do see a future and I do have plans. I'm going to take my first break since 1939 and have a couple of weeks back home in the Shetlands. When were you last back home in the Shetlands?"

"Not for years."

"Will you come with me, Janet?"

"Of course."

McKinnon went into Ward A and passed up the aisle to where Sister Morrison was sitting at her table. "How's the captain?"

"Well enough, I suppose. Bit dull and quiet. But why ask me? Ask him."

"I have to ask the ward sister's permission to take him out of the ward."

"Take him out—whatever for?"

"I want to talk to him."

"You can talk to him here."

"I can just see the nasty suspicious looks I'd be getting from you if we started whispering together and the nasty suspicious questions I'd be getting afterward. My dear Margaret, we have matters of state to discuss."

"You don't trust me, is that it?"

"That's the second time you've asked me that silly question. Same answer. I do trust you. Totally. I trust Mr. Kennet there. But there are five others I don't know whether to trust or not."

McKinnon took the captain from the ward and returned with him inside two minutes. After she'd tucked him back in bed, Margaret Morrison said: "That must rank as the shortest state conference in history."

"We are men of few words."

"And that's the only communiqué I'll be getting?"

"Well, that's the way high-level diplomacy is conducted. Secrecy is the watchword."

As he entered Ward B he was stopped by Janet Magnusson. "What was all that about, then? You and Captain Bowen, I mean."

"I have not had a private talk with the captain in order to tell all the patients in Ward B about it. I am under an oath of silence."

Margaret Morrison came in, looked from one to the other, then said: "Well, Janet, has he been more forthcoming with you than with me?"

"Forthcoming! Under an oath of silence, he claims. His own oath, I have no doubt."

"No doubt. What *have* you been doing to the captain?"

"Doing? I've been doing nothing."

"Saying, then. He's changed since he came back. Seems positively cheerful."

"Cheerful? How can you tell? With all those bandages, you can't see a square inch of his face."

"There are more ways than one of telling. He's sitting up in bed, rubbing his hands from time to time and twice he's said 'Aha.'"

"I'm not surprised. It takes a special kind of talent to reach the hearts and minds of the ill and depressed. It's a gift. Some of us have it." He looked at each in turn. "And some of us haven't."

He left them looking at each other.

McKinnon was wakened by Trent at 2 A.M. "The moon's out, Bosun."

The moon, as McKinnon bleakly appreciated when he arrived on the port wing of the bridge, was beautiful—and awful. A three-quarter moon and preternaturally bright—or so it seemed to him. At least half the sky was clear. The visibility out over the now almost calm seas was remarkable, so much so that he had no difficulty in picking out the line of the horizon: and if he could see the horizon, the bosun all too clearly realized, then a submarine could pick them up ten miles away, especially if the *San Andreas* were silhouetted against the light of the moon. McKinnon suddenly felt naked and very vulnerable. He went below, roused Curran, told him to take up lookout on the starboard wing of the bridge, found Naseby, asked him to check that the falls and davits of the motor lifeboats were clear of ice and working freely, and then returned to the port wing, where, every minute or two, he swept the horizon with his binoculars. But the sea between the *San Andreas* and the horizon remained providentially empty.

The *San Andreas* itself was a remarkable sight. Wholly covered in ice and snow, it glittered and shone and sparkled in the bright moonlight except for a narrow central area abaft of the superstructure where wisping smoke from the shattered funnel had laid a brown smear all the way to the stern post. The fore and aft derricks were huge glistening Christmas trees, festooned with thick-ribbed woolly halyards and stays, and the anchor chains on the fo'c's'le had been transformed into great fluffy ropes of the softest cotton wool. It was a strange and lovely world with an almost magical quality about it, almost ethereal; but one had only to think of the lethal dangers that lay under the surrounding waters and the beauty and the magic ceased to exist.

An hour passed and everything remained quiet and peaceful. Another hour came and went, nothing untoward happened and McKinnon could scarcely believe their great good fortune. And before the third uneventful hour was up the clouds had covered the moon and it had begun to snow again, a gentle snowfall only, but enough, with the hidden moon, to shroud them in blessed anonymity. Telling Ferguson, who now had the watch, to shake him if the snow stopped, he went below in search of sleep.

It was nine o'clock when he awoke. It was an unusually late awakening for him, but he wasn't unduly perturbed—dawn was still an hour distant. As he crossed the upper deck he noted that the conditions were just as they had been four hours previously— moderate seas, wind no stronger than force three and still the same gently falling snow. McKinnon had no belief in second sight but he felt in his bones that this peace and calm would have gone before the morning was out.

Down below he talked in turn with Jones, McGuigan, Stephen and Johnny Holbrook. They had taken turns, in pairs, to monitor the comings and goings of everybody in the hospital. All four swore that nobody had stirred during the night and that, most certainly, no one had at any time left the hospital area.

He had breakfast with Dr. Singh, Dr. Sinclair, Patterson and Jamieson—Dr. Singh, he thought, looked unusually tired and strained—then went to Ward B. Janet Magnusson looked wan, and there were shadows under her eyes.

McKinnon looked at her with concern. "What's wrong, Janet?"

"I couldn't sleep. I didn't sleep a wink last night. It's all your fault."

"Of course. Cardinal rule number one—when anything goes wrong blame the bosun. What am I supposed to have done this time?"

"You said the submarine, the U-boat, would attack if the moon broke through."

"I said it could, not would."

"Same thing. I spent most of the night looking out

through the porthole—no, Mr. McKinnon, I did *not* have my cabin light switched on—and when the moon came out at about two o'clock I was sure the attack must come any time. And when the moon went I was sure it would come again. Moon. U-boat. Your fault."

"A certain logic, I must admit. Twisted logic, of course, but not more than one would expect of the feminine mind. Still, I'm sorry."

"But *you're* looking fine. Fresh. Relaxed. *And* you're very late on the road this morning. Our trusty guardian sleeping on the job."

"Your trusty guardian lost a little sleep himself, last night," McKinnon said. "Back shortly. Must see the captain."

It was Sister Maria, not Sister Morrison, who was in charge in A Ward. McKinnon spoke briefly with both the captain and the chief officer, then said to Bowen: "Still sure, sir?"

"More sure than ever, Archie. When's dawn?"

"Fifteen minutes."

"I wish you well."

"I think you better wish us all well."

He returned to Ward B and said to Janet: "Where's your pal?"

"Visiting the sick. She's with Lieutenant Ulbricht."

"She shouldn't have gone alone."

"She didn't. You were asleep, so George Naseby came for her."

McKinnon looked at her with suspicion. "You find something amusing."

"That's her second time up there this morning."

"Is he dying or something?"

"I hardly think she would smile so much if a patient was slipping away."

"Ah! Mending fences, you would say?"

"She called him Karl twice." She smiled. "I'd call that mending fences, wouldn't you?"

"Good lord! Karl. That well-known filthy Nazi."

"Well, she said you asked her to make it right. No, you told her. So now you'll be taking all the credit, I suppose."

"Credit where credit is due," McKinnon said absently. "But she must come below at once. It's too exposed up there."

"Dawn." Her voice had gone very quiet. "This time you're sure, Archie?"

"This time I'm sure. The U-boat will come at dawn."

The U-boat came at dawn.

7

IT WAS LITTLE MORE THAN HALF-LIGHT WHEN THE
U-boat, in broken camouflage paint of various
shades of gray and at a distance of less than half
a mile, suddenly appeared from behind a passing snow
squall. It was running fully on the surface with three
figures clearly distinguishable on the conning tower
and another three manning the deck gun just for'ard
of that. The submarine was on a course exactly par-
alleling that of the *San Andreas* and could well have
been for many hours. The U-boat was on their starboard hand, so that the *San Andreas* lay between it
and the gradually lightening sky to the south. Both
bridge wing doors were latched back in the fully open
position. McKinnon reached for the phone, called the
engine room for full power, nudged the wheel to starboard and began to edge imperceptibly closer to the
U-boat.

He and Naseby were alone on the bridge. They
were, in fact, the only two people left in the super-

structure because McKinnon had ordered everyone, including a bitterly protesting Lieutenant Ulbricht, to go below to the hospital only ten minutes previously. Naseby he required and for two reasons. Naseby, unlike himself, was an adept Morse signaler and had a signaling lamp ready at hand; more important, McKinnon was more than reasonably certain that the bridge would be coming under attack in a short time, and he wanted a competent helmsman there in case he himself was incapacitated.

"Keep out of sight, George," McKinnon said. "But try to keep an eye on them. They're bound to start sending any minute now."

"They can see you," Naseby said.

"Maybe they can see my head and shoulders over the wing of the bridge. Maybe not. It doesn't matter The point is that they will believe that I can't see them. Don't forget that they're in the dark quadrant of the sea and have no reason to believe that we're expecting trouble. Besides, a helmsman's job is to keep an eye on the compass and look ahead—no reason on earth why I should be scanning the seas around." He felt the superstructure begin to shudder as Patterson increased the engine revolutions, gave the wheel another nudge to starboard, picked up a tin mug from the shattered binnacle and pretended to drink from it. "It's a law of nature, George. Nothing more reassuring than the sight of an unsuspecting innocent enjoying a morning cup of tea."

For a full minute, which seemed like a large number of full minutes, nothing happened. The superstructure was beginning to vibrate quite strongly now, and

McKinnon knew that the *San Andreas* was under maximum power. They were now at least a hundred yards closer to the U-boat than they had been when it had first been sighted, but the U-boat captain gave no indication that he was aware of this. Had McKinnon maintained his earlier speed, his acute angling in toward the U-boat would have caused him to drop slightly astern of the submarine, but the increase in speed had enabled him to maintain his relative position. The U-boat captain had no cause to be suspicious—and no one in his right mind was going to harbor suspicions about a harmless and defenseless hospital ship.

"He's sending, George," McKinnon said.

"I see him. 'Stop,' he says. 'Stop engines or I will sink you.' What do I send, Archie?"

"Nothing." McKinnon edged the *San Andreas* another three degrees to starboard, reached again for his tin mug and pretended to drink from it. "Ignore him."

"Ignore him?" Naseby sounded aggrieved. "You heard what the man said. He's going to sink us."

"He's lying. He hasn't stalked us all this way just to send us to the bottom. He wants us alive. Not only is he not going to torpedo us, he can't, not unless they've invented torpedoes that can turn corners. So how else is he going to stop us? With that little itsy-bitsy gun he's got on the foredeck? It's not all that much bigger than a pompom."

"I have to warn you, Archie, the man's going to get very annoyed."

"He's got nothing to be annoyed about. We haven't seen his signal."

Naseby lowered his binoculars. "I also have to warn you that he's about to use that little itsy-bitsy gun."

"Sure he is. The classic warning shot over the bows to attract our attention. If he *really* wants to attract our attention, it may be into the bows for all I know."

The two shells, when they came, entered the sea just yards ahead of the *San Andreas*, one disappearing silently below the waves, the other exploding on impact. The sound of the explosion and the sharp flat crack of the U-boat's gun made it impossible any longer to ignore the submarine's existence.

"Show yourself, George," McKinnon said. "Tell him to stop firing and ask him what he wants."

Naseby moved out on the starboard wing and transmitted the message; the reply came immediately.

"One-track mind," Naseby said. "Message reads 'Stop or be sunk.'"

"One of those laconic characters. Tell him we're a hospital ship."

"You think he's blind, perhaps?"

"It's still only half-light and the starboard side is our dark side. Maybe he'll think that we think he can't see. Tell him we're a neutral, mention Geneva conventions. Maybe he's got a better side to *his* nature."

Naseby clacked out his message, waited for the reply, then turned gloomily to McKinnon. "He hasn't got a better side to his nature."

"Not many U-boat captains have. What does he say?"

"Geneva conventions do not apply in the Norwegian Sea."

"There's little decency left on the high seas these days. Let's try for his sense of patriotism. Tell him we have German survivors aboard."

While Naseby sent the message, McKinnon rang down for slow ahead. Naseby turned in the doorway and shook his head sadly.

"His patriotism is on a par with his decency. He says: 'Will check nationals when we board. We commence firing in twenty seconds.'"

"Send: 'No need to fire. We are stopping. Check wake.'"

Naseby sent the message, then said: "Well, he got that all right. He's already got his glasses trained on our stern. You know, I do believe he's angling in toward us. Very little, mind you, but it's there."

"I do believe you're right." McKinnon gave the wheel another slight nudge to starboard. "If he notices anything he'll probably think it's because he's closing in on us and not vice versa. Is he still examining our wake?"

"Yes."

"Turbulence aft must have died away quite a lot by this time. That should make him happy."

"He's lowered his glasses," Naseby said. "Message coming."

The message didn't say whether the U-boat captain was happy or not, but it did hold a certain degree of satisfaction. "Man says we are very wise," Naseby said. "Also orders us to lower our gangway immediately."

"Acknowledge. Tell Ferguson to start lowering the gangway immediately but to stop it about, say, eight feet above the water. Then tell Curran and Trent to swing out the lifeboat and lower it to the same height."

Naseby relayed both messages then said: "You think we're going to need the lifeboat?"

"I quite honestly have no idea. But if we do, we're going to need it in a hurry." He called the engine room and asked for Patterson.

"Chief? Bosun here. We're slowing a bit, as you know, but that's only for the moment. The U-boat is closing in on us. We're lowering both the gangway and the lifeboat, the gangway on the U-boat's instructions, the lifeboat on mine. . . . No, they can't see the lifeboat—it's on our port side, their blind side. As soon as they are in position I'm going to ask for full power. A request, sir. If I do have to use the boat I'd appreciate it if you'd permit Mr. Jamieson to come with me. With your gun." He listened for a few moments while the receiver crackled in his ear then said: "Two things, sir. I want Mr. Jamieson because apart from yourself and Naseby he's the only member of the crew I can trust. Show him where the safety catch is. And no, sir, you know damn well you can't come along instead of Mr. Jamieson. You're the officer commanding and you can't leave the *San Andreas.*" McKinnon replaced the receiver and Naseby said, plaintive reproach in his voice: "You might have asked me."

McKinnon looked at him coldly. "And who's going to steer this damned ship when I'm gone?"

Naseby sighed. "There's that, of course, there's that. They seem to be preparing some kind of boarding party across there, Archie. Three more men on the conning tower now. They've armed with submachine guns or machine pistols or whatever you call those things. Something nasty, anyway."

"We didn't expect roses. How's Ferguson coming along? If that gangway doesn't start moving soon, the U-boat captain is going to start getting suspicious. Worse, he's going to start getting impatient."

"I don't think so. At least, not yet awhile. I can see Ferguson, so I'm certain the U-boat captain can too. Ferguson's having difficulty of some kind, he's banging away at the lowering drum with a hammer. Icing trouble for a certainty."

"See how the boat's getting on, will you?"

Naseby crossed the bridge, moved out onto the port wing and was back in seconds. "It's down. About eight feet above the water, as you asked." He crossed to the starboard wing, examining the U-boat through his binoculars, lowered them and turned back to McKinnon.

"That's bloody funny. All those characters seem to be wearing some kind of gas masks."

"Gas masks? Are you all right?"

"Certainly I'm all right. They're all wearing a horseshoe-shaped kind of life jacket around their necks with a corrugated hose attached to the top. They're not wearing it at the moment, it's dangling down in front, but there's a mouthpiece and goggles attached to the end of the tube. When did German submariners start using gas?"

"They don't. What good on earth would gas be to a U-boat?" He took Naseby's binoculars, examined the U-boat briefly and handed the glasses back. "Tauchretter, George, Tauchretter. Otherwise known as the Dräger Lung. It's fitted with an oxygen cylinder and a carbon dioxide canister, and its sole purpose is to help people escape from a sunken submarine."

"No gas?" Naseby sounded vaguely disappointed.

"No gas."

"That doesn't look like a sunken submarine to me."

"Some U-boat commanders make their crews wear them all the time they're submerged. Bit pointless in those waters, I would have thought. At least six hundred feet deep here, maybe a thousand. There's no way you can escape from those depths, Dräger set or not. How's Ferguson coming along?"

"As far as I can tell, he's not. Still hammering away. No, wait a minute, wait a minute. He's put the hammer down and is trying the release lever. It's moving, Archie. It's coming down."

"Ah!" McKinnon rang for full power.

Some seconds passed, then Naseby said: "Halfway." A similar length of time elapsed then Naseby said in the same matter-of-fact voice: "It's down, Archie. Eight feet, give or take. Ferguson's secured it."

McKinnon nodded and spun the wheel to starboard until he had maximum rudder on. Slowly, ponderously at first, then with increasing speed, the *San Andreas* began to come round.

"Do you want to get your head blown off, George?"

"Well, no." Naseby stepped inside, closed the wing door behind him and peered out through the little window in the door. The *San Andreas*, no longer riding with the sea, was beginning to corkscrew, although gently; but the entire superstructure was beginning to vibrate as the engines built up to maximum power.

"And don't you think you ought to lie down?"

"In a minute, Archie, in a minute. Do you think they've gone to sleep aboard that U-boat?"

"Some trouble with their eyes, that's for sure. I think they're rubbing them and not believing what they're seeing."

Except that there was no actual eye-rubbing going on aboard the U-boat, McKinnon's guess was very close to the mark. The reactions of both the submarine commander and his crew were extraordinarily slow. Extraordinarily, but in the circumstances, understandably. The U-boat's crew had made both the forgivable and unforgivable mistake of relaxing, of lowering their guard at the precise moment when their alertness and sense of danger should have been honed to its edge. But the sight of the gangway being lowered in strict compliance with their orders must have convinced them that there was no thought or possibility of any resistance being offered and that the taking over of the *San Andreas* was no more than a token formality. Besides, no one in the history of warfare had ever heard of a hospital ship being used as . . . as an offensive weapon. It was unthinkable. It takes time to rethink the unthinkable.

The *San Andreas* was so far round now that the U-boat was no more than 45 degrees off the starboard bow. Naseby moved from the starboard wing door to the nearest small window let into the front of the bridge.

"They're lining up what you call that itsy-bitsy gun, Archie."

"Then maybe we'd both better be getting down."

"No. They're not lining up on the bridge, they're lining up on the hull aft. I don't know what they intend to—" He broke off and shouted: "No! No! Get down, get down!" and flung himself at McKinnon, bringing both men crashing heavily to the deck of the bridge. Even as they landed, hundreds of bullets, to the accompaniment of the staccato chattering of several machine guns, smashed into the fore end and starboard side of the bridge. None of the bullets succeeded in penetrating the metal, but all four windows were smashed. The fusillade lasted no more than three seconds and had no sooner ceased when the U-boat's deck gun fired three times in rapid succession, on each occasion causing the *San Andreas* to shudder as the shells exploded somewhere in the after hull.

McKinnon hauled himself to his feet and took the wheel. "If I'd been standing there I'd have been very much the late Archie McKinnon. I'll thank you tomorrow." He looked at the central window before him. It was holed, cracked, starred, abraded and completely opaque. "George?"

But Naseby needed no telling. Fire extinguisher in hand, he smashed away the entire window in just two blows. He hitched a cautious eye over the bottom of where the window had been, saw that the *San Andreas* was arrowing in on the bows of the U-boat, then abruptly straightened in the instinctive reaction of a man who realizes that all danger is past.

"Conning tower's empty, Archie. They've all gone. Bloody funny."

"Nothing funny about it." The bosun's tone was dry. If he was in any way moved or shaken by the narrowness of his recent escape he showed no sign. "It's customary, George, to go below and pull down the hatch after you when you're going to dive. In this case, crash dive."

"Crash dive?"

"Captain has no option. He knows he hasn't the firepower to stop us and he can't possibly bring his torpedoes to bear. Right now he's blowing all main ballast. See those bubbles? That's water being blown from the ballast tanks by high-pressure air—something like three thousand pounds per square inch."

"But—but he's left his gun crew on deck."

"Indeed he has. Again, no choice. A U-boat is much more valuable than the lives of three men. See those valves they're twisting on the right-hand side of their suits? Oxygen valves. They're turning their Dräger lungs into life jackets. Much good it will do them if they run into a propellor. Will you go out on the wings, George, and see if there's any flame or smoke aft?"

"You could phone."

McKinnon pointed to the shredded phone in front of the wheel, shattered by a machine gun bullet. Naseby nodded and went out on both wings in turn.

"Nothing. Nothing you can see from the outside." Naseby looked ahead toward the U-boat, not much more than a hundred yards distant. "She's going down, Archie. Fore and aft decks are awash."

"I can see that."

"And she's turning away to her starboard."

"I can see that, too. Counsel of desperation. He's hoping that if he can turn his sub at an acute enough angle to us he'll be struck only a glancing blow. A glancing blow he could survive. I think."

"Hull's submerged now. Is he going to make it?"

"He's left it too late." McKinnon rang down for full astern and eased the wheel slightly to port. Five seconds later, with the top of the conning tower barely awash, the forefoot of the *San Andreas* tore into the hull of the U-boat some thirty feet for'ard of the tower. The *San Andreas* shook throughout its length but the overall effect of the impact was curiously small. For a period of not more than three seconds they felt rather than heard the sensation of steel grinding over steel. Then all contact was abruptly lost.

"Well," Naseby said, "so that's how it's done, is it?" He paused. "There's going to be a lot of jagged metal on that U-boat. If one of our props hits that—"

"No chance. The U-boat's been driven down, deep down—and they'll still be blowing main ballast. Let's just hope we haven't damaged ourselves too badly."

"You said the U-boat captain had no option. We didn't either. You think there'll be any survivors?"

"I don't know. If there are any, we'll find out soon enough. I question very much whether they would even have had time to close watertight doors. If they didn't, then that U-boat is on its way to the bottom. If anyone is going to escape, they're going to have to do it before it reaches the two-hundred-and-fifty-foot mark—I've never heard of anyone escaping from a submarine at a depth greater than that."

"They'd have to use the conning tower?"

"I suppose. There is a for'ard escape hatch—it's really an access hatch to the deck gun. But the chances are high that the fore part of the U-boat is completely flooded, so that's useless. There may be an after escape hatch, I don't know. The conning tower is probably their best bet, or would have been if we hadn't rammed them."

"We didn't hit the conning tower."

"We didn't have to. The compressive power of something like ten thousand tons deadweight has to be pretty fierce. The conning-tower hatch may have been jammed solid. Whether it would be possible to ease it or not I wouldn't know. Worse still, it may have sprung open and with a hundred gallons of water a second pouring down into the control room, there is no way anyone is going to get out. They'd probably be battered unconscious in the first few seconds. I'm going down on deck now. Keep going round to starboard and keep her astern till you stop, then heave to. I'll take the motorboat out as soon as you've lost enough way."

"What's the point in taking the boat if there are going to be no survivors?"

McKinnon led him out onto the port wing and astern to where three men were floundering about in the water. "Those three characters. The gun crew. As far as I could tell they were only wearing overalls and oilskins. Maybe the odd jersey or two, but that would make no difference. Leave them out there another few minutes and they'll just freeze to death."

"Let them. Those three bastards hit us aft three times. For all we can tell, some of those shells may have exploded inside the hospital."

"I know, George, I know. But I daresay there's something in the Geneva conventions about it." McKinnon clapped him lightly on the shoulder and went below.

Just outside the deck entrance to the hospital McKinnon found half a dozen people waiting for him—

Patterson, Jamieson, Curran, Trent, McCrimmon and Stephen. Patterson said: "I believe we've been in some sort of collision, Bosun."

"Yes, sir. U-boat."

"And?"

McCrimmon pointed downward. "I just hope we don't go the same way. For'ard watertight bulkheads, sir?"

"Of course. At once." He looked at McCrimmon and Stephen, who left without a word. "And next, Bosun?"

"We were hit three times aft, sir. Any damage in the hospital?"

"Some. All three hit the hospital area. One appears to have exploded when it passed through the bulkhead between A and B Wards. Some injuries, no fatalities. Dr. Sinclair is attending to them."

"Not Dr. Singh?"

"He was in the recovery room with the two injured seamen from the *Argos*. Door's jammed and we can't get inside."

"Shell explode in there?"

"Nobody seems to know."

"Nobody seems—but that's the next compartment to A Ward. Are they all deaf in there?"

"Yes. It was the first shell that exploded between the two wards. That deafened them all right."

"Ah. Well, the recovery room will just have to wait. What happened to the third shell?"

"Didn't explode."

"Where is it?"

"In the dining area. Rolling about quite a bit."

"Rolling about quite a bit..." McKinnon repeated

slowly. "That's handy. Just because it didn't go off on impact—" He broke off and said to Curran: "A couple of heaving lines in the motorboat. Don't forget your knives." He went inside and reappeared within twenty seconds, carrying a very small, very innocuous-looking shell, threw it over the side and said to Jamieson: "You have your gun, sir?"

"I have my gun. What do you want the heaving lines for, Bosun?"

"Same reason as your gun, sir. To discourage people. Tie them up if we have to. If there are any survivors, they're not going to feel very kindly disposed because of what we've done to their boat and their shipmates."

"But those people aren't armed. They're submariners."

"Don't you believe it, sir. Many officers carry hand guns. Petty officers, too, for all I know."

"Even if they had guns, what could they do?"

"Take us hostage, that's what they could do. And if they could take us hostage they could still take over the ship."

Jamieson said, almost admiringly: "You don't trust many people, do you?"

"Some. I just don't believe in taking chances."

The motorboat was less than fifty yards away from the spot where the U-boat's gun crew were still floundering in the water when Jamieson touched McKinnon on the arm and pointed out over the starboard side.

"Bubbles. Lots of little bubbles."

"I see them. Could be there's someone coming up."

"I thought they always came up in a great big air bubble."

"Never. Big air bubble when they leave the submarine, perhaps. But that collapses at once." McKinnon eased back on the throttle as he approached the group in the water.

"Someone's just broken the surface," Jamieson said. "No, by God, two of them."

"Yes. They've got inflatable life jackets on. They'll keep." McKinnon stopped the engines and waited while Curran, Trent and Jamieson literally hauled the gun crew aboard—they seemed incapable of helping themselves. The trio were young, hardly more than boys, teeth chattering, shivering violently and trying hard not to look terrified.

"We search this lot?" Jamieson said. "Tie them up?"

"Good lord, no. Look at their hands—they're blue and frozen stiff. If they couldn't even hang on to the gunwale, and they couldn't, how could they press the trigger of a gun? Even if they could unbutton their oilskins, which they can't?"

McKinnon opened the throttle and headed for the two men who had surfaced from the submarine. As he did, a third figure bobbed to the surface some two hundred yards beyond.

The two they hauled aboard seemed well enough. One of them was a dark-haired, dark-eyed man in his late twenties; his face was lean, intelligent and watchful. The other was very young, very blond and very apprehensive. McKinnon addressed the older man in German.

"What is your name and rank?"

"Obersteuermann Doenitz."

"Doenitz? Very appropriate." Admiral Doenitz was the brilliant Commander in Chief of the German submarine fleet. "Do you have a gun, Doenitz? If you say you haven't and I find one I shall have to shoot you because you are not to be trusted. Do you have a gun?"

Doenitz shrugged, reached under his blouse and produced a rubber-wrapped pistol.

"Your friend here?"

"Hans is an assistant cook." Doenitz spoke in fluent English. He sighed. "Young Hans is not to be trusted with a frying pan, far less a gun."

McKinnon decided to believe him for the moment and headed for the third survivor. As they approached, McKinnon could see that the man was at least unconscious, for his neck was bent forward and he was face down in the water. The reason for this was apparent: his Dräger apparatus was only partially inflated and the excess oxygen had gone to the highest point of the bag at the back of the neck, forcing his head down. McKinnon drew alongside, caught the man by his life jacket, put his hand under his chin and lifted the head from the water.

He studied the face for only a second or two then said to Doenitz: "You know him, of course."

"Heissmann, our first lieutenant."

McKinnon let the face fall back into the water. Doenitz looked at him with a mixture of astonishment and anger.

"Aren't you going to bring him aboard? He may just be unconscious, just half-drowned perhaps."

"Your first lieutenant is dead." McKinnon's voice

carried total conviction. "His mouth is full of blood. Ruptured lungs. He forgot to breathe out oxygen on the way up."

Doenitz nodded. "Perhaps he didn't know that he had to do that. I didn't know. I'm afraid we don't have much time for escape training these days." He looked curiously at McKinnon. "How did you know? You're not a submariner."

"I was. Twelve years."

Curran called from the bows. "There's one more, Bosun. Just surfaced. Dead ahead."

McKinnon had the motorboat alongside the struggling man in less than a minute and had him brought aboard and laid on the thwarts. He lay there in a peculiar position, knees against his chest, his hands hugging both knees and trying to roll from side to side. He was in considerable pain. McKinnon forced open the mouth, glanced briefly inside, then gently closed it again.

"Well, this man knew enough to exhale oxygen on the way up." He looked at Doenitz. "You know this man, of course."

"Of course. Oberleutnant Klaussen."

"Your captain?" Doenitz nodded. "Well, he's in pain, but I wouldn't think he's in any danger. You can see he's been cut on the forehead—possibly banged his head on the escape hatch on the way out. But that's not enough to account for his condition, for he must have been conscious all the way up or he wouldn't have got rid of the oxygen in his lungs. Were you traveling underwater or on the surface during the night?"

"On the surface. All the time."

"That rules out carbon dioxide, which can be poisonous but you can't build up carbon dioxide when the conning tower is open. From the way he's holding his chest and legs it would seem to be caisson disease; that's where the effects hurt most. But it can't be that either."

"Caisson disease?" Jamieson said.

"Diver's bends. When there's too rapid a build-up of nitrogen bubbles in the blood when you're making a fast ascent." McKinnon, with the motorboat under full throttle, was heading directly for the *San Andreas*, which was stopped in the water at not much more than half a mile's distance. "But for that you have to be breathing in a high-pressure atmosphere for quite some time. Your captain certainly wasn't below long enough for that. Perhaps he escaped from a very great depth, perhaps a greater depth than anyone has ever escaped from a submarine. Then I wouldn't know what the effects might be. We have a doctor aboard. I don't suppose he'll know either—the average doctor can spend a lifetime and not come across a case like this. But at least he can stop the pain."

The motorboat passed close by the bows of the *San Andreas* which, remarkably, appeared to be quite undamaged. But that damage had been done was unquestionable—the *San Andreas* was at least six inches down by the head, which was no more than was to be expected if the for'ard compartments had been flooded.

McKinnon secured alongside and half helped, half carried the semiconscious U-boat captain to the head of the gangway. Patterson was waiting for him there, as was Dr. Sinclair and three other members of the engine-room staff.

"This is the U-boat captain," McKinnon said to Dr. Sinclair. "He may be suffering from the bends, you know, nitrogen poisoning."

"Alas, Bosun, we have no decompression chamber aboard."

"I know, sir. He may just be suffering from the effects of having surfaced from a great depth. I don't know, all I know is he's suffering pretty badly. The rest are well enough, all they need is dry clothing and a little lesson in alertness." He turned to Jamieson, who had just joined him on deck. "Perhaps, sir, you would be kind enough to supervise their change of clothing?"

"You mean to make sure that they're not carrying anything they shouldn't be carrying?"

McKinnon smiled and turned to Patterson. "How are the for'ard watertight bulkheads, sir?"

"Holding. I've had a look myself. Bent and buckled but holding."

"With your permission, sir, I'll get a diving suit and have a look."

"Now? Couldn't that wait a bit?"

"I'm afraid waiting is the one thing we can't afford. We can be reasonably certain that the U-boat was in contact with Trondheim right up to the moment that he signaled us to stop—I think it would be very silly of us to assume otherwise. Flannelfoot is still with us. The Germans know exactly where we are. Till now, for reasons best known to themselves, they have been treating us with kid gloves. Maybe now they'll be feel-

ing like taking those gloves off, I shouldn't imagine
that Admiral Doenitz will take too kindly to the idea
of one of his U-boats being sunk by a hospital ship. I
think it behooves us, sir, to get out of here and with
all speed. Trouble is, we've got to make up our minds
whether to go full speed ahead or full speed astern."

"Ah. Yes. I see. You have a point."

"Yes, sir. If the hole in our bows is big enough, then
if we make any speed at all I don't see the watertight
bulkheads standing up to the pressure for very long.
In that case we'd have to go astern. I don't much fancy
that. It not only slows us down but it makes steering
damn difficult. But it can be done. I knew of a tanker
that hit a German U-boat about seven hundred miles
from its port of destination. It made it—going astern
all the way. But I don't much care for the idea of going
stern first all the way to Aberdeen, especially if the
weather breaks up."

"You make me feel downright nervous, Bosun. With
all speed, Bosun, as you say, with all speed. How long
will this take?"

"Just as long as it takes me to collect a rubber suit,
mask and flashlight, then get there and back again.
At the most, twenty minutes."

McKinnon was back in fifteen. Mask in one hand,
flashlight in the other, he climbed up the gangway to
where Patterson was awaiting him at the top.

"We can go ahead, sir," McKinnon said. "Full ahead,
I should think."

"Good, good, good. Damage relatively slight, I take it. How small is the hole?"

"It's not a small hole. It's a bloody great hole, big as a barn door."

Patterson stared at him.

"There's a ragged piece of that U-boat, about eight foot by six, imbedded in our bows. Seems to be forming a pretty secure plug, and I should imagine that the faster we go the more securely it will be lodged."

"And if we stop, or have to go astern, or run into heavy weather—I mean, what if the plug falls off?"

"I'd be glad, sir, if you didn't talk about such things."

8

"AND WHAT ARE YOU DOING THERE?" Mc-Kinnon looked down on the recumbent form of Janet Magnusson who, her face pale, was lying on the bed nearest the desk where she normally sat.

"I normally have a rest at this time of the morning." She tried to inject an acid tone into her voice, but her heart wasn't in it and she smiled albeit wanly. "I have been badly wounded, Archie McKinnon. Thanks to you."

"Oh, dear." McKinnon sat on her bedside and put his hand on her shoulder. "I am sorry. How—"

"Not there." She pushed his hand away. "That's where I've been wounded."

"Sorry again." He looked up at Dr. Sinclair. "How bad is badly?"

"Nurse Magnusson has a very slight graze on her right shoulder. Piece of shrapnel." Sinclair pointed to a jagged hole in the bulkhead about six feet above

216

deck level, then indicated the scarred and pock-marked deckhead. "That's where the rest of the shrapnel appears to have gone. But Nurse Magnusson was standing at the time and caught quite a bit of the blast effect. She was thrown across the bed she's in now— it was, providentially, empty at the time—and it took us ten minutes to bring her around. Shock, that's all."

"Layabout." McKinnon stood. "I'll be back. Anybody else hurt here, Doctor?"

"Two. At the far end of the ward. Seamen from the *Argos*. One in the chest, the other in the leg. Shrapnel ricocheting from the ceiling and pretty spent shrapnel at that. Didn't even have to dig it out. Not even bandages—cotton wool and plaster."

McKinnon looked at the man, restless and muttering, in the bed opposite. "Oberleutnant Klaussen— the U-boat commander. How is he?"

"Delirious, as you can see. The trouble with him— I've no idea. I tend to go along with your suggestion that he must have come up from a very great depth. If that's the case, I'm dealing with the unknown. Sorry and all that."

"I hardly think there's any need to be sorry, sir. Every other doctor would be in the same situation. I don't think anyone has ever escaped from a depth greater than two hundred and fifty feet before. If Klaussen did—well, it's uncharted territory. There simply can't be any literature on it."

"Archie."

McKinnon turned round. Janet Magnusson was propped up on an elbow.

"You're supposed to be resting."

"I'm getting up. What are you doing with that sledgehammer and chisel in your hand?"

"I'm going to try to open a jammed door."

"I see." She was silent for some moments while she bit her lower lip. "The recovery room, isn't it?"

"Yes."

"Dr. Singh and the two men from the *Argos*—the one with the multiple burns and the other with the fractured pelvis—they're in there, aren't they?"

"So I'm told."

"Well, why don't you go to them?" She sounded almost angry. "Why stand around here blathering and doing nothing?"

"I hardly think that's quite fair, Nurse Magnusson." Jamieson, who was accompanying McKinnon and Sinclair, spoke in tones of gentle reproof. "Doing nothing? The bosun does more than the whole lot of us put together."

"I'm thinking perhaps there's no great hurry, Janet," McKinnon said. "People have been banging on that door for the past fifteen minutes and there's been no reply. Could mean anything or nothing. Point is, there was no point in trying to force that door till there was a doctor at hand, and Dr. Sinclair has just finished in the wards."

"What you mean is—what you really mean, Archie—is that you don't think the people inside the recovery room will be requiring the services of a doctor."

"I hope I'm wrong. But, yes, that's what I'm afraid of."

She sank back in her bed. "As Mr. Jamieson didn't say, I was talking out of turn. I'm sorry."

"There's nothing to be sorry about." McKinnon turned away and went into Ward A. The first person to catch his attention was Margaret Morrison. Even paler than Janet Magnusson had been, she was sitting in her chair behind her desk while Sister Maria carefully tied a bandage around her head. McKinnon didn't immediately go to her but went to the far right-hand side of the ward where Lieutenant Ulbricht was sitting up in his bed while Bowen and Kennet lay flat in theirs.

"Three more victims," Sinclair said. "Well, unfortunates, I should say. While the blast in Ward B went upward I'm afraid it was slightly downward here."

McKinnon looked at Ulbricht. "What's the matter with you?" Ulbricht had a thick bandage round his neck.

"I'll tell you what's the matter with him," Sinclair said. "Luck. The devil's own luck. A piece of shrapnel—it must have been as sharp as a razor—sliced through the side of his neck. Another quarter inch to the right and it would have sliced through the carotid artery as well, and then he'd have been a corpse called Lieutenant Ulbricht."

Ulbricht looked at McKinnon with little in the way of expression on his face. "I thought you sent us down here for our own safety."

"That's what I thought, too. I was certain they'd concentrate their fire on the bridge. I'm making no excuses, but I don't think I miscalculated. I think the U-boat's gun crew panicked. I'm sure that Klaussen gave no instructions to fire into the hull."

"Klaussen?"

"Oberleutnant. The captain. He survived. He seems fairly ill."

"How many survivors altogether?"

"Six."

"And the rest you sent to the bottom."

"I'm the guilty party, if that's what you mean. I don't feel particularly guilty. But I'm responsible, yes."

"I suppose that makes two of us. Responsible but not guilty." Ulbricht shrugged and seemed disinclined to continue the conversation.

McKinnon moved to the captain's bed. "Sorry to hear you've been hurt again, sir."

"Me and Kennet. Left thighs. Both of us. Dr. Sinclair tells me it's only a scratch, and as I can't see it I have to take his word for it. Doesn't feel like a scratch, I can tell you. Well, Archie my boy, you've done it. I knew you would. If it weren't for these damned bandages I'd shake hands with you. Congratulations. You must feel pretty good about this."

"I don't feel good at all, sir. If there were any survivors and if they managed to find a sealed compartment they'll be gasping out their lives—now—on the floor of the Norwegian Sea."

"There's that, of course, there's that. But not to reproach yourself, Archie. Them or us. Unpleasant, but still well done." Bowen adroitly switched the subject. "Building up speed, aren't we? Limited damage up front, I take it."

"Far from limited, sir. We're badly holed. But there's a large chunk of the U-boat's casing imbedded in that hole. Let's just hope it stays there."

"We can but pray, Bosun, we can but pray. And regardless of how you feel, every person aboard this boat is deeply in your debt."

"I'll see you later, sir."

He turned away, looked at Margaret Morrison, then at Dr. Sinclair. "Is she hurt? Badly, I mean."

"She's the worst of the lot, but nothing dangerous, you understand. She was sitting by Captain Bowen's bedside at the time and was hit twice. Nasty gash on the upper right arm and a minor scalp wound—that's the one Sister Maria has just finished bandaging."

"Shouldn't she be in bed?"

"Yes. I tried to insist on it, but I can tell you I won't be doing it again. How about you trying?"

"No, thank you." McKinnon approached the young woman, who looked at him with reproachful brown eyes that were slightly dulled with pain.

"This is all your fault, Archie McKinnon."

McKinnon sighed. "Exactly what Janet said to me. It's difficult to please everybody. I'm sorry."

"And so you should be. Not for this, though. The physical pain, I can tell you, is nothing compared to the mental hurt. You deceived me. Our greatly respected bosun is exactly what he accused me of being—a fibber."

"Long-suffering bosun back in court again. What am I supposed to have done wrong now?"

"Not only that, but you've made me feel very very foolish."

"I have? I would never do that."

"You did. Remember on the bridge you suggested— in jest, of course—that you might fight the U-boat with a fusillade of stale bread and old potatoes. Well, something like that."

"Ah!"

"Yes, ah! Remember that emotional scene on the bridge—well, emotional on my part, I cringe when I think about it—when I begged you to fight them and fight them and fight them. You remember, don't you?"

"Yes, I think I do."

"He thinks he does! You had already made up your mind to fight them, hadn't you?"

"Well, yes."

"Well, yes," she mimicked. "You had already made up your mind to ram that U-boat."

"Yes."

"Why didn't you tell me, Archie?"

"Because you might have casually mentioned it to somebody who might have casually mentioned it—unknowingly, of course—to Flannelfoot, who would far from casually have mentioned it to the U-boat captain, who would have made damn certain that he would never put himself in a position where he could be rammed. You might even—again unknowingly—have mentioned it directly to Flannelfoot."

She made no attempt to conceal the hurt in her eyes. "So you don't trust me. You said you did."

"I trust you absolutely."

"Then why—"

"It was one of those then-and-now things. Then you were Sister Morrison. I didn't know there was a Margaret Morrison. I know now."

"Ah!" She pursed her lips then smiled, clearly mollified. "I see."

McKinnon left her, joined Dr. Sinclair and Jamieson and together they went to the door of the recovery room. Jamieson was carrying with him an electric drill, a hammer and some tapered wooden pegs. Jamieson said: "You saw the entry hole made by the shell when you went up to examine the bows?"

"Yes. Just on—well, an inch or two above—the waterline. Could be water inside. Or not. It's impossible to say."

"How high up?"

"Eighteen inches, say. Anybody's guess."

Jamieson plugged in his drill and pressed the trigger. The tungsten carbide bit sank easily into the heavy steel of the door. Dr. Sinclair said: "What happens if there's water behind?"

"Tap in one of those wooden pegs, then try higher up."

"Through," Jamieson said. He withdrew the bit. "Clear."

McCrimmon struck the steel handle twice with the sledge. The handle did not even budge a fraction of an inch. On the third blow it sheared off and fell to the deck.

"Pity," McKinnon said. "But we have to find out."

Jamieson shrugged. "No option. Torch?"

"Please." Jamieson left and was back in two minutes with the torch, followed by McCrimmon carrying the gas cylinder and a lamp on the end of a wandering lead. Jamieson lit the oxyacetylene flame and began to carve a semicircle around the space where the handle had been; McCrimmon plugged in the wandering lead and the wire-caged lamp burned brightly.

Jamieson said from behind his plastic face-shield: "We're only assuming that this is where the door is jammed."

"If we're wrong we'll cut away around the hinges. I don't think we'll have to. The door isn't buckled in any way. It's nearly always the lock or latch that's jammed."

The compartment was filled with stinging acrid smoke when Jamieson finally straightened. He gave the lock a couple of blows with the side of his fist, then desisted.

"I'm sure I've cut through, but the damn thing doesn't seem to want to fall away."

"The latch is still in its socket." McKinnon tapped the door with his sledge, not heavily, and the semi-circular piece of metal fell away inside. He hit the door again, heavily this time, and it gave an inch. With a second blow it gave several more inches. He laid aside the sledge and pushed against the door until, squeaking and protesting, it was almost wide open. He took the wandering lead from McCrimmon and went inside.

There was water on the deck, not much, perhaps two inches. Bulkheads and deckhead had been heavily starred and pockmarked by shrapnel from the exploding shell. The entrance hole formed by the shell in the outer bulkhead was a jagged circle not more than a foot above the deck.

The two men from the *Argos* were still lying in their beds while Dr. Singh, head bowed to his chest, was sitting in a small armchair. All three men seemed unharmed, unmarked. The bosun brought the light closer to Dr. Singh's face. Whatever shrapnel may have been imbedded in his body, none had touched his face. The only sign of anything untoward were tiny trickles of blood from his ears and nose. McKinnon handed the lamp to Sinclair, who stooped over his dead colleague.

"Good God! Dr. Singh." He examined him for a few seconds, then straightened. "That this should happen to a fine doctor, a fine man like this."

"You didn't really expect to find anything else, did you, Doctor?"

"No. Not really. Had to be this or something like this." He examined, briefly, the two men lying in their beds, shook his head and turned away. "Still comes as a bit of a shock."

McKinnon nodded. "I know. I don't want to sound callous, Doctor, I know it might sound that way, but you won't be needing those men any more. I mean, no post-mortems, nothing of that kind."

"Good lord, no. Deaths must have been instantaneous. Concussion. If it's any consolation, they died without knowing."

He paused. "You might look through their clothing, Bosun. Or maybe it's in their effects or perhaps Captain Andropolous has the details."

"You mean names, birth dates, things like that, sir?"

"Yes. I have to fill out the death certificates."

"I'll attend to that."

"Thank you, Bosun." Sinclair essayed a smile, but it could hardly have been rated as a success. "As usual, I'll leave the grisly part to you." With that he was gone, a man glad to be gone. The bosun turned to Jamieson.

"Could I borrow McCrimmon, sir?"

"Of course."

"McCrimmon, go and find Curran and Trent, will you? Tell them what's happened. Curran will know what sizes of canvases to bring."

"Needles and thread, Bosun?"

"Curran is a sailmaker. Just leave it to him. And you could tell him that it's a clean job this time."

McCrimmon left and Jamieson said: "A clean job? It's a lousy job. You always get the dirty end of the stick, McKinnon. I honestly don't know how you keep on doing it. If there's anything nasty or unpleasant to be done, you're number one on everybody's list."

"Not this time I'm not. This time, sir, you're number one on my list. Someone has to tell the captain. Someone has to tell Mr. Patterson. Worst of all—much the worst of all—someone has to tell the nursing staff. That last is not a job I'd care for at all."

"The girls. God, I hadn't thought of that. I don't care for it either. Don't you think, Bosun—seeing you know them so well, I mean—"

"No, I don't think, sir." McKinnon half smiled. "Surely as an officer, you wouldn't think of delegating to an underling something you wouldn't do yourself."

"Underling! God, that's rich. Very well, never let it be said that I shirked my duty. But as from now I feel one degree less sorry for you."

"Yes, sir. One other thing—when this place is clear would you have a couple of your men weld a patch over this hole in the bulkhead? Heaven knows they've had enough practice in welding patches recently."

"Of course. Just let's hope it's the last patch."

Jamieson left and McKinnon looked idly around him.

His attention was caught by a fairly large wooden box in one corner, and that only because its lid had been sprung by the shock of the explosion. McKinnon, not without some effort, lifted the lid and peered for some seconds at the contents. He replaced the lid, retrieved his sledge and tapped the lid securely back into place. Stamped on the lid in big red letters were the words CARDIAC ARREST.

McKinnon wearily sat down at the table in the dining area. The injured sister and nurse, both looking as if they should have been in bed—they had been relieved by Sister Maria and Irene—were sitting there, as was Lieutenant Ulbricht, who not only gave the impression of having completely forgotten his narrow brush with death but was sufficiently back on balance to have found himself a seat between the two girls. Sinclair, Patterson and Jamieson were clustered around one end of the table. McKinnon considered Ulbricht for a moment, then addressed himself to Dr. Sinclair.

"Not calling your professional competence into question, sir, but is the lieutenant fit to be up and around?"

"My professional competence is irrelevant." One could see that Dr. Sinclair had not yet recovered from the shock of the death of his colleague. "The lieutenant, like Sister Morrison and Nurse Magnusson, is uncooperative, intransigent and downright disobedient. The three of them would probably call it having minds of their own. Lieutenant Ulbricht, as it so happens, is in no danger. The injury to his neck couldn't even be described as a flesh wound. Torn skin, more like."

"Then perhaps, Lieutenant, you would be prepared to take another fix? We haven't had one since last night."

"At your disposal, Bosun." If the lieutenant harbored any ill will toward the bosun for the deaths of his fellow countrymen, he concealed it. "Any time. I suggest just on noon."

Patterson said: "You finished in the recovery room, Bosun?"

McKinnon nodded.

"Well, one gets tired of saying 'Thank you' so I'll spare you that. When do we bury them?"

"Your decision, sir."

"Early afternoon, before it starts to get dark." Patterson laughed without humor. "My decision. Chief Engineer Patterson is your man when it comes to making decisions on matters that are of no importance. I don't recall making the decision to attack that submarine."

"I did consult with Captain Bowen, sir."

"Ah!" It was Margaret Morrison. "So *that* was what that two-minute conference was about."

"Of course. He approved."

Janet said: "And if he hadn't? Would you still have rammed that U-boat?"

McKinnon said patiently: "He not only approved, he was enthusiastic. Very enthusiastic. With all respects to Lieutenant Ulbricht here, the captain wasn't feeling too kindly disposed toward the Germans. Not at that moment of time, anyway."

"You're being evasive, Archie McKinnon. Answer my question. If he *had* disapproved would you still have attacked?"

"Yes. No need to mention that to the captain, though."

"Nurse Magnusson." Patterson smiled at Janet to rob his words of any offense. "I hardly think Mr. McKinnon deserves either interrogation or disapproval. He deserves congratulations for a magnificent job well done." He rose, went to the cupboard and returned with a bottle of scotch and some glasses, poured a measure for McKinnon and set it before him. "I think Dr. Singh would have approved."

"Thank you, sir." McKinnon looked down at the glass on the table. Then he said, none too gently: "He won't be needing this any more."

There was silence round the table. Predictably, it was broken by Janet.

"I think, Archie, that that was less than a gracious remark."

"You think so now. Maybe. Maybe not." There was no hint of apology in his voice. He raised his glass and sipped from it. "Knew his scotch, did the doctor."

The silence was longer this time, longer and strained. It was Sinclair, embarrassed by the silence, who broke it.

"I'm sure we all echo Mr. Patterson's sentiments, Mr. McKinnon. A splendid job. But—to quote yourself, I'm not questioning your professional competence—you did take a bit of a chance, didn't you?"

"You mean I endangered the lives of all aboard?"

"I didn't say that." His look of discomfiture made it evident that he had thought it, if not said it.

"It was a calculated risk," McKinnon said, "but not all that calculated. The odds were on my side, heavily, I believe. I am quite certain that the U-boat was under orders that we were to be seized, not sunk. Which is why I am equally certain that the gun crew fired into the San Andreas without orders.

"The U-boat captain, Oberleutnant Klaussen, was the wrong man in the wrong place at the wrong time. He was tired or immature or inexperienced or incompetent or overconfident—he may have been all those things at the same time. What is certain is that an experienced U-boat commander would never have put himself in a position where he was running parallel to us and less than a half a mile away. He should have stayed at a couple of miles' distance—which in an emergency would have given him plenty of time to crash dive—ordered us to send across a boat, loaded it up with a half-dozen men with machine pistols and sent them back to take over the San Andreas. We could have done nothing to stop them. Even better, he should have closed up from astern, a position that would have made ramming impossible, then eased up alongside the gangway."

He sipped the whisky.

"And of course, he was too confident, too sure of himself, too relaxed by half. When he saw us lowering the gangway, he was convinced the game was over. It never even occurred to him that a hospital ship could be used as a man-o'-war. And he was either so blind or so stupid that he never even noticed that we were steadily closing in on him all the time we were in contact. In short, he made every mistake in the book."

There was a long and uncomfortable silence. Mario, unobtrusive and efficient as ever, had filled all the glasses on the table, but no one, with the exception of the bosun, had as yet touched them.

Sinclair said: "On the basis of what you say, the U-boat captain was indeed the wrong man for the job. And, of course, you wholly outmaneuvered him. But surely the danger still existed. In the actual collision, I mean. The U-boat could have sunk us and not vice versa. We are only made of thin sheet plating; the hull of the submarine is immensely strong."

"I would not presume to lecture you on medical matters, Dr. Sinclair."

Sinclair smiled. "Meaning I should not presume to advise you on matters maritime. But, Mr. McKinnon, you're a Bosun on a merchant vessel."

"Today, yes. Before that I spent a dozen in the submarine service."

"Oh, no." Sinclair shook his head. "Too much, just too much. This is definitely not Dr. Sinclair's day."

"I've known a good number of cases of collisions between merchant vessels and submarines. In nearly all cases those collisions were between friend and friend or, in peacetime, between a submarine and a harmless foreign vessel. The results were always the same. The surface vessel came off best.

"It doesn't seem logical, but it does make sense. Take a hollow glass sphere with walls, say, a third of an inch in diameter, submerge it to a very considerable depth—I'm talking about hundreds of feet—and it still won't implode. Bring it to the surface, give it a light tap with a hammer and it will shatter into a hundred pieces. Same with the pressure hull of a submarine. It can resist pressure at great depths, but on the surface a short sharp blow, as from the bows of a merchant ship, will cause it to rupture. Admittedly, the chances of the submarine are not improved by the fact that the merchant ship may displace many thousands of tons and be traveling at a fair speed. On the other hand, even a vessel as small as a trawler can sink a submarine. Point is, Dr. Sinclair, it wasn't all that dangerous; once we had our chance, I hadn't much doubt about the outcome."

"Point taken, Mr. McKinnon. You see before you a rueful cobbler who will stick to his last from now on."

Patterson said: "This ever happen to you?"

"No. If it had, the odds are very high that I wouldn't be here now. I know plenty of instances. When I was in the service, the trade as we called it, we had a maxim which said, in effect, never mind the enemy, just watch out for your friends. Back in the twenties, a British submarine—the M-1, it was—was accidentally struck by a merchant ship off the Devon coast. All died. Not long afterward the American S-1 was overrun by the Italian passenger liner *City of Rome*. All died. Some time later, another American submarine was overrun by a coastguard destroyer off Cape Cod. All died. The *Posiedon*, British, was sent to the bottom by a Japanese ship. Accident. Off the north China coast. A good number of survivors, but some died from the diver's bends. In the early years of the war, the *Surcouf*, crewed by the Free French and the biggest submarine in the

world—so big that it was called a submarine cruiser—
was sunk in the Caribbean by a ship in a convoy she
was escorting. The *Surcouf* had a crew of a hundred
and fifty. All died." McKinnon passed a hand across
his eyes. "There were others. I forget most of them.
Ah, yes, there was the *Umpire*. In forty-one, I think.
It took only a trawler, and not a very big one, to destroy
her."

Patterson said: "You've made your point, as Dr. Sinclair says, you've more than made your point. I accept
that the element of risk, after you made your move,
was not high. You'll just have to bear with us, Mr.
McKinnon. Amateurs all. We didn't know. You did. The
fact that the U-boat is at the bottom of the sea is
testimony enough to that." He took his drink and sam-
pled it. "I have to say, Bosun, that your achievement
doesn't appear to have given you any great satisfaction."

"It hasn't."

Patterson nodded. "I understand. To have been
responsible for the deaths of so many men—well, it's
hardly a cheerful thought."

McKinnon looked at him. "What's done is done. So
the U-boat's gone and its crew with it. It's no matter
for celebration but it's no matter for recrimination either.
The next Allied merchant ship to appear on the cross
hairs of Klaussen's periscope sight would surely have
gone to where Klaussen's U-boat is now. The only good
U-boat is a U-boat with a ruptured pressure hull at
the bottom of the ocean."

"Then why—" Patterson broke off, plainly at a loss
for both thought and words, then said: "The hell with

the pros and cons, it was still a splendid job. I didn't
fancy a prison camp any more than you. Well, I don't
feel as modest about your accomplishments as you
are." He looked around the table. "A toast to our bosun
here—and to the memory of Dr. Singh."

"I'm not nearly as modest as you think I am. I haven't
the slightest objection to drinking a toast to myself."
McKinnon looked slowly around the table at the other
six. "But I draw the line at drinking a toast to the
memory of Flannelfoot."

McKinnon was becoming very expert at causing
silences. This, the fourth such silence, was much
longer and much more uncomfortable than the ones
that had preceded it. The other six stared at him, looked
at each other with questioning, frowning glances, then
returned their exclusive attention to McKinnon. Again
it was Janet who broke the silence.

"You do *know* what you're saying, Archie? At least
I hope you do."

"I'm afraid I do. Dr. Sinclair, you had a cardiac-arrest
unit in the recovery room. Did you have another similar
unit elsewhere?"

"Yes. In the dispensary."

"And you were under strict instructions that, in an
emergency, the dispensary unit was the one that was
to be used first."

"That is so." Sinclair looked at him without understanding. "How on earth do *you* know that?"

"Because I'm clever." The normally calm and un-
emotional bosun made no attempt to conceal his bitterness. "After the event, I'm very clever." He shook
his head. "There's no point in you listening to me tell-

ing you how clever I haven't been. I suggest you go—
I suggest you all go—and have a look at the recovery-
room cardiac unit. The unit's not there any more. It's
in Ward A, by the sister's desk. The lid is closed but
the lock has been damaged, as has the seal. You can
wrench the lid open easily enough."

All six looked at each other, then rose, left and were
back within minutes. They sat in silence; they were
either stunned by what they had seen or could not
find the words to express their emotions.

"Nice, is it not?" McKinnon said. "A high-powered
radio transceiver. Tell me, Dr. Sinclair, did Dr. Singh
ever lock himself up in the recovery room?"

"I couldn't say." Sinclair shook his head quite violently, as if to clear it of disbelief. "May well have, for
all anyone would know."

"But he did frequently go into that room alone?"

"Yes. Alone. Quite often. He insisted on looking after
the two injured men personally. Perfectly within his
rights, of course—he was the man who had operated
on them."

"Of course. After I'd found the radio—I still don't
know what made me open up that damned cardiac
unit—I examined the lock on the door, the keyhole
part that Mr. Jamieson had burned away with his torch,
and the latch. Both were heavily oiled. When Dr. Singh
turned that key you would have heard no sound of
metal against metal or even the faintest click, not even
if you were listening outside a couple of feet away—
not that anyone could have had any conceivable reason
for lurking outside. After locking the door and check-
ing that his two patients were under sedation—and if

they weren't, he would make sure they very quickly were—he could use his radio to his heart's content. Not, I should imagine, that he used it very often; the primary purpose, the essential purpose of the radio, was that it kept on sending out a continual homing location signal."

"I still can't understand or bring myself to believe it." Patterson spoke slowly, a man still struggling to be free of a trance. "Of course it's true, it has to be true, but that doesn't make it any more credible. He was such a good man, such a kind man—and a fine doctor, was he not, Dr. Sinclair?"

"He was an excellent doctor. No question. And a brilliant surgeon."

"So was Dr. Crippen, for all I know," McKinnon said. "I find it as baffling as you do, Mr. Patterson. I have no idea what his motives could have been, and I should imagine that we'll never find out. He was a very clever man, a very careful man who seldom took a chance, a man who covered his tracks—if it weren't for a trigger-happy U-boat gun crew we'd never have found out who Flannelfoot was. His treachery may have had something to do with his background. Although he spoke of Pakistani descent he was, of course, an Indian, and educated Indians have little reason to love the British Raj. May have had something to do with religion; if he had Pakistani roots he was probably a Muslim. The connection—I have no idea. There are a dozen other reasons apart from nationality and politics and religion that make a man a traitor. Where did those cardiac-arrest units come from, Dr. Sinclair?"

"They were loaded aboard at Halifax, Nova Scotia."

"I know that. But do you know where they came from?"

"I have no idea. Does it matter?"

"It could. Point is, we don't know whether Dr. Singh installed the radio transceiver after the unit came aboard or whether the unit was supplied with the transceiver already installed. I would take long odds that the transceiver had already been installed. Very tricky thing to do aboard a boat. Difficult to smuggle the transceiver aboard, equally difficult to get rid of the cardiac unit that was inside the box."

Sinclair said: "When I said I didn't know where that unit came from, that's quite true. But I know the country of origin. Britain."

"How can you tell?"

"Stencil marks."

"Would there be many firms in Britain that make those things?"

"Again, no idea. Not a question that comes up. A cardiac unit is a cardiac unit. Very few, I should imagine."

"Should be easy enough to trace the source—and I don't for a moment imagine that the unit left the factory already equipped with the transceiver." He looked at Patterson. "Naval Intelligence should be very interested in finding out what route that cardiac unit took between the factory and the *San Andreas* and what stopovers it made en route."

"They should indeed. And it should take them no time at all to find out where it changed hands and who made the switch. Seems damned careless of our saboteur friends to have left themselves so wide open."

"Not really, sir. They simply never expected to be found out."

"I suppose. Tell me, Bosun, why did you take so long in getting around to telling us about Dr. Singh?"

"Because I had the same reaction as you—I had to work damned hard to convince myself of the evidence of my own eyes. Besides, you all held Dr. Singh in a very high regard—no one likes to be the bearer of bad news." He looked at Jamieson. "How long would it take, sir, to fix up a push button on sister's desk in Ward A so that it would ring a buzzer in, say, here, the bridge and the engine room?"

"No time at all." Jamieson paused briefly. "I know you must have an excellent reason for this—what shall we call it—alarm system. May we know what it is?"

"Of course—so that the sister or nurse in charge of Ward A can let us know if any unauthorized person comes into the ward. That unauthorized person will be in the same state of ignorance as we are at the moment—he will not know whether that transceiver is in working order or not. He *has* to assume that it is, he has to assume that we may be in a position to send out an S.O.S. to the Royal Navy. It's obviously all-important to the Germans that such a signal not be sent and that we remain alone and unprotected. They want us and they want us alive, so the intruder will do everything in his power to destroy the set."

"Wait a minute, wait a minute," Patterson said. "Intruder? Unauthorized person? What unauthorized person? Dr. Singh is dead."

"I've no idea who he is. All I know is that he exists. You may remember that I said earlier that I thought that we had more than one Flannelfoot aboard. Now I'm certain. Dr. Sinclair, during the entire hour before Lieutenant Ulbricht and hs Focke-Wulf made their appearance—and indeed for some time afterward—you and Dr. Singh were operating on the two wounded sailors—now the two dead sailors—from the *Agros*. That is correct?"

"That's so." Sinclair looked and sounded puzzled.

"Did he leave the surgery at any time?"

"Not once."

"And it was during this period that some unknown was busy tinkering with junction boxes and fuses. Thus, Flannelfoot Number Two."

There was a brief silence; then Jamieson said: "We're not very bright, are we? Of course you're right. We should have worked that out for ourselves."

"You would have. Finding Dr. Singh's dead body and then finding out what he was is enough to put any other thought out of your mind. It's only just now occurred to me. More time to get over the shock, I suppose."

"Objection," Patterson said. "Query, rather. If that set is smashed the Germans have no means of tracking us."

"They're not tracking us now," McKinnon said patiently. "Battery leads are disconnected. Even if they weren't, smashing the transceiver would be far the less of two evils. The last thing that Flannelfoot Two wants to see is the Royal Navy steaming over the horizon. They may have another transmitter cached away somewhere, although I very much doubt it. Dr. Sinclair, would you please check the other cardiac unit in the dispensary. I'm sure you'll find it okay."

"Well," Sinclair said, "there's at least some satisfaction in knowing that they've lost us."

"I wouldn't bet on that, Doctor. In fact, I'd bet against it. A submarine can't use its radio under water but you have to remember that this lad was trailing us on the surface and was almost certainly in constant contact with its shore base. They'll know our position and course at the time of the sinking of the submarine. I wouldn't even be surprised if there's another U-boat tagging along behind us—for some damned reason we seem to be very important to the Germans. And you mustn't forget that the further southwest we steam the more hours of daylight we have. The sky's pretty clear, and the chances are good that a Focke-Wulf or some such will pick us up during the day."

Patterson looked at him morosely. "You're still a bundle of cheer, Bosun."

McKinnon smiled. "Sorry about that, sir. Just reckoning the odds, that's all."

"The odds," Janet said. "You're betting against our chances of getting to Aberdeen, aren't you, Archie?"

McKinnon turned his hands palms upward. "I'm not a gambler, and there are too many unknowns. Any of your opinions is as good as mine. I'm not betting against us, Janet. I think we have a fair chance of making it." He paused. "Three things. I'll go and see Captain Andropolous and his men. I should think that 'radio' is a pretty universal word. If not, sign language should work. Most of the crew of the *Argos* survived, so the chances are good that there is a radio officer among them. He can have a look at this machine and see if we can transmit with it. Lieutenant Ulbricht, I'd be grateful if you could come up to the bridge when it's time and take a noon sight. Third thing—if the lights in Ward A fail at any time, whoever is in charge is to press the panic button immediately."

McKinnon made to rise, stopped, and looked at his unfinished drink. "Well, perhaps after all, a final toast to the departed. An old Gaelic curse, rather. Dr. Singh: may his shade walk on the dark side of hell tonight." He raised his glass. "To Flannelfoot."

McKinnon drank his toast alone.

9

LESS THAN TEN MINUTES AFTER MCKINNON'S ARrival on the bridge the phone rang.

"Jamieson here," the voice said. "Things do keep happening aboard this damned ship. There's been another accident."

"Accident?"

"Accident on purpose. Incident, I should have said. Your pal Limassol."

"Limassol" was the name that McKinnon had given to the man whom he had found to be the radio operator of the *Argos*. Apart from this discovery, the only thing that the bosun had been able to discover about him was that he was a Greek Cypriot from Limassol.

"What's happened?"

"He's been clobbered."

"Ah." McKinnon was not a man much given to exclamatory outbursts. "Inevitably. Who clobbered him?"

"You know better than to ask that question, Bosun.

How the hell should I know who clobbered him? Nobody ever knows who does anything aboard the *San Andreas*. The chief officer was more prophetic than he knew when he gave this ship its new name. It's a bloody disaster area. I can only give you the facts as I know them. Sister Maria was on duty when Limassol sat down to have a look at the transceiver. After a while he stood and made the motion of screwing his forefinger against the palm of his other hand. She guessed, correctly, that he wanted tools and sent for Wayland Day to take him down to the engine room. I was there and gave him the tools he wanted. He also took a bridge-megger with him. Gave every impression of a man who knew what he was doing. On his way back, in the passageway leading to the mess deck, he was clobbered. Something hard and heavy."

"How hard, how heavy?"

"If you'll just hang on for a moment. We have him down here in a bed in A Ward. Dr. Sinclair is attending to him. He can tell you better than I can."

There was a brief silence, then Sinclair was on the phone. "Bosun? Well, damn it, confirmation of the existence of Flannelfoot Number Two—not that any confirmation was needed, but I didn't expect such quick proof. This lad doesn't hang around, does he? Dangerous, violent acts on his own initiative, and his mind's working on the same wavelength as ours."

"Limassol?"

"Pretty poorly, to say the least. Some metallic object, no question, could easily have been a crowbar. I would guess that the attacker's intent was to kill him. With most people he might well have succeeded, but this

Limassol seems to have a skull like an elephant. Fractured, of course. I'll have an x-ray. Routine and superfluous but mandatory. No signs of any brain damage, which is not to say that there isn't any. But no obvious damage, not, at least, at this stage. Two things I'm pretty certain about, Mr. McKinnon. He'll live, but he's not going to be of much use to you—or anyone—for some time."

"As Dr. Singh said about Commander Warrington—two hours, two days, two weeks, two months?"

"Something like that. I've simply no idea. All I know is that even if he does recover rapidly he'll be of no possible use for days to come, so you can rule him out of any plans you may have."

"I'm fresh out of plans, Doctor."

"Indeed. We seem to be running out of options. Mr. Jamieson would like to have another word with you."

Jamieson came back on the phone. "This could have been my fault, Bosun. Maybe if I'd been thinking a bit more clearly and a bit quicker, this wouldn't have happened."

"How on earth were you to know that Limassol was going to be attacked?"

"True. But I should have gone with him; not for his protection, but to watch him to see what he did to make the set work. That way I might have picked up enough to have some knowledge—rudimentary, but some—so that we wouldn't have to rely entirely on one man."

"Flannelfoot would probably have clobbered you too. No point, sir, in trying to place blame where none exists. The milk's spilt and you didn't spill it. Give me enough time and I'll find out it was all McKinnon's fault."

He hung up and related the gist of his conversation to Naseby, who had the wheel, and to Lieutenant Ulbricht, who had declared himself to be feeling so fit that he no longer qualified as a bed patient.

"Disturbing," Ulbricht said. "Our friend seems to be resourceful, very quick-thinking and very much a man of decision and action. I say 'disturbing' because it has just occurred to me that *he* may have been Flannelfoot Number One and not Dr. Singh, in which case we can expect a great deal more trouble. In any event, it seems to rule out the crew of the *Argos*— none of them speaks English so they couldn't have known about the fake cardiac unit in A Ward."

McKinnon looked morose. "The fact is that none of them *appears* to understand a word of English. They're very good with their blank stares when you address them in that language—doesn't mean that one or two of them doesn't speak better English than I do. It doesn't rule out the crew of the *Argos*. And, of course, it doesn't rule out our own crew or the nine invalids we picked up in Murmansk."

"And how would they have known that the tampered cardiac unit had been transferred from the recovery room to Ward A? Only—let me see—only seven people knew about the transfer. The seven at the table this morning. One of us could have talked, perhaps?"

"No." McKinnon was very definite.

"Inadvertently?"

"No."

"You trust us that much?" Ulbricht smiled but there was no humor in it. "Or is it that you *have* to trust somebody?"

"I trust you, all right." McKinnon sounded a little weary. "Point is, it wasn't necessary for anyone to talk. Everybody knows that Dr. Singh and the two injured crewmen from the *Argos* are dead." McKinnon made a dismissive little gesture with his hand. "After all, we're going to bury them inside the half hour. Everybody knows that they were killed by an explosive blast inside the recovery room, and our surviving Flannelfoot must have known that the transceiver was there and may have guessed, or suspected, that the case of the cardiac unit had been damaged sufficiently to reveal the existence of the transmitter. It had not, in fact, but that was pure luck on my part."

"How do you explain the attack on the Greek radio officer?"

"Easily." McKinnon looked and sounded bitter. "Flannelfoot didn't have to know where the radio was, all he had to know was that we had developed a certain interest in radio. Mr. Jamieson tried to take some of the blame for the attack. Totally unnecessary when mastermind McKinnon is around. My fault. My fault entirely. When I went down to find a radio officer the crew of the *Argos* were, as usual, in a corner by themselves. They weren't alone in the mess deck—several other men were there, but not close enough to hear us talking. Not that there was any talking. I just said the word 'radio' several times, low enough not to be overheard, and this lad from Limassol looked at me. Then I made a motion of tapping my forefinger as if sending a signal in Morse. After that, I spun the handle of an imaginary electrical generator. None of this could have been seen except by the crew of the *Argos*. Then I made my stupid mistake. I cupped my hand to my ear as if listening to something. By this time Limassol had got the message and was on his feet. But very likely our new Flannelfoot had got the message too. Just one little movement of my hand and he got it. He's not only violent and dangerous but smart. An unpleasant combination."

"Indeed it is," Ulbricht said. "You have it right, and I can't see any reason for self-reproach."

Naseby said: "Do you by any chance remember who exactly was in the mess deck when you were there?"

"I do. Every crew member who wasn't on watch. On the deck side, only two were on watch—you and Trent down in the captain's cabin there keeping an eye on the sextant and chronometer. All the off-duty engine-room staff. Two cooks and Mario. Seven of the seventeen invalids we picked up in Murmansk—the three who were supposed to be tubercular cases, the three who are supposed to be suffering from nervous breakdowns and one of the exposure cases. He's so wrapped in bandages that he can barely walk, so he doesn't come into consideration. A couple of nurses—they don't come into consideration either. And there's no doubt you're right, Lieutenant—the crew of the *Argos* has to be in the clear."

"Well, that's something," Ulbricht said. "A moment ago you were expressing reservations against them which I found rather puzzling, as in that long talk in the captain's cabin we had more or less agreed that the crew of the *Argos* was in the clear. The original suggestion, you may remember, came from you."

"I remember. Next thing you know I'll be looking into the mirror and saying '...and I don't trust you, either.' Yes, I know I made the suggestion, but I still had this tiny doubt. At the time I more than suspected that we had another Flannelfoot aboard, but I wasn't certain until less than half an hour ago. It's impossible that it wasn't our new Flannelfoot who blew the hole in the for'ard ballast room when we were alongside that sinking corvette. And it's unthinkable—and for me this is the clincher—that a member of the *Argos* crew would deliberately set out to murder a person who was not only a crew mate but a fellow country-man."

"At least it's something," Naseby said. "Brings it down to our own crew, doesn't it?"

"Yes, our crew—and at least six allegedly physical and mentally disturbed cripples from Murmansk."

Naseby shook his head sorrowfully. "Archie, this trip is going to be the ruination of you. Never known you to be so terribly suspicious of everybody—and you just said you could find yourself not even trusting yourself."

"If a nasty suspicious mind is any kind of hope for survival, George, then I'm going to keep on having just that kind of mind. You will remember that we had to leave Halifax in a tearing hurry, in a cargo ship little more than half converted to a hospital. Why? To get to Archangel, and that with all possible speed. Then, after that little accident when we were alongside that corvette, it became equally essential that we be diverted to Murmansk. Why?"

"Well, we were listing a bit and down by the head."

"We had stopped making water, weather conditions were fair, we could have reached the White Sea, crossed it, and made Archangel without much trouble. But, no, it was Murmansk or nothing. Again why?"

"So that the Russians could place that explosive charge in the ballast room." Ulbricht smiled. "I recall your words—our gallant allies."

"I recall them too. I wish I didn't. We all make mistakes, I'm certainly no exception, and that was one of my biggest. The Russians didn't place that charge. Your people did."

"The Germans? Impossible!"

"Lieutenant, if you imagine Murmansk and Archangel aren't crawling with German spies and agents, you're living in Alice's Wonderland."

"It's possible. But to infiltrate a Russian naval working party—that's impossible."

"It's not impossible, but it doesn't even have to be necessary. People are capable of being suborned, and while it may not be true that every man has his price, there are always those who have."

"A Russian traitor, you suggest?"

"Why not? You have your traitors. We have our traitors. Every country has its traitors."

"Why should we—the Germans—want to place a charge in the *San Andreas*?"

"I have no idea. In the same way as I have no idea why the Germans have attacked, harassed and pursued us—but not tried to sink us—ever since we rounded the North Cape. What I'm suggesting is that it's very likely the same German agent or agents suborned one or more of the invalids we picked up in Murmansk. An alleged psychiatric case or mental-breakdown patient, who is sick of both the war and the sea, would make an ideal choice for the traitor's part. The price wouldn't have to be very high."

"Objection, Mr. McKinnon. It was a last-minute decision to detach the *San Andreas* from the convoy. You can't suborn a man overnight."

"True. At the most, highly unlikely. Maybe they knew a week or two ago that we would be detached to Murmansk."

"How on earth could they have known that?"

"I don't know. The same way I don't know why someone in Halifax knew quite a long time ago that Dr. Singh would be in need of a transceiver."

"And you don't think it extraordinary that the Russians—if they were not responsible for placing that charge—should have brought the *San Andreas* into Murmansk apparently for the sole benefit of your mysterious German agents?"

"They're not my agents, but they're mysterious, all right. The answer again is that I simply don't know. The truth appears to be that I don't know anything about anything." He sighed. "Ah, well. Close to noon, Lieutenant. I'll go get the sextant and chronometer."

Lieutenant Ulbricht straightened up from the chart. "Still, remarkably, holding the same course—213. Precisely 64 degrees north. Ideally, we should steer due south now, but we're near enough to Trondheim as it is, and that would only bring us closer. I suggest we maintain this course for the present, then turn due south sometime during the night, midnight or thereabouts. That should bring us down the east coast of your native islands tomorrow, Mr. McKinnon. I'll work it out."

"You're the navigator," McKinnon said agreeably.

In marked contrast to the conditions that had existed exactly forty-eight hours previously, when the mass burial had taken place, the weather was now almost benign. The wind was no more than force three, the sea calm enough to keep the *San Andreas* on an all but steady keel, and the cloud cover consisted of a wide band of white, fleecy, mackerel sky against the light blue beyond. McKinnon, standing by the starboard rail of the *San Andreas*, derived no pleasure whatsoever from the improvement; he would greatly have preferred the blanketing white blizzard of the previous burial.

Besides the bosun, the only other attendants or witnesses—by no stretch of the imagination could they have been called mourners—at the burial were Patterson, Jamieson, Sinclair and the two stokers and two seamen who had brought up the bodies. No one else had asked to come. No one was going to mourn Dr. Singh, and only Sinclair had known the two dead crewmen from the *Argos*, and even then as no more than unconscious bodies on operating tables.

Dr. Singh was unceremoniously tipped over the side—not for him the well-wishing for his journey into the hereafter. Patterson, who would obviously never have made it as a clergyman, quickly read the liturgy from the prayer book over the two dead Greek seamen and then they too were gone.

Patterson closed the prayer book. "Twice of that lot is twice too often. Let's hope there's not going to be a third time." He looked at McKinnon. "I suppose we just plod on on our far from merry way?"

"All we can do, sir. Lieutenant Ulbricht suggests that we alter course by-and-by to due south. That'll take us on a more direct route to Aberdeen. He knows what he's about. But that will be approximately twelve hours yet."

"Whatever's best." Patterson gazed around the empty horizon. "Doesn't it strike you as rather odd, Bosun, that we've been left unmolested, or at least not located, for the better part of three hours? Since all communication from the U-boat has ceased in that time, they must be very dense if they're not aware that something is far wrong with it."

"Admiral Doenitz's U-boat fleet commander in Trondheim is far from dense. I've the feeling they know where we are. I understand that some of the latest U-boats are quite quick under water, and one could easily be trailing us by Asdic without our knowing anything about it." Like Patterson, only much more slowly, he looked around the horizon, then stood facing the port quarter. "In fact, we are being tailed."

"What? What's that?"

"Can't you hear it?"

Patterson cocked his head and soon nodded. "I think I can. Yes, I can."

"Condor," McKinnon said. "Focke-Wulf." He pointed.

"I can see it now. It's coming straight out of the east, and Trondheim is about due east of us now. The pilot of that plane knows exactly where we are. He's been told, probably via Trondheim, by the U-boat that's trailing us."

"I thought a submarine had to surface to transmit?"

"No. All it has to do is to raise its transmitting aerial above the water. It could do that a couple of miles away and we wouldn't see it. Anyway, it's probably a good deal farther distant than that."

"One wonders what the Condor's intentions are."

"Your guess, sir. We're not, unfortunately, inside the minds of the U-boat and Luftwaffe commanders in Trondheim. *My* guess is that they're still not going to try to finish us off. If they wanted to sink us, one torpedo from the U-boat I'm sure is out there would do the job nicely. Or, if they wanted to sink us from the air, they wouldn't use a Condor, which is really a reconnaissance plane. Heinkels, Heinkel IIIs or Stukas with long-range tanks could do the job much more efficiently—and Trondheim is only about two hundred miles from here."

"What's he after, then?" The Condor was two miles distant now and losing height rapidly.

"Information." McKinnon looked up at the bridge and caught sight of Naseby out on the port wing looking aft toward the approaching Condor. He cupped his hands and shouted: "George!"

Naseby swung round.

"Get down, get down!" McKinnon made the appropriate gesture with his hand. Naseby raised an arm in acknowledgment and disappeared inside the bridge. "Mr. Patterson, let's get inside the superstructure. Now."

Patterson knew when to ask questions and when not to. He led the way, and within ten seconds they were all in shelter except the bosun, who remained in the shattered doorway.

"Information," Patterson said. "What information?"

"One moment." He moved quickly to the side of the ship, looked aft for no more than two seconds, then returned to shelter.

"Half a mile," McKinnon said. "Very slow, very low, about fifty feet. Information? Shell holes, say, on the sides of superstructure, something to indicate that we had been in a fight with some vessel. He won't see any holes on the port side."

Patterson made to speak, but whatever he had to say was lost in the sudden clamor of close-range fire by machine guns, in the cacophonous fury of hundreds of bullets striking the superstructure and side in the space of seconds and in the abrupt crescendo of sound as giant aero engines swept by not more than fifty yards away. Another few seconds and all was relatively quiet again.

Jamieson said: "Well, yes, I can see now why you told Naseby to get his head down."

"Information." Patterson sounded aggrieved, almost plaintive. "Bloody funny way they set about getting information. And I thought you said they weren't going to attack us."

"I said they wouldn't sink us. Knocking a few of the crew off would be grist to their mill. The more of us they can kill, the more they think they'll have us at their mercy."

"You think they got the information they wanted?"

"I'm certain of it. You can be sure that every eye on that Condor was examining us very closely as they passed by fifty yards away. They won't have seen the damage to our bows because it's under water, but they can't have helped seeing something else that's under water up for'ard—our load line. Unless they're completely myopic they're bound to have seen that we're down by the head. And unless they're equally dense they're bound to realize that we've either hit something or been hit by something. It couldn't have been a mine or torpedo or we'd be at the bottom now. They'll have known at once that we must have rammed and there won't be much guessing about what that was."

"Dear, oh dear," Jamieson said. "I don't think I like this one little bit, Bosun."

"Nor me, sir. Changes things quite a bit, doesn't it? Question of the German High Command's priorities, I suppose. A question of alive or dead. Is it more important to us that they take us more or less alive or do they take revenge for their lost U-boat?"

"Whichever they choose, there's damn all we can do about it," Patterson said. "Let's go and have lunch."

"I think we should wait a moment, sir." McKinnon remained still and silent for a few moments then said: "It's coming back."

And back it came, flying at the same near-wave-top height. The second fly-past was a mirror image of the first: instead of flying stern to stem on the port side it flew stem to stern on the starboard side, again to the accompaniment of the same fusillade of machine-gun fire. Some ten seconds after the firing ceased, McKinnon, followed by the others, left the shelter and went to the port rail.

The Condor was off the port quarter, climbing steadily and flying away from them.

"Well, well," Jamieson said. "We seem to have got off lightly. Bound to have seen those three shell holes on the starboard side, weren't they, Bosun?"

"Couldn't have missed them, sir."

"They could be gaining bombing altitude before turning back to settle accounts with us?"

"He could bomb us from a hundred feet without the slightest bit of danger to himself."

"Or maybe he just isn't carrying any bombs?"

"No. He'll be carrying bombs all right. Only the Focke-Wulfs on the big half circle from Trondheim to Lorient in France around the British Isles, or the ones who patrol as far out as the Denmark Strait, don't carry bombs. They carry extra fuel tanks instead. The ones on shorter patrols always carry bombs—250-kilo bombs, usually, not the smaller ones that Lieutenant Ulbricht used. The pilot of the Condor is, of course, in direct radio communication with Trondheim. He's told them why they're not hearing from the U-boat any more, but still has been told to lay off us. For the meantime, anyway."

"You're right," Patterson said. "He's not coming back. Funny. He could have spent all day—till nightfall at least—circling us and reporting our position. But no, he's off. I wonder why."

"No need to wonder, sir. The Condor's exit is all the

proof we require that we are being tailed by a U-boat. No point in having a U-boat and a plane tailing us at the same time."

"Isn't there anything we can do about that damned U-boat?"

"Well, we can't ram him because we don't know where he is, and we can be certain that there's no chance that he'll surface because he's bound to have heard by now—or will hear very soon—what happened to the other U-boat. We can, just possibly, shake him off, but not at this moment. Sure, by shutting off our engines and generators we could make him lose contact, but that wouldn't be for very long—he'd just raise his periscope, traverse the horizon and nail us again."

"Not at this moment—you mean, after it gets dark?"

"Yes, I thought we might try then. We lie doggo for half an hour, then steam away on a new course at very low engine revolutions—the less racket we make, the less chance there is of our being picked up. Might take us the better part of an hour to reach full speed. At the best it's only a gamble, and even if we do win that gamble it's still no guarantee that we're free and clear. The U-boat will just radio Trondheim that they've lost us. They still know approximately where we are, and a Condor with a few dozen flares can cover an awfully big area in a very short time."

"You do my morale a power of good," Jamieson said. "Their tactics puzzle me. Why do they have a Condor fly out here, fly back again and then, as you suggest, fly out here at dusk. Why doesn't it stay? It doesn't make sense to me."

"It does to me. Although we're still a long way from Aberdeen, the German brass hats in Norway may well be making a decision as to whether or not to try to stop us again. My feeling—it's no more than that—says they will. No way a Condor can stop us without sinking or crippling us. It's become quite clear that they have no wish to sink us or cripple us to the extent that we can no longer proceed under our own steam. The U-boat can surface about a mile off, watching carefully for even a couple of degrees' deviation in our course—and they'll be watching for that very, very carefully—then proceed to pump shell after shell into the superstructure and hospital zone until we run up the little white flag."

"Sounds plausible," said Patterson. "You're a great comfort to me, Bosun."

As McKinnon entered the bridge, Naseby handed him a pair of binoculars.

"Starboard door, Archie. No need to go outside. A bit for'ard of midships. Near enough west, I would say."

McKinnon took the glasses, studied the area indicated for about ten seconds then handed the glasses back.

"Mile and a half, I would say. Looks like a mirror. Only, of course, it's not a mirror, just a U-boat's periscope reflecting the sun. We, George, are being subjected to psychological warfare."

"Is that what you call it?"

"Meant to see it, of course. By accident, of course.

Carelessness, of course. Slowly, very slowly, George, round to port until we're heading more or less due east, then keep it on that bearing. While you're doing that I'll call up the chief engineer and ask his permission."

He located Patterson in the mess deck, told him the situation and asked for permission to head east.

"Whatever you say, Bosun. Doesn't exactly get us nearer home, does it?"

"That's what will make the Germans happy, sir. It's also what makes me happy. As long as we're heading for Norway, which is where they want us anyway, and not to Scotland, they're hardly likely to clobber us for doing exactly what they want us to do. Come darkness, of course, it's heigh-ho for Scotland again."

"Satisfactory, Bosun. Do we make the news public?"

"I suggest you tell Mr. Jamieson and Lieutenant Ulbricht, sir. As for the rest, any more talk about U-boats would only put them off their lunch."

10

"**H**AVE I THE WARD SISTER'S PERMISSION TO have a few words with the captain?"

"The captain is only two beds away." Margaret Morrison eyed the bosun speculatively. "Or do you have another secret session in mind?"

"Well, yes, it is rather private."

"More U-boat ramming, is it?"

"I never want to see another U-boat in my life." McKinnon spoke with some feeling. "The only thing that heroics will get us is an early and watery grave." He nodded toward the bed where Oberleutnant Klaussen was lying, moving restlessly and mumbling to himself in a barely audible monologue. "Is he like this all the time?"

"All the time. Never stops rambling on."

"Does any of what he says make sense?"

"Nothing. Nothing at all."

* * *

McKinnon guided the captain into a chair in the small lounge off the crew's mess.

"Mr. Patterson and Mr. Jamieson are here, sir. I wanted them to hear what I have in mind and to have your permission to—perhaps—carry out certain things I have in mind. I have several suggestions to make.

"The first concerns our destination. Are we absolutely committed to Aberdeen, sir? I mean, how ironclad are the Admiralty orders?"

Captain Bowen made a few pointed but unprintable observations about the Admiralty, then said: "The safety of the *San Andreas* and of all aboard her are of paramount importance. If I consider this safety to be in any way endangered I'll take the *San Andreas* to any safe port in the world and the hell with the Admiralty. We're here, the Admiralty is not. We are in the gravest danger. The biggest peril facing the Admiralty is falling off their chairs in Whitehall."

"Yes, sir." The bosun half smiled. "I did think those questions rather unnecessary but I had to make them."

"Why?"

"Because I'm convinced there's a German espionage network in Murmansk." He outlined the reasons he had given to Lieutenant Ulbricht less than an hour previously. "If the Germans know so much about us and our movements then it's nearer a certainty than a possibility that they also know that our destination is Aberdeen. Maintaining any kind of course for Aberdeen is like handing the Germans a gift from the gods.

"Even more important, from my way of thinking, anyway, is *why* the Germans are so very interested in us. We probably won't know until we arrive in some safe port and even then it might take some time to find out. But if this unknown factor is so very valuable to the Germans, might it not be even more valuable to us? It is my belief—I can't give any solid grounds for this belief—that the Germans would rather lose this valuable prize than let us have it. I have the uncomfortable feeling that if we got anywhere near Aberdeen the Germans would have a submarine, maybe two, loitering somewhere off Peterhead—that's about twenty-five miles nor'-nor'-east of Aberdeen—with orders not to let us move any farther south. That could mean only one thing—torpedoes."

"Say no more, Bosun," Jamieson said. "You've got me convinced. Here's one passenger who wants Aberdeen struck right off our cruise itinerary."

"I have a feeling you're right," Bowen said. "Maybe a hundred percent. Even if the chances were only ten percent, we wouldn't be justified in taking the risk. I do have a complaint to make. Against myself, Bosun. I'm supposed to be the captain. Why didn't I think of that?"

"Because you had other things on your mind, sir."

"And where does that leave me?" Patterson said.

"I've only just thought of it myself, sir. I'm sure that when Mr. Kennet and I were ashore in Murmansk we missed something. We must have. What I still don't understand is why the Russians pulled us into Murmansk, why they were so prompt and efficient in repairing the hole in the hull and completing the hospital. If I had the key to answer that question I'd know the answer to everything, including the answer to why the Russians were so helpful and cooperative, in marked contrast to their standard behavior. But I don't have that key."

"We can only speculate," Bowen said. "If you've had time to consider that, Bosun, you've had time to consider alternative ports. Safe ports. Bolt holes, if you like."

"Yes, sir. Iceland or the Orkneys—that is, Reykjavik or Scapa Flow. Reykjavik has the disadvantage of being half as far away again as Scapa; on the other hand, the farther west we go, the more we steam out of the reach of the Heinkels and Stukas. Heading for Scapa, we should be within easy reach, practically all the way, of the Heinkels and Stukas based in Bergen. And there's the other disadvantage that ever since Oberleutnant Prien sank the *Royal Oak* up there, the mine defenses make entry impossible. But it has the advantage that both the Navy and the R.A.F. have bases there. I don't know for certain, but I should think it very likely that they maintain frequent air patrols round the Orkneys—after all, it is the base of the Home Fleet. I have no idea how far out those patrols range—fifty miles, a hundred, I don't know. I think there's a good chance that we would be picked up long before we're even near Scapa."

"Tantamount to being home and dry, is that it, Bosun?"

"I wouldn't quite say that, sir. There are always the U-boats." McKinnon paused and considered. "As I see it, sir, four things. No British pilot is going to attack a

British hospital ship. We'd probably be picked up by a patrol plane like a Blenheim, which wouldn't waste much time in calling up fighter supports, and no German bomber pilot in his senses is going to risk meeting up with Hurricanes or Spitfires. The patrol plane would also certainly radio Scapa to have them open a minefield passage for us. Lastly, they'd probably send out a destroyer or frigate or sloop—something fast, anyway, with enough depth charge to discourage any U-boat that might be around."

"Not a very enviable choice," Bowen said. "Three days to Scapa, you would say?"

"If we manage to shake off this U-boat which I'm pretty sure is following us. Five days to Reykjavik."

"What if we don't manage to shake off our shadower? Aren't they going to become very suspicious indeed when they see us altering course for Scapa Flow?"

"If they do succeed in following us, they won't notice any course alteration for a couple of days or more. During that time we'll be on a direct course to Aberdeen. Once we get south of the latitude of Fair Isle we'll alter course southwest or west-southwest or whatever for Scapa."

"It's a chance. It's a chance. You have any preference, Mr. Patterson?"

"I think I'll leave my preferences to the bosun."

"I second that," Jamieson said.

"Well?"

"I'd feel happier in Scapa, sir."

"I think we all would. Well, Bosun, suggestion number one dealt with. Number two?"

"There are six exits from the hospital area, sir, three for'ard and three aft. Don't you think it would be wiser, sir, if we had *everybody* confined to the hospital area, except of course, for those on watch in the engine room and on the bridge?" We know Flannelfoot Two is still with us, and it seems a good idea to confine his sphere of operations—if he has any left, which we don't know—to as limited an area as possible. I suggest we seal up four of those doors, two aft, two for'ard, and post guards at the other two doors."

"Weld them up, you mean?" Jamieson said.

"No. A bomb *might* hit the hospital. The two doors not sealed off *might* buckle and jam. Everyone would be trapped. We just close the doors in the usual way and give them a couple of moderate taps with a sledge."

Patterson said: "And maybe Flannelfoot has access to his own private sledgehammer."

"He'd never dare use it. First metallic clang and he'd have the whole ship's company on his back."

"True, true." Patterson sighed. "I grow old. You had another point?"

"Yes, sir. Involves you, if you will. I don't think it would do any harm if you were to assemble everybody and tell them what's going on—not that you can get across to Captain Andropolous and his crew—because I'm sure most have no idea what's going on. Tell them about Dr. Singh, the transceiver, and what happened to Limassol. Tell them that another Flannelfoot is at large and that's why we've closed off four doors so as to limit his movements. Please tell them that although it's not a very nice thing they are to watch each other like hawks—it is, after all, in their own survival interests—and to report any suspicious behavior. It might just cramp Flannelfoot's style, and it will at least give them something to do."

Bowen said: "You really think, Bosun, that this—the sealing off of the doors and the warning to the ship's company—will keep this man in check?"

"On the basis of our performance to date," McKinnon said gloomily, "I very much doubt it."

The afternoon and the early evening—and, even although they were now more than three hundred miles south of the Arctic Circle, early evening in those latitudes was still very early—passed away as peacefully as McKinnon had expected. There was no further sign of the U-boat. But he had been certain that the U-boat would not show itself. There was no sign of any reconnaissance Condor, which only served to further underscore his belief in the enemy concealed below, nor did any Heinkels or Stukas appear over the eastern horizon, for the hour of the coup de grâce had not yet come.

Half an hour after sunset the night was as dark as it was likely to become on the Norwegian Sea. Cloud cover was patchy and the rest of the sky hazy, although a few small stars could be seen.

"Time, I think, George," McKinnon said to Naseby. "I'm going below. When the engines stop—that should be in seven or eight minutes—bring her around 180 degrees till we're heading back the way we came. You should be able to pick up our wash even though it is dark. After that—well, we can only hope that you'll pick up a star. I should be back in about ten minutes or so."

On his way down he passed the captain's cabin. There was no longer anyone there to guard the sextant and chronometer: with two of the for'ard exits from the hospital area closed off and the third under guard it was impossible for anyone to reach the upper deck and so the bridge. On the deck it was so dark, the bosun was pleased to note, that he had to use the guide line to find his way to the hospital. Stephen, the young stoker, was there, acting the part of sentry; McKinnon told him to join the others on the mess decks. When they got there McKinnon found Patterson waiting for him.

"Everybody here, sir?"

"Everybody. Not forgetting Curran and Ferguson." Those two had been holed up in the carpenter's shop in the bows. "Riot act duly read. Anybody making the slightest sound after we stop—after the engines have stopped, rather—inadvertently or not, will be silenced. Talking only in whispers. Tell me, Bosun, is it really true that you can pick up the sound of a knife and fork on a plate?"

"I don't really know. I don't know how sensitive the listening devices on a modern U-boat are. I do know that the sound of a hammer being dropped on a steel deck is easily detectable. No chances."

He went into the two wards, checked that everybody had been told of the need for absolute silence, switched on the emergency lamps and went down to the engine room. Ony Jamieson and McCrimmon were there.

Jamieson looked at him and switched on an emergency lamp.

"Now, I take it?"

"It's as dark as it's going to get, sir."

Even by the time McKinnon had reached the mess decks the engine revolutions had fallen away. He sat at a mess table next to Patterson and waited in silence until the engines had stopped and the sound of the generator had died away. With the complete silence and only the feeble light from the emergency lamps to illuminate the area, the atmosphere abruptly held elements of both the eerie and the sinister.

Patterson whispered: "No chance that the U-boat will think that their listening apparatus has failed?"

"No, sir. You wouldn't have to be a very efficient Asdic operator to know when engine revolutions are falling, then dying away."

Jamieson and McCrimmon appeared, each carrying an emergency lamp. Jamieson sat beside McKinnon.

"All we need now, Bosun, is a ship's chaplain."

"A few prayers wouldn't come amiss, sir. Especially a prayer that Flannelfoot hasn't got a bug sending out a location signal."

"Please. Don't even talk about such things." He was silent for some moments, then said: "We're heeling, aren't we?"

"We are, yes. Naseby is making a 180-degree turn, heading back the way we came."

"Ah!" Jamieson looked thoughtful. "So that he will overshoot us. Turning back on our tracks. But won't he do the same? I mean, wouldn't that be the first thing that would occur to him?"

"Quite honestly, I don't and wouldn't have the faintest idea as to what his first, second or tenth thoughts are. His first thought might be that our reversing course is so obvious a ploy that he's not even going to consider it. He might even think that we're carrying straight on for the Norwegian coast, which is so ludicrous a possibility that he may even be considering it. Or we might be heading back northeast again for the Barents Sea. Only a madman would do that, of course, but he'll have to consider the fact whether we think he thinks we're mad or not. Alternatively—and there are a lot of alternatives—he may figure that once *we* figure we're clear of his Asdic clutches we'll just continue on course to Aberdeen. Or some place in north Scotland. Or the Orkneys. Or the Shetlands. There are an awful lot of options open to us, and the chances are that he will pick the wrong one."

"I see," Jamieson said. "I say this in admiration, Bosun, and not in reproof: you have a very devious mind."

"Let's just hope the Oberleutnant in charge of that U-boat out there hasn't an even more devious mind." He turned to Patterson. "I'm going up top to join Naseby and see if there's any sign of life around."

"Sign of life? You mean you think the U-boat may have surfaced and is looking for us."

"May have."

"But it's dark, you said."

"He'll have a searchlight. Two of them, for all I know."

Jamieson said: "And you think he'll be using them?"

"It's a possibility. Not a probability. He's bound to

know by this time what happened to his fellow U-boat this morning."

Patterson touched his arm. "You wouldn't—ah—be considering another possibility—another collision?"

"No. I don't really think the San Andreas could survive another bump like that. Not, of course, that the captain of that submarine is to know that. He may well be convinced that we're desperate enough for anything."

"And we're not?"

"It's a long way down to the bottom of the Norwegian Sea." McKinnon paused reflectively. "What we really need now is a nice little old blizzard."

"Still the Condor, still the flares. Is that it, Bosun?"

"It's not a thought that goes away easily." He turned to Jamieson. "Under way in half an hour, sir?"

"Half an hour it is. But gently, gently?"

"If you would, sir."

McKinnon examined the sea from both sides of the upper deck, but all was black and quiet and still. He climbed to the bridge and went out on the wings, but even from this higher perspective there was nothing to be seen, no sweeping finger of a searchlight, nothing.

"Well, George, this makes a change. Silent night, unholy night. All is calm, all not very bright."

"Is that a good sign or a bad one?"

"Take your pick. Still under way, aren't we?"

"Yes. I've just picked up our wake. And I've just

located a couple of stars, one off the port bow, the other off the starboard. No idea what they are, of course, but it should keep us heading more or less west until we come to a halt."

In just under fifteen minutes the *San Andreas* was dead in the water and fifteen minutes after that she came to life again, albeit very slowly. From the bridge any sounds from the engine room were quite inaudible; the only indication that they were under way once more came from the faintest vibration of the superstructure. After a few minutes McKinnon said: "Any steerage way yet, George?"

"Barely. We're about ten degrees off course right now. To the south. A couple of minutes and we'll be heading west again. I wonder, I wonder."

"You wonder, I wonder, we all wonder—are we alone in the Norwegian Sea or do we still have company, company that has no intention of making its presence known? I just guess and hope that we're alone. Beyond a certain distance a submarine is not very good at picking up a slow-turning engine and prop. What it can pick up is a generator—which is why there will be no lights down below for another fifteen minutes yet."

Just under half an hour after McKinnon had arrived on the bridge the telephone bell shrilled. Naseby answered and handed the phone to the bosun.

"Bosun? This is Ward A. Sinclair speaking. I think

you had better come down." Dr. Sinclair sounded weary or dispirited, or both. "There's been an accident. No need to break your neck though—nobody's been hurt."

"We've been far too long without an accident." The bosun felt as weary as Sinclair. "What happened?"

"Transceiver's wrecked."

"That's just splendid. I'm on my way. At a leisurely pace." He replaced the phone. "Flannelfoot's at it again, George. It seems that the transceiver in Ward A is not quite what it was."

"Oh, Jesus." It wasn't an exclamation of shock, horror or anger, just a sigh of resignation. "Why wasn't the alarm buzzer pressed?"

"I'll find out when I get there. I'll send Trent to relieve you. I suggest you broach Captain Bowen's supplies. If it's any comfort, George, life aboard the *San Andreas* is like life everywhere: just one damned thing after another."

The first thing that took McKinnon's eye in Ward A was not the transceiver in the cardiac-arrest box but the sight of Margaret Morrison, eyes closed, lying on a bed with Janet Magnusson bending over her. The bosun looked at Dr. Sinclair, who was sitting disconsolately in the chair normally occupied by the ward sister.

"I thought you said nobody had been hurt."

"Not hurt in the medical sense, although Sister Morrison might take issue with me on that matter. She's been chloroformed. But she'll be fine in a few minutes."

"Chloroformed? Flannelfoot doesn't seem to have a very original turn of mind. He's repeating himself."

"He's a callous bastard. This girl has just been wounded, once quite nastily, but this character seems to have been missing when they handed out humanitarian instincts."

"You expect delicacy and a tenderness of feeling from a criminal who tries to murder a man with a crowbar?" McKinnon walked to the side of the table and looked down at the mangled remains of the transceiver. "I'll spare you the obvious. Naturally no one knows what happened because of course there were no eyewitnesses."

"That's about it. If it's any use, Nurse Magnusson here was the person to discover this."

McKinnon looked at her. "Why did you come through, Janet? Did you hear a noise?"

She straightened on the bed and looked at him with some disfavor.

"You *are* a cold-blooded fish, Archie McKinnon. This poor poor girl lying here, the radio smashed and you don't even look upset or annoyed, far less furious. *I* am furious."

"I can see that. But Margaret will be all right and the set is a total ruin. I see no point in getting angry about things I can do nothing about, and what passes for my mind has other things to worry about. Did you hear anything?"

"You're hopeless. No, I heard nothing. I just came in to talk to her. She was crumpled over her table. I ran for Dr. Sinclair and we lifted her into this bed here."

"Surely *someone* saw *something*. They couldn't all have been asleep."

"No. The captain and the chief officer were awake." She smiled in mock sweetness. "You may have noticed, Mr. McKinnon, that the eyes of both Captain Bowen and Chief Officer Kennet are heavily bandaged."

"You just wait," McKinnon said sotto voce, "until I get you to the Shetlands. They think a lot of me in Lerwick." She made a moue and the bosun looked across to Bowen. "Did you hear anything, Captain?"

"I heard something that sounded like the tinkling of glass. Wasn't much, though."

"You, Mr. Kennet?"

"Same, Bosun. Again it wasn't much."

"It didn't have to be. You don't require a sledge-hammer to crush a few valves. A little pressure from the sole of the shoe would be enough." He turned to Janet again. "But Margaret wouldn't have been asleep. She'd have been bound to—no, he couldn't have come that way. He'd have had to pass through your ward. I'm not being very bright today, am I?"

"No, you're not." She smiled again but this time without malice. "Not our usual hawkeyed selves this evening, are we?"

McKinnon turned and looked past the sister's table. The door to the recovery room was about an inch ajar. He nodded.

"It figures. Why should he bother to close it when it would be obvious to anyone with half an eye—he must have forgotten about me—that there was no other way he could have entered? Mess deck, side passage, operating room, recovery room, Ward A—simple as that. Every door unlocked, of course. Why should they have been otherwise? Well, we don't bother locking them now. When did this happen, anyone know—sometime between engine start-up and the lights coming back on again?"

"I think it had to be that," Sinclair said. "It would have been the ideal opportunity. About ten minutes after start-up but five minutes before the generator came on, Mr. Patterson gave permission for people to talk normally and move around as long as they didn't make any loud noise. The emergency lights are pretty feeble at the best of times, everyone was talking excitedly—relief of tension I suppose, hopes that we had slipped the submarine, thankfulness that we were still in one piece, that sort of thing—and lots of people moving around. It would have been childishly simple for anyone to disappear unnoticed and return again after a minute, still unnoticed."

"Had to be that," the bosun said. "Anyone of the crew, or that lot from Murmansk—in fact anyone who was out there. Still no nearer the identity of the man with the key to the dispensary. Captain, Mr. Kennet, I am wondering why you didn't call Sister Morrison. Surely you must have smelled the chloroform?"

Janet said: "Oh, come on Archie, you can see that their noses are bandaged up. Could you smell anything with a handkerchief to your nose?"

"You're just half right, Nurse," Bowen said. "I did smell it, but it was very faint. The trouble is that there are so many medical and antiseptic smells in a ward that I paid no attention to it."

"Well, he wouldn't have gone back to the mess deck

with a sponge reeking of chloroform. Hands too, for that matter. Back in a moment."

The bosun unhooked an emergency light, went into the recovery room, looked around briefly, then passed into the operating theater, where he switched on the lights. Almost immediately, in a bucket in a corner, he found what he was looking for and returned to Ward A.

"A sponge—duly reeking—a smashed ampoule and a pair of rubber gloves. Quite useless."

"Not to Flannelfoot, they weren't," Sinclair said.

"Useless to us. Useless as evidence. Gets us nowhere." McKinnon perched on the sister's table and looked in slight irritation at Oberleutnant Klaussen, who was muttering away to himself, unintelligibly, incessantly.

"He still like this? Always like this?"

Sinclair nodded. "Goes on nonstop."

"Must be damned annoying. To the other patients and to the sister or nurse in charge. Why isn't his bed wheeled into the recovery room?"

"Because the sister in charge—that's Margaret, remember?—doesn't want him removed." Janet was being cool and tolerant. "He's her patient, she wants to keep a close eye on him and she doesn't mind. Any more questions, Archie?"

"You mean why don't I be on my way or keep quiet or go and do something? Do what? Do some detecting?" He looked gloomy. "There's nothing to detect. I'm just waiting till Margaret comes round."

"Signs of grace at last."

"I want to ask her some questions."

"I might have known. What questions? It's as certain as can be that the assailant crept up behind her unseen and had her unconscious before she knew anything about it. Otherwise she'd have reached for the button or called for help. She did neither. There are no questions you can ask her that we can't answer."

"As I'm not a gambler I won't take your money. Question number one. How did Flannelfoot know— and he *must* have known—that, apart from Captain Bowen and Mr. Kennet, who are effectively blind at the moment, everyone else in Ward A was asleep? He would never have dared to do what he did if there was even a remote possibility of someone being awake. So how did he know? Answer, please."

"I—I don't know." She was obviously taken aback. "That had never occurred to me before. But I don't think it occurred to anyone else either."

"Understandable. Such questions occur only to stupid old bosuns. You're just being defensive, Janet. Question number two. *Who* told him?"

"I don't know that either."

"Maybe Maggie does. Number three. What solicitous member of the crew or passengers carried out solicitous inquiries about the state of health of the patients in Ward A?"

"How should I know?"

"Maggie might know, mightn't she? After all, she would be the obvious choice to be asked, wouldn't she? And you said you could answer any question that she could. Bosh! Question number four."

"Archie, you're beginning to sound like a prosecuting counsel. I'm not guilty of anything."

"Don't be daft. You're not in dock. Fourth question and the most important of all. Flannelfoot, as we all know to our costs, is no fool. He must have taken into account the possibility that someone would ask the question of Maggie: with whom, Sister Morrison, did you discuss the state of health of your patients? He *had* to assume that Maggie was in the position to put the finger on him. So my question is why, to protect his anonymity, did he not, after rendering her unconscious, slit her throat? A nice sharp knife is just as silent as a chloroform sponge. It would have been the logical thing to do, wouldn't it, Janet? But he didn't. Why didn't he murder her?"

Janet had gone very white and when she spoke her voice was barely above a whisper.

"Horrible," she said. "Horrible, horrible."

"Are you referring to me again? Goes well, I must say, with what you last called me—a heartless fiend."

"Not you, not you." Her voice was still unsteady. "It's the question. The thought. The possibility. It—it could have happened that way, couldn't it, Archie?"

"I'm more than mildly astonished that it didn't. But I think we'll find the answer when Maggie wakes up."

The silence that fell upon the ward was broken by Bowen.

"Very gallant of you, Bosun, very gallant indeed. Not to have reproached the young lady for being unable, as she had claimed she could, to answer the questions you asked. If it's any consolation to your friend, Janet, not one of those questions occurred to me either."

"Thank you, sir," she said. "That was very kind of

you. Makes me feel more than halfway better already. See, Archie, I can't be all that stupid."

"Nobody ever suggested you were. How long will it take her to come round, Dr. Sinclair?"

"Five minutes, twenty-five? Impossible to say. People vary so much—I'm beginning to sound like a broken record—in their recovery times. And even when she does come out of it she'll be fuzzy for some time, not mentally clear enough to remember or answer what might be difficult questions."

"When she is, call me, please. I'll be on the bridge."

11

HALF AN HOUR LATER MCKINNON JOINED MAR-
garet Morrison in the small lounge off the mess
deck. She was pale and unsmiling but looked
composed enough. He sat down opposite her.

"How do you feel now?"

"Bit sick. Bit nauseated." She half smiled. "Dr. Sinclair seemed to be more concerned about the state of
my mind. I think that's well enough."

"Fine. Well, not fine, it was a damnable thing to
happen to you, but I feel less like commiserating with
you than congratulating you."

"I know. Janet told me. I'm not one for shudders,
Archie—but, well, he could have, couldn't he? I mean,
cut my throat."

"He could have. He should have."

"Archie!"

"Oh, God, that wasn't very well put, was it? I meant
that for his own sake he should have. He may just

possibly have given away enough rope to hang him-self."

"I don't understand what you mean. I don't think anyone understands quite what you mean." She smiled to rob her words of offense. "Janet says you're a very devious character."

"Be you white as snow, et cetera. Only the truly honest get maligned in this fashion. A cross one has to bear."

"I have difficulty in seeing you in the role of martyr. Janet said you had questions to ask me."

"Just one. Well, a few, but all the same question. Where were you this afternoon before we stopped?"

"In the mess deck. Out there. Then I went to relieve Irene just before the lights went out."

"Anyone inquire about the health of the patients in Ward A when you were out there?"

"Well, yes." She seemed faintly surprised. "I often get asked about the patients. Natural, isn't it?"

"This late afternoon, I meant."

"Yes. I told them. Also natural, isn't it?"

"Did they ask if anyone was asleep?"

"No. Come to think of it, they didn't have to. I remember telling them that only the captain and first officer were awake. It was some sort of joke." She broke off, touched her lips with her hand and looked thoroughly chagrined. "I see. It wasn't really such a joke, was it—it let me in for half an hour's involuntary sleep, didn't it?"

"I'm afraid it did. Who asked the question?"

"Wayland Day."

"Ah. Our pantry boy—ex-pantry boy, I should say, and now your faithful shadow and worshiper from afar."

"Not always as far away as you might think. Gets a little embarrassing at times." She smiled and then was suddenly serious. "You're barking up the wrong tree, Archie. He may be a bit of a pest, but he's only a boy and a very nice boy. It's unthinkable."

"Agree, unthinkable. Our Wayland would never be a party to anything that might harm you. Who were the others at your table? Within hearing distance, I mean."

"How do you know there was anyone else at my table?"

"Margaret Morrison is too clever to be stupid."

"That *was* stupid. Maria was there—"

"Sister Maria?" She nodded. "She's out. Who else?"

"Stephen. The Polish boy. Can't pronounce his surname. Then there were Jones and McGuigan, who are nearly always with Wayland—I suppose because they are the three youngest members of the crew. Two seamen by the name of Curran and Ferguson—I hardly know them because I hardly ever see them. And, yes, I seem to remember there were two of the sick men we picked up in Murmansk. I don't know their names."

"You *seem* to remember?"

"No. I do. It's because I don't know their names, I suppose. I'm sure one's a TB case, the other a nervous breakdown."

"You could identify them again?"

"Easily. Both had red hair."

"E.R.A. Hartley and L.T.O. Simmons." McKinnon opened the lounge door. "Wayland!"

Wayland Day appeared within seconds and stood at respectful attention. "Sir."

"Go and find Mr. Patterson and Mr. Jamieson. Oh, yes, and Lieutenant Ulbricht. My compliments to them and ask them if they would please come here."

"Yes, sir. Right away, sir."

Margaret Morrison looked at the bosun in amusement. "How did you know that Wayland was so close?"

"Ever tried to lose your shadow on a sunny day? I can prophesy things—nothing to do with the second sight—such as that Lieutenant Ulbricht will be the first along."

"Do be quiet. Has this been of any good to you? Ah, another stupid question. Must have been or you wouldn't have sent for those three."

"Indeed it has. Another little complication but I think we can manage it. Ah, Lieutenant Ulbricht. That was quick. Please sit down." Ulbricht took his seat by the side of Margaret Morrison and McKinnon contemplated the ceiling.

She said in a vexed voice: "There's no need for that."

Ulbricht looked at her. "What do you mean, Margaret?"

"The bosun has a warped sense of humor."

"Not at all. She just doesn't like me being right." He looked round, greeted Patterson and Jamieson, then rose and closed the door with a firm hand.

"As serious as that, is it?" Patterson said.

"I'd rather we weren't overheard, sir." He gave them a brief résumé of the talks he'd had with Janet Magnusson and Margaret Morrison. "One of those nine people within hearing distance of Sister Morrison knew that Captain Bowen and Mr. Kennet were the only two patients in Ward A who were awake and made the fullest use of that information. Agreed?"

No one disagreed.

"We can rule out Sister Maria. No hard reason, except that it's inconceivable."

"Inconceivable." Both Patterson and Jamieson spoke at the same time.

"Stephen? No. He's pro-British enough to make us all feel ashamed, and he'll never forget that it was the Royal Navy that saved his life in the North Sea."

Margaret Morrison looked up in surprise. "I didn't know that."

"Neither did we, Sister, even although he is in the engine-room department. Not till the bosun told us. His agents are in every nook and cranny." Patterson seemed slightly aggrieved.

"Wayland Day, Jones and McGuigan. No. They're hardly out of kindergarten and haven't lived enough or have been steeped enough of sin to make junior grade saboteurs. That leaves us with four suspects."

"Curran and Ferguson are out. I know them. They are shirkers and malingerers of the first order and haven't the energy, interest or intelligence to make the grade. That apart, they spend all their spare time holed up in the carpenter's shop in the bows and leave it so seldom that they can hardly know what's going on in the rest of the ship. Final proof, of course, is that though they may not be very bright they're hardly stupid enough to set off an explosive charge in the ballast room while they are sleeping in the carpenter's shop directly above. That leaves Simons and Hartley, two of the sick men—or allegedly sick men—that we picked up in Murmansk. Don't you think we should have them up here, Mr. Patterson?"

"I do indeed, Bosun. This is becoming interesting."

McKinnon opened the door. "Wayland!"

If possible, Wayland Day made it in even less time than the previous occasion. McKinnon gave him his instructions and added: "Have them here in five minutes. Tell them to bring their paybooks." He closed the door and looked at Margaret Morrison.

"Wouldn't you like to leave now?"

"No, I wouldn't. Why should I? I'm as interested and involved in this as any of you." In a wholly unconscious gesture, she touched her throat. "More, I would say."

"You might not like it."

"A Gestapo-type interrogation, is that it?"

"How they are treated depends entirely on Mr. Patterson. I'm only venturing an opinion, but I wouldn't think that Mr. Patterson goes in much for thumb-screws and racks. Not standard engine-room equipment."

She looked at him coldly. "Facetiousness does not become you."

"Very little does."

"Hartley and Simons," Jamieson said. "We had them on our list of suspects. Well, more or less. Remember, Bosun?"

"I remember. I also remember that we agreed that the C.I.D. were in no danger of a takeover from us."

"Something I have to say," Ulbricht said. "Discouraging, but I have to say it. I was here from the time the generator lights went out until they came on again. With their red heads, those two men are unmistakable. Neither of them left their seats in that time."

"Well, now." Margaret Morrison had an air of satisfaction about her. "Rather puts a damper on your theory doesn't it, Mr. McKinnon?"

"Sad, Sister, very sad. You really would like to prove me wrong, wouldn't you? I have the odd feeling that I will have been proved wrong before this trip is over. Not by you, though." He shook his head. "It's still sad."

Sister Morrison could be persistent. She put on her best ward sister's face and said: "You heard what the lieutenant said—neither of those two men left their seats during the crucial period."

"I should be astonished if they had."

Margaret Morrison's prim frown gave way to perplexity, which in turn yielded to a certain wariness.

McKinnon looked at Ulbricht. "Lieutenant, we are not just dealing with Number Two: we are dealing with Numbers Two and Three. We have established that it was Number Two, a crew member, who blew the hole in the ballast room when we were alongside that sinking corvette. But no crew member under suspicion was within hearing range of Sister Morrison. So the finger points at Hartley or Simons. Maybe both. It was clever. There was no way we could reasonably associate them with the misfortunes of the *San Andreas*, for at the time the first hole was blown in the ballast they were still in hospital in Murmansk, where one or both had been given their assignments. Of course neither was going to leave his seat during the time of the attack. That could have been too obvious."

Ulbricht tapped his head. "The only thing that is obvious to me is that Lieutenant Ulbricht is not at his brightest and best today. Hit me over the head with a two-by-four long enough and I'll see the point as fast as any man. Of course you have the right of it. Obvious." He looked at Margaret Morrison. "Don't you agree?"

There was a distinct tinge of red in the normally pale face. "I suppose so."

"There's no supposing." The bosun sounded slightly weary. "What happened was that the information was passed on before—well before—the engines stopped. How long before the engines stopped did Wayland Day ask you the question about Ward A?"

"I don't know. I'm not sure."

"Come on, Margaret. Can't you see it's important?"

"Fifteen minutes?" she said uncertainly. "Maybe twenty. I'm really not sure."

"Of course you're not. People don't check their watches every five minutes. But during those fifteen or twenty minutes one of those two men left his seat and returned?"

"Yes." Her voice was very low.

"Which one?"

"I don't know. I really don't. Please believe me. I know I said earlier that I could easily identify them—"

"Please, Margaret. I believe you. What you meant is that you could identify them as a pair, not individually. Both look uncommonly alike, both have red hair and you didn't even know their names."

She smiled at him, a grateful little smile, but said nothing.

"You do have the right of it, Bosun. Apart from that, I'm convinced of it because there's no other explanation." Patterson rubbed his chin. "This interrogation business. Like Mr. Jamieson and yourself I don't really think I'm C.I.D. material. How do we set about it?"

"I suggest we first try to establish their bona fides—if any—to see if they are what they say they are. Hartley claims to be an engine-room artificer. I'll leave him to you. Simons says he's a leading torpedo operator. I'll speak to him." He looked at his watch. "The five minutes are up."

Patterson didn't invite either man to sit. For some seconds he looked at them coolly and thoughtfully, then said: "My name is Chief Engineer Patterson. I am in temporary command of this vessel and have some questions to ask. The reasons for the questioning can wait. Which of you is E.R.A. Hartley?"

"I am, sir." Hartley was slightly taller, a bit more heavily built than Simons, but otherwise the resemblance was remarkable; Margaret Morrison's confusion was more than understandable.

"You claim to be an E.R.A. Can you prove it?"

"Prove it?" Hartley was taken aback. "What do you mean 'prove it,' sir? I don't have any certificates on me if that's what you're after."

"You could pass a practical test?"

"A practical test?" Hartley's face cleared. "Of course, sir. I've never been in your engine room but that's no matter. An E.R.A. is an E.R.A. Take me to your engine room and I'll identify any piece of equipment you have. I can do that blindfolded—all I have to do is touch. I'll tell you the purpose of that or any piece of equipment and I can strip it down and put it together again."

"Hm." Patterson looked at Jamieson. "What do you think?"

"I wouldn't waste our time, sir."

"Neither would I." He nodded to the bosun, who looked at Simons.

"You L.T.O. Simons?"

"Yeah. And who are you?"

McKinnon looked at the thin arrogant face and thought it unlikely that they would ever be blood brothers.

"You're not an officer," Simons said.

"I'm a seaman."

"I don't answer questions from a Merchant Navy seaman."

"You will, you know," Patterson said. "Mr. McKinnon is hardly the equivalent of the Royal Navy's ordinary seaman. The senior seaman aboard, the equivalent of your warrant officer. Not that it matters to you what he is. He's acting under my orders and if you defy him you defy me. You understand?"

"No."

McKinnon said in a mild voice: "'No, *sir*,' when you're talking to a senior officer."

Simons sneered; there was a blur of movement, and Simons was doubled over, making retching sounds and gasping for breath. McKinnon looked at him unemotionally as he gradually straightened and said to

Patterson: "May I have an option as regards this man, sir? He's an obvious suspect."

"He is. You may."

"Either irons, bread and water till we reach port or a private interrogation with me."

"Irons!" Simons's voice was a wheeze. A McKinnon jab to the solar plexus was not something from which one made an instant recovery. "You can't do that to me."

"I can and if necessary will." Patterson's tone was chillingly indifferent. "I am in command of this ship. If I choose, I can have you over the side. Alternatively, if I have proof that you are a spy, I can have you shot as a spy. Wartime regulations say so." Wartime regulations, in fact, said nothing of the kind but it was most unlikely that Simons knew this.

"I'll settle for the private interrogation," McKinnon said.

A horrified Margaret Morrison said: "Archie, you can't—"

"Be quiet." Patterson's voice was cold. "I suggest, Simons, that you will be well advised to answer a few simple questions." Simons scowled and said nothing.

McKinnon said: "You an L.T.O.?"

"Course I am."

"Can you prove it?"

"Look, like Hartley here I haven't any certificates with me. And *you* don't have any torpedoes to test me with. Not that you would know one end of a torpedo from another."

"What's your barracks?"

"Portsmouth."

"Where did you qualify L.T.O.?"

"Portsmouth, of course."

"When?"

"Early '43."

"Let me see your paybook." McKinnon examined it briefly. "Very new and very clean."

"Some people look after their things."

"You didn't make a very good job of looking after your old one, did you?"

"What the hell do you mean?"

"This is either a new one, a stolen one or a forged one."

"God's sake, I don't know what you're talking about!"

"You know all right." The bosun tossed the paybook on the table. "That's a forgery, you're a liar, and you're not an L.T.O. Unfortunately for you, Simons, I was a Torpedo Gunner's Mate in the Navy. No L.T.O.s qualified in Portsmouth in early 1943, or for some considerable time before and after that. They qualified at Roedean College near Brighton—used to be the leading girls' school in Britain before the war. You're a fraud and a spy, Simons. What's the name of your accomplice aboard the *San Andreas*?"

"I don't know what you're talking about."

"Amnesia." McKinnon stood and looked at Patterson. "Permission to lock him up, sir?"

"Permission granted."

"Nobody's going to bloody well lock me up," Simons shouted. "I demand—" His voice broke off in a scream as McKinnon twisted his forearm high up behind his back.

"You'll stay here, sir?" McKinnon said. Patterson

nodded. "I won't be long. Five, ten minutes. We won't be needing E.R.A. Hartley any more?"

"Of course not. Sorry about that, E.R.A. But we had to know."

"I understand, sir." It was quite apparent that he did not understand.

"You don't. But we'll explain later." Hartley left, followed by McKinnon and Simons, the latter with his right wrist still somewhere up in the vicinity of his left shoulder blade.

"Ten minutes," Margaret Morrison said. "It takes ten minutes to lock up a man?"

"Sister Morrison," Patterson said. She looked at him. "I admire you as a nurse. I like you as a person. But don't presume to pass judgments on things you know nothing about. The bosun may only be a bosun but if it weren't for him you'd be either a prisoner or dead. Instead of constantly sniping at him you'd be better occupied at giving thanks for a world where there's still a few Archie McKinnons around." He broke off and cursed in silent self-reproach as he saw tears trickling down the lowered head.

McKinnon pushed Simons inside an empty cabin, followed him in, locked the door, pocketed the key, turned and hit Simons in exactly the same spot as previously, although with considerably more force. Simons staggered backward across the floor, smashed heavily into the bulkhead and slid to the deck. McKinnon picked him up, held his right arm against the bulkhead and struck his right biceps with maximum power. Simons screamed, tried to move his right arm and found it impossible: it was paralyzed. The bosun repeated the process on the left arm and let him slide down again.

"I am prepared to keep this up indefinitely," McKinnon's voice was conversational, almost pleasant. "I'm going to keep on hitting you, and, if necessary, kicking you anywhere between your shoulders and toes. There won't be a mark on your face. I don't like spies, I don't like traitors, and I don't care too much for people with innocent blood on their hands, especially my shipmates'."

McKinnon returned to the lounge and resumed his seat. Ulbricht looked at his watch and said: "Four minutes. You do keep *your* word, Mr. McKinnon."

"A little dispatch, that's all." He looked at Margaret Morrison and the still visible tear stains. "What's wrong?"

"Nothing. It's just this whole horrible ugly business."

"It's not nice." He looked at her for a speculative moment, made as if to say something, changed his mind. "Simons has come all over cooperative and volunteered some information."

"Volunteered?" Margaret said incredulously.

"Never judge a man by his appearances. There are hidden depths in all of us. His name is not Simons, it's Braun, 'a-u,' not 'o-w.'"

"German, surely," Patterson said.

"Sounds that way, but he *is* RN, Royal Navy. His

passport is a forgery—someone in Murmansk gave it to him. He couldn't be more specific than that, I assume it must have been a member of what *must* now be that espionage ring up there. He's not an L.T.O., he's an S.B.A., a Sick Bay Attendant, which ties in rather nicely with the chloroform used twice and the drugging of Captain Andropolous." He tossed two keys on the table. "I'm sure Dr. Sinclair will confirm that those are the dispensary keys."

Jamieson said: "You have not been exactly idle, Bosun. He—Braun—must have been most communicative."

"He was indeed. He even gave me the identity of Flannelfoot Number Two."

"What!"

"Remember, Margaret, that I said to you only a few minutes ago that I would be proved wrong about something before the trip was over. Well, it hasn't taken long for me to prove I was right about being wrong. It's McCrimmon."

"McCrimmon!" Jamieson was half out of his seat. "McCrimmon. That bloody young bastard!"

"You are sitting—well, more or less—next to a young lady." McKinnon's tone of reproof was mild.

"Ah! Yes. So I am. Sorry, Sister." Jamieson sat again. "But—McCrimmon!"

"I think the fault is mainly mine, sir. I've been on record as saying that although he was a criminal, I regarded him as a trustworthy criminal. Serious flaw in judgment. But I was half right."

"I can accept that it was McCrimmon." Patterson's tone was calm and if he was upset it wasn't showing.

"Never liked him. Truculent, offensive, foul-mouthed. Two terms in Barlinnie, the maximum security prison outside Glasgow. Both for street violence. The feel of an iron crowbar in his hand is nothing new to that man. The Royal Navy would never have accepted someone with his record. One can only assume that we have lower standards." He paused and considered. "We pull him in?"

"I wonder. I'd love to have a little chat with him. Point is, Mr. Patterson, I don't think we'd get any useful information out of him. The men who hired him would be far too clever to tell a character like McCrimmon any more than he needed to know. They certainly wouldn't tell him what their plans, their end was. It would be a case of 'just do so-and-so and here's your cash.'

"Also, sir, if we leave him loose, we can watch every move he makes. Without his knowing that we are watching. We can put together some excuse for why Simons is out of action. It's quite possible McCrimmon has something more up his sleeve, and if we can watch him in the act of what he's doing it might give us some very valuable information. I have the feeling that we should give him that little more rope."

"I agree. If he's bent on hanging himself, we ought to be generous with the line and the tree and anything else he needs."

Lieutenant Ulbricht had found them a star to steer by. He was on the bridge with McKinnon as the *San Andreas* headed due west at full speed, Curran at the wheel. Cloud cover was patchy, the wind light and the sea relatively calm. Ulbricht had just caught a brief but sufficient glance of the polestar and had established that they were in almost exactly the same place as they had been at noon. He had remained on the bridge, where he seemed to prefer to spend his time— except, the bosun couldn't help noticing, during those periods when Margaret Morrison was off duty.

"Think we've shaken him now, Mr. McKinnon? Three and a half hours, maybe four…"

"No hide nor hair of him, and that's a fact. But because we can't see him, as I keep on saying, doesn't mean that he's not there. But, yes, I do have this odd feeling that we may have slipped him."

"I have learned a certain respect for your 'odd feelings.'"

"I only said 'may.' We won't know for certain until the first Condor comes along with its flares."

"I wish, Mr. McKinnon, you wouldn't talk about such things. Anyway, it's possible that we may have lost him *and* that the Focke-Wulf may fail to find us. How long do you intend to maintain this course?"

"The longer the better. *If* they have lost us, then they'll probably reason that we're heading back on a course to Aberdeen. As far as we know, they have no reason to believe that we're not heading for Aberdeen and would therefore opt for someplace else. So they may still think that we're on a roughly south-southwest course instead of due west. Or will, in any case, come around to south-southwest soon. I have heard it said, Lieutenant Ulbricht, I can't remember who it was, that some Germans at some times have one-track minds."

"Nonsense. Look at our poets and playwrights, our composers and philosophers." Ulbricht was silent for a few moments, and McKinnon could imagine his smiling to himself in the darkness. "Well, yes, maybe now and again. I sincerely hope that this is one of those times. The longer they keep combing the area in the direction of Aberdeen and the longer we keep heading west, the less chance they will have of locating us. So we keep this course for an hour or two more?"

"Longer. We maintain this course throughout the night; then, shortly before dawn, lay off a course directly for Scapa Flow."

"Sounds very wise to me. Even if"—was there another smile in the dark?—"a bit one-track. In any case, that'll mean leaving the Shetlands on our port hand. May even have a glimpse of your islands. Pity you can't drop in while we're passing."

"There'll come a day. Dinner time, Lieutenant."

"So soon? Mustn't miss that. Coming?"

"Yes. Curran, get on the phone and ask Ferguson to come up here. Tell him to keep a constant look-out on both wings. Three hundred and sixty degrees, you understand."

"I'll do that. What's he supposed to be looking out for, Bosun?"

"Flares."

McKinnon met Jamieson just after they'd entered the mess deck and drew him to one side.

"Our traitorous friend been up to anything he should not have been up to, sir?"

* * *

"No. Guaranteed. Chief Patterson and I had a discussion and we decided to take all the engine-room staff into our confidence—well, all except one, Reilly, who seems to be the only person who talks to him. Reilly apart, McCrimmon would win any unpopularity contest without trying. He's the most cordially detested person in the engine room. We spoke to each man individually, told them the score, and told them not to discuss the matter with any other member of the crew. So he'll be under constant supervision, both in the engine room and in the mess decks." He looked closely at McKinnon. "We thought it a good idea. You don't seem quite sure?"

"Whatever you and Mr. Patterson decide is okay by me."

"Damn it!" Jamieson spoke with some feeling. "I suggested to the chief that we talk to you, but he was sure you'd think it a good idea."

"I really don't know, sir." McKinnon was doubtful. "It *seems* a good idea. But—well, McCrimmon may be a villain, but he's a clever villain. Don't forget that he's gone completely undetected and unsuspected so far and would have kept on that way but for a lucky accident. Being a crude, violent and detestable person with a penchant for crowbars and breaking bodies doesn't mean that he can't be sensitive to atmosphere, to people being over-casual on the one hand and too furtively watchful on the other. Also, if Reilly is on speaking terms with him, shouldn't he be under observation, too?"

"It's not all bad, Bosun. Even if he does suspect he's under observation, isn't that a guarantee of good behavior?"

"Either that or a guarantee that when—if—he does something he shouldn't, he's going to make damn sure that there's no one around when he does it, which is the last thing we wanted. If he believed he was still in the clear he might have betrayed himself. Now he never will." McKinnon looked at their table. "Where's Mr. Patterson?"

Jamieson looked uncomfortable. "Keeping an eye on things."

"Keeping an eye on things? Keeping an eye on McCrimmon, you mean. Mr. Patterson has never missed dinner since joining this ship. You know that, I know that—and you can be sure McCrimmon knows that. If he has the slightest suspicion that we have the slightest suspicion I can just hear those alarm bells clanging in his head."

"It *is* possible," Jamieson said slowly, "that it may not have been such a good idea after all."

Patterson wasn't the only absentee at the table that night. Janet Magnusson was on duty, and both Sister Maria and Dr. Sinclair were engaged in the ticklish and rather painful task of rebandaging Captain Bowen's head. Captain Bowen, it was reported, was making a considerable amount of noise in response.

Jamieson said: "Does Dr. Sinclair think he'll be able to see again?" Jamieson, like the three others at the table, was nursing a glass of wine while waiting for the first course to be served.

"He's pretty sure," Margaret Morrison said. "So am I. Some days yet, though. The eyelids are badly blistered."

"And the rest of the ward sound asleep as usual?" She winced and shook her head, and Jamieson said hastily: "Sorry, that wasn't a very tactful question, was it?"

She smiled. "It's all right. It's just that it'll take me a day or two to get Simons and McCrimmon out of my head. As usual, only Mr. Kennet is awake. Perhaps Oberleutnant Klaussen is too—it's hard to say. Never still, keeps rambling on."

"And making as little sense as ever?" McKinnon said.

"None. All in German, of course, except for one word in English which he keeps repeating over and over again, as if he was haunted by it. It's odd how on board, on this ship, Scotland keeps cropping up all the time." She looked at Ulbricht. "You know Scotland well. We're headed for Scotland. I'm half Scots. Archie and Janet, although they claim to be Shetlanders, are really Scots."

McKinnon said: "And don't forget the lad with the chloroform pad."

She grimaced. "I wish you hadn't said that."

"Sorry. Stupid. And what's the Scots connection with Klaussen?"

"The word he keeps repeating. Edinburgh."

"Ah! Edinburgh. The Athens of the North!" Ulbricht sounded very enthusiastic. "Know it well, quite well.

Better than most Scots, I daresay. Edinburgh Castle. Holyrood Palace. The shrine. The Gardens. Princes Street, the most beautiful of all—" His voice trailed off, then he said in a sharp tone: "Mr. McKinnon! What's the matter?"

The other two looked at the bosun. The eyes were those of a man who was seeing things at a great distance and the knuckles of the big hand around the glass were showing white. Suddenly the glass shattered and the red wine flowed over the table.

"Archie!" The young woman reached across the table and caught his wrist. "Archie! What is it?"

"Well, now that was a damn stupid thing to do, too, wasn't it?" The voice was calm, without emotion, the bosun back on balance again. He wiped away the blood with a paper napkin. "Sorry about that."

She twisted his wrist until the palm showed. "You've cut yourself. Badly."

"It doesn't matter. Edinburgh, is it? He's haunted by it. That's what you said, Margaret. Haunted. So he damn well ought to be. And I should be haunted, too. All my life. For being so blind, so bloody well eternally stupid."

"How can you say such a thing? If you see something that we can't see, then we're all more stupid than you are."

"No. Because I know something that you don't know."

"What is it, then?" There was curiosity in her voice, overlaid by a deeper apprehension. "What is it?"

McKinnon smiled. "Margaret, I would have thought that you of all people would have learned the dangers of talking shop in public. Would you please bring Captain Bowen to the lounge?"

"I can't. He's having his head re-dressed."

"I should have mine examined," McKinnon said.

"I think Margaret, you should do what the bosun suggests." It was the first time that Ulbricht had used her Christian name in company. "Something tells me that the captain will need no second invitation."

"And bring your pal," McKinnon said. "What I have to say may well be of interest to her."

She looked at him for a long moment, then nodded and left without a word. McKinnon watched her go, an equally thoughtful expression on his face, and turned to Jamieson. "I think you should ask one of your men to request Mr. Patterson to come to the lounge also."

Captain Bowen came into the lounge accompanied by Dr. Sinclair, who had no alternative but to come, for he was still only halfway through rebandaging Bowen's head.

"It looks as if we'll have to change our minds again about our plans," McKinnon said. He had a certain air of resignation about him, due not to the change in plans but to the fact that Janet was firmly bandaging his cut palm. "It's certain now that the Germans, if they can't take us, will send us to the bottom. You see, the *San Andreas* is no longer a hospital ship."

"Why is that?" Bowen said.

"It's more of a treasure ship. We are carrying gold."

"How?" someone said. "How much?"

"I don't know how much, but I would guess at something between twenty and thirty million pounds sterling."

Nobody spoke. There wasn't much one could make in the way of comment about such a preposterous statement, and the bosun's relaxed certainty didn't encourage what might have been any more of an expected exclamatory chorus of surprise, doubt, or disbelief.

"It is, of course, Russian gold, almost surely in exchange for Lend Lease materiel supplied to them. The Germans, of course, would love to get their hands on it. I suppose gold is gold no matter what the country of origin, but if they can't get it they're going to make damned sure that Britain doesn't get it either, and this is not just out of spite or frustration, although I suppose that that would play some part. But what matters is this. The British government is bound to know that we're carrying this gold—you've only got to think about it for a moment to see that this must have been a joint planned operation between the Soviet and British governments."

"Using a hospital ship as a gold transport!" Jamieson's disbelief was total. "The British government would never be guilty of such a pernicious act."

"I am in no position to comment on that, sir. I can imagine that our government can be as perfidious as any other, and there are plenty of perfidious governments around. Ethics take a back seat in war—if there are any ethics left in war. All I want to say about the government is that they are going to be damned suspicious of the Russians and would put the worst possible interpretation on our disappearance—they may well arrive at the conclusion that the Russians intercepted the ship after it had sailed, got rid of the crew, sailed the *San Andreas* to a port in northern Russia, unloaded the gold, and scuttled the ship. Alternatively, they might well believe the Russians didn't even bother to load any gold at all but just lay in wait for the *San Andreas*. The Russians do have a submarine fleet, small as it is, in Murmansk and Archangel.

"Whichever the government prefers to believe, and it's highly likely that they will believe one or the other, the result will be the same, and one that would delight the hearts of the Germans. The British government is going to believe that the Russians welshed on the deal and so will be extremely suspicious not only of this but of any future deal. They'll never be able to prove anything, but there is something they *can* do—reduce or even stop all future Lend Lease aid to Russia. This could be a more effective way of stopping Allied supplies to Russia than all the U-boats in the North Atlantic and Arctic."

There was quite a long silence, then Bowen said: "It's a plausible scenario, Bosun, attractive—if one may use that word—even convincing. But it does rather depend on one thing. What makes you think we have this gold aboard?"

"I don't think, sir. I know. Only a few minutes ago, just after we had sat down to dinner, Sister Morrison here happened to mention again Oberleutnant Klaussen's constant delirious ramblings. In his delirium one word kept recurring—Edinburgh. Sister says he seemed to be haunted by that word. And presumably by the city. But it's not the city he's ranting about. I should damn well think he was haunted. It was not so very long ago that a U-boat sent the cruiser *Edinburgh* to the bottom on her way back from Russia. The *Edinburgh* was carrying at least twenty million pounds of gold bullion in her holds."

"Good God!" Bowen's voice was no more than a whisper: "Good God above. You have the right of it, Archie, by heavens you have the right of it."

"It all ties in too damn nicely, sir. It had been dunned into Klaussen that he was not to repeat the exploits of his illustrious Nazi predecessor who had dispatched the *Edinburgh*. It also accounts—the sinking of the *Edinburgh*, I mean—for the rather underhanded British decision to use the *San Andreas*. Any cruiser, any destroyer can be sunk. By the Geneva conventions, hospital ships are inviolate."

"I only wish I had told you sooner," Margaret Morrison said. "He'd been muttering about Edinburgh ever since he was brought aboard. I should have realized that it must have meant something."

"You've nothing to reproach yourself with," McKinnon said. "Why should the word have had any significance for you? Delirious men rave on about anything. It wouldn't have made the slightest difference if we had found out earlier. What does matter is that possibly we have found out before it's too late. At least, I hope it's not too late. If there are any reproaches going, they should come in my direction. At least I *knew* about the *Edinburgh*—I don't think anyone else did—and shouldn't have had to be reminded of it— Spilt milk."

"It does all mesh together, doesn't it?" Jamieson said. "Explains why they wouldn't let you and Mr. Kennet see what was going on behind that tarpaulin when they were repairing the hole in the ship's side. They didn't want you to see that they were replacing that ballast they'd taken out to lighten ship by a different sort of ballast altogether. I suppose you knew what the original ballast looked like?"

"As a matter of fact, I didn't. I'm sure Mr. Kennet didn't know either."

"The Russians weren't to know that and took no chances. Oh, I'm sure they'd have painted the bullion gray or whatever the color of the ballast was; the size and shape of the blocks and bars of the gold would almost certainly have been different. Hence the 'No Entry' sign at the tarpaulin. Everything that has happened since can be explained by the presence of gold."

Jamieson paused, seemed to hesitate, then nodded as if he had made up his mind. "Doesn't it strike you, Bosun, that McCrimmon poses a bit of a problem?"

"Not really. He's a double agent."

"Damn it!" Jamieson was more than a little chagrined. "I'd hoped, for once, that I might be the first to come up with the solution to a problem."

"A close-run thing," McKinnon said. "The same question had occurred to me at the same time. It's the only answer, isn't it? Espionage history—or so I am led to believe—is full of accounts about double agents. McCrimmon's just another. His primary employer— his only really true employer—is, of course, Nazi Germany. We may find out, we may not, how the Germans managed to infiltrate him into the service of the Russians, but infiltrate him they did. Sure, it was the Russians who instructed him to blow the hole in the ballast room, but that was even more in the Germans' interest than the Russians'. Both had compelling reasons to find an excuse to divert the *San Andreas* to Murmansk: the Russians to load the gold, the Germans to load Simons and that charge in the ballast room."

"A tangled story," Bowen said, "but not so tangled when you take the threads apart. This alters things more than a little, doesn't it, Bosun?"

"I think it does, sir."

"Any idea what the best course—I use that word in both its senses—to take for the future?"

"I'm open to suggestions."

"You'll get none from me. With all respects to Dr. Sinclair, his ministrations have just about closed down a mind that wasn't working all that well in the first place."

"Mr. Patterson?" McKinnon said. "Mr. Jamieson?"

"Oh, no," Jamieson said. "I have no intention of being caught out in that way again. It does my morale no good to have it quietly explained to me why my brilliant scheme won't work and why it would be much better to do it your way. Besides, I'm an engineer. What do you have in mind?"

"On your own heads. I have in mind to continue on this course, which is due west, until about midnight. This will help to take us even farther away from the Heinkels and Stukas. I'm not particularly worried about them. They rarely attack after dark, and if we're right in our assumption that we've slipped that U-boat, then they don't know where to look for us, and the absence of any flares from a Condor would suggest that, if they are looking, they are looking in the wrong place."

"At midnight, I'll ask the lieutenant to lay off a course for Aberdeen. We must hope that there will be a few helpful stars around. That would take us pretty close to the east coast of the Shetlands, you said, Lieutenant?"

"Very close, I should say. Hailing distance. You'll be able to wave a last farewell to your homeland, Mr. McKinnon."

"Mr. McKinnon isn't going to wave to any place." The voice was Janet Magnusson's, and it was pretty positive. "He needs a holiday, he tells me, he's homesick and Lerwick is his home. Right, Archie?"

"You have second sight, Janet." If McKinnon was chagrined at having his thunder stolen, he showed no signs of it. "I thought it might be a good idea, Captain, to stop off a bit in Lerwick and have a look at what we have up front. This has two advantages. We're certain now that the Germans will sink us sooner than permit our safe arrival in any British port. The farther south we go, the greater the likelihood of being clobbered, so we make as little southing as possible. Secondly, if we are found by either plane or U-boat before getting there, they'll be able to confirm that we're still on a direct course to Aberdeen and so have plenty of time in hand. At the appropriate moment we'll turn west, round a place called Bard Point, then northwest and north to Lerwick. From the time we alter course till the time we reach harbor shouldn't be much more than an hour, and it would take longer than that for the German bombers to scramble from Bergen and reach us."

"Sounds good to me," Jamieson said.

"I wish I could say the same. It's far too easy, too cut and dried. There's always the possibility of the Germans' figuring out that that's exactly what we will do. Probability would be more like. It's close to a counsel of desperation, but it's the least of all the evils I can imagine—and we have to make a break for it some time."

12

THE TIME WORE ON TO MIDNIGHT AND STILL THE Condors kept away. Apart from two men on watch in the engine room, Naseby and Trent on the bridge, Lieutenant Ulbricht and McKinnon in the captain's cabin and two hospital lookouts and two night nurses, everyone was asleep or appeared to be asleep or should have been asleep. The wind, backing to the north, had freshened to force four and there was a moderate sea running, enough to make the *San Andreas* roll as she headed steadily west but not enough to inconvenience anyone.

In the captain's cabin Lieutenant Ulbricht looked up from the chart he had been studying, then glanced at his watch.

"Ten minutes to midnight. Not that the precise time matters—we'll be making course alterations as we go along. I suggest we take a last sight and head for the Shetlands."

* * *

Dawn came, a cold and gray and blustery dawn, and still the Condors did not appear. At ten o'clock, a weary McKinnon—he'd been on the wheel since 4 A.M.—went below in search of breakfast. He found Jamieson having a cup of coffee.

"A peaceful night, Bosun. Does look as if we've shaken them off, doesn't it?"

"So it would seem."

"Seem? Only 'seem'?" Jamieson looked at him speculatively. "Do I detect a note of something less than cheerful confidence? A whole night long without a sign of the enemy. Surely we should be happy with our current circumstances?"

"Sure, I am. The current's just fine. What I'm not so happy about is the future. It's not only quiet and peaceful at the moment, it's too damn quiet and peaceful. As the old saying goes, it's the lull before the storm, the present the lull, the future the storm. Don't you feel it, sir?"

"No, I don't!" Jamieson looked away and frowned slightly. "Well, I didn't, not until you came along and disturbed the quiet and even tenor of my ways. Any moment now and you'll be telling me I'm living in a fool's paradise."

"That would be stretching it a bit, sir."

"Which? Fool or paradise? Anyhow, too quiet, too peaceful? Maybe it is at that. Cat and mouse, again— with us, of course, in the role of mouse. They have us pinned and are waiting for a convenient moment— convenient for them, that is—to strike? Is that it?"

"Yes. I've just spent six hours on the wheel and I've had plenty of time to think about it—two minutes should have been enough. If there's any fool living in paradise it's been me. How many Condors do you think they have in the Trondheim and Bergen airfields, sir?"

"I don't know. Too damn many for my liking, I'm sure."

"And for mine. Three or four of them acting in concert could cover ten thousand square miles in a couple of hours, all depending upon how high they are and what the visibility is. Bound to locate us—us, the most valuable prize on the Norwegian Sea. But they haven't, they haven't even bothered to try. Why?"

"Because they know where we are. Because we didn't manage to slip that submarine after sunset."

McKinnon nodded and propped his chin on his hands. His breakfast lay untouched before him.

"You did your best, Bosun. There was never any guarantee. You can't reproach yourself."

"Oh, yes I can. It's a thing I'm getting pretty good at—reproaching myself, I mean. But, in this case, not for the reason you think. Given only the slightest degree of luck, we should have shaken him yesterday evening. We didn't. We forgot the Factor X."

"You sound like an advertisement, Bosun. Factor X, the secret ingredient in the latest ladies' cosmetics."

"What I mean, sir, is that even if we slipped him— moved out of his Asdic listening range—he could still have found us, Asdic or not, Condors or not. A good archer always carries a second string for his bow."

"What second string?" Jamieson put his cup down

very carefully. "You mean we have another of those damned location transmitter bugs aboard?"

"Can you think of any other solution, sir? Luck has made us too smug, too self-confident, to the extent that we have been guilty of gravely underestimating the ungodly. Singh or McCrimmon or Simons—all three of them, for all I know—have been smarter than we have, smart enough, anyway, to gamble on the likelihood of our missing the glaringly obvious, just because it was too obvious. Chances are high that this won't be a transceiver, just a simple transmitter no bigger than a lady's handbag."

"But we've already searched, Bosun. Very thoroughly. If there wasn't anything there then, there won't be anything now. I mean, transmitters just don't materialize out of thin air."

"No. But there could have been one before we made our search. It could have been transferred elsewhere before that—it's entirely possible, it's likely, that any or all of the three Flannelfeet or their masters may have anticipated just such a search. Sure, we combed the area of the hospital, cabins, store rooms, galleys, everything—but that's all we did search."

"Yes, but where else—" Jamieson broke off and looked thoughtful.

"Yes, sir, the same thought had occurred to me. The superstructure is not more than an uninhabited warren at the moment."

"Isn't it just?" Jamieson put down his cup and rose. "Well, heigh-ho for the superstructure. I'll take a couple of my boys with me."

"Would they recognize a bug if they saw one? I don't think I would."

"I would. All they've got to do is to bring me any piece of equipment that has no place aboard a ship."

After he had gone, McKinnon reflected that Jamieson, in addition to his engineering qualifications, was also an A.M.I.E.E. and, as such, an expert in matters electrical, probably would be able to spot any intrusive, alien device.

Not more than ten minutes later Jamieson returned, smiling widely and in evident satisfaction.

"The unfailing instinct of your true bug hunter, Bosun. Got it first time. Unerring, you might say."

"Where?"

"Cunning devils. Suppose they thought it would be ironic and the last place we would look. What more fitting place for a radio device? A wrecked radio room. Not only had they used one of the few undamaged batteries there to power it, they'd even rigged up a makeshift aerial. Not that you would ever know that it was an aerial of any kind, just to look at it."

"Congratulations, sir. That was well done. Is it still in place?"

"Yes. First instincts, of course, were to rip the damn thing out. But then, wiser counsels, if I can finally use that term about myself, prevailed. If they have us on that transmitter, then they have us on their Asdic."

"Of course. And, if we'd dismantled our set and stopped the engine and generator, they'd just have poked their periscope above the surface and located us in nothing flat. There'll be a better time and better place to dismantle that bug."

"During the night, you mean, Bosun—if we're still afloat by nightfall?"

"I'm not rightly sure, sir. As you imply, it all depends upon what condition we're in, come the dark."

Jamieson looked at him but said nothing.

McKinnon, in a cabin next to that of Captain Andropolous, was sound asleep when Johnny Holbrook shook him half an hour after noon.

"Mr. Naseby is on the phone, sir."

McKinnon sat up in his bunk, rubbed his eyes and looked with something less than favor at the teen-age ward orderly who, like Wayland Day, walked in awe of the bosun.

"Couldn't somebody else, somebody in charge, have spoken to him?"

"Sorry, sir. Specially asked for you."

McKinnon moved out into the mess deck, where people were already gathering for lunch. Patterson was there with Jamieson and Sinclair, together with Margaret Morrison and Nurse Irene. He picked up the phone.

"George, I was in a better world."

"Sorry about that, Archie. Thought you'd better know." Naseby could have been talking about the weather. "We have company."

"Ah!"

"Starboard. About two miles. A bit under, perhaps. Says to stop or he will fire."

"Oh."

"Also says that if we try to alter course he will sink us."

"Is that so?"

"So he says. May even mean it. Shall I turn into him?"

"Yes."

"Full power?"

"I'll ask for it. Up in a minute." He replaced the phone.

"My word!" Margaret Morrison said. "That was an intriguing conversation. Full of information."

"Bosuns are men of few words. Mr. Patterson, could we have full power?" Patterson nodded heavily, rose without speaking and crossed to the telephone.

Jamieson said in a resigned voice: "No need to ask, I suppose?"

"No, sir. Sorry about your lunch."

"The usual—ah—direct tactics?" Sinclair said.

"No option. Man says he's going to sink us."

"He's going to say more than that when he sees us altering course toward him," Jamieson said. "He's going to say that the *San Andreas* is crewed by a bunch of unreconstructed lunatics."

"If he does, he could well be right." As he turned to go, Ulbricht put out a restraining hand.

"I'm coming too."

"Please not, Lieutenant. I don't believe our new acquaintance is going to sink us, but he's sure as hell going to try to stop us. The primary target will be the bridge, I'm sure. You want to undo all the good work

Dr. Sinclair and the nursing staff have done, the stitching and bandaging all over again? Selfish. Margaret!"

"You stay where you are, Karl Ulbricht."

Ulbricht scowled, shrugged, smiled slightly and stayed where he was.

When McKinnon reached the bridge the *San Andreas*, under maximum helm, was already starting to slew around to starboard. Naseby looked round as McKinnon entered.

"Take the wheel, Archie. He's sending."

Naseby moved out on the starboard wing. Someone on the conning tower of the U-boat was using an Aldis lamp but transmitting very slowly—almost certainly, McKinnon guessed, because a non-English speaking operator was sending letter by given letter. For'ard of the conning tower three men were crouched around the deck gun, which, as far as the bosun could judge at that distance, was pointed directly at them. The signaling ceased.

"What does he say, George?"

"'Regain course. Stop or I fire.'"

"Send him that bit about a hospital ship and the Geneva conventions."

"He won't pay a blind bit of attention."

"Send it anyway. Distract him. Give us time. The unwritten rules say you don't shoot a man when you're having a conversation with him."

Naseby started transmitting but almost immediately jumped back inside the bridge. The puff of smoke from the gun was followed by the shock and sound of a shell exploding inside the superstructure almost immediately afterward. Naseby gave McKinnon a reproachful look.

"They're not playing by your rules, Archie."

"So it would seem. Can you see where we've been hit?"

Naseby went out on the starboard wing and looked below and aft.

"Crew's mess deck," he said. "Well, what was the crew's mess deck. Nobody there, of course."

"Not what they were aiming for, you can be sure of that. A force four is nothing to us, but it makes for a very unstable gun platform on a submarine. I don't like that much, George: they're liable to hit anywhere except where they're aiming for. We can only hope that the next one is as high above the bridge as that one was below it."

The next one came straight through the bridge. It shattered the starboard for'ard window — one of those that had been replaced after Klaussen's machine gunners had destroyed them — penetrating the thin sheet metal that separated the bridge from what had been the wireless office and exploding just beyond. The sliding wooden door, now in a hundred jagged fragments, blew forward into the bridge and the concussive blast of the explosion sent both men staggering, McKinnon against the wheel, Naseby against a small chart table: but the razor-sharp shards of the shell casing had flown in the other direction and both men were unhurt.

Naseby recovered some of the air that had been driven from his lungs. "They're improving, Archie."

"Fluke." The *San Andreas*, its superstructure beginning to vibrate badly as engine revolutions built up, was now bearing down directly on the conning tower of the U-boat, which, however, was still considerably more than a mile distant. "Next one will miss the bridge by a mile."

The next one, in fact, missed the ship completely and went into the sea a hundred yards astern of the *San Andreas*. It did not detonate on impact.

The following shell struck somewhere in the vicinity of the bows. Where it had exploded was impossible to tell from the bridge, for there was no visible uplifting or buckling of the fo'c's'le deck, but that it had done damage was immediately beyond doubt: the furious rattling of chain as one of the fore anchors plunged down to the floor of the Norwegian Sea could be heard a mile away. The rattling ceased as abruptly as it had begun, the fastening torn from the floor of the chain locker.

"No loss," Naseby said. "Who's ever anchored in a thousand feet or whatever?"

"Who cares about the anchor? Point is, are we open to the sea?"

Yet another shell buried itself in the bows, and this time a small area of the fo'c's'le deck, port side, lifted upward almost a foot.

"Open to the sea or not," Naseby said, "this is hardly the time to investigate. Not as long as they're zeroing in on the bows, which is what they appear to be doing. We're all that closer now, so they're getting all the more accurate. They seem to be going for the water line. It can't be that they want to sink us. Don't they know the gold is there?"

"I don't know what they know. Probably know there's gold aboard; no reason why they should know where. Not that a little shrapnel lowers the value of gold. Anyway, I suppose we should be grateful for small mercies: at this angle of approach it's impossible that they can hit the hospital area."

A third shell struck and exploded in the bows in almost the same position as the previous one—the already uplifted section of the fo'c's'le had heaved up almost another foot.

"That's where the paint and carpenter's shops are," Naseby said absently.

"That's what I've been thinking."

"Were Ferguson and Curran in the mess deck when you left?"

"That's why I've been thinking. Can't remember seeing them although that's not to say they weren't there. They're such an idle couple they might well have passed up lunch for an hour's nap. I should have warned them."

"There wasn't time for you to warn anyone."

"I could have sent someone. I did think they'd concentrate their fire on the bridge but I should still have sent someone. My fault. Slipping, as I told Jamieson." He paused, narrowed his eyes in concentration and said: "I think they're turning away, George."

Naseby had the glasses to his eyes. "They are. And there's someone on the bridge, captain or whoever, using a loud-hailer. Ah! The gun crew are working on their gun and—yes—they're aligning it fore-and-aft. This means what I think it means, Archie?"

"Well, the conning tower's empty and the gun crew are going down the hatch, so it must mean what you think. See any bubbles coming up?"

"No. Wait a minute. Yes. Yes, lots."

"Blowing main ballast."

"But we're still a mile away from them."

"Captain's taking no chances, and I don't blame him. He's not a clown like Klaussen."

They watched for moments in silence. The U-boat was now at a 45-degree angle, the decks barely awash and vanishing quickly.

"Take the wheel, George. Give the chief engineer a ring, will you, tell him what's happened and ask him to drop down to normal speed. Then back on the course we were on. I'm going to check on any flooding for'ard."

Naseby watched him go and knew that flooding was secondary in the bosun's mind. He was going to find out whether Curran and Ferguson had elected to miss lunch.

McKinnon was back in about ten minutes. He had a bottle of scotch in his hand, two glasses, and no smile.

Naseby said: "Their luck run out?"

"Abandoned by fortune, George. Abandoned by McKinnon."

"Archie, you must stop it. Please stop blaming yourself. What's done is done." Janet had intercepted him as he had entered the mess deck—he had come down with Naseby and left Trent on the wheel with Jones and McGuigan as lookouts—and pulled him into a corner. "Oh, I know that's trite, meaningless, if you want. And if you want another, you can't bring back the dead."

"True, true." The bosun smiled without humor. "And speaking of the dead—and one should speak no ill of the dead—they were a couple of moderately useless characters. But both were married, both had two daughters. What would *they* think if they knew that the gallant bosun, in his anxiety to get at a U-boat, completely forgot them?"

"The best thing would be if *you* forgot them. Sounds cruel, I know, but let the dead bury their dead. *We* are alive: when I say 'we' I'm not just talking about you and me, I'm talking about every other person aboard. Your duty is to the living. Don't you know that every single person on this ship, from the captain and Mr. Patterson down, depends on you? We're depending on you to take us home."

"Do be quiet, woman."

"You'll take *me* home, Archie?"

"Scalloway? Hop, skip and jump. Of course I will."

She stood back at arm's length, hands on his shoulders, and searched his eyes. "You know, Archie, I really believe you will."

He smiled in return. "I'm glad of that." He didn't for a moment believe it, but there was no point in spreading undue despondency.

They joined Patterson, Jamieson and Ulbricht at the table. Patterson pushed a glass in front of him. "I would say that you have earned that, Bosun. A splendid job."

"Not so splendid, sir. I had no choice but to do what I did. Can't say I feel sorry for a U-boat captain, but he's really up against a nearly impossible problem, faced with a hiding to nothing. He's under orders not to sink us, so the best he can do is to try to incapacitate us. We run at him and he hides. Simple as that."

"The way you put it, yes. I hear you had a very narrow escape on the bridge."

"If the shell had passed through metal and exploded in the bridge, that would have been it. But it passed through the hospital glass instead. Luck."

"And up front?"

"Three holes. All above the water line. What with those and the damage that the U-boat did to us— rather, the damage we inflicted on ourselves—there's going to be a fair old job for the ship repairers when we get into dry dock. The watertight bulkheads seem sound enough. That's the good part. The bad part— and I'm afraid this is all my fault—is that—"

"Archie!" Janet's voice was sharp.

"Oh, all right. You'll have heard—Ferguson and Curran are dead."

"I know and I'm sorry. Damnable. That makes twenty now." Patterson thought for a few moments. "You reckon this situation will continue for some time?"

"What situation, sir?"

"That they keep on trying to stop us instead of sinking us."

McKinnon shrugged. "It is much more important to the Germans that they discredit the Russians with our government than that they get the gold. As things stand at the moment they want to both have their cake and eat it. Factor of greed, really."

"So as long as they remain greedy we're relatively safe?"

"Safe from sinking, yes. Not safe from being taken."

"But you just said—"

"All they have to do is to bring up another U-boat and they'll have us cold. With two U-boats we have no chance. If we go after one the other will parallel our course and pump shells into us at their leisure. Not the engine room, of course; they want to take us under our own steam to Norway. The hospital area. First shell in there and the white flag flies—if we've any sense we'd fly it before the first shot. Next time I go up to the bridge I'll take a nice big bedsheet with me."

"There are times, Bosun," Jamieson said, "when I wish you'd keep your keenest thoughts to yourself."

"Merely answering a question, sir. And I have another thought, another question, if you like. Only a tiny handful of people would have known of this operation, the plan to use the *San Andreas* as a bullion carrier. A Cabinet minister or two, an admiral or two. No more. I wonder who the traitor is, who sold us down the river. *If* we get back and *if* some famous and prominent person unaccountably commits suicide, then we'll know." He rose. "If you'll excuse me, I have some work to do."

"What work, Archie?" It was Janet. "Haven't you done enough for one day?"

"A bosun's work, like a woman's, is never done. Routine, Janet, just routine." He left the mess deck.

"Routine," Janet said. "What routine?"

"Curran's dead," Jamieson said.

She looked puzzled. "I know that."

"Curran was the sailmaker. It's the sailmaker's job to sew up the dead."

Janet rose hastily and left the table. Patterson gave Jamieson a sour look.

"There are times, Second, when I wish *you* would keep your thoughts to yourself."

"True, true. Delicacy? A water buffalo could have done it better."

13

PATTERSON FINISHED SPEAKING—BY THIS TIME HE was getting distressingly professional at reading burial services—planks tilted and the shrouded forms of Curran and Ferguson slid down into the city waves and wastes of the Norwegian Sea. It was then that the engine-room noise faded away and the *San Andreas* began to slow.

Nearly all the crew were on deck—the dead men had been an amiable enough pair and well liked. The cooks and stewards were below, as were the nursing staff and three stokers. Trent and Jones were on the bridge.

Jamieson was the first to move. "It looks," he said, "as if we have made a mistake." He walked away, not quickly, with the air of a man who knew that this was not a moment that called for any particular urgency.

Patterson and McKinnon followed more slowly. Patterson said: "What did he mean by that? That we've made a mistake, I mean."

"He was being kind, sir. What he meant was that the all-wise bosun has made another blunder. Who was on watch down below?"

"Just young Stephen. You know, the Polish boy."

"Let's hope he's not the next to go over the side."

Patterson stopped and caught McKinnon by the arm. "What blunder?"

"The one thing ties up with the other." McKinnon's voice sounded dull. "Maybe I'm tired. Maybe I'm not thinking too well. Did you notice who *wasn't* at the funeral, sir?"

Patterson stared at him. "The nursing staff. Kitchen staff. Stewards. Men on the bridge." His grip tightened on the bosun's arm. "And McCrimmon."

"Indeed. And whose brilliant idea was it to let McCrimmon roam around on the loose?"

"I see. All right, it just worked out the wrong way. You can't think of everything. No man can. He's a slippery customer, this McCrimmon. Do you think we'll be able to pin anything on him?"

"I'm certain we won't. Nevertheless, sir, I'd like your permission to lock him up." McKinnon shook his head, his face bitter. "If we get to him in time. Nothing like locking the door when the horse has ruined the stable."

Stephen was lying on the steel plates, covered with oil gushing from a severed fuel line. There was a rapidly forming bruise, bleeding slightly, behind his right ear. Sinclair finished examining his head and straightened.

"I'll have him taken to hospital. X-ray, but I don't

think it necessary. He'll wake up with nothing more than a sore head." He looked at the two steel objects lying on the deck plates beside Stephen. "You know who did this, Bosun?"

"Yes."

"The Stillson wrench that laid him out and the fire axe that slashed the fuel line—there could be finger prints."

"No." With his toe McKinnon touched a clump of engine-room waste. "He used that, and there'll be no prints on it." He looked at Patterson. "This line can be replaced, sir?"

"It can. How long, Second?"

"Couple of hours," Jamieson said. "Give or take."

McKinnon said: "Would you come along with me, Mr. Patterson?"

"It will be a pleasure, Bosun."

"You could have killed him, you know," McKinnon said conversationally.

From his bench seat in the mess deck McCrimmon looked up with an insolent stare. "What the bloody hell are you talking about?"

"Stephen."

"Stephen? What about Stephen?"

"His broken head."

"I still don't know what you're talking about. Broken head? How did he get a broken head?"

"Because you went down to the engine room and did it. And cut open a fuel line."

"You're crazy. I haven't left this seat in the past quarter of an hour."

"Then you must have seen whoever went down to the engine room. You're a stoker, McCrimmon. An engine stops and you don't go down to investigate?"

McCrimmon chewed some gum. "This is a frame-up. What proof you have?"

"Enough," Patterson said. "I am putting you under arrest, McCrimmon. When we get back to Britain, you'll be tried for murder and high treason, convicted and certainly shot."

"This is absolute rubbish." He prefaced the word "rubbish" with a few choice but unprintable adjectives. "I've done nothing and you can't prove nothing." But his normally pasty face had gone even pastier.

"We don't have to add anything to what we have," McKinnon said. "Your friend Simons or Braun or whatever his name is—has been, well, as the Americans say, singing like a canary. He's willing to turn king's evidence on you in the hope of getting less than life."

"The bastard!" McCrimmon was on his feet, lips drawn back over his teeth, his right hand reaching under his overalls.

"Don't," Patterson said. "Whatever it is, don't touch it. You've got no place to run, McCrimmon—and the bosun could kill you with one hand."

"Let me have it," McKinnon said. He stretched out his hand and McCrimmon, very slowly, very carefully, placed the knife, hilt first, in the bosun's palm.

"You haven't won." His face was both scared and vicious. "It's the man who laughs last that wins."

"Could be." McKinnon considered the face before him. "You know something that we don't?"

"As you say, could be."

"Such as the existence of a transmitting bug in the wireless office?"

McCrimmon leaped forward and screamed, briefly, before collapsing to the deck. His nose had broken against the bosun's fist.

Patterson looked down at the unconscious man and then at McKinnon. "That give you a certain kind of satisfaction?"

"I suppose I shouldn't have done it, but—well, yes."

"Me, too," Patterson said.

What seemed, but wasn't, a long day wore on into the evening and then into blackness, and still the Germans stayed away. The San Andreas, under power again, was again on a direct course to Aberdeen. Stephen had regained consciousness and was suffering from no more than the predicted headache. Sinclair had carried out what were no better than temporary repairs to McCrimmon's broken face, but it was really a job for a plastic surgeon, and Sinclair, though daily becoming more versatile and flexible, was no plastic surgeon.

Ulbricht, a chart spread out on the table before him, rubbed his chin thoughtfully and looked at McKinnon, who was seated opposite him in the captain's cabin.

"We've been lucky so far. Lucky? Never thought I'd

say that aboard a British ship. Why are we being left alone?"

"Because we're just that. Lucky. They didn't have a spare U-boat around and our friend who's trailing us isn't going to try it on his own again—so far. Also, we're still on course to Aberdeen. They know where we are and have no reason to believe that we still aren't going where we're supposed to be going. And we think they have no means of knowing what's happened aboard this ship."

"Reasonable, I suppose." Ulbricht looked at the chart and tapped his teeth. "If something doesn't happen during the night, something is going to happen to us tomorrow. That's what I think. At least, that's what I feel."

"I know."

"What do you know?"

"Tomorrow. Your countrymen aren't clowns. We'll be passing close to the Shetlands tomorrow. They'll suspect that there is a possiblity that we might make a break for Lerwick or some such place and will act on that possibility."

"Planes?"

"It's possible."

"Does the R.A.F. have fighters there?"

"I should imagine so. But I don't know. Haven't been there for years."

"The Luftwaffe will know. If there are Hurricanes or Spitfires there, the Luftwaffe would never risk a Condor against them."

"They could send long-range Messerschmitts as escort."

"If not, it could be a torpedo?"

"That's not something I care to think about."

"Nor me. There's something very final about a torpedo. You know, it's not necessary to sail south around Bressay and turn around Bard Head. We could use the north channel. Maryfield is the name of the village, isn't it?"

"I was born there."

"That was stupid. Stupid of me, I mean. We make a sharp turn for the north channel and it's a torpedo for sure?"

"Yes."

"And if we steam steadily south past Bressay they may well think that we're keeping on course to Aberdeen?"

"We can only hope, Lieutenant. A guarantee is out of the question. There's nothing else we can do."

"Nothing?"

"Well, there's something. We can go down below and have dinner."

"Our last, perhaps?"

McKinnon crossed his fingers, half smiled and said nothing.

Dinner, understandably, was a rather solemn affair. Patterson was in a particularly pensive mood.

"Has it ever occurred to you, Bosun, that we might outrun this U-boat? Without bursting a few steam valves, we could get two or three knots more out of this tub."

"Yes, sir. I'm sure you could." The tension in the air was almost palpable. "I'm also sure that the U-boat would pick up the increased revolutions immediately. He would know that we were on to him, know that we know he's following us. He would just surface— that would increase his speed—and finish us off. He's probably carrying a dozen torpedoes. How many do you think would miss us?"

"The first one would be enough." Patterson sighed. "Rather desperate men make rather desperate suggestions. You could sound more encouraging, Bosun."

"Rest after toil," Jamieson said. "Port after stormy seas. There's going to be no rest for us, Bosun. No safe harbor. Is that it?"

"Has to be a harbor, sir." He pointed at Janet Magnusson. "You heard me promise to take this lady back home."

Janet smiled at him. "You're very kind, Archie McKinnon. Also, you're lying in your teeth."

McKinnon smiled back. "Ye of little faith."

Ulbricht was the first to sense a change in the atmosphere. "Something has occurred to you, Mr. McKinnon?"

"Yes, Lieutenant. At least, I hope it has." He looked at Margaret Morrison. "I wonder if Captain Bowen could come to the lounge again?"

"*Another* secret conference? I thought there were no more spies or criminals or traitors left aboard."

"I don't think so. But—no chances." He looked around the table. "I would like it if you all joined us."

Just after dawn the next morning—still a very late

dawn in those latitudes—Ulbricht gazed out through the starboard wing doorway at low-lying land that could be intermittently seen through squalls of sleety snow.

"So that's Unst, is it?"

"That's Unst." Although McKinnon had been up most of the night he seemed fresh, relaxed and almost cheerful.

"And that—*that* is what you Shetlanders break your hearts over?"

"Yes, indeed."

"I don't want to give any offense, Mr. McKinnon, but that's probably the most bare, bleak, barren and inhospitable island I've ever had the misfortune to clap my eyes on."

"Home sweet home," McKinnon said placidly. "Beauty, Lieutenant, is in the eye of the beholder. Besides, no place would look its sparkling best in weather like this."

"And that's another thing. Is the Shetland weather always as awful as this?"

McKinnon regarded the slate-gray seas, the heavy cloud and the falling snow with considerable satisfaction. "I think the weather is just lovely."

"As you say, the eye of the beholder. I doubt whether a Condor pilot would share your point of view."

"Right. It's unlikely." McKinnon pointed ahead. "Fine off the starboard bow. That's Fetlar."

"Ah!" Ulbricht consulted the chart. "Within a mile— or two at the most—of where we ought to be. We haven't done too badly, Mr. McKinnon."

"We? You, you mean. A splendid piece of navigation,

Lieutenant. The Admiralty should give you a medal for your services."

Ulbricht smiled. "I doubt whether Admiral Doenitz would approve of that. Speaking of services, you will now, I take it, be finished with mine. As a navigator, I mean."

"My father was a fisherman, a professional. My first four years at sea I spent with him around those islands. It would be difficult for me to get lost."

"I should imagine." Ulbricht went out on the starboard wing, looked aft for a few seconds, then hastily returned, shivering and dusting snow off his coat.

"The sky—or what I can see of it—is getting pretty black up north. Wind's freshening a bit. Looks as if this awful weather—or, if you like, wonderful weather—is going to continue for quite some time. This never entered your calculations."

"I'm not a magician. Nor a fortuneteller. Reading the future is not one of my specialities."

"Well, just let's call it a well-timed stroke of luck."

"Luck we could use. A little, anyway."

Fetlar was on the starboard beam when Naseby came up to take over the wheel. McKinnon went out on the starboard wing to assess the weather. As the *San Andreas* was heading just a degree or two west of south and the wind was from the north, it was almost directly abaft. The clouds in that direction were dark and ominous, but they did not hold his attention for long: he had become aware, faintly at first but then more positively, of something a great deal more ominous. He went back inside and looked at Ulbricht.

"Remember our talk about luck?" Ulbricht nodded. "Well, our little luck has just run out. We have company. There's a plane out there."

Ulbricht said nothing, just went outside on the wing and listened. He returned after a few moments.

"I can hear nothing."

"Variation in wind force or direction. Something like that. I heard it all right. Up in a northeasterly direction. I'm quite sure that the pilot didn't intend that we should hear him. Some passing freak of wind. They're being either very careful or very suspicious or maybe both. They have to consider the possibility that we might make a break for some port in the Shetlands. So the U-boat surfaces before dawn and calls up the Focke-Wulf. Pilot's doubtless been told to stay out of sight and hearing. He'll do that until he hears from the U-boat that we've suddenly changed direction. Then he'll come calling."

"To finish us off," Naseby said.

"They won't be dropping rose petals, that's for sure."

Ulbricht said: "You no longer think that it will be torpedo bombers or glider bombers or Stukas that will come and do the job?"

"No. They wouldn't get here in time, and they can't come earlier and hang around waiting. They haven't the range. But that big lad out there can hang around all day if need be. Of course, I'm assuming there's only one Condor out there. Could be two or three of them. Don't forget we're a very, very important target."

"It's a gift not given to many." Ulbricht was gloomy. "This ability to cheer up people and lighten their hearts."

"I second that." Naseby didn't sound any happier than Ulbricht. "I wish to hell you hadn't gone out on that wing."

"You wouldn't like me to keep the burden of my secrets alone? No need to tell anyone else. Why spread gloom and despondency unnecessarily, especially when there's damn all we can do about it?"

"Blissful ignorance, is that it?" Naseby said.

McKinnon nodded. "I could do with some of that."

Shortly after noon, when they were off a small and dimly seen group of islands which McKinnon called the Skerries, he and Ulbricht went below, leaving Naseby and McGuigan on the bridge. The snow, now more sleet than snow, had eased but not stopped. The wind, too, had eased. The visibility, if that was the word for it, varied intermittently between two and four miles. Cloud cover was about two thousand feet, and somewhere above that the unseen Condor lurked. McKinnon had not heard it again, but he didn't for a moment doubt that it was still there.

The captain and Kennet were sitting up in bed and the bosun passed the time of day with them and Margaret Morrison. Everybody was being elaborately calm, but the tension in the air was stretching to a breaking point. It would have been even more considerable, McKinnon reflected, had they known of the Condor patrolling above the clouds.

He found Patterson and Sinclair in the mess deck.

Sinclair said: "Singularly free from alarums and excursions this morning, aren't we, Bosun?"

"Long may it continue." He wondered if Sinclair would consider the accompanying Condor an alarum or an excursion. "The weather is on our side. Snowing, poor visibility—not fog but not good—and low cloud cover."

"Sounds promising. May yet be that we shall touch the happy isles."

"We hope. Speaking of happy isles, Doctor, have you made preparations for off-loading our wounded when we reach the isles?"

"Yes. No problem. Rafferty is a stretcher case. So are four of the men we picked up in Murmansk—two with leg wounds, two frostbite cases. Five in all. Easy."

"Sounds good. Mr. Patterson, those two rogues, McCrimmon and Simons or whatever his name is. We'll have to tie them up—at least behind their backs—before we take them ashore."

"If we get the chance to take them ashore. Have to leave it to the last minute—double-dyed criminals they may be, but we can't have a couple of men on a sinking ship with their hands tied."

"Please don't talk about such things," Sinclair said.

"Of course, sir. Have they been fed? Not that I really care."

"No." It was Sinclair. "I saw them. Simmons says he's lost his appetite and McCrimmon's face is too painful to let him eat. I believe him; he can hardly move his lips to speak. It looks, Bosun, as if you hit him with a sledgehammer."

"No sledge—and no tears for either."

McKinnon had a quick lunch and rose to go. "Have to relieve Naseby."

McKinnon said: "Two hours or so. Perhaps earlier if I can see a convenient bank of low cloud or snow or even fog—anything we can disappear into. You or Mr. Jamieson will be in the engine room about then?"

"Both, probably." Patterson sighed. "We can only hope it works, Bosun."

"That we can, sir."

Shortly after three o'clock in the afternoon, on the bridge with Naseby and Ulbricht, McKinnon made his decision to go. He said to Ulbricht: "We can't see it, but we're near enough opposite the south tip of Bressay?"

"I would say so. Due west of us."

"Well, no point in putting off the inevitable." He lifted the phone and called the engine room. "Mr. Patterson? Now, if you please. George, hard a-starboard. Due west."

"And how am I to know where west is?"

McKinnon went to the starboard wing door and latched it open. "Going to be a bit chilly—and damp—but if you keep the wind fair and square on your right cheek that should be it near enough." He went into the wrecked radio room, disconnected the transmitting bug, returned to the bridge and went out on the port wing.

The weather had changed very little—gray skies,

gray seas, moderate sleet and a patchy visibility extending now to not more than two miles. He returned to the bridge again, leaving the door open so that the north wind had a clear passage through the bridge.

"One wonders," Ulbricht said, "what thoughts are passing through the mind of the U-boat captain at this moment."

"Probably not very pleasant ones. All depends whether he was counting on the transmitting bug or the Asdic or both to keep tabs on us. If it was the bug, then he might trail us at a prudent distance so that he could have his aerial raised to pick up the transmitting signal without being seen. In that case he might have been out of Asdic listening range. And if *that* is the case, he might well believe that the transmitter has failed. He has, after all, no reason to believe that we might have stumbled on the bug and that we know of McCrimmon's shenanigans."

The *San Andreas*, silent now, was heading approximately west, still with a good turn of speed on.

"So he's in a quandary," McKinnon said. "Not a position I would like to be in. So what decision does he make? Does he increase speed on the same course we've been following in the hope of catching us up or does he think we might be running for shelter and go off on an interception course for Bard Head in the hope of locating us? All depends how crafty he is."

"I just don't know," Ulbricht said.

"I know," Naseby said. "We're just assuming that he hasn't been tracking us on Asdic. If he's as crafty as you are, Archie, he'll set off on an interception course—*and* he'll ask the Condor to come down and look for us."

"I was afraid you'd say that."

Fifteen minutes passed in an increasingly eerie silence; then McKinnon went out on the port wing. He didn't remain there long.

"You were right, George." The bosun sounded resigned. "He's out there, searching for us. I can hear the Condor's engines quite clearly, but he hasn't seen us yet. But he will, though, he will. He's only got to quarter the area long enough—and that won't be long—and he'll nail us. Then a signal to the U-boat, a cluster of bombs for us and the U-boat comes to finish us off."

"That's a very depressing thought," Naseby said.

Ulbricht went out on to the port wing and returned almost immediately. He said nothing, just nodded his head.

McKinnon picked up the engine-room phone. "Mr. Patterson? Would you start up, please? And please don't bother working her up slowly. Quickly, if you would, and to the maximum power. The Condor is down searching for us and it can only be a matter of minutes before he finds us. I'd like to make tracks out of here with all speed."

"You're not as fast as a Condor," Naseby said.

"I'm sadly aware of that, George. But I don't intend to remain here like a sitting duck while he comes and clobbers us. We can always try a little evasive action."

"He can also turn and twist a damn sight faster than we can. You'd be better off trying a few prayers."

* * *

The Condor pilot took another twenty minutes to find them, but find them he did and wasted no time in making the plane's presence felt as well as heard. In the classic fashion he approached from astern, flying low, as Naseby had predicted he would, certainly at not more than three hundred feet. Naseby gave the rudder maximum helm to port, but it was a wasted effort: as Naseby had also said, the Condor could turn much faster than they could.

The bomb, certainly not the size of a 500-pounder, struck the deck some sixty feet for'ard of the super-structure, penetrated and exploded in a first flash of flame and a large jet of oily black flame.

"That was odd," Naseby said.

The bosun shook his head. "Not odd. Greed."

"Greed?" Ulbricht looked at him then nodded. "Gold."

"They haven't given up hope yet. How far would you say it was to Bard Point?"

"Four miles?"

"About that. If they don't get us—stop us, I mean—by that point then they're going to sink us."

"And if they stop us?"

"They wait till the U-boat comes up and takes us over."

"It's a sad thing," Naseby said. "This love of money, I mean."

"I think," McKinnon said, "that they'll be back in a minute or so to show us some more love."

And, indeed, the Condor was executing a very tight

turn and heading back to pass the *San Andreas* on the port side.

"Some of you Condor pilots," McKinnon said to Ulbricht, "do have one-track minds."

"There are times when one wishes we hadn't."

The second attack was an exact replica of the first. The pilot—or his navigator—was evidently a precision bombardier of some note, for the second bomb landed in exactly the same place with the same sort of result.

"These are not very big bombs," McKinnon said, "but it's for sure we can't take much more of this. Another one like that and I think we'll call it a day."

"The white bedsheet, is that it?"

"That's it. I have it up here. I wasn't kidding. Listen! I hear an aero engine!"

"So did I," Ulbricht said. "Made in Germany."

"Not this one, it's not. Different note altogether. It's a fighter plane. My God, how foolish can I be! Come to that, how foolish can you be? Or the pilot of that Condor? Of *course* they've got radar on the island. Place is probably crawling with the stuff. Of course they've picked us up, and they've picked the Condor up. So they've sent out someone to investigate. No. Not one. I hear two." McKinnon reached out and flooded the decks and side of the *San Andreas* with its red cross lights. "We'd better not be mistaken for the *Tirpitz*."

"I can see them now," Ulbricht said. His voice was without expression.

"Me, too." McKinnon looked at Ulbricht and managed to keep the elation out of his voice. "Recognize them?"

"Yes. Hurricanes."

"Sorry, Lieutenant." The regret in the bosun's voice was genuine. "But you know what this means?"

"I'm afraid I do."

It was no contest. The Hurricanes rapidly overhauled the Condor from the rear and fired simultaneously, one from above, the other from below. The Focke-Wulf didn't blow up or disintegrate or burst into flames. Trailing clouds of smoke, it crashed steeply into the sea and vanished at once below the waves. Lieutenant Ulbricht's face remained empty of all expression.

The two fighter planes returned to the *San Andreas* and began to circle it, one close in, the other at the distance of about a mile. Although it was difficult to see what they could do against a submarine about to launch a torpedo except blow its periscope off, their presence was immensely comforting and reassuring.

McKinnon stepped out on the port wing and waved at one of the planes, the one making a close circuit of the ship. The Hurricane waggled its wings.

Jamieson answered the telephone when McKinnon called. "I think you can reduce to normal speed now, sir. The Condor's gone."

"Gone where?" There was, as there might well have been, bafflement in Jamieson's voice.

"Under the sea. A couple of Hurricanes shot him down."

The Hurricanes remained with them until they were within a mile of Bard Point, when a lean, purposeful frigate approached out of the gathering dusk and slid effortlessly alongside. The bosun was on the deck.

A man aboard the frigate—presumably the captain—used a loud-hailer.

"Are you in need of care and protection, friend?"

"Not now we're not."

"Are you badly damaged?"

"Some. A few shells and bombs. But we're a going concern. There's a nasty old U-boat hanging around."

"Not now he won't be. He'll be all to hell and gone."

McKinnon saw the cargo they were carrying. The depth charges were lined up, ready to roll.

"Well, well." The bearded naval commodore shook his head in wonderment and looked at the others gathered in the small lobby of the hotel. "The story is impossible, of course. But on the evidence of my eyes—well, I've just got to believe you. Your crew and passengers all taken care of, Mr. Patterson?"

"Yes, sir. Here and in nearby houses. We have everything we want."

"And there's somebody very high up in either the Cabinet or Admiralty who have been telling tales. We'll want him. Shouldn't take too long to root him out. Bosun, we'll be wanting to say a number of things to you later—rather good things. You're quite sure about this gold?"

"Your pension against mine, sir. I should imagine there's a considerable difference."

He rose, took Janet Magnusson's arm and helped her to her feet. "And if you will excuse me, everybody. I made a promise. Now it is time for me to take this lady back home."

About the Author

Alistair MacLean has been thrilling readers with great adventure tales for twenty-five years. Today, H.M.S. ULYSSES, THE GUNS OF NAVARONE, WHERE EAGLES DARE, and ICE STATION ZEBRA are considered classics, while such recent bestsellers as PARTISANS and FLOODGATE continue to earn MacLean an enthusiastic international following.